THE
TURKISH
CONNECTION

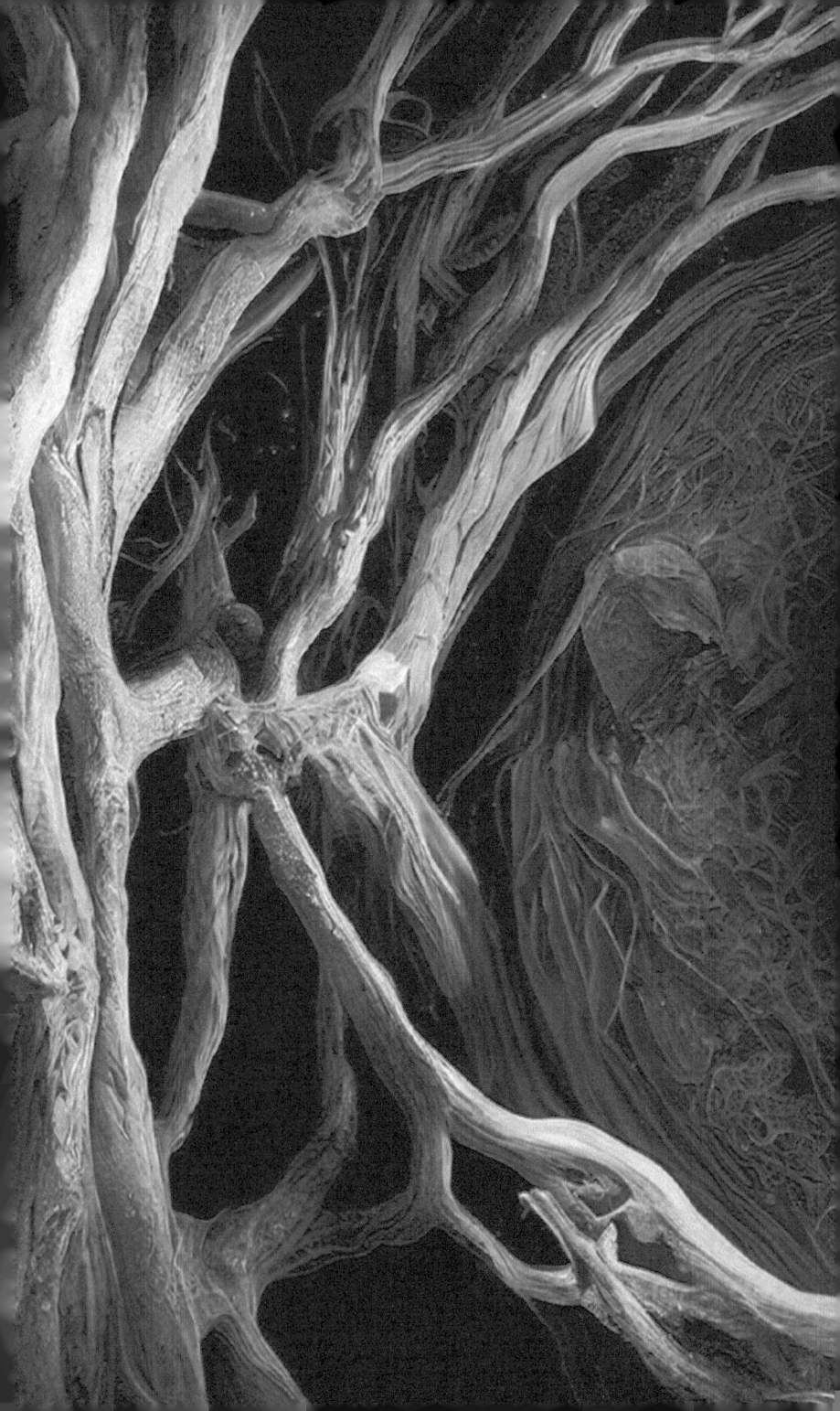

THE TURKISH

SLEUTHING WITH MORTALS

CONNECTION

D. A. SPRUZEN

4 Horsemen
Publications, Inc.

4 Horsemen
Publications, Inc.

4 Horsemen Publications, Inc.
1497 Main St. Suite 169
Dunedin, FL 34698
4horsemenpublications.com
info@4horsemenpublications.com

Cover & Typesetting by Autumn Skye
Edited by Joseph Mistretta

Library of Congress Control Number: 2023934147

Paperback ISBN-13: 978-1-64450-897-8
Hardcover ISBN-13: 978-1-64450-898-5
Audiobook ISBN-13: 978-1-64450-899-2
Ebook ISBN-13: 978-1-64450-900-5

Acknowledgements

I am forever grateful to my mentor, author and professor Fred Leebron, who has offered so much wise advice and guidance over the years. I also send love and thanks to my writing group buddies, Gwynyth Mislin and Josh Hagy, who are ever-encouraging and ever-vigilant.

Table of Contents

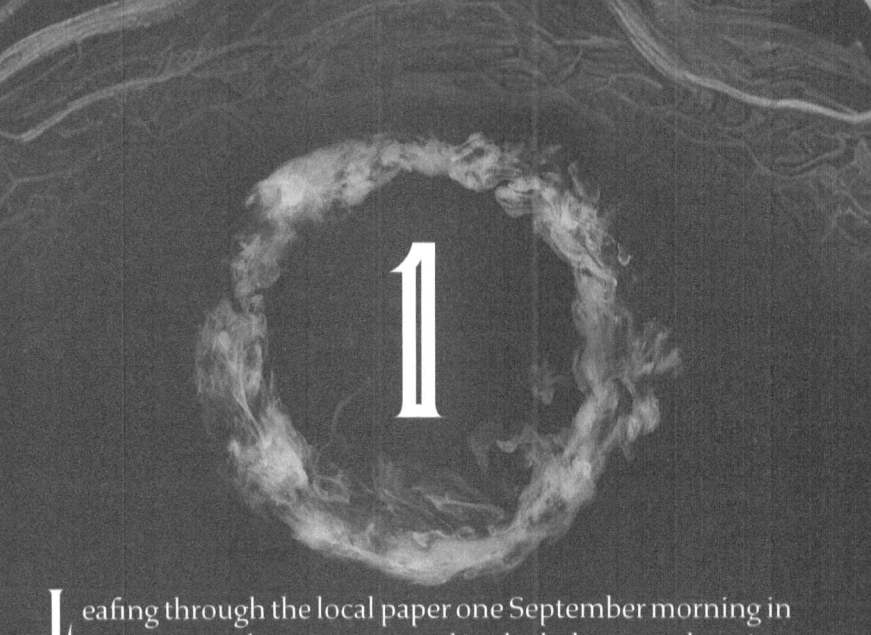

Leafing through the local paper one September morning in 2017, I spotted an intriguing ad in the help wanted section.

> Ghostwriter for memoir. Live-in, good pay, generous leisure time. Call for appointment.

Funny, it didn't mention experience or educational requirements. But what the heck, it was a job. I called immediately and met Lin Thoren the next morning.

I had never seen anyone like her. She looked like a fairy-tale ice princess—her cascade of pale golden hair framed a face stunning in its carved symmetry. I suppose my awe was obvious because her smile bordered on a smirk.

The first thing she did was show me the basement suite that had been set aside for the lucky candidate.

"As you can see, it's a walk-out. I'll order some patio furniture next week. We had this space completely renovated after we moved in. The previous owners had a particular use for it that was quite unsuitable..." Frowning, Lin closed her eyes and took a deep breath as if pushing down a bad memory. A sudden draft raised the hair on my arms. "But it's spacious, and you'd have your own bathroom and plenty of closet space. We had a little suite built for the maid above the garage, so she won't intrude on your privacy. I can provide a computer if you need one. You are always welcome to spend time upstairs with us or to enjoy the garden."

"Actually, my laptop is on its last legs," I said, hoping that didn't sound too eager.

We went upstairs and settled down. We established that I had a Master of Fine Arts in creative writing, that I had had some short stories published, and that I was working on a novel, which I might finally be able to finish.

"I have had an unusual life," she said, clasping her hands on her lap. "I own a detective agency in town, although I'm semi-retired now. My former assistant—now partner—takes care of most cases, only calling me in as needed. Our specialty is missing persons, and we've developed quite a good reputation."

"My aunt, Peggy Lambert, wrote to me about a case a few years ago involving girls brought over from Syria. Was that you?"

A smile lit up her fine Nordic face, but that was all that moved. It creeped me out a bit. "Yes, it was. Well, I want my story told. Not just my cases, but my life. No one must know, not even my husband. When no one else is home, I will come down to you and talk. You will record it. Your job is to put everything together in a bookish-kind-of-way. You know, good English, chapters, and all that." She shrugged. "I have the education, but not the patience. We will begin with a brief explanation of my origins, then cover my first major case. That will probably be a whole book in itself. If all goes well, we can move on to another."

"Why the secrecy?"

She lowered her voice and leaned toward me, although no one was around that I could see. "As I said, my life has been unusual ... to say the least. You will understand as we begin our work together. My husband, Hunter, is fanatical about privacy. He would not approve. Ever since Venice. But I'll tell you about that later." Returning to her normal volume, she added, "I've met your aunt, by the way. A nice woman. Sweet dog. The job is yours if the terms suit."

The terms suited. I couldn't believe my luck. A well-paid job, a place to live, a new computer. Move in Sunday, start work Monday. And close to Aunt Peggy. Too good to be true? That crossed my mind, only to be shunted aside. My twenty-four-year-old mind didn't go for hitches and hurdles.

"One more thing. These memoirs cannot be published until my lawyers notify you. That may be many years from now. We will have left the area by then. If you find a publisher, you may take full credit and ownership."

"That's very generous and ... well, a little odd."

She shrugged again. "I know. Everything about us is a little odd by your standards. Anyway, I've been on the board of the Salton Symphony for about five years. We have a concert tomorrow, and I'd like you to come as my guest. The little theater we use has been my pet project since I more-or-less retired. It opened nine months ago. The competition for stage time from all our local arts groups is fierce, as I've worked hard to keep the rental reasonable. I love to show it off. When can you start?"

"I have nothing going on at the moment, so any time."

"Great! The season's first concert is tomorrow evening at eight. Why don't you meet me in the foyer at 7:15, and I'll show you around. You can move in Sunday."

"Thank you. I look forward to it. Will your husband be there?"

"No, classical music isn't his thing. You'll meet him on Monday."

Lin handed me a $100 bill for "a little starting money," as she put it, and I hurried off home to tell Auntie Peggy. I'd miss her, especially her spaniel Sam's warm body at the bottom of my bed every night.

I shared my good news with Auntie while she frantically knitted woolly hats for the homeless as if winter might descend tomorrow. I asked if she remembered meeting a Mrs. Thoren.

"Why yes, dear, I did. It was at a reception after the symphony's holiday concert last year. We had a lovely chat about Sam. She loves dogs, but her husband wouldn't let her have one. So sad." Auntie's knitting needles stilled for a moment before flying across the rows once more. "She came to tea the next day. Of course, the attraction was Sam rather than me. Beautiful woman. I'm so pleased you're going to stay around." We hugged, and despite a knitting needle poking my ribs, I felt as if my world had righted itself. "I know you'll be in good hands, Mary." When Sam came nosing between us, he got a hug too.

I'd come to Salton to stay with Auntie Peggy, my mother's sister. I loved her dearly, and she always came when I needed reassurance and comfort. Mom had died only six months before in Scranton, my hometown. Daddy died when I was nine. My sister had left home at eighteen to get married. She lives in a small house in Wilkes-Barre, weighed down by wet diapers and money worries.

After I finished my master's degree in Philadelphia and wrapped up the small estate, at nearly twenty-four, I found myself in a vacuum of sorts. No writing jobs in Pennsylvania, no friends left in town, boyfriend gone with the wind. After my friends went away to college, none of them came back. I hung out a few times with a few high school acquaintances who hadn't gone on to university, but after the first half-hour, we couldn't find anything to talk about anymore.

I called Auntie Peggy, who urged me to stay with her until I "got myself straight." Thanks to Mom, I had a little nest egg, so I could coast for a while. Auntie was a healing soul. I started feeling better after a few days of home cooking, gentle conversation, and snuggling with her Cavalier King Charles spaniel, dear little Sam.

I arrived as planned in the foyer of Salton's small community theater, where I found Lin chatting with friends. She greeted me warmly, introducing me as her "writer in residence." Everyone looked suitably impressed, but she pulled me away to a quiet spot by the ticket desk before the inevitable inquisition could begin.

Still holding my arm, she leaned close and whispered, "I'm afraid there's a pickpocket in the house. I'll deal with it. Just bear with me." She gestured with her chin toward a pear-shaped woman in magenta silk who stood chatting with a disheveled young man, who blithely ignored her air of bored endurance accompanied by sighs and eye-rolling. He threw his arms around a great deal.

We wandered over. Lin nudged me to the puny youth's side while she stood opposite, next to the lady. My heart beat faster, anticipating a little drama.

"Good evening, Laura. May I introduce Mary Lambert? Mary, this is Laura Kalich, a long-time and very generous supporter of the symphony."

Mrs. Kalich shook my hand with unusual enthusiasm, no doubt sensing a reprieve.

"Charming. My young friend here is a writer. The silly boy wants to work on a biography of my husband," she drawled, her voice dripping with condescension.

Young Friend looked put out.

Lin locked his eyes in one of her uncomfortably pene-trating gazes. "Do you, now? Well, my friend Mary here is a writer. She will be staying with Hunter and me for a while to work on some of her projects. Maybe you two should get to know each other."

Why do people think writers belong to some sort of coven that draws its members together like fridge magnets? I stuck out my hand. "I'm Mary."

He looked at it without raising either of his and said, "I know. She said." *Graceless brat.*

"Well, please excuse us, Laura. I have to check on a few details at the box office," Lin said, her gaze finally moving off the young man to smile at her friend.

We moved toward the theater doors, then swept around to the back of the foyer. We chatted about the Salton Symphony and the new little theater, all the time watching Mrs. Kalich from behind. We edged closer.

One of Young Friend's emphatic gestures sent Mrs. Kalich's bag crashing to the floor, where it burst open. Apologizing profusely, he bent down to retrieve it, shoveling everything back in as fast as he could. Mrs. Kalich made a few abortive attempts to bend down that far, only achieving a head-butting for her pains before leaving him to it.

With the bag retrieved and returned to Mrs. Kalich's grasp, I saw Lin sprint to Young Friend's side. At least, I did, and I didn't. She moved so fast she seemed to arrive before my brain could catch up—like seeing it in slow-motion replay. I scurried toward them, fearing I might be hallucinating.

"Laura, dear, what happened to your beautiful sap-phire pendant?"

The woman clutched at her neck and let out a little screech. "It must have fallen. Help me look!"

People started to gather. In another snaky move, Lin grabbed Young Friend's wrist and pulled his hand out of his pocket. His bone snapped with sickening crispness. He screamed and turned white.

The lobby became quiet as my stomach churned unquietly.

"Let go—you've broken my arm. What are you doing?" He bawled like a banshee.

Lin maintained her grip, although some in the crowd murmured concern. She fished in his pocket with her other hand. "Here you are, dear." The pendant sent syncopated shafts of light over the crowd as she swung it back and forth.

Mrs. Kalich grabbed it. "You little sneak thief," she huffed in tones of tragic betrayal.

Lin fished around in his other pockets. He offered no resistance, looking about ready to pass out. Sweat ran through his eyebrows and over downy cheeks, pooling in patches on a grubby collar. I wasn't doing so well myself.

One tightly permed woman said in a quavering voice, "He's only a kid. You're hurting him." Murmurs ran through the little crowd, some for and some against.

"Anyone missing this?" Lin brandished a hunter-green leather wallet.

A portly gentleman, one of those tut-tutting Lin's conduct loudest, squawked, "That looks like mine." He felt around his inside pockets, found them bereft, and marched up to the boy in a markedly less sympathetic frame of mind. "Thief!" he spluttered, snatching his wallet from Lin's hand without so much as a thank you.

Lin said, "All right, we're done here. I'm going to show this young man outside. I think he's learned his lesson. Time to go on into the auditorium, everyone!" She looked over at me. "Wait here. I'll be right back."

She marched the wilting boy outside. Naturally, I followed, reeling in my challenged state of mind.

She pulled him round to the rear, near a clutch of trash cans, and wedged him into a corner. A reproduction Victorian gas lamp dappled the duo in sepia light and shadow as he wept and pleaded. Letting go of his wrist, she gazed into his face while starting to grow like the Nutcracker Christmas tree. Her arms morphed into hovering black wings, and her face contorted into a chalk-white demonic grimace as she hovered far above him. The boy's panting and gasping were all that broke the silence.

The creature bared her teeth and growled as a big wet spot appeared on the front of his pants. She looked madly hungry. I wanted to scream, but my throat wouldn't cooperate. My knees felt unsupportive too.

"If I ever see you or hear about you plying your dirty little trade again, I will pay you a visit. You will not enjoy it. Go." Her voice could have sliced granite.

She pushed him away. Sobbing once more, he stumbled over the concrete, clutching his wrist against his chest. In the minute or so it took Lin to sort of dissolve back to her normal state, I tried to back away, but shock rendered me clumsy on the loose gravel.

Her head whipped around. "So, you saw."

"Yes."

"When you start work on Monday, I will explain. Now, we have a concert to enjoy."

She grabbed my hand, and we strode back into the now mostly empty foyer. The few who remained congratulated her, except one man, who approached, frowning.

"Lin, what's going on? Why didn't you call me?"

"Oh, Joe, just a silly young pickpocket who thought he could get away with it. Don't worry; he won't be back."

"I thought your detecting days were over. You should have called me to deal with it."

Lin patted his cheek, which didn't seem to improve his outlook, and led me into the auditorium, more-or-less holding me up. Joe, she explained, was a police detective assigned to this district and had served on the symphony board for some time, having initially become involved to catch a notorious serial killer who'd been on the symphony board. That rang a bell. I'd have to ask Auntie Peggy.

The orchestra was already tuning up. A group of seats in the front row had been reserved for board members. We claimed the last two.

I was still trembling, and Lin must have felt it. Her constant side glances and amused smirk got on my nerves. My mouth was dry as a Sunday sermon. I pulled a small bottle of water out of the bag still slung across my body and took a couple of swigs before shoving it back in. I decided to sit on my hands. The crack of that bone still careened around the caves of my memory.

"Did you ever see those Harpy Girl comics?" she whispered in my ear.

"Yes. My cousin loved them." I could visualize the character now that she mentioned it. "Oh, I see. Good job! You looked just like her." *I just congratulated a demon?*

"My daughter loved it too. It took a lot of practice to get it right."

I considered her pride unseemly.

The conductor arrived to the enthusiastic applause of everyone except me because my wrists still felt horribly vulnerable. The music began. The noise washed over me, and my hands started to ache. Here I was, sitting next to God-knew-what and moving into her/its house tomorrow.

Should I? Dare I turn her down? I need the job!

Fricking nightmare.

And so it was that I first saw Lin Thoren in action.

Auntie Peggy treated me to a white-knuckle drive to the Thoren's house on Sunday afternoon while telling me all about the local serial killer, Rose Hale. She frequently turned to me while explaining the sequence of events, gesticulating as the story got more exciting, mercifully, with only one hand. I vaguely remember hearing something on the news. At least it took my mind off the possible nightmare I faced.

One suitcase carried most of my worldly possessions. I'd even fit my old laptop into it but stuffed a few books into a plastic shopping bag. Lin had promised a new laptop, but I had too many files with all kinds of writing samples, not to mention my novel—such as it was. I'd gone for the "write what you know" mantra and set the book in a small Pennsylvania town. A working-class girl goes to college and broadens her horizons. I struggled to find anything interesting to say about that. I badly wanted to write a so-called literary work, but my favorite reading material had always been more in the mystery and fantasy genres. Perhaps a nice juicy murder would help. But would it still be literary? My MFA colleagues looked down their noses at genre.

I stopped brooding about my masterpiece when we screeched to a halt in front of the house.

"I'll miss you, dear. I hope it all works out."

"Thank you, Auntie. I'll miss you too." I gave her a hug and scrambled out, retrieving my case from the back seat, where Sam stood wagging his tail anxiously. I leaned in to kiss his silky head. "Goodbye, boy. Be good." I felt like crying. I loved that dog. Auntie too. Would I ever see them again?

As I mounted the steps to the front door, Auntie's car zoomed away. The door opened before my finger touched the bell. My heart pounded faster.

"Hello, Mary. Welcome!"

"Hello, Lin."

We went straight through to the kitchen, where a huge blond man nursed a mug in a beefy fist. He stared at me as if I were a monster.

"Hunter, this is Mary. Remember I told you she'd be staying with us for a while?"

"Hello, Mary," he said gruffly. "I am afraid I have work to do." He rose to reveal astounding height and bulk. More of a hunk than I've ever seen.

"Hello." I stood there like an awkward teen with what must have been a sloppy grin on my face.

"Coffee or tea?" asked Lin.

"Tea would be lovely, thank you."

"Earl Grey, green or oolong?"

"Er, I'm not sure. Whatever you're having.

"I'm fond of Earl Grey."

The tea improved the more I sipped. Strangely scented at first, it became comforting and luxurious. I accepted a second cup.

"I'm glad you like it. First time?"

"Yes. It's unusual and lovely."

"This blend is from Sri Lanka."

"Don't they have it in India?" I thought all tea came from India.

"Oh, yes. The tea tastes slightly different depending on where it was grown and blended."

I was clearly going to be exposed to some of the little luxuries in life ... all new to me. I hoped I wouldn't make a fool of myself.

When we'd finished, she took me downstairs, where we'd had our interview. Along the corridor, she opened the door to my room. The furniture was plain in that undefinable way of expensive elegance. Solid wood, fine bed linens, and highly polished hardwood floor softened by a Persian rug. Two small windows sat high in the wall.

"I didn't put a desk in here for you," Lin said. "I felt you'd prefer to sit in the living room where you can see the garden. That's where we'll have our sessions too. Now, remember, not a word to Hunter."

"I remember." I set my suitcase down next to the bed. She showed me a small modern bathroom with textured beige and ivory tiling before leading me back into the living area. She pointed to the desk set against what must be the bedroom's side wall, near sliding glass doors that led to a patio lined with pots full of annuals, most of which were geraniums and petunias in different shades of red and pink. I appreciated the cheerful and uplifting colors.

In the center of the room, two identical chintz sofas faced each other with a bistro table and two chairs at one end, close to the wall opposite the patio.

"During our sessions, you will sit at that table with a tape recorder, and I will lie on one of the sofas. I like to keep my eyes closed while traveling through my memories. And I don't like to be interrupted."

"I understand" *Tape recorder?*

"I'll leave you to freshen up and settle in. Dinner is at seven, but come up earlier if you like. We don't mind at all." She went upstairs.

I sat on my bed and bounced a couple of times. Nice and soft. My dorm had had horrid hard mattresses, and the one at home wasn't much better. Auntie Peggy's was comfy, though. Everything about Auntie was comfy, come to think of it. If you didn't count her driving. I unpacked and lay on the bed. I must have dozed off because twilight had settled in by the time I opened my eyes. I looked at my watch in panic—quarter of an hour to spare. I washed my hands and combed my hair before venturing upstairs to the kitchen, where a plump woman with dark hair and elfin features was pulling something out of the oven. Startled, she splashed some hot sauce on herself when she saw me.

"Ouch! Who the hell are you?" She slammed the pan down on the counter, causing more sauce to splash here and there.

"I'm Mary. I'm so sorry I startled you. Lin didn't tell you I was here? They've invited me to stay for a while."

"Yes, she did mention it, but she didn't say when. I made up the bed a few days ago."

"I'm sorry if it makes dinner difficult."

A voice behind me said, "You know perfectly well I told you Mary would be coming today, silly girl." Lin stood beside me. "Lin, this is Dora, our maid."

Dora's frown clenched furiously. Did she think I was going to make more work? Or didn't she like being called a maid? I hoped she wouldn't hate me.

"Come into the dining room, Mary. Hunter will be along shortly."

We went into another designer room (as I naively thought of it), and Lin asked me to sit opposite her next to the end chair, which I assumed was reserved for Hunter.

"Are you all settled in now?"

"Oh, yes, thank you. I lay down for a few minutes and somehow fell asleep. I don't usually take naps. The bed is super comfortable, though."

"Well, good. We're going to watch a movie tonight. You are welcome to join us."

"That sounds like fun."

"Well, it's Hunter's turn to choose, so I make no promises."

Just then, the hunk ambled into the room and sat in his allotted place.

"How is my lovely wife this evening?" Lin treated him to a dazzling smile. "And how is our lovely guest?"

"I am well, thank you. Your house is lovely."

He didn't reply but wore the look of a man who's received very good news. Lin grinned and winked at me.

Dora brought in several dishes on a trolley and placed them on the sideboard. "Here's dinner," she announced before trundling off again. The clattering and banging of pots and utensils emanated from the kitchen.

"In one of her moods," said Lin as she strode to the kitchen door. "Be quiet, Dora." Things calmed down.

Hunter seemed oblivious as he loaded his plate from the array of dishes. "Come along, Mary, fill your plate," he said, flashing me a smile that made my knees go weak. It came as a shock. I mean, sure, I'd noticed his attractions, but I hadn't expected that kind of frisson. I glanced at Lin, who was looking at me with a funny smile. *Careful.*

Hunter didn't speak until he'd demolished an astonishing number of helpings of horribly rare roast beef and potatoes. I think he managed a broccoli spear too. Lin tucked into a few filets of fish, potatoes cooked with dill, and a selection of other vegetables. I ate a little of everything, careful to avoid looking at Hunter's bloody plate. Surely they didn't eat like this every night? Lin and I enjoyed a couple of glasses of icy white wine. Hunter, needless to say, drank wine of an extraordinarily vivid red that complemented his steak.

"I have to check how my stocks did today," Hunter said as he pushed back his chair and left the room. "I will see you later."

"Thank you, Lin. That was a fantastic meal."

"Yes, Hunter eats a great deal. He is a big man who needs to keep up his energy. He is a man of many appetites, as you can imagine." She smirked suggestively after this last statement.

"I see. Yes, he is a very big man," was my brilliant rejoinder.

"Let's go to the living room and see what's on TV. Hunter should return soon." Lin filled our glasses again, and we took them with us.

I sat on a deep side chair when Lin perched prettily on the middle cushion of the sofa. Lin had just turned on the TV when Hunter came in, carrying a DVD, which he loaded into the player.

"New one, dearest?" asked Lin.

"Yes, it is a thriller."

It was one of those blood-and-gore affairs, although I quite enjoyed it. Lots of action and plenty of black humor that made you laugh at things you shouldn't.

"Hope you enjoyed it. Goodnight," Hunter said when it ended.

"Goodnight," we chorused.

"He's a man of few words, I'm afraid. I think I'll go up and read. Are you all right for books, Mary? I don't know if you noticed, but there's a small bookshelf in the living room downstairs. Lots of novels."

"Well, I do have a book going, but I'll be sure to take a look. Thank you, Lin. It's been a lovely day."

"You're welcome. I'm glad you're here. I'll see you at breakfast. We usually have it around nine."

Perfect. I hated getting up early.

Breakfast the next morning was strange. Yesterday at dinner, Hunter tucked into the biggest and bloodiest steak I've ever seen. Absolutely revolting. The next morning at breakfast, I was surprised to find several such steaks on the sideboard.

"Yes, he has meat for breakfast too," Lin said, clearly amused by my look of disgust. Looking at bloody slabs of meat didn't sit too well on an empty stomach. "Eggs?"

"Yes, thank you."

"Fried eggs on toast for us," she called out to Dora through the open kitchen door.

"Oh, all right," was the sulky answer.

Dora was such an unpleasant woman; I wondered why Lin put up with her.

Hunter came in and ate only steak before disappearing without a word. After breakfast, Lin opened a drawer in the sideboard and got out a big old tape recorder and a plastic bag.

"Here, take this down and plug it in. There's a fresh tape in it. There's a stock of tapes in this bag. I won't be long."

I was ready and waiting when she came down.

Lin set the rules while she settled herself on the sofa as if ready to be psychoanalyzed. "I want to just talk as much as I feel like for each session. Please try not to interrupt or disturb my train of thought."

"Yes, I quite understand." *Why so harsh?*

"You may have heard a few tales about the end of our worlds." Clenched fists and slightly raised shoulders betrayed Lin's tension, but soon her eyes closed, her body relaxed, and she clasped her hands, becoming as still as one of those marble likenesses on top of a queen's tomb. "They got some of it wrong, probably because no one could really know the truth. We were never sure how they knew as much as they did—those old people who told and retold our story through the ages. I have my suspicions now, but more of that later. The horror will always be with us. I don't think anyone can forget their own war—the loss, the pain— however hard they try."

Her face crumpled momentarily but soon recomposed into statue mode.

"This part will be one of the hardest. But I want it known. I want it out in the open."

Tape 1

I won't go into all the details of the final battle, as most of it is rather well-known to humans who are interested in such things. But it wasn't true that all the gods perished. Hunter and I survived, as did a few others, although I didn't find that out until eons later.

I was born in paradise and ended up in Hel for almost an eternity—that's only one "L" in my language, by the way. Prophecies had long foretold Ragnarök, the downfall of the universe, together with its gods and goddesses. We all knew what was coming when the first of these prophesied events came to pass—Loki killed our sweet god Baldur—and we prepared for the end. Odin chose the best human warriors to join him in the final battle against the giants, even though he knew none of these actions could save us. As a precaution, he chained up his blood brother Loki, a half-giant, and Loki's son, the monstrous wolf Fenrir, to stop them from wreaking more havoc.

Some of our gods had strayed badly. They had broken oaths and fallen short of honorable behavior on several occasions. We referred to the realm of humans as Midgard, and even there, people had abandoned their traditional way of life and no longer honored the bonds of kinship. Their culture sank into willful apathy. Three winters came in a row with neither spring nor summer between, a long, devastating season of icy darkness that the prophecies had called the *Fimbulwinter*

Eventually, Loki and Fenrir broke free of their fetters and began inflicting the kind of destruction we'd all feared.

Yggdrasil, the great tree that held the Nine Worlds in its branches and roots, began to tremble as its leaves wilted and turned brown. Seeing such nobility wither demoralized all of us.

The far-seeing watchman, Heimdall, was the first to spot a vast army of giants headed for our celestial stronghold. Amid the throng came Loki at the helm of the ship Naglfar. Heimdall blew and blew his *Gjallarhorn* to alert us.

The giants not only set about destroying the abode of the gods but the entire universe along with it. The great wolf, Fenrir, loped across the land with his lower jaw on the ground and his upper jaw in the sky, consuming everything in between. He even dragged the sun from its mooring and into his stomach. Surt, a giant bearing a flaming sword, strode across the earth, leaving a deadly inferno in his wake.

The gods fought valiantly to the death, immortality vanquished by weapons poisoned in a cursed well. Thor and Odin were killed, although they took a fair number of the enemy with them. Even the giants fell out among themselves until everything fell into silence.

The goddesses tried to flee to Hel, but I was the only one who made it. My poor mistress Frigg died in my arms.

A tear or two rolled down Lin's face. I wanted to ask her if she needed a glass of water, but her mind was far away on that battlefield. I decided to keep quiet, especially after her comment about interruptions. She hadn't spoken for a few minutes, but her eyes stayed closed, although her hands now lay on her thighs. Had she finished for now? She shifted a fraction, clasping her hands as if in prayer. She spoke again.

Frigg whispered her instructions before closing her eyes forever. Her faithful handmaiden, I followed them to the letter. I first snapped a small branch off Yggdrasil and wrapped it in Frigg's blood-soaked shawl, concealing it under my robe. Frigg's bag contained a set of golden chessmen she'd plucked from the field of Ida to hide them from the giants, and I strapped that to my back. Devastated by the loss of everything dear to me, I stumbled through a never-ending thicket of charred stumps that had once been a lush forest. There, I found Thor's brother, the god Hoenir, grievously wounded by Loki's poisoned sword, crawling along the charred path just ahead of me. To his credit, he'd slain Loki before he fell. I slung him over my shoulder and carried him to Hel.

I should explain that my vocation as Frigg's handmaiden had been to go down to *Midgard* and assist humans under the goddess's protection when they were in dire peril. Clearly, my new role was to assist Hoenir, the last remaining god of the *Aesir.*

Reversing the process of creation, our ruined world sank back into the ocean and vanished below the waves. Soon, the ocean itself sank into the void. The perfect darkness and silence of the void reigned once more. Hel, which has always been and always will be, is ruled by a ravenous goddess of the same name. She created a dark, chill space divorced from life and hope—from anything at all. There were no healing herbs, no immortal nectars, only rest and quiet for what seemed like ever, although probably it was not much more than a millennium. Hoenir gradually gained strength. I thought I'd go mad. I dreamed of green tree canopies against a brilliant blue sky, flowing rivers teeming with darting fish, and scented flowers colored like jewels.

This age of death was not eternal, however. The earth once again rose from the ocean, and the fresh land became more lush and bountiful than before. A new human couple awakened from their deep slumber where they'd taken refuge among Yggdrasil's dead branches, and the human race again lay claim to the land.

I gradually sensed human breath and babies' cries, smelled the greening of the earth, and heard water lapping a distant shore. I lost no time in helping Hoenir ascend the eight hundred steps to the black river, fighting off mangled spirits that clung to my hair, moaning and pleading for release. Hel would never have allowed them to escape her hungry clutches, and I had no wish to incur her wrath. As fellow gods, she never took her portion of us, as Odin had allowed her to do with mere mortals. When we reached the riverbank, a faceless demon ferried us to an earthly shore.

We first checked on Yggdrasil. It was still dead, or possibly dormant, along with eight of its realms. The sprig I'd kept wrapped all these years had not withered, however, so perhaps our world could rise again. There was nowhere left to go but Midgard. We turned south and journeyed for days. Eventually, Hoenir managed to run with me for a few hours at a time as his stamina began to reassert itself. We found a fire-filled mountain with warm caves. Aetna, as she came to be known, was a grumpy old thing even then, spewing fire and lava when in one of her moods, but she seemed protective of us. I enjoyed walking barefoot up her slopes, roaming at will across a land rich in all that fertile soil has to offer. After Hoenir had fully recovered, although neither of us was as strong as before, we began to explore the rest of the world. So many changes from place to place, century to century. The memories flood back sometimes. All our children, so many children. But that's another story, not the one I want to tell right now.

Maybe Yggdrasil will bring back our heavens one day, especially if humans despoil their world irreparably. I'd kept the sprig in a dormant state in Hel and plant it in the garden everywhere we live. It hasn't died, but it hasn't rooted or leafed out, either. I feed it sometimes. One morning in London, I found a dead baby nightingale under a tree—it must have fallen out of its nest—and buried it amidst Yggdrasil's roots in the hope of encouraging growth. That evening, an angelic song rang out at the bottom of the garden. A nightingale perched on one of Yggdrasil's twigs poured out its little heart. I was enchanted, then came to my senses and frantically dug into the soil with my bare hands. No baby bird. Now my heart soared. Yggdrasil might be dormant, but its magic lives.

I never managed to scrub the blue bloodstain out of Frigg's shawl. I still have it, wrapped in white silk, in a dresser drawer. It once lay across my dear lady's shoulders. If Yggdrasil flourishes again and the stain fades, perhaps we can go home, and the earth plunderers will be vanquished for good. I yearn to bear immortal children.

I could weep for days thinking back to our charmed existence and how it all shattered, how evil almost triumphed. But it does no good to cry; all we can do is persevere. The story I want to tell is of the successful life I made for myself in this suburban bubble. Hardly the sort of place you'd expect to find murder and mayhem. At least I have Hoenir. We call him Hunter now.

Lin rose and left without a word, obviously overcome by her loss. I was overcome, too. Fairytales or truth? Were there really Norse gods? Valhalla and all that? What about our God? I was raised Presbyterian. No stained glass or incense, just plain-jane faith. Could our God be a latecomer to the party?

My mind raced vertiginously. Were they mad? Was I? Were they dangerous? Lin clearly could be. Hunter was big enough to do serious damage. Good or bad? Or just somewhere in between, like the rest of us? So many questions I didn't dare ask. Not yet.

It was all very confusing. I spent the afternoon lying on my bed, thoughts tumbling like a waterfall over sharp rocks.

Dinner was even better than the previous evening, with a wonderful spread of Greek cuisine (so I was informed). Plus steak. We watched a couple of cop shows before heading off to bed, where I read for an hour or so. It all seemed like a normal family day. If you didn't count Lin's morning revelations, which I tried not to think about. Unfortunately, my dreams wouldn't let them go. I dreamed of monsters that chased me through Salton and all the way back to Pennsylvania. They wafted away as soon as I crossed the border. I woke up out of breath and exhausted.

The next morning, Lin explained that the children were away at school, so they were empty nesters. Hunter was polite yet did not seem the slightest bit interested in what I might be doing in his house.

Breakfast for Hunter, this time, consisted of a smaller steak that, like at dinner, had been seared on the outside but otherwise left to its own devices. I kept my eyes averted again as I found it so hard to deal with on an empty stomach. Their sullen maid, Dora, asked me what I wanted. She sniffed at my request for oatmeal.

"Haven't got any."

"I'll buy some today," Lin said. "Do you like toast? Raisin bread? Orange juice?"

I was fine with all that; my protestations that I didn't want to be any trouble brushed aside. Hunter soon disappeared—as I later discovered, he retreated to his study most mornings. Dora just stomped around and served me none too graciously. Resenting the extra work?

I followed Lin downstairs after breakfast and switched on the recorder as she arranged herself for another session. She could have been a mummy—the ancient Egyptian dead kind—the way she stayed motionless while she talked. Most people fidget, at least a little. Not her. Pure focus.

"Hunter will be in his study all morning because the stock market is acting funny. He is very clever in matters of finance, limited as he is in other areas."

Well, that was a snarky thing to say about her own husband. Although he was definitely limited in the conversational area.

"Salton is only the latest of many places we have landed in over the millennia. It's nice enough, but there's not much life in people here. They are so wrapped up in their status symbols and fixating on their children being above average. I became very bored until I got involved in detection. It was Hunter's idea. He surprises me sometimes."

Hunter seemed to get on Lin's nerves a lot. Well, if you've been married for that long...

Tape 2

Olive Goodall hated me. She insisted I threw her son off a ladder while he was trying to sneak through his bedroom window, in spite of the police and I pointing out the preposterous nature of her accusation. Look at me! Petite, golden-haired, and—my real sin—beautiful, clearly not up to heaving grown men off ladders. Chad, expelled from college yet again, had arrived without due notice, drunk yet again, and found no one home. Hence the ladder.

Bob was my companion on the neighborhood watch that night. We got bored with cruising our patch, so we pulled up in a dark and thankfully undeveloped dead-end just beyond Olive's house. We had gotten into the habit of relieving a tedious shift with a little "hanky-panky," as he liked to call it. He'd been married for about twenty-five years, and me, well, I can't remember how many hundreds and hundreds now. A change is as good as a rest, they say.

Anyway, my godly ears registered her doorbell ring several times. The back gate clanged, followed by several more clangs and bangs, and over Bob's shoulder, I caught sight of a shadow moving up the wall. It suddenly vanished, and judging from the thud and curses, the intruder had come to grief. Not a professional, then. I pulled away from Bob, to his annoyance.

"Shush, there's something going on at the Goodall's. I'm going to check it out."

He said, "Lin, call 911. You know the rules. We don't intervene. You could get hurt." His voice came across as adolescent-plaintive rather than manly-protective, which irritated me to no end.

"Shut up! I'll be right back. I'm only going to look." He made no reply, no doubt offended by my brusque reply. I'd overheard someone describe me as brusque a couple of months before and rather liked the sound of it.

Once I'd crept deep enough in shadow that Bob couldn't see me, I vaulted the fence and crawled up the wall of the house like a gecko until I came up right behind the man just as he had reached a second-floor window. He reeked of booze and urine. I wondered why he hadn't tried the ground-floor windows until I remembered that when the house was under construction and windows were being installed, the company truck sported a logo new to me. I'd been playing around with the foreman on and off for a while, and he told me that the lower-level windows were all made of some special glass that is nearly impossible to break. He swore me to secrecy. Anyone would think the Goodalls kept gold bullion in there. I decided that one of these days, I would go in and have a good poke around. Olive's husband was a mid-level executive and shouldn't need to fit his house out with drug-king defenses. Granted, it was a little grander than the rest of the houses in our bailiwick, but still. Fishy.

I scooted around the intruder and drew level with him. His face was partially shadowed by a hoodie, though when he turned to face me, his look of shock and horror was clear enough. If I hadn't been distracted by his nose rings, not to mention the overpowering reek of stale liquor wafting from his open mouth, I might have recognized him. He shook like Aetna before she loses her temper. That tends to happen on the rare occasions I employ what few divine powers remain to me. When I bared my teeth and snarled, he squealed like a piglet and tried to punch me. He missed, instead breaking the window before making a desperate attempt to get inside and away from the monster. With that, the alarm went off. "Naughty, naughty, time to go," I whispered and picked him up with my right arm, flinging him off the ladder to the ground, where he screeched, writhed, and called for his mom. My work complete, I sped back to Bob. He asked me if I'd had fun playing cop, sounding like the parent of a recalcitrant daughter.

"Thank you, yes." I told him that the intruder had broken an upstairs window, then fell off the ladder. The alarm company would call 911. But I thought that Bob should too, if only to tell them we needed an ambulance.

Bob called. He thinks I'm a Neanderthal because I don't use a cell phone, which is hilarious when I think about how some of my best friends were Neanderthals. I told him I didn't want my husband to be calling me all the time. The truth is, when I hold a cell phone the battery drains within minutes. The first couple of times it happened, I returned the phone for a replacement. The third time, I realized it was me. Same with anything electronic. Godliness has its drawbacks.

When the sirens drew close, we drove to the front of the house and met the cops.

The older cop asked, "What's going on?" He was a sergeant, if I remember the stripe thing correctly.

Bob started to explain. "We are members of the neighborhood watch..." and I said, "Yes, well, we were in that lane by the side of the house. As we turned around to go back the way we came, we heard noises coming from the side of the house, then a sort of crash, and the alarm went off. I went to check and saw a man on the ground. He'd clearly fallen off a ladder. We called 911."

The sergeant said, "I see," and told his partner to take our names. "Follow me," he told the EMTs, who had just arrived.

I ignored the note-taker and joined the procession into the yard. They pulled back the burglar's hood, and that's when I realized it was young Chad. *Oops!* His wallet seemed to be missing, but I told the cops who he was, mentioning that I hadn't recognized him at first because, and so on and so forth.

He woke up for a few minutes when the EMTs did their checks and loaded him onto the stretcher. Right leg and left wrist broken was the tally so far. He started rambling about this woman monster in a blue and white dress who picked him up and threw him to the ground. I tiptoed backward, but not fast enough. He opened his eyes, caught sight of me in the headlights between the cars, and started screaming for his mother again.

I wouldn't wear that dress again for a long time—a pity because it was very striking and one of my favorites. My people love blue, the color of the sky. I still remember Yggdrasil's magnificent canopy outlined against our brilliant Norse heaven. We were still powerful then. We ruled the world.

"Turn that thing off, Mary. I'm done for the day."

"So that's why we're using this old recorder."

"Yes, it's almost embarrassing. I'm like a doomsday machine for modern electronics."

"What happened to Chad?"

"Oh, nothing till much later. He spent a few days in the hospital, of course. But he never did amount to anything. Too indulged. And not too bright. You'll hear about him again soon enough. I'll be busy next week, by the way, so just relax. Maybe work on your novel."

I was free to work on my own stuff for a while but couldn't settle down to it. I had to keep reminding myself that this could all be a giant hoax. *But I saw her shape-shift with my own eyes.* She couldn't have faked that. Everything I thought was real had to be questioned, not to mention everything I thought to be folklore and myth.

Well, everything real is still real, I guess. It was what I always thought was unreal that was the problem. I think I was in shock. Moving like a robot, just going through the motions.

I wonder if she ever met Jesus?

I thought she might not come down as we'd finished breakfast more than an hour ago. I'd been poking around in my
novel for a week but still couldn't concentrate after what I'd
heard the week before. Good grief!

Suddenly, she was peering over my shoulder.

"Okay, Mary, let's get on with it. I've only got half an hour.
Hunter wants me to join him at the mall after he's met with
our bank manager. I hate the mall. Full of annoying people."

She flung herself onto the sofa, heaved a great sigh, and
began talking. I barely had time to switch on the recorder
and grab my notebook and pencil. Later, when I replayed
the tape to type up the session, the first few sentences were
missing, but I'd made good notes.

I planned to go out too. Lunch with Aunty Peggie and a
good walk with Sam. I can't wait to see Sam—he will always
hold a special place in my heart. Dogs get under your skin,
burrow into your soul.

Tape 3

The night after the Chad debacle, our neighborhood watch committee called an emergency meeting at the house of Olive's best friend, Diane. She brought up the fact that I had breached protocol. Her sallow, pinched face presented a perfect picture of benign concern. She perched like a queen on the middle cushion of a cream velour sofa. Her throne stood at the end of a not-quite-matching cream wool carpet, which ran down the center of a rectangular room littered with spindly tables and chairs. The rest of the committee members squirmed on those chairs as they tried to get comfortable.

"I just went to make sure there really was an intruder." I readjusted myself in a chair I had selected for its distance from the sofa. "We called 911," I added, picking at a bowl of peanuts on the wobbly table next to me, which teetered on stilettos rather than actual legs.

Diane said, "Olive feels there was more than that. You must have frightened the boy."

I said, "Oh, come on, Diane, he was drunk and hurt. He never saw me until the police arrived. He's confused."

Then Bob chimed in, "I did tell you, stay in the car and call." He looked at me like a triumphant tomcat after it's serviced the local purebred. Apt analogy. Casanova would live to regret it, or maybe not.

"We very much appreciate your service Lin," Diane said, "but do you think perhaps a little break might be a good idea?"

Fury rendered me silent for a minute. It was important not to let these people see my fury. It's impressive, but I have to live among them. No one can ever know I'm a goddess, albeit a minor one. Although, with the others gone, possibly not so minor anymore? Our powers are much weaker but still terrifying to humans if we let ourselves go. Why should I put up with that kind of shit?

"I resign then! I wanted to avoid troubling the police unnecessarily, and this is the thanks I get." I swept out of there, only just managing to restrain myself from slamming the front door off its hinges.

Mortals can be so petty.

I needed to walk and think, so I ambled across to the community center park, where a path meanders around the perimeter. No one goes there after dark unless they're up to no good, but I'm a match for any local punk who feels like messing with me. I had another lifetime to get through, this one here in Salton, a Northern Virginia suburb of the nation's capital. We were nobodies in a nice enough neighborhood, our section by no means high-end, condemned to live out another lifetime before moving on. In the good old days—I mean the really, really old days—I used to be docile and often invisible when I descended and went about my business here on earth, but I'd changed. I craved excitement. My husband, ostensibly an entrepreneur, was as bored with me as I with him. Our servant girl Dora, a washed-up Greek nymph, resented her demotion from maiden to maid, although she had no choice in the matter— long story. She provoked me whenever she thought she could get away with it.

I'd arrived back at the park entrance but still felt restless and confused, so I set off again, in the opposite direction this time. Maybe going widdershins would shake up my brain. Widdershins means going in the opposite direction to the sun's course. Counterclockwise. I learned the word from an old friend who claimed to be a witch. Maybe she was; I was never sure. I met a real witch later, and she was the real deal.

My children were always in trouble. I enrolled them in Tae Kwon Do to work off their natural—okay, unnatural—exuberance. The instructor was excited by their prowess but mentioned tactfully that they didn't seem to know their own strength. We still haven't told the children what and who we are. You'd think they'd notice our uniqueness, but I guess it's all normal to them. We are just Mom and Papa. They used to complain a lot about not having grandparents or family photos like everyone else. I told them, truthfully, that their grandparents are all dead, as are their aunts, uncles, and cousins, to the best of our knowledge. They still harp on it.

To my everlasting sorrow, immortality passes our children by. Most people have a friend or relative who has experienced the agony of losing a child. Imagine how it is with us. One or two every lifetime. We have learned to let go and leave them when they are well set on their course in life. Our slow aging always raises questions, you see. We leave "on vacation," telling them some good reason for the trip, and stage an accident. At first, we would simply disappear but realized that put them through their own agony—that of never knowing. They are always well provided for. Hunter takes it in his stride and rarely looks back. I keep track for a while, though, and my heart will ache dreadfully forever. I still remember many of them with a pang, although they fade into a misty grayness, eventually. We don't care to keep likenesses. Never have. No point.

I sat under a tree, hoping for suggestions. Unfortunately, this wasn't an oak, so I waited in vain. Silver birches are too cute and flighty to be nurturing like oaks. I hugged my knees, trying to come up with a game plan.

I have never adapted to mediocrity. We've still got plenty of money but must not risk drawing attention to it. How could I earn enough to justify a higher lifestyle? I've been to the best schools and universities in the world. Things change so fast, and you have to keep up, even though it's tiresome to have to sit through classes, learn new languages and take exams every century or so if you don't want to come off like a moron. Sometimes I have to brush up on science, but that's easy enough. Even history keeps changing, depending on who's telling and who's forgetting. I have the brains to accomplish greatness. Hunter always panics about us drawing unwelcome attention. What's the point of living, then? He is so insecure, very handsome, but rather slow-thinking, and he knows it. His brother-gods called him stupid often enough. He doesn't want me getting ahead of him. That's the truth of it.

She closed her eyes and sighed. Was she done? Hunter actually talked to me at dinner last night. Asked me what I was writing about. He is very handsome. And deliciously big. And rather sweet. He seemed puzzled by the idea of fiction, which I found odd. Had he never had stories read to him as a child? At breakfast, he asked me if I would prefer tea or coffee. The Thorens' coffee is so rich and smooth, I've never had better, and I told him that. He responded with a big, big smile. So sweet.

I shouldn't be writing such things in my notes. Thank heavens for the recorder, although that might not be so safe either.

Pay attention. She started talking again.

Our immortality took a hit after *Ragnarök*, and we have to endure the pain of rebirth at regular intervals. I always come back the way I was created—a girl of sixteen or so—and don't lie down for rebirth until around one hundred and fifty. Hunter gets quite decrepit around one hundred and thirty and is reborn as a baby, which works out quite conveniently. I get him a nanny and don't have to have much to do with him day-to-day. How many times could I stand raising the kid, knowing what I'm ending up with? It's not as if he evolves much, and I'm certainly not going to potty-train my own husband. After I've fired the household help so I can be reborn in private, he's on his own for a couple of weeks. It takes me at least a month before I'm back to full strength, so we have the most awful rows about the state of the place and who's going to see to the meals. The concept of responsibility eludes him. When you've been worshipped and waited on for thousands of years, it tends to go to your head, you know.

Anyway, my needs were changing. I yearned for fulfillment. What could I do? Politics? No, that would invite close scrutiny, although think what I could achieve, the people I could bring to heel. I got up, patted the pretty bark, and left.

When I got home that night, I went into the living room, where Hunter lounged in his recliner, watching TV. He's loved crime dramas ever since he discovered the small silver screen. This one had lots of shooting and chasing—right up his alley. Our godly king, Odin, used to stalk anyone who upset him badly enough and smite them with thunderbolts. Such fun. Having only one eye, his focus was unerring, so he never missed. Odin's son, Thor, Hunter's brother, crafted the bolts in his forge and presented him with a new supply every summer solstice. Zeus and his ilk, who came to power long after we were vanquished, learned about thunderbolts from all the old stories.

Hunter asked, "How was your meeting?" He couldn't have cared less but believes in observing the traditional hypocrisies. He sighed regretfully as the show ended with the hero gloating over a swathe of dead bodies.

"I quit. They didn't like me going to see what was happening before we called the cops."

"You should not have hurt him like that. It makes people talk."

"But they don't know I did. Olive believed her son, but no one else did. They're all jealous of my beauty, you know that. And Bob is being vindictive because he made a pass at me, and I turned him down."

Dumb as he is, in some ways, Hunter can be impressive. He hoisted himself out of the recliner and seemed to have grown a couple of feet as he thought through this insult. Bob would find him terrifying.

I said, "Now, then, dearest, we mustn't draw attention to ourselves. Be subtle." Asking Hunter to be subtle is like asking a charging rhinoceros to tip-toe so as not to wake the birdies. I'll prod him along until we find the right moment.

Hunter breathed out slowly, deflated back into his recliner, and started watching a new show. An elderly English lady bustled around solving a murder—not his usual fare.

He suddenly turned to me. "You are always complaining about being bored," he said, pointing at the screen. "Why not go out and solve things like her?"

The idea began to take root. I thought about it all evening and most of the night. But where would I find clients? I'd have to get some credentials, too. Maybe one good case under my belt would do it. I should seduce one of our local detectives, get him talking about his unsolved cases. TV shows seem to be full of amateurs who help the police, but I supposed it never happened that way in real life. A kidnapping? Drugs? I remembered reading in the paper about a new strain of heroin that had found its way into our region. If I could just bust that. Could I do it as me, Lin? Hunter would not like the notoriety, so maybe not.

Olive had to be punished, too. Why those windows? Maybe I should start there.

"So, you found out why they had those funny windows?"

"I certainly did, but you're going to have to wait to find out!"

So annoying!

"I want to go to the mall after lunch. Come with me. Let's get ourselves something new."

And we did. She insisted I get this really expensive pant-suit, navy with red piping, then some shoes to match. She wouldn't let me pay.

"I can see you love the way you look in it. I can't tell you how much pleasure that gives me."

So generous. I was beginning to like them both. A lot.

Lin told me Hunter would be out that evening. "He some-times likes to have a few drinks with friends. Funny thing is, I've never met any of them. Probably a woman."

She shrugged and settled down. I wondered at such equanimity. She didn't mind? Interesting.

"So, if it is a woman, you really don't mind?"

"Of course not. When you have been with someone for thousands of years, you have to give them a little leeway. Relationships get stale, need goosing up a bit from time to time. We will always be together."

Sage advice but not suited to the everyday mortal mar-riage, perhaps.

Tape 4

I'd watched the Goodall house for more than a week from the middle of a cluster of spiky evergreen bushes, zipping home from time to time, always mindful that I shouldn't neglect my domestic responsibilities. Hunter is mostly laid back, but if he feels unappreciated, there's hell to pay. He still misses the sacrifices, too, and if he broods on that for too long, he gets tetchy. I'd left Dora with strict instructions about dinner. Hunter is the consummate carnivore, demanding slabs of barely cooked meat and a token spoonful or two of vegetables. A couple of large baked potatoes always hit the spot, too. He's a big man, a very big man.

Dora was lazy and got away with a lot because Hunter had a soft spot for her. They were probably disporting themselves in our gazebo while I slaved away at my new job. They seemed to think I didn't know, thought I would care, which was strange. Gods have always taken liberties with lesser beings. It's in their genes; I know the score, and anyway, Hunter is a higher-ranked god than me as the brother of Thor and son of Odin—although I'm not sure ranks matter anymore. In all these millennia, we hadn't yet come across any of the others. Maybe they were lying low, like us. Anyway, I really didn't care because everyone I've ever deeply cared about—except my children—was killed in the last battle. I saw their ravaged bodies with my own eyes.

No wonder Dora didn't like me. She considered me competition. And why not? I wasn't bad looking. Slim. Not a patch on Lin, but who was? I was tall and had dark hair. That might be a plus. She said a change is as good as a rest.

Oops, she's talking again.

I shook myself loose from sad memories and reread my notes on the Goodall's visitors—who came and went and when. They'd had people over every other Friday night to play bridge, or so she claimed, for years. No one from around here had ever been invited, and people sometimes wondered who their guests were, these strangers in big, black cars, some with chauffeurs. Someone occasionally brought it up, but Olive always changed the subject. People Jerry went to school with, she said once in my hearing. This was one of those Fridays, and I wanted to know who her guests might be. It was late April, and the days were getting longer. They began to arrive at eight, not quite dark.

The first car rolled up, and a chunky young man in uniform sprang out and around to open his passenger's door. A Japanese gentleman barely out of his twenties rushed out. The front door opened as soon as he reached it. He slid inside without a word. The next car parked in the driveway, and an emaciated, pale man, about six-four, unfurled himself from his seat and loped along the side path, peering from side to side before he, too, was sucked through the portal. Four more cars arrived, discharging a motley group, none of whom I could imagine went to school with Jerry. For one thing, two were at least twenty years younger than him, and three maybe ten years older.

Anyway, these men made me realize that there was definitely something strange going on at the Goodall residence.

I decided to wait and see how long they stayed. I'd go back on the next bridge night and hide inside.

Three hours later, the men straggled out and left. I had jotted down their license plates to get them checked out when I could. I'd been flirting with one of the cops who answered the call when Chad had his little accident. Recently separated, he'd be ripe for seduction. He could run them for me once I'd gotten him sufficiently enchanted. As it happened, I never got around to it.

I crept close to the front door while they were inside. Large boxwoods provided good concealment, but I felt I should make sure all was quiet before leaving. I had just made up my mind to go home when the garage door opened. Jerry sat in the car, and he and Olive quarreled in whispers. My hearing is inhumanly good, so I caught every word.

Olive hissed, "Don't let anyone see you."

"I don't intend to. That guy's nuts! I don't want him back."

Olive's whisper slipped into a squeal. "We have no choice."

The car left, and the garage door lowered. As soon as Olive was out of sight, I ran after Jerry. He went for about a half-hour before I decided to conserve my strength by perching on the Beemer's roof the rest of the way.

He went down some dirt tracks in a heavily wooded park and stopped at a picnic area along a creek of the Potomac. I leaped into an oak tree that offered me a good view of the action. He opened the trunk and lugged out a large object wrapped in a sheet. I smelled the blood before I saw the stains—the blood of a woman.

He trudged to the bank and rolled her in. The splash occurred a few seconds later. The spot he chose must have been higher than I realized.

I didn't wait to see any more but sped off home. Hunter was already in bed, snoring and grunting. I could hear him from the living room, even with the doors closed. I was glad not to have to put up with his sulking because I'd been gone so long. It's not that he minds my absence, more that he resents my attention focusing on something other than him.

I looked in on the children—Husky Sven, still slightly grubby and Margareta, still unaware of her incipient Norse beauty. Their serenity in sleep gave no hint of their rambunctious natures. I tried to fix the images in my memory. Should I allow myself to take one photo? Would it help eighty years from now, or would it slice too deep? I took a photo with my old camera but would never tell Hunter.

I had to plan my next move. Jerry clearly knew that spot by the river well. I could start with that. And I'd scan news reports for a body being washed up. I needed to run those license plates. If necessary, I could try putting the cop into a trance. It doesn't always work these days, but I sometimes succeed. I needed to get inside the house while Olive and Jerry were out, look around for clues, and search out a hiding place, and then I must get inside the day of the next party. I felt excited and nervous. I had to do this right and get the credit. And not get sent to prison myself. Of course, no one can hold me for long, but then we'd have to disappear, making Hunter and the children really mad. I hate Hunter when he's mad, although it's pretty great when we make up.

6

Lin missed a couple of days because her partner called her in to assist with a case. I didn't even see her at breakfast, but rather enjoyed getting to know Hunter better. The first morning, he became downright loquacious by his standards.

"Do you not have a boyfriend, Mary?"

"No, not at the moment."

"You are such a charming young lady; I find that hard to believe." *Flatterer.*

"I was seeing someone in college, but I had to go back to Pennsylvania to sort things out after my mother died. He went on to graduate school in California."

"Do you miss him?"

"Actually, I don't. I think we just got used to doing things together."

"He is a very silly boy, letting a lovely lady like you get away."

I giggled like a teen.

Such a charming man in so many ways. We had plenty of uninterrupted time for conversation. Hunter wanted to know all kinds of things about me. I tried to ask him about his life, too, but he answered in very general terms, such as monitoring his investments, taking care of the family, and so on. He gave nothing away, soon turning the conversation back to me.

He smiled at me quite often, his face lighting up like a beacon—an unusually magnetic one. My thoughts began to stray to fantasyland.

Dora acted unusually sulky, even for her.

Lin didn't discuss the case when she reappeared, except to say that it was solved and it hadn't been pleasant. She was pretty snappy with us all, so it had clearly upset her. I read about it in the paper a few days later. She'd found the missing person dead, missing a few fingers.

She said nothing to me when she did come downstairs but lay down and started to talk. I'd arrived at my station a few minutes before, so she found me ready and waiting.

Tape 5

I'd had a busy week. I suffered through two Salton Symphony board meetings, where just about all anyone could talk about was the Rose Hale affair. I knew Rose slightly and tailed her once or twice as I sensed that she was not what she seemed. I saw her murder a young woman in the garden by stabbing her while she sunbathed. She was a psychopath, a serial killer. I chose not to interfere. From what I've read, those people almost never get away with it.

I was appointed to the board after she was arrested, as half the trustees had either been murdered or resigned. Not many people wanted to have anything to do with the symphony after the scandal made national headlines. I didn't mind. I like music. I used to be a virtuoso on the lyre, but only weird people play it now, and they manage to make it sound like a cat with a thorn in its paw.

Inevitably, donations dried up to a large extent, and the symphony found itself in dire straits. We were interviewing new conductors, too, as the other little fellow had had enough after an embarrassing incident when a rat ran amok on the stage, causing no end of chaos, not to mention an undignified and abrupt end to the concert. I'm pretty sure Rose engineered it. She looked very smug as well as amused, but then almost the entire audience was just about rolling in the aisles, tears of laughter running down their cheeks.

I made a very large donation, a quarter of it from Hunter and me and the rest anonymous. People would have wondered why we lived in a 1960s split-level if we had that kind of money. I wondered myself, but Hunter was adamant about keeping a low profile. At least our donation would keep the group afloat for another year while we set the organization on a firm footing.

Best of all, the detective who worked the case had started volunteering with the Symphony when he was surveilling Rose. After the arrest and her conviction, Joe kept on because he enjoyed it. We invited him to join the board—quite a windfall from my point of view.

At last, Olive went to Roanoke for an overnight visit with her married daughter. Her housekeeper Kate told Dora, who told me. I'd instructed Dora to keep in with Kate so I could keep abreast of their movements. Unfortunately, the woman was always off Friday noon to Sunday night, so there was no dirt on the "bridge night" guests. Jerry spent his days at the office and often enjoyed a cocktail or two at the end of the day.

Friday after twelve, then. I ran to the Goodall house to stay invisible, scaled the fence, and waited for the housekeeper to leave. She opened the door, and I confronted her.

She asked, "Mrs. Thoren, how can I help you?"

I gazed into her eyes as intently as I could.

"Mrs. Thoren! Whatever is the matter? I just set the alarm. I'm going home."

The damn woman was tough. "It's all right, Kate. I saw something strange in your eye. Does it hurt? Keep your eyes open."

I went on gazing and concentrating until I thought I'd pop my brain. She'd just opened her mouth to speak again when the telltale glaze shuttered her face. Phew! Old age is no fun. I slipped through the door before the alarm went off.

"What is the alarm code?"

"Chad21." *Pathetic.*

I closed the door. She'd come to herself in a few minutes. I checked that I'd gotten in fast enough that I didn't need to turn off the alarm. Most people have the exit set for thirty or forty-five seconds. That shambolic mesmerizing must have taken at least a minute. Blessed silence.

I searched the study first, rummaging through mahogany desk drawers and the matching file cabinet, scanning hundreds of documents over the next quarter hour. Nothing except bills, family letters, and a couple of terse communications from schools that had expelled Chad. Where was the safe? I looked behind gold-framed paintings and drew back the Turkish rug. Maybe in the basement.

I went downstairs, freezing for a few minutes when I heard female voices, some weeping. I tiptoed the rest of the way, peering around the last bend. The recreation room was empty, small, and spartan for a house this size. Three doors. One led to a washroom and a second to the utility room. The third door bore a huge padlock. The voices lay beyond it. I felt along the top of the doorframe and found the key. Too easy made me feel … uneasy. When the lock released, the voices fell silent. I found myself in a narrow hallway with six doors, three along each side. I gently opened the first on the right, half expecting someone to cosh me. Five frightened girls huddled on a bed that took up most of the space. Purple velvet cushions lay stacked on the floor.

"It's all right. I won't hurt you. Who are you?"

One of them started to speak in Arabic. Educated at Victoria College in Alexandria, Egypt, only one lifetime ago, I speak Arabic, albeit that of an earlier era.

"We are prisoners," said one. "Kept here to please men."

So that was what it was all about.

"How many of you are there?"

"There were seven, even though there is only room for six. Muna and Zara had to take turns sitting in the kitchen while the other was entertaining and then share a room to sleep. After the last visit, Yasmin was hurt. We heard her screaming, and then she disappeared. We think one of the men killed her. One girl who was still here when we came said they will change us out, sending one or two away each month. Then they bring replacements. Only they brought us six together. The first girl was taken away the same night. I don't know where they took her."

This was delivered in a monotone, a drone of despair. She'd be gorgeous if she smiled.

"I will help you, but you'll have to stay a little longer until I can get help."

"What does it matter now? We cannot go home. Our families will not want us. And America will not want us."

I understood. The ownership concept. Lost virginity, second-hand goods.

"How did you come here?"

"A woman promised us refuge. We are Syrians and were living in a refugee camp after we fled our town. One of the aid ladies told us all the same story. She would get us to America, and after a while, we could bring our families. It was a lie. I should have realized. But we were desperate. Laila and I left together. The others joined us in Cyprus."

"And these men come every two weeks to lie with you?"

"Yes. The lady asked us if we were virgins. She said she wanted to be sure we were of good character. Men pay a lot for virgins; that is why she asked. But we are no longer virgins, so I am sure we will be moved soon."

"This woman at the camp, what was her name?"

"She called herself Mrs. Mary Wilder."

"And are there many camps in that area?"

"Yes, and there are more going up every week. Ours was in Turkey, just across the Syrian border, a three-day walk from our town. Life there is so bad, so dangerous. But not as bad as here."

"I'll try to get you out before they move you on."

"Nazli and I have been lucky … if you can call it that." She pointed at a girl sitting on the floor with her knees pulled up to her chest, sobbing piteously. "Nazli is only fifteen, and the old man likes her. And I put up a fight. The Japanese fellow likes that. I started that way to try to save myself, but now the fight is perhaps saving me from worse."

"What is your name?"

"Reema. That is Iman." She pointed to a plump girl with thick black eyebrows and lashes framed by a mane of dark curls. "She is Muna," pointing to a fair-haired girl huddled on the floor next to Nazli. "And this is Zara next to me. We know each other from home."

"Hello, ladies," I said, with a bright smile to all. They nodded and muttered polite replies but couldn't bring themselves to smile back.

"I had just started medical school when the war broke out. I have more education than the others. But it did not save me from my own stupidity."

Hearing the name "Reema" felt like a stab to my heart. Reema, my beautiful daughter of Egypt. The name, coupled with this cruel tale, fueled incandescent fury in my gut. Perhaps the *Norns*—the fates—sent me to these young women.

"It's not your fault," I said. "You wanted to help your family."

The one named Iman said, "I told my family what I was doing, and they were eager, too. We have to write letters home full of lies. One each month." Her voice sounded even more desolate than Reema's.

I asked if they had enough food. They told me they had a little kitchen with a refrigerator and a bathroom. The word for refrigerator had me stumped until Reema explained that it was a cupboard to keep food cold. She looked puzzled, obviously wondering why I didn't know that word. The fact is, refrigerators weren't thick on the ground when I learned Arabic.

Muna said there was a cupboard with beans and rice and a few other things. "It is not in their best interests to let us go hungry."

I asked, "What is in the other rooms?"

"There is a room for each of us so we can entertain our guests." Reema said this with a bitterness that lifted the monotone to something more spirited. I don't know why I asked. It should have been obvious.

"Sometimes, I suppose when his wife is out, the man comes for one of us. Yesterday, it was his son. His mother brought him down, lined us up, and told him to pick one as a special treat. He chose Nazli and kept her all afternoon." Nazli cried harder as Muna comforted her.

My cue to get out. Since Olive was out, Jerry might come back early to enjoy himself.

"I am so, so sorry. I will try to help you. But don't tell anyone about me."

They chorused, "We will not."

"Do you know when letters will be sent again?"

Muna said, "Tomorrow. We were told to write them today."

"All right. I will see you again."

"Goodbye, lady." Reema's eyes welled, and she held out her hand as if begging. I patted her shoulder. In spite of everything, she had found hope.

I wouldn't let them down. It's what I was born to do—help humans in dire peril. It's what my dear lady Frigg would expect of me. What she always expected and what I had always done until she passed over in that fearsome battle. She used to send me to earth to save those under her protection when they were in danger.

This was danger of the worst kind, and I could almost hear her gentle voice telling me the story as she pointed into her silver pool and showed me these unlucky creatures. I would say, "Yes, my lady, I am ready," and close my eyes. When I opened them, only moments later, I found myself among those unfortunates, although they could not yet see me. It was time to fulfill my destiny once more. I wondered suddenly if Frigg could be watching me in some secret world. The other worlds we knew of had perished after the battle, all except Hel and Midgard. Could another have existed? A sort of heaven for gods? None of us could know. So much might come to light if Yggdrasil were to live and grow once more.

I left the hidden rooms and locked them in, replacing the key where I found it. The alarm sounded, then silenced when someone disarmed it. I darted into the utility room, footsteps already clumping down the stairs as I pulled the door ajar. Jerry. He crossed my field of vision on his way to the girls, pausing and turning briefly when a mousetrap snapped shut on my toe. It took all my resolve to keep quiet and still. He shrugged and turned back. The padlock rattled, the key turned, and he locked the door from the inside. It turned my stomach to think what would happen next. Jerry was a plump, sweaty fellow, who I'm sure behaved as crassly in bed as he did socially. A self-made man, as he liked to proclaim himself, he prided himself on having "pulled myself up by my bootstraps" and saying, "My family never went on welfare; we all worked our butts off." He'd boasted about his state scholarship for college often enough, which didn't quite seem to square with his "always paid my own way" mantra. My stomach turned again as my toe cried out for attention.

Intercepting those letters the next day and finding out who they were addressed to, and where, was of crucial importance. They might get put in the mail, or they might be handed off to someone. It couldn't be easy to smuggle people into the U.S. without quite a support network. This was way bigger than I had dreamed of. Way bigger. Could I handle it alone?

I did pretty well tiptoeing upstairs and out of the house, considering the goddamn mousetrap clamped on my big toe, but I had to get out pronto and couldn't wait around to deal with it. I'd just closed the front door when the mailman opened the gate. Nothing for it but to sprint home. The mailman had raised his hand in greeting but suddenly realized no one was there after all, just a funny clicking noise.

If I stopped running, I'd be visible, so on I went. No one else saw me, of course, but the clacking mousetrap and the occasional agonized grunt from me confused an elderly man taking his mutt for a walk. The dog wasn't confused at all but gave chase, pulling his old master behind him until he let go of the leash. I took care not to cross the road if a car was coming. I like dogs. He couldn't keep up, of course, but the stout-hearted fellow gave it his best shot. I doubled back and picked him up. I'd take care of him until the lost dog notices showed up.

I ran around the back of our house and pried off the mousetrap. I resolved to always wear shoes for sleuthing in the future, stealth be damned. The dog licked my toe. I kissed him and read the collar tag. Simon, together with a phone number. I'd call the old man after a decent interval. The kids mustn't meet him, though. I don't know why Hunter is so opposed to getting a dog. I really wanted one. They know how to cuddle without seeking a reward beyond the occasional biscuit.

"Oh, yes," I broke in. "Auntie Peggy's Sam is such a sweetheart. I love him so much. Have you asked Hunter why he doesn't like them?"

Lin reacted as if I'd interrupted an anointing. Her eyes snapped open, and she glared at me.

"I don't like to have my train of thought interrupted. No, he won't talk about it."

"Sorry, Lin."

"Huh."

She squirmed around before continuing.

I kneeled down and petted Simon. He rubbed his head against my cheek for a while before struggling out of my arms and bolting out through the front gate. He would find his way home, of course—dogs and gods always do. But I wanted him.

I felt like crying. Part of it was about hearing the name Reema. I straightened my shoulders. I would save those girls. And hobble-sprinting home through time with a mousetrap compressing my toe proved one of my most heroic endeavors ever. The old Lin was still on the job.

Olive put the letters in the mailbox near their home, so I waited for the mailman to open it. I'd meditated that morning for two hours to focus my mind.

"Good afternoon! I'm afraid I posted a bill too early. Could you let me have it back?" I gazed into the mailman's eyes. He looked acutely uncomfortable. Heck, *I* was acutely uncomfortable. It should have worked after all that effort.

"We are not allowed to do that, Madam. I'd get fired if anyone found out."

"Oh, dear, I wouldn't want that to happen." I squeezed some tears into the corners of my eyes and stared into his eyes again. This time, his face stilled, and his eyes lost their light. He would remember nothing. Hopefully. I soon spotted the fat brown envelope Olive slid through the slot, grabbed it, and walked away. It took a while to decipher the address, but I managed with help from Google. I stashed them with my precious mementos in a fireproof chest in the garden shed.

Lin sighed with evident satisfaction. "I cooked their gooses. All of them. By the way, I've decided I can't do this every single day. I'll let you know when I'm ready for one of our sessions. You'll have plenty of time to yourself. Is that okay with you?"

"Of course," I said. "I just don't want you to feel you're paying a lot and not getting enough in return."

"Oh, we all like you, Mary. You're a great addition to our household."

Already! These people were strange. *Well, they're not people, are they?*

Lin had been almost silent at breakfast. Hunter seemed preoccupied, too. I ate my oatmeal quickly and brought my coffee down with me.

"This is going to be another difficult one," Lin said as she arranged herself for our session. "It may sound as if I'm a bad mother, but a few children have been more precious to me than others. I'm afraid I don't even remember some—it's been so long, and, needless to say, they mostly look alike. I've loved them all, mind you, cried for them all, but there are those who are burned into my memory. Reema is one of them, and hearing this young captive's name brought back the loss."

"How old are your children? You didn't say."

"Sven is 16, and Margareta is nearly 18. They'll both soon be in college, although Margareta is taking a break. They are away at boarding school in Connecticut. It became clear that when they wanted to invite their friends home and for sleepovers and such, things could get awkward ... if you know what I mean."

"You mean they might see strange occurrences?"

"Yes, of course. Look how you reacted when you saw Hunter eating rare meat for breakfast. And that's just a small thing. We both have godly sight, hearing, and occasionally move much faster than usual. We are very strong by human standards, too. It's easy to forget and give ourselves away when we're in our own home."

"Such a shame you had to send them away."

"Oh, they're perfectly happy. They love us, but none of us are very sentimental."

Clearly. "I look forward to meeting them."

"They'll be home for Thanksgiving."

Tape 6

Egypt—my fondest memory since my homeland. I'd attended Victoria College, an elite private boy's school, disguised as a boy. I never showered with the others and kept strict privacy, which caused speculation, as you can imagine. I actually managed to shift into a boy shape once, but there were too many vulnerable appendages—at least we women have bras in this modern age. I found it so disorienting; I changed right back. However, I licked them all at sports and gave out a few bloodied noses, too, so they didn't pursue the matter. A grand time, that. And a first-class education. Rubbing shoulders with the nobility of the Middle and Far East came in handy, too. It wasn't much help later after reclaiming womanhood, but I reveled in some splendid vacations in fabulous places for a few years. Later, I claimed to be the twin sister of their friend who had tragically died of typhoid—which plenty did in those days—so I didn't forfeit all my contacts. I had to fend off a few marriage proposals, though.

After graduation, I moved to Cairo. Hunter was by now sufficiently matured—physically, at least—and soon Reema came along. I spent many jasmine-scented moonlit evenings reclining in a dhow as it plied the Nile, picking up my friends from this dock and that for an evening of music and dance. Hunter usually went out carousing with his own friends.

Reema would often accompany me, falling asleep in the crook of my arm until our faithful boatman Nasser lifted her from me and laid her in the little quilted nest he'd made under the awning. A blonde beauty; she was a great favorite in our circle. As was I.

My headstrong, fiercely loving girl developed an iron will, married young, and divorced after giving birth to a daughter Nabila, who, I was happy to see, became as high-spirited and difficult as her mother. Karma! Reema had refused to go to university, but now that her daughter was going, she decided to follow suit. I, of course, was no longer around as I looked as young as my granddaughter at that time. Nabila was special to me, too, but never as much as her mother. Pretty as a picture, even at fifty, Reema never knew I still watched over her. She thought we were dead, victims of an anarchist bombing. She eventually became a famous writer. That was my last life before this one. I'll suffer like that again and again.

I never hung on to the others like I did Reema. Our relationship always felt different, but I'm not sure why or how she held my heart like she did. I would kiss her while she slept. I was nowhere close to the end of that life before I realized I must let Reema go. She was nearly sixty, and I couldn't face watching her grow old and die. That last night I entered her dreams to bid her goodbye. Her mouth puckered and stretched, and she laughed softly. As her hand reached close to my face, I lowered my cheek to it briefly before pulling back. My love swelled unbearably.

Reema is long gone. I don't think Hunter misses them the way I do. When I said that final goodbye, he was running around Tunisia, doing heaven knows what or whom. At around one hundred, I decided to will an early rebirth, and Hunter could do as he pleased. We usually try to transition about twenty years apart, as I explained. Me first, since he comes back as a baby, and a very demanding one, I might add. I supposed I'd have to track him down to explain the arrangements. It was going to be almost impossible if he wouldn't play along.

I found him at a grand hotel in Tunis. The manager shuffled from one foot to the other as he tried to stall me. The sounds of a vicious fight assailed my godly ears, although no one else in the lobby could hear it. However, the manager clearly knew his generous client had a guest.

I said, "Give me the key to my husband's room immediately."

"But Madame …"

Jumping the counter and lifting him off his feet by his old-boy British necktie did the trick. I didn't let him down until I marched over to the cubby and retrieved the old-fashioned iron key. Room 307. Taking the stairs three at a time soon got me to my destination, where a little crowd had gathered outside the door. A woman screeched, Hunter alternately roared and wheedled, and crockery flew and smashed as a grand spectacle played itself out.

"You promised me marriage."

"My little pigeon, I only said I would try. I have a wife already, you know that."

"Get rid of her!"

"It is complicated…"

Nothing so complicated a little brute force couldn't fix. I kicked in the door. Hunter looked like a man beaten down by the fates, what with macaroni festooning his hair, red sauce running down his face, and the sudden appearance of his irate wife looking as if she might do him the kind of mischief only a pissed-off goddess could devise.

"What do you want? Get out! Mind your own business!" Doing her fishwife act, the woman, a blowsy type, stood, arms akimbo, taking an unwisely aggressive stance.

"I'm the wife you'd like to get rid of. Out you go!"

I picked her up and threw her into the crowd outside. She shrieked some more.

"Take a shower, dear husband. I'll wait. I want to go home and transition." Hunter stopped pacing and looked at me as if I'd said Odin wanted a word.

"So early? Why? I do not want to."

"I can't bear missing Reema anymore. I need to get away."

"You do it to yourself."

"Don't you want to lose that harridan? Don't you feel even a shred of shame?"

"You never play around?"

"That's beside the point. I just heard her yell she's going to call the police because you assaulted her."

"You assaulted her. Why not just run away?"

That made me mad. And I made sure I looked mad, picking up a large brass pot and swinging it over my head.

"All right, all right, quick shower, and then back to Egypt." He started for the bathroom.

"No, I moved everything to our new home. America." He braked again.

"What? That is a wild country. I like civilized places. Luxury."

"San Francisco isn't that bad."

"And I will not be able to make love to you for weeks."

"It's been weeks. Anyway, you won't be making love to me for years … or to anyone else. You will also transition."

"I do not want to. Why are you doing this to me?" He looked like a sulky little boy.

"Don't make me mad."

Hunter disappeared into the shower. I laid out his clothes and packed his belongings. He is much stronger than me, so I found it interesting he'd been so easily intimidated. It probably had more to do with what I could withhold than what I could do. Not only the sex but we were bound by the loneliness of being utterly marooned in our secret godliness.

Three tiresome weeks later, we arrived at our new home in San Francisco. I had arranged for the place to be cleaned and food delivered. All our trunks had arrived. We unpacked and set things up ourselves, as we did not want anyone to lay eyes on us. Time enough to hire servants after the transition. We ran over to the other end of town to have dinner on our last evening and made love most of the night.

At dawn, I bathed and donned a white nightgown before lying down on a clean bedsheet in a spare bedroom. Hunter came in and gave me a sweet, lingering kiss before leaving the room. Eyes closed, my mind traveled back in time, flew over the millennia through happy celebrations in Asgard where I stood behind my lady Frigg, keeping her plate and wine glass replenished, enjoying the colorful robes, the aromas of roasting meats, precious perfumes, and fragrant blossoms, the merriment, the joy. I didn't need food or drink then, and desire had not yet touched my soul. I needed only my lady, my companions, and my mission. Those were my joys.

Tearing nerves and cramping organs interrupted the beautiful dreams, ten times worse than usual because it was not near my time. Hunter said I didn't cry out, so the screams must have been in my head. The normal process is bad enough, but this was torture. My skin rolled and stretched unbearably, knives stabbed joints, bees stung toes and fingers, and rats gnawed my flesh. Finally, I sank into oblivion. When I awoke, it was night. Almost too weak to give voice, I called Hunter. He rushed in with water telling me three days had passed. He promised to be back soon with fruit and broth. He looked eager in the way he did when ready for lovemaking, but I wasn't up to it. Not yet. In a week or two I would be back to normal, free and sweet sixteen.

After a few weeks of enjoying married life once more, it was Hunter's turn. He suffered greatly, too. He howled and flailed through it all before ending up cute, demanding, ravenous, and exasperating. He would pretty much stay that way while he grew like Jack's beanstalk. I'd be back to a life of bringing up baby with the help of a nanny and a couple of servant girls. I had a new country to get used to and a new life to shape. To the outside world, we'd be a couple of orphans.

"That sounds like a terrible ordeal," I said.

"Transitioning or losing my Reema?"

"Er—both, I guess."

She sprang up and ran upstairs. I wondered if I'd done irreparable harm to our relationship with that comment. I didn't want to leave. To lose Lin. To lose Hunter too soon. *What are you thinking? Stop it. Stop it.*

8

Lin didn't come downstairs the next day. At breakfast, she said she didn't feel well and would go back to bed. Hunter didn't seem too concerned and stayed at the table longer than usual as we chatted. The morning after that, she told Hunter she had decided to do some reading, so she had been spending some time downstairs each morning where it was quiet. She planned to continue as she found it calming.

Phew! We were still on.

Hunter looked pensive while he masticated. "Oh, that is so strange. What are you reading that is so fascinating?"

"Memoirs," she said.

"What are these?"

"Stories about people's lives. True stories, that is."

"It sounds very boring."

"Some people have led extraordinary lives, wouldn't you say?"

He opened his mouth to answer, shut it abruptly, and sent her a warning look. I concentrated on munching my cereal and chasing a stray banana slice around the bowl.

"Some kings and queens have led fascinating lives. And what about the actors in the TV shows you like? Wouldn't you like to know something about them?" I asked.

"No, they just playact. It is the characters who are interesting," Hunter replied.

Well, that sounded sensible. "You are quite right, of course," I said, laughing.

"I know," he said.

"Well, I am interested in other people's lives, especially if they are less boring than mine!" Lin said, clearly irritated.

Hunter glared at her and said nothing. Lin seemed to be spoiling for a fight.

Sure enough, Lin arrived downstairs clutching a veritable tome, which she set on the floor beside the sofa.

"Some Russian epic. I'll read a few pages each day so I can say something about it if he asks."

She grinned, pleased with herself, and took several minutes to arrange herself, making sure her hair was spread on the cushion becomingly. What a princess! She really shouldn't have lied to Hunter. But then, this whole setup was a lie. Layered secrets. I deceived Auntie. Lin and I deceived Hunter. Lin and Hunter deceived their children and all their friends. And Lin and Hunter cheated on each other, or so Lin gave me to understand.

But I was beginning to feel bad about deceiving Hunter like that. He was so sweet, such a teddy bear. The kind of teddy bear one likes to cuddle. *Stop it.*

Tape 7

Well, I was determined about the private eye thing. The Freya Agency was duly registered by our lawyer. I'd thought first of calling it the Frigg Agency after my beloved mistress, but it didn't quite set the right tone in the context of American culture, so I used the name she assumed in her role of seer and sorceress. Becoming a private detective turned out to be a royal pain in the neck. I thought I could put a nice sign on an office door and an ad in the paper. Not so fast. A license was required, meaning school, forms, and tests. Oh well ... the office and receptionist, not to mention clients, could come later.

I was worried the girls might be moved from the Goodall's in my absence, or I might have lost track of them. I checked on the house every evening, although that didn't tell me much. I hit on the idea of anonymously reporting a Peeping Tom and flasher to the cops with convincing detail—matching traitorous Bob to a tee—to ensure regular police and neighborhood watch patrols. The Goodalls surely wouldn't risk a big move with all that going on. My training would take eighty hours—two whole weeks before a long journey to the Middle East.

So, back to school. I'd found a training school that not only offered the required basic training course but self-defense and handgun certification, too. I have always been able to defend myself but needed to learn to make moves more along human lines. I had expected to ace everything, but boredom is a dangerous state of mind for someone like me.

I used to be calm and cast a warm glow over people, but then everyone died except Hunter and me. No pure goddess to guide me, no predestined mission, no uninterrupted immortality. Things used to be straightforward. Then they got complicated—the understatement of the century. I just couldn't concentrate in that gray, sterile room with hateful desks with their attached chairs.

My mind kept wandering away from "Applicable Sections of the Code of Virginia" and "Basic Law," so when the buzz-cut goon instructor Reg Moore called on me, it often came as if out of the blue. He subjected me to the full weight of clumsy sarcasm to the point that all I could think about was unique ways to make him suffer. "Lin seems to confuse unlawful entry with data entry."

The smirks of my classmates didn't help, either. In any event, I passed the section tests because I memorized the book, but not with flying colors, which hurt my ego. Legal issues aren't necessarily black and white, so rote memory didn't always serve, especially when it seemed the test setter's sole aim was to trip up the students. Anyway, there was still the final exam to cram for, so I didn't worry about it.

The other tests were fun, especially shooting, with a different instructor, thank heavens, a lanky pock-marked Vietnam vet called Sandy. My anger was so palpable by that point I visualized each target as Reg's crotch. Naturally, I outperformed the rest of the class. Not so much smirking anymore. Sandy fancied me; I could tell by the flash in his eyes and the way the corners of his mouth relaxed when he saw me each day. I didn't fancy him, though. Too skinny.

Reg and a young Asian man called Sam Lee alternated instruction on self-defense. Sam's slight build gave no hint of his strength and skill. He was fun, too. We studied throws and holds and a variety of evasive measures. I performed quite well but avoided being outstanding as I couldn't risk drawing too much attention to myself as I had with the weapons training. But then we came to the final class.

"This afternoon, we are going to practice fending off a sudden aggressive move." Reg turned to me, beaming with fake bonhomie. "Come on forward, little Lin, show us your moves," he said, lumbering to the middle of the floor like an arthritic dancing bear. I walked toward him in what I hoped looked a timid fashion. He made a sudden lunge and found himself looking up at me, momentarily in shock, before letting out a roar of anguish.

"You broke my frickin' back, yer stupid bitch!" he wailed.

"I'm so sorry. I thought that was the move you taught us." I said in a chastened voice as I watched him struggle to get up. "Perhaps you should lie still until the ambulance arrives," I said, my breathy voice turning all milk and honey. He slumped back. I turned to the class.

"Has anyone called 911?" A youngish man called Paul Drake (as he loudly declared our first day as if it meant something special) sidled to his backpack, apparently unwilling to turn his back on me, and retrieved his phone. The eerie silence and the appalled gaze of the others became annoying.

"What's the matter? Beginner's luck. Could have happened to anyone."

Lettie, a burly young woman with curly red hair who'd always been friendly, said, "You moved so fast I could hardly see your hands. You must have done this before. You're an expert."

"Well, yes, it's not my first time. You have to admit that Reg is hardly the person to be teaching us how to guard against a surprise attack."

Reg roused himself sufficiently to add, with a touch of the Irish, "Feckin bitch!"

The sirens halted their bawling outside the ground-floor window below. A minute later, an EMT poked his head around the door. "You called?"

I moved aside and pointed to Reg, now panting with little moans like a woman well along in labor. "A little training accident," I said, as seriously as I knew how. "He thinks his back is broken." The EMT yelled over his shoulder, "Bring the stretcher and brace, Bert."

Steph, the office manager, clattered up the hall and rushed into the room. "I was in the powder room when I heard sirens. What's going—Reggie! Darling! Are you all right?" She flung herself to her knees beside him, wincing only slightly as her kneecaps bounced on the hard surface, Bert the EMT wincing rather more when she knocked the stretcher into his shin.

"Does it look as if I'm all right? That bitch broke my back!"

"Which bitch, dearest?"

Bert told her to move aside and let them do their job in a dangerously testy tone. She rose—an unsightly move given her tight skirt and high heels, backing away as she mangled a lace-edged embroidered handkerchief. I didn't know they made those anymore.

The medics loaded Reg on the gurney to the accompaniment of much cursing and squawking, rolling him toward the elevator.

"Call my wife!" Reg bellowed at Steph on his way out the door.

"Yes, dearest," she called, waving her hankie. She ran over to the window to watch their departure.

CHAPTER 8

It was the last session of the day, so we all collected our bags and left. Most of the students gave me a wide berth, but Lettie gamely strode beside me. "Coffee?"

"Sure," I said, strangely grateful for friendship. "Why not?"

Hunter would be waiting to hear about my day. He seemed fascinated by the course. I hoped he wasn't thinking of trying it himself. First of all, being as thick as a plank, he couldn't pass the written tests, which would make him petulant, always an unpleasant state of affairs. Second, unleashing him on the general public could only end in catastrophe. I wouldn't mention this Reg incident but play bored. Actually, I was bored for the most part. I figured I could be a half-hour late without incident. I'd blame it on paperwork.

"So, where did you learn to fight like that?" Lettie asked, eyes wide with admiration.

I sucked foam off my cappuccino while considering my reply.

"I went to a marvelous martial arts studio in New York a few years ago. Chinatown. It's not there anymore," I said, by way of opening a window and closing a door.

"Wow!"

"I try not to overuse my skills. It's not done. But you know how Reg picked on me. You saw him mock me before I threw him. He thought he'd make a fool of me. I hope he's learned his lesson."

"Why is a classy woman like you taking this course? What will you do when you get your license?" Lettie sounded puzzled.

"Since you're wondering, yes, I am a bored housewife, but I've traveled the world and found myself in many difficult situations. I am well-educated and intelligent and intend to open a detective agency, probably in Fairfax City near the courthouse. But I have to go on a long trip first. You?"

"I don't have the money to hang my own shingle. I'll look for a job. Maybe in security or something like that."

"Well, if I make a go of it, perhaps I'll be able to offer you a job."

"Wow!"

She'd have to get well beyond the "wow" phase to work for me, but Lettie had shown herself to be competent and stout-hearted. And I liked her. She seemed the loyal type, too. But she could never know the real me.

"Well, I must get home. Dinner and all that. See you tomorrow, Lettie."

The next morning, we all filed into the classroom where we were to sit for our final exam. A representative from the licensing board would monitor the room to ensure all was on the up and up, so we sat in tense silence, waiting for that personage to appear. First came Steph, her eyes puffy, her shoulders slack.

"You will be happy to know that Reg has signed the papers attesting that you have all passed your self-defense and containment section. I took them to the hospital last night. The other segments had already been signed off. So, after this exam, you are done. Good luck to you all." A brave little speech with only a couple of catches in her throat.

"How is Reg?" I asked.

"Nothing broken. Bruised kidneys. He's in traction. They had to give him morphine, he was in so much pain." She started to say something that began with "You should be more..." her voice rising in indignation and accusation before dropping into a quiver. She dug around her pocket, presumably for another lace-edged handkerchief, before making a dash for the door, almost bowling over the dapper young fellow sauntering in.

"Good morning," he said, setting a plastic shopping bag on the desk and rubbing his hands together with an air of merriment. "What have you been doing to that poor lass?"

I took it upon myself to reply. "Nothing at all. She's just upset because her boss met with a little accident yesterday. He's going to be fine."

"Good, good. Well, I'm Pat Rourke, and I'm your test monitor today. I'll pass out the papers now, and we'll get started. You've all got pens?" He drew a handful of somewhat mauled booklets out of the bag and passed them out before retrieving another handful for the back row. "Now, be sure to read every question twice. Some of them are tricky. Ready? He paused dramatically for a few seconds. Begin!"

Multiple choice isn't always the easiest way to go. It makes life easier for the graders, for sure, but doesn't really get the job done. Those buggers who probably wear pointy wizard hats while they think up ways to confuse the students should be boiled in oil. *Read each question twice.*

I knew I'd done well. We'd get the results in a few days. Meanwhile, as Pat Rourke told us at the end, this would be a good time to get fingerprints taken. He passed out the applicable forms.

Crap! I'd forgotten about fingerprints. I don't have any. Norse gods are smooth all over.

Only one thing for it. I'd have to steal some. But suppose we had to get them done at the police station in front of someone? If there was just one person in the room, I could hack it. If there were others hanging around, I was screwed. I wasn't good enough yet to mesmerize more than one person at a time. My friend Joe from the Symphony Board—I'd ask him to do it as a special favor. At home? Cocktails? That might work.

I decided to assume there was a way to handle things with just any old signature. There was always a way for someone with my powers. I could only think of one place to find a spare set of fingerprints.

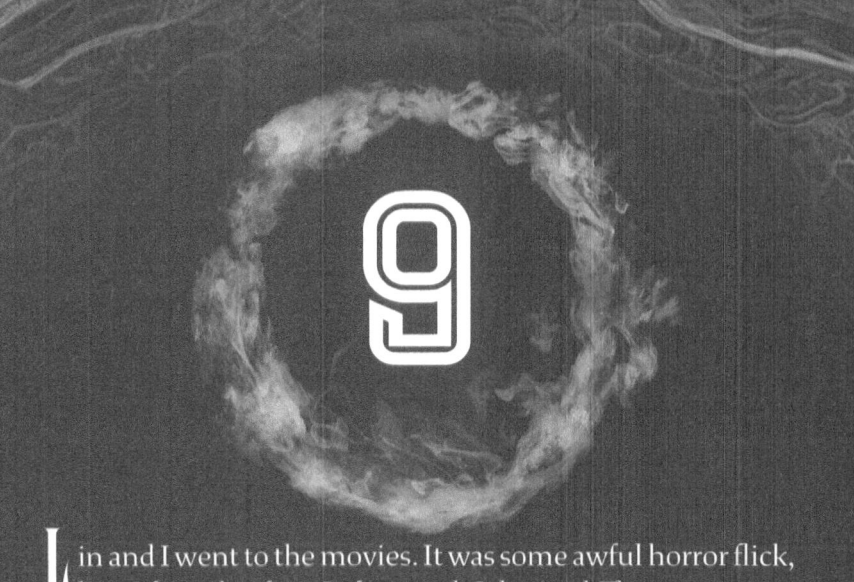

9

Lin and I went to the movies. It was some awful horror flick, but I found it fun. It featured Odin and Thor, so it was obvious why Lin chose it. She giggled all the way through to the extreme aggravation of anyone within earshot.

"Stop it," I whispered once. "You're annoying people."

Odin started to deliver a hokey speech about destiny that had her in stitches. I gave up and let the rest of the audience shush and complain all they wanted.

In the car home, she was still laughing.

"Odin would have sent the director a thunderbolt!" She said. "And he would have turned the cast into cockroaches. We didn't have cockroaches in Asgard, although the Jotuns— you know, the ice giants—did. Filthy creatures."

"The movie wasn't that bad, was it?"

"Oh, it was ridiculous. When Thor lost his hammer! Thor never let that thing from his hand! And he never wooed a human maiden in his life!"

"Didn't fancy humans, then?"

"Oh, no, he fancied them plenty. If he wanted one, he just took her. They were gods, Mary. Gods are to be worshipped and indulged in every way."

"My, how things have changed," I muttered.

"Yes, sadly, the order has collapsed."

"Is that a bad thing?"

Lin's face froze. I'd gone too far. She turned to me. "Is the world any better under your god, Mary?" she asked, her voice soft and sad.

"Not really," I had to admit. "Evil abounds." And I wasn't sure there was anyone to put it right. Saying "everything is for a purpose and is God's will" seems such a cop-out.

So, here we were in the next morning, ready for another session.

"You didn't have breakfast this morning, Lin?"

"I had it in bed. I didn't sleep very well. Besides, it annoys Dora, and it does her good to serve me once in a while, understand who's boss."

"Good idea." Dora needed to be kept in check. She could be really nasty.

"This one I'm going to tell you about today was a bit of a laugh, Mary," she giggled a little as she settled herself.

"Great! You know ... you sound almost British sometimes. Did you live there?"

"A few times, yes. But at Victoria College in Alexandria—Egypt, not Virginia—we were taught English by British teachers, and I went to a British School in India, too. So, yes, there's plenty of Britishness in my English." She laughed, so I followed suit, although I wasn't sure what was so funny.

Tape 8

I'd visited Quentin & Price, a big funeral home in the next town over, when a neighbor died in a multi-car crash on the Capital Beltway. A place like that would surely have all kinds of security, which would be a significant drawback. I looked them up in the Yellow Pages and found a full-page ad listing an enticing range of services, including "Planning Ahead." That would provide a great pretext to case the joint. You'll notice I was getting into the jargon groove, Mary.

Shapeshifting really took it out of me while my powers were still weak, even though I'd been practicing every day, so I opted for a mousy wig and old sweatpants with a tee and sneakers. No make-up, hair hidden under one of those dreadful baseball caps. Wire-rimmed glasses. My name would be Lynne Eddy. I'd first settled on Edda but realized that would be overdoing the Norse thing. Renting a car was a pain since it meant driving out to Dulles Airport.

I drove up in a gray Corolla in front of a colonially columned building. It was surrounded by viciously manicured boxwoods fronted by cunning little diamonds of white begonias. I parked in the area marked for visitors. Who the hell else would park there? Surely deliveries went around the back.

A bell chimed softly as I entered the empty reception hall. I was about to call out when a pimply youth in a black suit reared up from under the desk, giving me quite a start.

"I beg your pardon, madam. I dropped my paper clips. How may I assist you?" He fed the paper clips into a container shaped like a gaping cow.

"I would like to inquire about your Planning Ahead program and take a tour of your facility."

"Please take a seat, madam. I will summon Mr. Quentin."

I sat in an overstuffed armchair and leafed through a casket catalog. No prices. Bad sign.

"Good morning, madam!" Mr. Quentin was a huge, blond man, one of those who walks as if he has baseballs taped in his armpits. He shook my hand in a crushing grip, which I returned in kind, enjoying his manfully suppressed agony. "Let me show you around," he said, his luxuriant mustache quivering as he massaged his knuckles.

He first showed me the Gathering Lounge, furnished in peachy chintz and Queen Anne, complete with a bookstand holding a thin white leather guest book. This room opened into the Memorial Service Hall, set up with rows of chairs—somehow, I'd expected pews—an empty bier, an empty wreath stand, and a cloth-covered dais, also unoccupied.

The Memorial Service Hall had a wide exit door opening into a corridor that led mourners back to the reception area. But before we got that far, Mr. Quentin opened a door to a small Peace Room with walls painted chalk white and the ceiling sky blue. Why hadn't they painted fluffy white clouds on the ceiling? Why stop short of the finish line? A bier, this one supporting a richly carved casket, stood in the center of the room amid a scattering of vacant upright chairs upholstered in a bilious shade of sludge green.

"We have a visitation this evening," said Mr. Quentin in a booming voice that could awaken the dead but didn't. I cocked my head at the casket and raised my eyebrows. "Yes," he said, his voice dropped almost to a whisper. "The wife and daughter will be here shortly to sit with their beloved husband and father. I persuaded them to leave it closed. Nasty accident, you see; there wasn't much we could do. The funeral is tomorrow morning."

I'm afraid I beamed at this revelation, causing Mr. Quentin some astonishment. "I don't want you to think me facetious, Mr. Quentin, but I just think it's so beautiful that the family can enjoy a peaceful sojourn with their loved one."

"Ah, yes, quite." His frown didn't entirely disappear, hovering between his eyebrows like a frayed rag. "Why don't we go back to my office to discuss our services."

His office was also a showcase of Queen Anne, this time dressed in pink roses. I suppose a soft, family look is comforting to some, a welcome distraction from the hard edge of mortality and decay. I discovered that dying is an expensive business in the United States. Caskets can cost a few thousand, and then there's transportation. Embalming is optional unless there's a viewing or unless you dilly-dally and don't get them buried pronto. Make-up and hair are optional but quite a bit more expensive for the dead than the living. And men can have a suit open at the back, for which no one should pay such a princely sum. The cemetery plot and lining are not optional unless the deceased is cremated. On it went, adding up to a tidy sum.

"We have various payment options, Mrs. Hawkins. Some very doable for those who may find the outlay ... er ... onerous."

"We will be paying the usual in full, naturally," I said, haughtily. I guess my appearance didn't suggest much in the way of liquidity.

"Oh, very good, madam, of course, yes, quite." At least he had the grace to blush.

"I assume you have good security here," I said, hoping they hadn't. "I mean people are sometimes buried with valuables, aren't they, like wedding rings?"

"We have double locks on every door, and we are negotiating a security alarm contract right now. It should be in place within the month."

I tell you, it was as if our gods still dwelt in their heavens.

I nodded gravely. "That sounds most satisfactory. I must discuss all this with my husband. He's not well, you see..." I whipped a tissue off Mr. Quentin's desk and held it to my eyes, which I screwed close to suggest the reluctant tears I couldn't quite squeeze out.

"My dear lady. Dear lady..." Unctuous platitudes were about to flow my way, so I shoved my glasses into my canvas tote, put on my sunglasses, and rose suddenly, bringing the pitch to a sudden halt. He darted around the desk, pushed some pamphlets and price sheets into my hands, and opened the door. "Allow me to help you to your car."

"Please don't trouble yourself. I'll be quite all right."

He stood in the door of his castle, hands in pockets, and rocking on his heels as he watched the brave little lady depart. I hoped he didn't notice I drove a rental.

Tonight.

Hours later, I parked on a dark side street. The funeral home sat on a corner of Sycamore Avenue, the main drag, and Oak Lane, so I looked for a way into the property around the side and back. The wide gate for hearses was padlocked and a worse option than a wall because a smashed padlock would signal a break-in. The gate might have splinters, too. Nothing for it—over the top I had to go. I saw a movie about Dracula once. The image of him scaling the wall of his castle like a lizard, his red cloak spread out behind him, stuck with me because I do it just like that. I'm not sure how I do it. I just think "up," and up I go. I've never done it in a cape, of course. What a ridiculous drama queen he was, with his white hair all puffed out at the sides and that cloak billowing out into space.

I hadn't had a chance to walk around there that morning, so I had no idea if motion lights guarded the approach to the working areas as they did the front entrance. I lay on my stomach on top of the wall, which proved most uncomfortable as it curved down and arched in further imitation of residential aesthetics. Fortunately, I see well in the dark. They'd left a dim light on over one of the doors, so probably no motion light. A car approached slowly enough to suggest a police patrol, prompting me to drop down onto the concrete apron right in the middle of an oil spill. My feet slid away from me as my arms flailed, and it was only with heroic effort and concentration that I levitated enough to move a yard away onto dry land, as it were. Doing the splits in the middle of an oil puddle would have been a messy and possibly painful business. I wiped my feet on a grass strip next to the building. The skies opened as May compensated for our lack of April showers with wanton enthusiasm. I darted under the eaves.

I tried the door. Locked, as expected. Private detectives in books always have skeleton keys, but they hadn't proved easy to come by, at least not the kind that work. I took out the various implements I'd gathered: an old credit card, tweezers, a small screwdriver, and an awl. I decided to start with the handle lock, which would be much easier than a deadbolt. I tinkered with the awl for about five frustrating minutes before trying the credit card. At last, after sawing and lifting, jiggling and pushing, I heard a welcome click. Now the deadbolt, which wouldn't be so easy. I couldn't move it. I could easily break in, but I didn't want to leave any traces. I took a break and leaned against the door, which slowly swung open, catapulting me into a dark void. The last person out had been remiss; bless him.

I righted myself and closed the door gently before shaking myself dry. Mary, I once did that in front of an old char-woman in Paris, resulting in her having a nervous break-down. Try to imagine "The Exorcist" kid in an earthquake. My right hand scraped along the wall for the light switch, which soon resulted in the typical spluttery humming of cheap fluorescent lights. I don't know why I bothered. I could have managed perfectly well without. I squeezed past a steel gurney toward a sliding door that opened into an arctic room that stank of chemicals.

The wall to the left had six large doors set into it, three up and three below. A couple of metal canisters that looked like paint cans sat in front of one of the bottom doors. This room had to be where they kept the bodies. I opened one drawer to check. The tray slid out remarkably smoothly to reveal a mottled old lady, not yet prettied up.

Wending my way through a hallway leading to the front, I marveled at the commercial thoroughness of the enter-prise. I passed three large rooms without doors way up the passage that I hadn't seen on my first visit when we'd entered farther down on our way to the reception area. The first room contained plain caskets littering the floor and plastic urns crammed on shelves. An adjacent closed door turned out to be the janitor's closet.

The next room showed off pale wooden shelves holding urns made of marble, fused colored glass, and metalwork, some of which I considered works of art. One, in partic-ular, took my fancy, featuring carved and pierced brass that reminded me of the lanterns in my house in Egypt. Strangely, it lacked a lining, which I would have thought quite a drawback given its purpose. In the last, largest showroom, several mahogany caskets lined with white satin and sporting brass fittings took pride of place next to more fanciful creations. With not a little revulsion, I noted a child-sized pink enameled container complete with a lace-edged pink silk pillow and two little boxes shaped like teddy bears. How exploitative! I've felt grief so many times, but I can't imagine indulging in this kind of escape from life's gritty business.

At last, I reached the front and made my way to the Peace Room. I fished a miniature toolbox out of my pocket and took out a small screwdriver before setting it on the chair nearest the bier. It only took a minute to open the casket's stiff hasps and lift the lid. Empty! They must have put him back in the fridge. Which meant they'd see any mischief done to him when they hauled him out again. Now what?

On the other hand, if they put him back, that meant he wouldn't keep, so he was never embalmed. After slamming and fastening the lid, I ran back to the cold room and started opening drawers. I'd already seen the old lady. I found an emaciated middle-aged woman next to her. A plump bottle blonde with a nasty gash on the side of her head made three. The first two bottom drawers were empty. The only place left lay behind the canisters. I stacked them to one side to slide it open and was startled enough by the contents to knock one over. The lid popped off and a cloud of dust exploded over the room. I had no time to waste and turned back to the drawer's yucky contents.

Purple plastic bowls contained all kinds of gory bits and pieces. The torso lay behind it, arms and legs piled on top. No head. I smelled a rat—among other things. But it made my job easier because no one would notice I'd shaved off his prints. I went to work, carefully unrolling each finger pad onto a specimen slide and sealing them in an airtight glass container. I hadn't thought through how I'd use them, especially as they were a lot larger than mine would have been. I'd find a way. I always find a way. I shut away the mess and crunched my way to the janitor's closet to look for a vacuum cleaner.

It felt weird to be vacuuming up someone, but I managed, starting with the bottom of my shoes and the hall carpet before moving on to the cold room. The sharp bits really wanted to stick to the wet soles of my shoes. My mouth felt gritty, and that was just nasty. As I put the machine away, it occurred to me that those canisters were fairly heavy. I'd have to weigh the empty one with something. Well, drawer number three could again be useful. Some of his odd bits wouldn't be missed, although I didn't fancy touching them. Oh well, needs must.

I'd just pushed my dismembered savior back into his slot when I heard noises up near the foyer. After wiping my hands down the side of my pants, I tiptoed out and stopped partway up the corridor. Someone had opened the front door. A male voice boomed, "Welcome to my humble abode, little lady." A throaty giggle ensued, followed by, "We're not gonna do it in a casket, are we?" in the ripe tones of a wannabe southern belle.

I retreated hastily, gingerly set the canisters in their former location, packed my tools and precious glass box into various pockets, and hightailed it out of there, careful to secure the handle lock behind me. I darted away from the light over the door and across the apron before scaling the wall and dropping onto the street. The rain had stopped, the clouds had cleared, and the short walk provided a welcome breath of fresh air. Before unlocking the car, I shook myself again and watched dust motes waft this way and that in the light of the moon.

Now, how to use these prints? I'd have to get an ink pad and put them onto the card myself before they dried up. Then maybe I'd have to mesmerize Joe. My skills in that department still lacked finesse. I needed practice, but who would play guinea pig? And where? The problem swirled around my brain all the way home.

Hunter was still up watching a movie. "How did it go?"

"Not too bad. But I don't know how to use the prints."

"Ask the Internet."

"Of course! Why didn't I think of that?" Why not, indeed. I wasn't yet used to scouring the Internet for every piece of information I needed. I must get more sophisticated about it, too.

"So, I am not so dumb, huh?" Hunter smiled uncertainly, head dipped a little, peering at me from under his shaggy eyebrows.

"Of course not, dearest. Whoever said you were?"

"My brothers and just about everyone else."

"Well, Hoenir, you are here, and they are not, so you didn't do too badly." I still call him by his real name on special occasions.

"Yes, I was the one who made it. That is the nicest thing you have ever said to me, Lin."

I smiled sweetly, seething because he overlooked my role in his survival, and he squeezed my hand, which hurt a lot. I held onto the smile to save the moment.

The Internet turned up a revelation. Fingerprint scanners were available to businesses that needed to have their employees checked. I could buy one, but my agency wasn't fully set up yet, so I wasn't entitled. And wouldn't be until I'd sent my prints to the county. Some businesses still used the ink pads, though. Did I know anyone with the sort of business that required fingerprinting the employees?

I went to check on the children, so gentle in sleep, and tucked them in. They tended to toss and turn a lot while dropping off, resulting in tangles of sheets and blankets cascading to the floor. I went to my bed, hoping Hunter wouldn't be up any time soon. I closed my eyes and drifted off. I dreamed of Steph and Reg, Mr. Quentin, and some faceless floozie. They flirted and danced and sang and shouted, "No fingerprints! No fingerprints!"

I woke up in a sweat. Hunter still wasn't in bed. I picked up my phone to check the time. I'd only been asleep a half-hour or so. Then it hit me. Didn't PI instructors have to have their fingerprints checked? And funeral directors and morticians? Tomorrow I'd get back to the Internet.

"I can't believe you did that. Weren't you disgusted touching those body bits?"

"No, not really. When you've seen the wars I have, you get hardened to it. It's usually males who do these awful things, and it has always been so."

"Did anyone find out?"

"Not really."

She didn't sound sure but didn't elaborate. I'd probably heard enough shocking revelations for the day, anyway, although I was beginning to find a lot of these stories falling into the range of acceptable, even normal. Maybe Lin was a witch who had cast a spell on me.

See what I mean?

10

"Where there's a will, there's a way. That's what I always say." *And so many others before you, Lin.* I felt irritable that morning. Hunter had whispered in my ear the afternoon before that he might visit me in the evening, just for a little chat. But he didn't. What was I getting myself into? Hoping to get myself into.

Tape 9

I found out that funeral directors and morticians had to have fingerprint checks to be licensed, but Mr. Quentin wouldn't need to have the paraphernalia on hand. That left the training school. They hired people like Sam Lee, who didn't have a PI license. Maybe they'd have a scanner or at least a pad. Steph didn't like me, so not much help to be found there. I'd have to break in. Or should I try to talk my way in?

I armed myself with an enormous bunch of flowers and called on her at around 11:30. Her first reaction was to scowl and act snippy.

"Yes?"

"Steph, I brought these for you. I'm truly sorry if you thought me insensitive. You are so good to us all. I didn't mean to hurt Reg. Can you forgive me?"

I thrust the flowers at her chest so she couldn't help embracing them.

"May I take you out to lunch?"

"Well..."

"I want to make things right, Steph. I know it's hard for you, you know, this situation."

"Well, all right then." She gathered her purse and jacket, lips still pursed.

So far, so good. I peered over her shoulder while she set the alarm.

We wandered up to a local bistro where I'd booked a quiet corner table.

"How about a glass of Prosecco?" I asked.

"Pro what?"

"It's Italian champagne."

"Oh, all right." She wasn't unbending quite yet. The wine should help.

"How is Reg?" I tried to sound deeply concerned.

"I think he's all right. He's at home now, so I really can't call except for business stuff, and there isn't much of that. We're between sessions." Her lower lip trembled a little. "His wife's a bit of a dragon. She doesn't like me."

"Oh, she's probably just jealous because you're young and beautiful." Talk about laying it on with a trowel.

"Oh, I don't know about that," she said, with a hint of simper. *Bingo!*

"You know, I'm confused about the fingerprint thing. Do I go to the police station?"

"Yes, didn't Pat tell you about all of that?"

"Probably, but my mind was in such a tizzy after the exam. Do your employees have to do it, too?"

"Yes, but because we are in the business, we take them ourselves and send in the cards." That was good news.

"Oh, that's convenient. They trust you not to get things mixed up, then?"

"Well, the employee has to sign, and the business manager has to sign. That would be me. And a small photo has to go along with it. It has to have our stamp, too, of course, to make it really official."

"Fascinating. I remember that class on fingerprints. If I set up my agency and hire people, I might have to do it."

I asked her about herself. That's always a winning topic. As I suspected, she lived in a small apartment with a cat, waiting for Reg to manage an evening when he could get away. Classic. She chattered on.

"You know, you're really nice and easy to talk to. I reckoned you were just one of those bored housewives. You seem so together. I thought you were a bit snooty, to be honest."

"Oh, Steph, I'm sorry if I gave that impression. I'm very ordinary, really."

"Yes, I can see that now." *Really missy?* "Oh, goodness, I must get back. Thanks ever so for the lovely lunch. And the flowers."

"You are most welcome, Steph. See you soon, I hope. Give my best to Reg."

I almost sang on the way home. Piece of cake. My license wasn't through yet, but the agency was registered as a business. I'd get the prints done at the school, sign it with my new name, sign it with my husband's name as business owner, get a passport photo taken, and Bob's yer uncle, as the Brits say! In other words, a piece of cake. I didn't think I'd need a notary.

That night, I entered the school by way of the front door and found the pad in one of Steph's desk drawers. I rolled each of my purloined prints onto the card by laying them over my fingertips with tweezers. They looked ludicrously large. Well, who'd be looking that closely? I wiped my hands as best I could, but that was not good enough if I wanted to keep the card clean while I signed and put it back in the envelope. A good scrub with soap and water in the washroom solved the problem. Clean now, I affixed the photo I'd had taken that afternoon, signed my name, and forged Hunter's signature. Hunter was secretary of the agency, now promoted to office manager so he could officially be the signatory. All ready to go. Except for the stamp. I searched the drawers again and found it, one of those that embossed the paper. Stupid of me; it must have my own agency name on it. I'd get one made at once.

The front door opened. *Again?* I replaced the stamp and shut the drawer slowly.

"You stupid woman, you forgot to set the alarm!"

"I'm sure I put it on, Reg, I'm sure."

"Silly cow."

I scooped up my envelope and scurried to the walk-in closet that held boxes of forms and filing cabinets. A great deal of scuffling started to happen outside.

"Ouch, my back!" Reg squealed.

"It's so much more comfortable at my place, Reg."

"Not with that damn cat of yours. I'm allergic, remember? Why don't you get rid of it?"

"Oh, Reg, he's all I've got besides you, and you're not around much, are you? I love him a lot, and he loves me. I couldn't be so cruel."

"Huh. Well, help me off with my things. My back still hurts bad. Then I'll watch you."

"All right, Reg."

I very quietly slid down into a corner and pressed my hands over my ears. I hoped they'd be quick. Reg seemed the slam-bang type. A plague on these randy old businessmen. Why couldn't they stay home nights?

I awoke with a start, all senses alert. Silence. I can hear the slightest movement, even breath, if I put my mind to it. I emerged from the closet and looked around. Crushed cushions on the armchair, sofa untouched, and that was about all.

I got out and remembered to set the alarm.

A couple of miles from home, on an impulse, I called the police anonymously from a payphone, adopting an English accent. I thought they'd be terribly interested in a funeral taking place the next morning directed by Quentin & Price in Vinston. The body had been interfered with—that is, the head was missing. Not one of my most sensible ideas, as it turned out. I thought it funny at the time.

I came home to find Hunter watching television for a change. "How'd it go?"

"Like a charm."

"Well done, old girl." Hunter actually slapped my bottom. It stung a lot. Nothing used to hurt in the good old days.

The next morning's post brought my letter from the Commonwealth of Virginia. I'd passed. Mission almost accomplished. Just some paperwork and an official rubber stamp for my agency, then a very long journey.

The next day, the news was full of it. They couldn't identify the body because the head was missing, and its fingerprints had also been removed. Two vital organs were also missing, so organ trafficking couldn't be ruled out. The deceased's family declined to try to identify the body and asked that their privacy be respected. The funeral home would be closed for an undetermined duration. They didn't mention what they'd done with the other three corpses. That was about it. With any luck, the story would develop into a tale of intrigue and murder. They clearly hadn't opened the canisters. Careless of them. I'd been sure to tamp the lid down firmly and stow it underneath the others, so the secret of the missing organs would be safe unless someone saw fit to decant the contents into something more decorative.

The feature reminded me to burn the fingerprint bits in the glass case. They, too, would soon become unpleasant.

Ugh! Just ugh! Lin seemed to take it all in her stride. Who was she? Worried about the girls, kind to me, a loving mother, adulterer, desecrator of corpses. She operated under a different set of principles.

Clearly, I was willing to countenance a little adultery, too. Was it catching, this disregard for the moral code? It was all so unsettling. Too many tricky gray areas.

11

Hunter had whispered at breakfast that morning—Lin had hers in bed again—that it was sometimes hard to get away. But he'd love to spend some time with me. If that would be all right. My whispered, rather feverish assent brought on his devastingly wide smile.

"I have bought a new car yesterday for you to use, also Sven and Margareta when they are home. Lin and I discussed it last night. It will be easier for you to visit your auntie."

I gasped. "You don't have to do that."

"But I have done it."

When Lin came down, I thanked her.

"You need it to be able to get around," she said, sitting in a corner of the chaise. "Children can be wonderful and terrible, all within the space of hours. You'll see one day."

Would I? I'd never met anyone eligible that I fancied. Right now, I fancied Hunter. Angering Lin didn't seem like a good idea—but would she be angry? They seemed to have an open marriage.

They both gave me the quivers ... for different reasons.

"I sometimes wonder if I'll ever have a family," I told her.

"Of course, you will. And for now, you have your aunt, Sam, and us. Not so bad."

Tape 10

Sven and Margareta became very clingy the day I left for Istanbul. My flight didn't leave until evening as I was connecting in London, so I let them stay home from school and took them to a bowling alley. This could be tricky as Sven always hurled the balls too hard, and they tended to stray, airborne, into other lanes.

"Sven, I want you to concentrate. The aim is to knock over the pins gently. When you send the balls over the edge, you lose." He hates to lose, as does his father.

Margareta won the first round. She had great powers of concentration and could place the ball with almost mathematical precision. It drove Sven crazy, so he pushed her over. I held his arms against his body and picked him up since there was no one around to see. I shook him. He cried.

"Sven, I'm going away for a week or so. Can't we just have a nice time together?" I put him down and wiped his nose. He played better next time but still lost. Margareta put her arm around him.

She said, "You are much better than me at art and chess, Sven. You can't be the best at everything. You are the best brother in the world, though." She can be so sweet. And so disturbingly manipulative.

We had lunch at Sven's favorite hamburger joint, then went home for a quick game of chess before I left. Playing with our golden chessmen was a very special treat. We usually only let the children play with wooden ones. They are forbidden to ever tell anyone about Lady Frigg's golden set. Anyway, I should have known better. Sven was better at chess than Margareta and nearly always beat her. He'd lower his icy eyes to the board until his white-blond hair fell across his forehead and shut out the world. His normally rosy cheeks would pale until he looked almost ill. Funnily enough, Hunter is also very good at chess. At the beginning of time, he gave humankind the gift of reason—his reason, which is probably why he doesn't have a whole lot left. But he has this uncanny feel for the game and the ability to hyper-focus. So now Margareta sulked, her little pink lips pouting, her eyes shining with unshed tears. She was more of a golden girl, like me. Deep blue eyes, fair skin, and golden hair. A real beauty whom Hunter would soon feel he had to protect from any member of the male population who might get too close. God help them. I've seen it all before, and it's not pretty.

"Margareta, when I get ready to go to the airport, would you like to put on some of my lipstick? And maybe a dab of my perfume?" Problem solved. I love my children but found them exhausting at that age—not that Hunter was any easier.

At the airport, we kissed and hugged and kissed some more. "Take care of Papa, now."

"We will," they chorused. Hunter pecked at each cheek and slapped me on the back, almost sending me headlong over a pile of suitcases.

I flew to Istanbul as Lin Thoren. As much as it pained me, my hair would have to appear dark to fit in where I must soon go. Inky black like Penelope Gaylord's. I would be striking, but in quite a different way, and tall. I've always wanted to be tall. Picturing Penelope clearly would be the key to success, but it was early days yet. Holding it overnight would be a major issue.

Once I passed through customs and immigration in Istanbul, I entered the ladies' toilet and emerged as a clone of Penelope Gaylord, ready to step out into the muggy landscape. Too bad I hadn't made it over there earlier to avoid the most searing heat of the summer.

"So, who is this Penelope Gaylord?"

"I'll tell you tomorrow. She was a dear friend who died too young."

"Oh. Sorry. Do you mind if I go to Auntie's for lunch?"

"No, of course not! Stay the night if you want. I might have a lie-in, so shall we say eleven?"

12

"Did you have a nice day at your aunt's?"

"Lovely, thanks. I walked quite a few miles with Sam. Lots of new smells to keep him happy. I found a dog park where he can run around and play with other dogs off the leash."

"Dogs are easily pleased, it seems."

"They are. Sam is a happy dog in general, wags his tail all the time. I sometimes wonder if he'll wag it off."

"I wish ... but never mind. Let's get on. Now we come to the place where British English was drilled into me," Lin said. "Our teachers insisted on correct upper-class pronunciation, and it sticks, even after all this time. It's true, I sound rather American now, but I often relapse."

I envied her wealth, her travels, and her vast experience. I was getting itchy feet. One day I'd get to some of these places. One day.

Where was Hunter? He hadn't even come down to breakfast. Avoiding me?

Tape 11

I hadn't thought about Penelope Gaylord for years, an Anglo-Indian girl I was at school with in Simla—this was before we moved to Egypt in my last life. Penelope had creamy coffee skin, finely etched features, and a curtain of black hair that shone in sunlight like polished lava. Her slanted, amber eyes were extraordinary, compelling people to look into them. She was my best friend during those lonely years at Ashley College, an English boarding school in the dreamy foothills of the Himalayas.

Anglo-Indians had a rough go of it in those days, despised and distrusted by both sides. Our headmistress picked on her terribly, often making her cry with cutting remarks that British schoolmarms hone to a fine point. Her mother's people wouldn't have her in their main compound, only in the servants' quarters. Her mother was lucky she wasn't kicked out entirely after consorting with a white man—life on the streets being tantamount to a sentence of death. The father, a retired British Army officer who worked for the East India Company, couldn't officially acknowledge her either, as frolicking with the natives was frowned upon, although freely enjoyed. He paid for her schooling, but the poor child was forced to spend the entire year at school. I spent the holidays with Hunter, still a toddler, whom I'd parked with an amah in a little white bungalow in Calcutta I'd bought. After the first term, I took

Penelope home with me, forging a letter of invitation from my fictitious mother.

I spent three years in that school, graduating when I was twenty-one, although they thought I was eighteen. I grew quite fond of the place, got used to most of the girls, and they to me after some early misunderstandings. I even liked most of the teachers. The rigorous academics suited me fine. I always knew what to expect and what was expected of me. When I felt down, all I had to do was sit in one of the sturdy rocking chairs on a rarely used side veranda, gazing out at distant purple mountains capped with snow and listening to the parrots and monkeys creating their chorus of screech and squawk. A leopard added a roar or two occasionally. Looking back, perhaps I only fancied it was leopards because they rarely make themselves known. More likely tigers.

One particular monkey first came to me as a baby. His mother sat on the railing with him and his sister clinging to her back. She stared at me long and hard. We weren't allowed to feed them, but she no doubt knew a scofflaw when she saw one and hoped I would break the rules. I remembered an orange in my pocket left over from lunch and offered it to her. She bounded down, snatched it, and leaped back onto her perch. Her little boy fell off as she retreated and rolled on the floor a couple of times, squeaking—crying, I suppose—in distress. I picked him up and cuddled him, glancing over to the mother, hoping she wouldn't take exception to my interference. Macaques can get nasty. She didn't quite sit but crouched, ready for action. "It's all right, Mama. I won't hurt your baby," I said in a low sing-song voice. She relaxed. He felt so good, so warm, as he slept peacefully in my arms. They came every day for months after that and waited for me. One day, it was only him. In spite of his size, I knew him from the kink in his tail. He seemed to want that cuddle even more than the treat. I had to be sneaky with my offerings, so no one would tell on me, but those moments offered me joy in its purest form. I didn't even let Penelope in on my secret because I wanted him all to myself. Sometimes, skinny little local boys would sneak around to see what was going on. We weren't allowed to feed them, either.

Penelope excelled in academics, as did I. Her father secured her a place in a teacher's training college in London. We spent a wonderful couple of weeks together in Calcutta before she embarked for "Home," as the Raj, stubbornly nostalgic, called it. We laughed a lot, went to the club, had pretty dresses made, flirted with pink, young Englishmen, and danced most nights away. It was with real regret that I waved goodbye at the port that stifling July morning.

It took over a month before the news reached me of a collision at sea between Penelope's liner and a merchant ship with a drunken captain at its helm. I hope she didn't suffer much. Which is worse? Pain or terror? I wouldn't know.

"That's so sad, Lin. Auntie and I were watching *Passage to India* last night. It's very well done. So many injustices. All so unfair. What happened to the monkey?"

"He simply didn't show up one day. Life in the wild is dangerous."

"I'm disappointed. I thought you might have taken him home to that little bungalow in Calcutta."

"No, Mary. Wild creatures shouldn't be caged. They should be allowed their own perilous freedom. That goes for people, too. Even us. Especially us."

13

"**Y**ou know, I was getting back to my life's mission, back to saving people. I felt good about that. I'd been selfish for too long. It took me eons to realize how empty it left me."

"Sometime I'd like to hear about some of your good deeds in the old world," I said.

"Yes, all right, there have been one or two concerning young women held against their will. But that's for another day. Now I want to talk about Syria and Turkey. I did rather well."

Her self-congratulation sometimes got on my nerves. Unreasonable, but I felt grouchy after Hunter failed to show up last night—again.

When Lin went into the kitchen to make more coffee that morning, Hunter walked behind me and bent down to whisper in my ear, "Sorry, I cannot always get away."

My heart leaped. So, he really meant to come to me.

Calm down.

Tape 12

I rented a room in an upscale Indian hotel, paid in advance, and informed them I'd be away for at least a week. Needing to find a place to change before slipping away, I explored the spa area and found a convenient back door. I undressed in my room the next afternoon, put on one of their plush bathrobes, and carried what I needed in a laundry bag down to the changing rooms closest to the back exit. After changing into the garb of a typical poor woman—thread-bare caftan and hijab, accessorized with a cheap canvas tote—I stuck my head out of the curtain only to see an Amazonian female striding down the corridor. I drew back and listened. She seemed to be standing at the exit. The door hadn't opened.

I peeked again. After a light knock, she opened it up to let in a young man who looked pretty shady, judging by his faux leather jacket and oil-slicked hair. He didn't belong there any more than the new me did. They conversed in whispers, and she passed him a card before whisking him through the corridor and, presumably, to the men's section. I tip-toed out and had just made it to the exit when a thunderous voice stopped me in my tracks. Not speaking Turkish didn't prevent the certain knowledge that she meant me no good. I turned and put my finger to my lips. Working in a place like this, she was sure to speak English.

"I won't tell if you don't."

"What the 'ell's that s'posed to mean?" I was right; English and a cockney, no less.

"I saw you let in that young thief and give him a key card."

Her face passed through a gamut of emotions. "Get out!"

I left quickly, clutching the tote as if it contained treasure. My money and papers were safely stored around my body, but I still needed a change of clothes, water, and a snack or two. I soon found a bus to take me in the direction I wanted to go.

And so my pilgrimage began, sometimes as a refugee and sometimes as a beggar. I hitched rides on a number of carts and trucks, bumping over rutted dirt roads and raising dust almost all the way to the Syrian border. I got used to feeling and looking grimy. I didn't smell bad because goddesses never do. I gave a few coins to the drivers, who usually accepted my offerings without comment, so poor they were grateful for anything they could get.

Those who made untoward moves found themselves temporarily disabled. I only left one more seriously damaged. People like him have no business procreating, anyway. I sprinted down that stretch of track until his yowls and curses were no more than a buzzing in my ears.

I slowed down to a hobble close to a sorry-looking hamlet of lean-to shacks with corrugated tin roofs, where I found a man with an ancient delivery truck who was willing to take me closer to the border. His son would also accompany him, so I had to wedge myself between crates of panicked chickens in the back. It didn't take long for the tangy reek and raucous clamor of those birds to dampen my sympathy for their plight. After disembarking, I wound my way to the marketplace in what seemed no more than a shanty town, picking feathers off myself and looking for a café where I might find food and a lead on transportation across the Syrian border.

There seemed to be only one, so I found myself a spot in a dark corner.

"Dinner, please," I said in Arabic, foolishly expecting a menu. A few minutes later, a plate of rice and beans and a mug of steaming tea were plonked down in front of me by a taciturn man sporting an absurd Dali mustache. He held out his palm, into which I placed a five lira coin. He shook his head and waggled his fingers, so I tried one more. His fist closed.

"Please, I must find my son. I have to cross into Syria. Can you help me?" I asked. He looked at me with contempt and said nothing. He presumably didn't speak Arabic, and I never had any reason to learn Turkish. I demolished my rice and beans, mopping up the remaining sauce with fresh bread. Closing my eyes and sipping tea, I gradually became aware of the raspy breath of someone behind me. I whipped around, recklessly godlike, and a large man stumbled back a few paces. He drew himself up again while I stared at him, silent.

"You want to cross? Twenty lira. Show me." I handed over a note. "Come now."

I tried to make small talk with this fierce and silent driver, as he was an Arab.

"Do you make this crossing often? Is it dangerous?"

He glared at me and shook his head. "If I do not ask questions of this woman who moves like a djin, speaks a strange dialect, and smells clean under her dirty old clothes, she should not be curious about my business."

I don't know where we crossed the border into Syria. We encountered no checkpoints, merely bumped across dirt tracks into a straggle of small houses that became a crowd of crumbling tenements leading into the center of a ruined town, whose name I never did learn. My driver made me get out into a dark alley of jagged concrete ruins where the ground seemed to shift underfoot. He offered no advice, no goodbye.

Heavy-hearted, I started to explore the terrain, listening for the sounds of people gathered together. There is nothing more depressing than a bombed-out town with its haze of smoke and stench of burned dwellings and people. I stumbled across a coffee house off the main square that still operated amidst the rubble, despite its missing door. I stepped over the threshold and stood for a few seconds looking around at this dismal hole with blown-out windows and half-broken furniture. A few men nursed tiny coffee cups and smoked hookahs. No doubt, most of their neighbors had died or moved away.

"Peace be with you, sirs," I called out. A shocked silence fell. This was a male preserve, after all, jealously hoarding its reek of cheap cigarettes, stinky armpits, and political opining.

The man behind the counter said, "What do you want here?"

"Dear sirs, take pity on a poor woman who has journeyed far. My neighbors took my son to a camp. They thought I had been killed when our house was bombed, but I was at the hospital with my dying mother. I must find my son. He is the only one I have left." I managed to squeeze out a sob. "It is a place with an American lady in charge."

The owner came around the counter and said, "I do not know about an American. There are two camps just inside Turkey, a few days' walk from here."

"Oh." I let my head droop. I sighed.

"Here, sit down. We do not have much to spare these days, even water not so much, but have some coffee, at least." He gestured to a table apart from where the others sat. He went behind the counter and brought back a tiny cup of Turkish coffee and a dry cookie. "Where have you come from? How did you get here?"

"Thank you, kind sir." I felt guilty accepting his hospitality. "From near Damascus, although I was born in Cairo. I paid a delivery truck driver to let me sit in the back with his boxes."

Another man chimed in. "There is a group leaving for one of the camps tomorrow. Perhaps you can join them. No one wants to stay here. Those dogs come back again and again with their bombs." His voice rose to a roar as he shook his fist toward the sky. "But some of us will never leave our homes!" The others mumbled agreement, although most sounded half-hearted.

The man who had mentioned the group walking to a camp said, "I am Ali. I will take you to my wife's sister. You can rest there until they leave."

Ali's sister-in-law Susu was none too pleased to see me. I didn't blame her as her little stone house was crammed with friends and relatives saying goodbye, not to mention her anxious children. She and Ali exchanged angry, whispered words, but I couldn't be bothered to eavesdrop at this point. I sat in a corner, hugging my knees, and kept my mouth shut, closing my eyes to avoid curious glances. I'd begun to itch unbearably too, a signal that my body wanted to morph back to Lin. I held out for longer and longer each day, but concentration was key. The real test would be holding onto Penelope for several days with little privacy to maintain my deception.

The noise rose to deafening proportions as everyone talked, and no one listened.

I slept in that corner after the house emptied out and the family went to bed. They rose at dawn, and everyone except me was handed a few bites of bread and cups half full of water. I understood—they had none to spare. I waited outside to save them embarrassment. They came out silently, avoiding looking me in the face.

"Come along," Susu said, a rough edge in her voice. I followed behind, and we soon fell in with a crowd that straggled slowly toward the border and, I hoped, the refugee camp I sought. I retold my story so many times, about wandering the streets after my house was bombed, not being able to remember my name or who my parents were, or even at first whether I had a husband or children. Now I remembered they'd all been killed except one son, whom I was desperate to find. I still could not remember my name. One of them called me Noor—light—and it stuck.

Exhausted though these people were, I caught a few men looking at me and almost licking their lips. Their women caught it too and resented my youth and beauty. My accent again had to be explained away. I murmured something incoherent about being born near the pyramids of Giza, but I couldn't remember how or when. They accepted that. Most of them were simple people, although a few had a little education, but all were too debilitated by the trek, hunger, and fear to think about it. Even the children were too tired to cry. They merely grizzled for a few minutes before falling asleep.

Dispirited guards at the border waved us through. They had worries of their own. We plodded on for hours, our weary shuffling kicking up dust that lodged in our eyes, noses, and mouths. Even I spat from time to time.

Eventually, we stopped for the night in a village square. All doors and windows were closed and barred against marauders. Even well out of Syria, the air still swirled with dark smoke, the moon no more than a plaintive suggestion. All of Syria was on fire, according to my companions.

Despite my strength, even I dragged my feet by the third day as we wound along a hard sandy track that would lead us into the camp. One morning, military planes roared overhead once, and everyone threw themselves to the ground, many whimpering in fright. They let us be, so people struggled to their feet again, weary almost beyond bearing, a faded column of patchwork rags. No one had spoken more than a word or two for at least a day.

We settled in for another night in the dry cold of the desert. The sound of footsteps near my head woke me. Someone stood looking down at me. I sprang to my feet and grabbed the person, assuming it would be a man. In the muddy moonlight, I saw it was Susu.

"I knew there was something wrong about you."

"What do you mean?" I kept hold of her.

"You are a foreigner, a spy! Let me go, or I'll scream. What will you give me to keep your secret?"

I did indeed feel different. I looked down at the golden hair spilling over my shoulders. I had to get rid of this woman and concentrate on shifting back to Noor. I didn't want to kill her. She had children. I clamped my hand over her mouth, picked her up, and ran with her out to the desert and out of earshot. She put up a good fight, scratching and biting and punching my back. Now I'd have to will those marks away in addition to everything else. I dumped her between a couple of rocks.

"I'm going to leave you here. You have a long walk ahead. When you get back to the camp, you will see you are mistaken. If you try to make trouble, they will think you mad."

She hugged herself, scared witless—not surprising given my inhuman strength, our lightning journey, and the prospect of being all alone in the desert in the dark.

"Are you really going to leave me here?"

"Yes, you brought it on yourself. Start walking."

I ran back to the group and huddled in my spot. Concentration so intense is exhausting, but Noor must reappear before daylight.

After a couple of hours sleep, I woke to the clamor of people getting ready to move off. A small group stood off to one side, seeming to search for something. Or someone.

"What has happened?" I asked the woman next to me.

"That man's wife is missing," she said, pointing with a shrug at a man gesticulating in the middle of the commotion, Susu's husband.

"Isn't that her?" I pointed at Susu, who came limping toward them, crying. I must have taken her farther than I realized.

Everyone settled down for a while so that Susu could rest. She put the story around that she went out to get some privacy to do the necessary, then got lost trying to get back. She never looked in my direction after an initial glance confirmed my dusky appearance.

We started trudging along once more, most hardly looking ahead, instead staring at their feet as though willing them to advance. We passed through several burned-out hamlets, empty of life. The blue sky reasserted itself once we got clear of razed dwellings, but the sun was unrelenting, whether clouded over or not.

Finally, more smoke curled up ahead, but from cooking fires this time. I smelled food, although nothing appetizing unless one were starving. I hadn't come to that point yet, but everybody else had. The pace picked up, and waves of chatter rose to a shaky crescendo. As we came nearer, other smells wafted our way, a mixture of distasteful elements I didn't care to analyze. I thought only of Mary Wilder, the fiend who trafficked desperate girls into prostitution.

A couple of ragged men guarded the camp entrance. One of them sauntered off to announce our arrival. The group sank to the ground, almost as one. After a lengthy wait, a lopsided old woman with a milky eye arrived with a few teenage boys. She separated us into family groups, each of which were escorted by one of the boys to their allotted space. As I was alone, she accompanied me herself through a maze of tent-lined alleys. She assigned me to a tent with three other young women, who clearly resented having to make room for me. They greeted me politely with stony faces and immediately continued their conversation. The old woman handed me a tin plate and a cup.

"Someone will bring you a mattress."

"May I ask who is in charge here?" I asked.

"An American woman. Madame Wilder."

"Thank you." She looked askance at my suddenly happy face.

"The water pump is over there," she said, pointing a palsied finger into the setting sun. "Your tent has buckets, so you must take it in turns to bring enough back to last the day. The others will show you where the showers are. Your shower time is on Thursday afternoons. We give everyone rice and bread, other food when we have it. You must cook for yourselves. There is little oil. You can boil the rice over a fire and add whatever else we can get."

That sounded grim enough, but I had to ask. "The toilets?" I remembered not to ask for the bathrooms in the American way, as a bathroom in the rest of the world does not necessarily include a lavatory.

She laughed—if that's what her strange cackle implied amusement. "They'll show you."

One of the girls pointed the way, but I didn't get far before the stomach-turning stink drove me into the desert with godly speed.

A private spot behind a massive rockslide looked ideal, so I pulled down my underwear, squatted, and let the stream flow. A frantic scritch-scratching had me doubling over to peer between my legs. A big, black scorpion stood to attention with its stinger arched over its body, ready to nail my rear end. A slick sideways leap and a large stone solved the problem. After all those years in Egypt, I should have known better, but one forgets.

My panties lay close to the scorpion's body. I shook them, checked for little intruders, slipped them on, and adjusted my clothing. My major regret was failing to put toilet tissue in my pocket. In my original immortal form, these issues did not occur, and I still found them burdensome. That is one of the drawbacks to embracing earthly pleasures. I take in food and drink, it gets processed, then the leftovers have to be disposed of—a rather disgusting procedure. I guess you can't have it both ways.

"It's funny to think you gods didn't always have to do that." Before she told me about the Aetna episode, it hadn't occurred to me to think about gods and bodily functions. Not that I'd ever thought about gods at all. I couldn't help being fascinated.

"Well, yes. If we eat, it all has to be processed. In our old world, I never ate or drank. The big gods did, but it was our own food and drink, grown on Asgard, with magical properties. It was different. We don't actually need to eat or drink, but who can resist? So, yes, we gods shit and pee, just like you humans, except it doesn't smell as bad."

"Wow," was my feeble response to this riveting information.

"The whole childbirth thing isn't much better. In this day and age, I can't appear with a new child without explanation, and I certainly can't give birth in the presence of a doctor or nurse due to my lack of red blood, not to mention the way they just pop out with no particular effort on my part, attached to a pale blue placenta. Nowadays, governments want records and certificates for every significant thing you want to accomplish. Think of the amount of work it took to get our passports without any birth certificates or finger-prints. Thank God we got them way before 9/11, so it's only a matter of renewal now. You've no idea the finagling we have to do to get around these impediments, not to mention the expense." She gazed at the ceiling for a few minutes. "But I don't think I can go back to being that chaste hand-maiden again. No caviar, no champagne, no lovemaking. No, can't do that."

"I must say, it sounds very complicated." *Jesus. Fake passports, birth certificates, everything.*

"Yes, well, let's get back to the story."

I started to run back toward the camp but stopped dead as something stabbed my ankle. I'd stepped too close to another, more dangerous scorpion, a small creature the color of sand. I killed it right away. One should always be on full alert in such a place; perhaps because the desert is so empty of normal life and movement, it's easy to over-look the dangerous nature of what little there is.

A burning pain shot through my ankle. This was not a good time or place to be reborn. Could a scorpion actually kill me? Before my long exile in Hel and Aetna, I never felt pain, never suffered hunger or thirst, never had to be reborn, and was truly immortal. Now pain, occasional hunger pangs, weakened powers, and a traumatic rebirth every century and a half was my lot. I wondered if—or that day—I might sink into nothingness like humans.

I sat on one rock, propped my foot on another, closed my eyes, and willed the poison down my veins and out of the puncture wound. A wet trickle ran down my foot. A scrap of torn hem wiped off any remaining traces. Will or skill?

I was itching again. Time for another imaging session. I found a large flat rock upon which I could sit cross-legged after searching the surroundings for scorpions and snakes.

Only one little green snake wriggled frantically toward a crevice. He didn't make it. I leaped onto the rock, closed my eyes, and focused on dear Penelope.

When I got back, one of the girls, who introduced herself as Mariam, looked at me curiously.

"Are you ill? You were gone for a long time. We were worried about you." Hoping I wouldn't return, more likely.

"No, I am quite all right, thank you. I went for a little walk, finding my way around."

Mariam, sharp-featured with fair hair, had gathered kindling and started a fire to boil water for rice. "That is the last of our water."

"I will go for more now," I said. "Tell me where."

As one might expect, I made it there and back in good time without getting out of breath. The only hold-up was standing in line as one tap served a large number of tents. Everyone clearly regarded any water at all as a gift, so they didn't complain. To the girls' amazement, I took the second bucket to fetch more, suggesting we might want to wash ourselves tomorrow morning since this was only Monday. Americans call that sucking up. It works.

I had briefly explained my lost family and faulty memory the first day but discarded the part about searching for a son because it was crucial to pose as a virgin. After a week, I fit right in. The water business got old fast, but I needed these girls to trust me, especially the other two, who were not inclined to be kind. Pretty, fat Didi went on about roast lamb, dolma, and all her other favorite foods so much I wanted to smack her, and I could tell the others did, too.

One day she said, "Dearest Noor, you look too healthy and plump to be a refugee."

"But my dearest Didi, you still look as if you eat a whole chicken every day. I believe our current diet will improve our figures, don't you agree?"

And Houdah, with her chestnut brown hair and cat-green eyes, could have been a top model had her culture allowed it. She was no doubt used to outshining any other young woman in her sphere—until I came along.

"Noor, my dear, when we get back to civilization, we can become glamorous once more. Have you ever thought about taking a little of that curve off your nose?"

"No, Houdah, I haven't. Have you? A significant nose is something we seem to have in common."

Things cooled to sub-zero after that, although we observed the niceties.

I wandered the camp a good bit the first couple of days, hoping to run into Mary Wilder. She proved elusive, but a few days after my arrival turned up at our tent with the old milky-eyed woman in tow. The Wilder woman looked like my old headmistress at that English boarding school in India. Pigeon chested, she was dressed in a white high-necked starched blouse that held up a face I can only describe as craggy. She bore gifts of stew meat and beans. A couple of girls I hadn't seen before joined us. She talked about jobs available in the United States and pitched the deal. She spoke Arabic fluently, albeit with a thick accent. The others were hesitant, unsure about moving so far from home. She was very persuasive, ending by asking them in her gravelly masculine voice, "What home?" She had a point. I acted enthusiastic, and they followed my lead.

"Of course, it is not easy to get out of here and into the United States. And you will have to be hidden. But we have people who know how to get you in. It is a long journey and sometimes uncomfortable. You will have to pay us out of your salary, just a little each month for a year."

She asked us a lot of questions, beginning with ascertaining that none of us had any family still living as far as we knew—I suppose the letters had become a nuisance. She ended up with coy references to "character," by which I realized she wanted to know if we were virgins. I think the others found it a reasonable question, and lying is second nature to me. It was hard not to laugh. After all, the most successful courtesan couldn't claim as many conquests as me—although maybe that's an unfair comparison, as they haven't had the benefit of eons of opportunity.

We would leave the following Sunday. Mary Wilder even managed to crack a smile after we all agreed to the plan. I made a mental note to track down her bank account and empty it.

About two hours before our departure, I made my way to the men's quarters. I sought Ali Muhammed, a middle-aged man I had noticed often held court in a group of his peers, clearly much respected.

"Good evening, Mr. Muhammed."

He looked astonished, as did the few men sitting around the cooking fire.

"You don't know me, but I am an American."

They didn't like that. "How do you come you speak our language?"

"I was born in Egypt. I am here on a mission. I must warn you. There is someone in your camp luring young women into a life of shame. They are told they will have good jobs and be able to save money to bring their families to America. But they are being tricked. They are smuggled into the country to become slaves. I do not need to tell you how they are used."

They murmured angrily.

"Do you have proof?" Ali Muhammed asked.

"Yes, I found six young women locked in a house in America used in this way. They came from this camp. I am here to stop this evil trade. I only know their first names. Perhaps you know young women who have gone to America? Or perhaps they kept it secret. But some of the families would know. They were told their daughters would eventually send them money. They do send letters, although that is strictly controlled." I reeled off the six names, noticing some starts of dismayed surprise as I did. "I'm sorry to say that Yasmin died at the hands of one of those men."

"I will make inquiries," Ali Mohammed said. "Who is doing this?"

"Mrs. Mary Wilder."

"But she works so hard here. She helps us all."

"And she is getting quite rich," I said. "Just make some discrete inquiries."

I turned and left, again becoming the waif who was soon to be smuggled into the United States of America.

Lin seemed quite buoyant, happy, and bouncy. What was up?

"Mary, yesterday you asked me to tell you about one of my missions for my lady Frigg. This one seems quite relevant to the situation I've been telling you about. And it's one I performed brilliantly."

"I'm sure you did. You do everything well."

She looked gratified, unaware of any tinge of sarcasm. I really had to stop these little darts of resentment before they backfired. Hunter was her husband, after all.

"I was sort of what you might call a fairy godmother to this family, you see. I protected them for many years until I knew it was time to let them go."

Suddenly, she seemed subdued, settling herself silently and quickly. I was eager to hear what new bombshell was coming my way, even though I wanted to know about this journey she'd told me about yesterday.

Tape 13

My lady Frigg called me to the silver pool one day, not long after I'd returned from dealing with another tricky situation on her behalf. I didn't mind, for that was my destiny.

The good woman who needs our help now is Gyr, widowed a few years ago but left well provided for. She married Ulf, a newcomer to her village, last summer. A woman needs protection in *Midgard,* and she felt her little girls needed a father. He was charming and treated her kindly. Even her family liked him. But all he wanted were the comforts her money could provide and a son of his own—certainly not these three girls who were not of his blood. He was angry because she had not yet borne him a son. Her father prayed to me for assistance. The husband owns his wife down in their world, so the father could not interfere other than talk to the wretch, which only made him angrier. The father heard her cries as he walked away.

As I gazed into the glinting water, it darkened before shining a white light over three emaciated girls in rags who huddled on the dirt floor of a bare room, weeping and shaking with cold. The youngest had a hacking cough. Snowflakes drifted through a small, uncovered window set high in the wall.

We next viewed the main hall, where a fire blazed in a vast hearth. A beautiful woman who held herself like a queen placed a platter of meat in front of a huge man who sat on a carved wooden throne at the head of a long table. As we watched, he guzzled half the dish before throwing it at the woman. The meat stained her gown as it tumbled to the floor. She stood stock still; her head bowed.

"You miserable wench who can only birth useless daughters. Your food tastes like animal dung." He rose and struck her across the face, knocking her to the floor. She lay there, clenching her teeth, refusing to cry.

"Your daughters will soon be useful after all. Some of my friends like a little entertainment now and then. That's all you and your spawn are good for."

The woman sprang up, crying, "But they are so thin. Your friends prefer more comely women, do they not?"

"Fine, fatten them up. Two weeks and they go to that big house at the forest's edge. Then I won't have three worthless mouths to feed. Tonight, you may give them this food from the floor. Nothing more."

The woman bowed her head again as the man stomped out of the house. She picked up the plate and used the side of her hand to scrape the meat splattered across the floor onto it. She took it to the room where the girls waited, but it was locked. She called to the girls that she had food and would find the key. As our picture faded, she scurried here and there, searching for a key that her husband had probably taken with him.

My soul ached with deep sorrow for this good mother and her poor daughters. I closed my eyes and waited.

I stood in that hall wearing a thick cloak over a woolen gown, fur-lined boots, and bearing a large pouch of foodstuffs. I watched Gyr for a moment. She staggered back, gasping when I materialized.

"Who are you?"

"My name is Lin, handmaiden to our lady Frigg. Your father prayed to my lady to save you from this terrible man. We saw what he did just now."

"But what can you do? I am married; I cannot leave. My home belongs to him now. What will become of my poor girls?"

"You and your daughters will be quite safe, Gyr. He will not. He will pay for his wickedness.

"You know my name!"

"We know everything. I will bring your girls into the warm now and feed them."

Gyr shook her head wildly. "He will beat them if he finds them here."

"No, he will not."

She shook her head again, too proud to cry. "But you are only a frail girl. What can you do against this tyrant? He is huge and strong."

I stroked her arm, fixing my eyes onto hers until she calmed. "You have the gods by your side now. Do you know where he is?"

"He might have gone to a house where his friends drink together. I am not sure."

"No mind, I will follow his scent. Come to your girls now."

She led me to their prison, crying out in wonder when I crushed the lock in my fist and pushed open the door.

"Feed them and take them to bed. He will not bother you again."

I waited until she had seated her daughters in front of the fire. They were too spent to do anything but stare into the flames and warm their hands. They still shivered under their blankets, although the little one hacked less often.

Gyr held herself with more confidence now, looking more like the proud lady she had once been. How humiliated she must have felt when Ulf denigrated her day after day in front of her children.

"I brought you food that is not too rich for their empty stomachs." I pointed to the pouch on the table. "I will be back soon. Without Ulf. He will never return."

The girls and their mother stared at me as I left, too awed to respond. I always intend to be comforting, but at the same time, can't help being frightening.

Tall pines, whipped by the wind, dropped chunks of snow on my head as I floated over the almost impassable track, sniffing out traces of Ulf. His scent had been pervasive in the house, a mixture of rank sweat and fury.

I soon came to a rough dwelling from which emanated the shouts of men in their cups and women whose job it was to entertain them. I opened the door and slammed it closed. Everything went quiet. Several of the men stood and started to approach. I raised both hands, freezing their limbs, although they soon began muttering and exclaiming in fearful anger. Ulf ordered a vicious-looking dog to do its job and take care of me.

"Yes, come here, boy," I cooed. "I've got a little treat for you." The dog ambled over, licked my hand, and gobbled a piece of meat I'd liberated from the plate on Gyr's table. The dog sat leaning against my leg, baring his teeth at Ulf.

"Leave us, girl! You are not welcome here." Ulf tried to sound commanding. The other men hushed him, understanding I was the one in command. The women sat at the tables, transfixed.

"Now then," I said. "I have been sent by my lady Frigg to take care of a problem. That problem is Ulf. He is cruel and faithless. He beats his wife and starves her daughters."

"Lies! She lies," Ulf yelled, managing to raise his fist a little before it dropped uselessly to his side.

"Do you think the gods sent me here because of lies? We gazed into our silver pool and watched your actions after Gyr's father prayed to Frigg for assistance."

"What do you want?" said another man, his voice shaking with fear.

"Ulf is to return to the village from which he came," I said.

"I can't, not there," Ulf squeaked, looking as panicked as his frozen body tried to escape.

"Why not?" I asked.

"I have my reasons," he mumbled.

I moved closer. "Look into my eyes," I commanded.

"No."

I stared at him until he could no longer resist. "You will tell the truth. What did you do to make you leave your village." He was now incapable of lying, transfixed by my intensity.

"I married a rich widow. There was an accident, and she and her son died. They thought it was my fault, although they couldn't prove anything. They ran me out anyway."

"Did you kill them?"

He swiveled his eyes away. "No, of course not."

"Look at me."

He set his mouth tight but could not resist my will for more than a minute. "I set a fire."

The room broke into a swell of angry voices.

"So, now you are starving your stepdaughters and planning to sell them to a house of pleasure. What are your plans for their mother, may I ask?"

"Well, she is my wife..." His voice, weaker now, dispersed into the rafters.

"You will continue to beat her and use her until you get what you want? And what delights do you have planned for her then?"

He hung his head. I released them all from their immobile state. Ulf started to splutter and explain himself to his friends, only to be met with stony silence.

"Leave," said one.

"But I have nothing."

"Leave," chorused the others. The women started to chant. "Leave, leave, leave!"

"Ulf, look at me." His face turned back to me, eyes sizzling with hatred. "You will walk out of here now. Find another village. If you persist in your wickedness, I will find you again."

With a curse, the brute flung his cloak over his shoulders and strode to the door, trying to knock me over as he pushed past. He halted and aimed a kick at the dog, who crouched in front of him, growling. The animal sprang aside and rushed in for the finish.

"Not now, boy," I said. "Go and wait in the corner." The dog slunk off, keeping up a low continuous growl as he stared at Ulf with murder in his heart.

Before Ulf could move again, I picked him up and levitated. "Open the door, someone." I threw him into a snowdrift. After my willing helper slammed the door behind him, his friends all stared at me, waiting for another dramatic flourish. I just smiled sweetly, wished them good evening, patted the dog, and left.

I sensed Ulf on the path ahead, perhaps waiting for me or perhaps on his way home to wreak vengeance on his wife. Certainly not to do as I'd commanded. I lifted my head, yipping and yowling to the wolves I knew couldn't be far away. "In the name of my lady Frigg, I ask for your protection. Ulf is an evil man who wishes his family harm, and me, too." The cold wind sliced across my face and throat, plucking at my hair like an impish child as I awaited their reply—a single sharp bark, very close. Ulf couldn't harm me, of course, but I knew suggesting he intended to would play well with the wolves.

I replaced my hood and floated toward Ulf, following his scent, now ripe with fear. The soft padding of wolves approached from all sides. When I rounded a bend, Ulf turned round, saw me, and made a run for his house—Gyr's house. I let him outstrip me momentarily. When I came to his hiding place, a woodshed, I called, "You must come out now, Ulf. Meet your destiny."

After a while, he emerged, fists raised, ready to charge, but found himself surrounded by a multitude of seemingly disembodied eyes glowing fiery yellow in the dark night. Even the stars had turned away. He spun this way and that, looking for an opening, but the hut had disappeared. As I floated back to Gyr to tell her she was free, the howls and screams began.

I forgot to turn off the recorder for a few minutes. Lin reposed peacefully, a satisfied smile curving her lips slightly. I could only sit, stunned. She set wolves on a man so they would rip him to pieces. He'd done evil things, but still. But still. My breath felt ragged as I realized how afraid of this woman I should be.

Lin rose and sat facing me.

"You are shocked. Perhaps a little frightened? Don't think me a cruel god. Sometimes there is no other way. A tyrant's cruelty is his pleasure. That kind of tormented soul never heals, knows only how to wound the innocent. Turn that thing on again; I haven't finished."

This was turning into our longest session yet.

This is the only family I kept up with until they were settled and free from fear. Usually, I would complete my mission and leave. But these people touched me, and I wanted to see the girls, especially, settled and happy.

Gyr was too good a catch to be left unprotected. Her father lived an hour's walk away, and he was getting on, as well as having his own small holding to farm. I visited them at the end of each season with gifts of food and cloth, usually linen or silk. They owned sheep, so didn't need wool. I'd warned off the wolves that night they disposed of Ulf, so they didn't suffer any losses from that quarter.

One day I stood outside their door, ready to knock, when I heard raised voices, most unusual in this quiet group of women. When I knocked, the youngest daughter, Anna, opened the door. Her eyes were red-rimmed, and her mouth turned down in a pout. I crossed the hallway toward the fire where Gyr stood, eyes hard and teeth clenched.

"What is it?"

"Anna wishes to marry. She is only fifteen, too young, and I don't like the boy. His family is not trustworthy."

I turned to Anna. "Is this true?"

"Yes, I want to marry Bjorn. He is very big and handsome, and I trust him completely. I love him, and he loves me."

"Your late stepfather was big and handsome," I said. "It means nothing."

Anna flounced up to the loft where they all slept. She usually treated me with reverence, but I suppose love had warped her judgment. The two other girls, Sigrun and Margret, gaped at me, horrified by Anna's rudeness, muttered their apologies, and followed her.

"Why do you think this young man is untrustworthy?" I asked Gyr.

"His family is suspected of stealing sheep from other farmers, and other things go missing, too. She's been slipping away from her chores to meet him, and I caught them making love once in the barn, fortunately before they'd gone too far. She is too young and very naïve."

"Don't worry, I'll look into it."

"Thank you. I'd go to see the boy's father, but he's a very rough sort of man."

I sat and chatted with Gyr for a while. I treasured those human moments with a good woman in front of a warm fire in a quiet house. The gods can get quarrelsome, and goodness knows most are self-centered. Some are downright cruel. After an hour or so, Gyr called up to the girls to finish their chores before the sun set. They came downstairs and stood in a line before me.

Gyr rose. "I believe you have something to say to Lin," she said to Anna, who looked scared.

"I am sorry for my rudeness," Anna said, bobbing a curtsey.

"I will excuse it this time, Anna, but you know it is never wise to anger the gods." I saw Gyr's look of concern out of the corner of my eye, mirrored by the girls' fear. "Go to your work now."

They filed out of the house in silence.

"Don't worry, Gyr, you know I'd never hurt them. The child needed to be put in her place."

"I know, I know. We owe you so much."

"It is my destiny to aid those under my lady's protection. But your family is special." She kissed my hand. I felt a sudden urge to hug her and kiss her cheeks, but gods don't do that. Dignity must be upheld, come what may. Sadly, those days are long gone.

I dematerialized, but instead of flying to Asgard, I made for the milking shed. Sigrun and Margret wrestled with half a dozen ewes to get them to give up their milk. No Anna. I left and floated this way and that to catch her scent. At last, I smelled a faint whiff of her mixed with male sweat. More than one male. I found them in the old shed where Ulf had tried to take refuge a few years ago. One young man held her down while the other untied his belt and pulled up her skirt. She cried and writhed, trying to kick the young man I guessed was her "big handsome" Bjorn. I materialized and tapped him hard on the shoulder. He swung around.

"What do you want? Some of the same?" He leered—his big mistake. "Her mother thinks she's too good for me. So, I'll just take her this way."

"Stop this at once."

He straightened himself and raised his hand, but forgot to retie his belt, causing his trousers to puddle at his ankles. As he bent to pull them up, I threw him against the wall, then banged his head on a beam for good measure. The other young man had backed himself into a corner, holding the now hysterical Anna by her throat.

"You come near me, and she's dead," he growled.

He had no idea who I was and how fast I could move. He soon found himself with a couple of broken ribs and no fair maiden to bargain with.

"Anna, go back to your mother at once. Tell her you are finished with Bjorn and that I have taken care of everything."

"Yes, Lin. Thank you, Lady Lin." She scurried out.

I asked the boy nursing his ribs, "What's your name?"

"Kurt."

"You will take me to your father. Pick up your brother and lead the way."

It was a long, slow walk, with Kurt holding his brother over his right shoulder and hugging his ribs with his left arm. He flagged from time to time until I kicked him in the backside. We finally arrived at a poorly kept farmyard where mud and dung clogged even the pathway. A couple of pigs wandered up to sniff the boys, only to be met with a vicious kick.

"Kurt, put down your brother and get inside." He dumped his brother in a particularly odiferous pile.

"Father will not be pleased. You may have met your match."

"I'm sure he won't be pleased at all. Do you seriously think he's any match for me?" He didn't answer. "Will your mother be inside?"

"My mother died last year. We need someone to keep house."

"And that someone would be Anna."

"Well, why not? She's young and strong. Years of work in her."

I pushed him through the door. A huge man sat next to the fireplace in the big room that served as kitchen, living room, and, as far as I could tell, bedroom. He rose when he saw us. Kurt hugged his ribs.

"What is going on?" he asked in a voice rather like Odin's when he cursed Loki, as he often had cause to do.

"I found your other son Bjorn, who is unconscious in the dung outside, trying to rape the widow Gyr's daughter Anna. This one," I poked Kurt painfully in the ribs, "was holding her down."

"Well, what of it? They'll be married soon enough."

"Gyr has not approved the match. And now that I see the state of things, and having heard about some of your other bad habits, I'm not surprised."

His face engorged with rage, and he rushed me. I stood my ground and pushed him into the fire. He stumbled out of it, hardly seeming to feel the burns in his frenzy. I ran around him this way and that so fast he became dizzy and sank to the floor. It was only then that he felt the fire licking up the back of his jacket and threw it off, moaning in pain.

I went outside. Bjorn had come to and was on his knees. "Get inside," I ordered. He staggered through the door.

The three sorry creatures, two on the floor, stared at me, their faces full of hate and fear.

"Know that Gyr and her daughters are under the protection of the gods. If you go near any of them again, you will die. And not quickly."

I slowly dematerialized—because I knew it would unnerve them—happy to leave the mucky farm for sweet-smelling Asgard.

The girls all married well, and I attended all their weddings. Gyr was sad when the two eldest left her for their new homes, but she was relieved they were secure. Anna finally met a young man she loved. I naturally checked him out, as I had her sisters' beaux. He was the youngest son of a farmer, so would not inherit, but I judged him to be honest and kind. He wasn't tall but stocky and strong with almost black hair not seen often in those parts. When he asked Gyr for her daughter's hand in marriage, she asked him if he would consider taking care of her small farm. She'd had enough of backbreaking work. He was delighted, and so was Anna. They would live with her and manage the farm. Gyr would manage the house while Anna helped her husband. Later, of course, Gyr would find herself surrounded by grandchildren, and that's backbreaking work, to be sure.

Gyr had her suitors but had gone off the idea of marriage, entailing as it did the loss of independence. "Enough is enough," she told me. I know what she means now.

Anna's wedding felt special. I arrived at Gyr's house when she and her two married daughters had almost finished dressing Anna. I thought they'd be in the loft but heard their excited chatter toward the back of the house. Anna's betrothed and his brothers had built a large room onto the house where the newlyweds would sleep. Very sensible. I'd been wondering about that because the loft was so open plan.

They all greeted me with smiles and curtsies, radiating happiness. It made me unusually happy, too. In those days, I was simply contented and rarely let any other emotion cloud my horizon—except where injustice was concerned. That could arouse my wrath, as you've heard. But even then, it was a cold anger, nothing hot.

I hung a heavy gold chain around Anna's neck. A gold and silver pendant showing a likeness of my lady Frigg hung from it. Her sisters had received the same gift upon their marriages, too, and they wore them now.

"As you know, Anna, your family is under the protection of my lady Frigg. Be sure to wear this when traveling or when you are near those who may try to do you harm. Also, be sure to wear it if you are ill and especially whilst giving birth. It will protect you."

"Oh, thank you, Lady Lin, thank you!" She twirled around, excited and happy.

I walked with them to the little white building that served as a gathering room where the villagers marked any special occasion, be it birth, marriage, or death. The ladies of the village had filled it with wildflowers that bloom in profusion at the end of May, even in that cool world. The warmth of a huge log in the fireplace, its flames glinting off golden wood walls and rafters, created an aura of safe haven and goodwill.

Anna's beloved gasped when he saw her, a bride with the glow most brides seem to acquire when they turn princess on their special day. A village elder performed the ritual of laying a cloth over their hands, placing a ring, first on her thumb and then on his, while intoning the prayers. He held up a wood tablet bearing their names—which neither of them could read—and asked them to kiss it.

The guests cheered and applauded when he declared them man and wife before tucking into a huge meal remarkable for a modest village.

I squeezed Gyr's hand and left that simple heaven for my home in the heaven of the gods. I never returned. My work was done.

I spent the afternoon with Sam in the park before going back to dinner. I'd been shaken to the core by Lin's revelation about setting the wolves on Ulf, but the carefree, bouncing Sam soon smoothed me out. Maybe Hunter would be able to sneak away, so that was something to look forward to.

There was a senior in high school I had a crush on when I was a freshman. I could hardly think about anything else for weeks. My stomach fluttered whenever I saw him, and his voice sent me into raptures. He barely noticed my existence. One day, I found him behind the gym, forcing himself on another girl. She was whimpering, "No, don't, stop it." He slapped her and kept on pushing while the girl cried. His face had taken on an ugly, cruel look. He left school shortly afterward, as did the girl he raped. He was not even allowed to attend graduation. So that was that. I hadn't felt those crush symptoms again—until now. And this was probably equally hopeless.

15

Lin could be truly monstrous. She saved a woman and her children by throwing a man to the wolves. Literally. It was unsettling to listen to those gruesome things, but I had to understand that she and Hunter lived by a moral code so different from ours that one could only accept rather than judge. That was her concept of justice.

I was suddenly struck by how different she sounded when telling her stories. She became almost lyrical sometimes. She could have made a good literary account if she had the patience. And if she didn't drain the computer each time she touched it. How was it that Hunter could use a computer without that problem? He had a cell phone, too; I'd seen him use it.

This dainty monster composed herself in revelation mode, statue still, eyes closed.

"I used to love boating. The sound of waves lapping is so soothing, the rocking motion almost hypnotic. But the next part of the journey back to America with those girls put me right off." Lin wrinkled her nose.

I'd always loved the water, too, especially the sea. We used to go to the beach on vacation every year when I was a child. My father would take a fishing trip at least once. I would lie around enjoying the sun and usually dozed off. I never fished. Poor things—such cruel hooks.

Tape 14

Stained blankets covered the dented truck's floor. In addition to Mariam, Houdah, and Didi, two other girls joined us, Sussann and Nadia. The girls were all depressed and wide-eyed after saying goodbye to their few acquaintances, to whom they'd presented small gifts of the food provided by Mary Wilder. I hoped it wouldn't be too long before that woman would only be able to suck sustenance from a straw.

After a valiant stint of trying to tune out their sniffles, I told them Arab legends I'd heard in Egypt. We used to have an old doorman who was very fond of my little girl Reema, carving her toys and telling her stories. I liked to listen in whilst sipping mint tea on the verandah.

I was beginning to get maudlin and told the girls, more abruptly than intended, to go to sleep. Sleep is my only escape from memory. I never dream. But no sleep for me that night. I guessed we were going to the coast, where we'd be stowed on some old freighter for the next leg. I had to commit everything to memory—routes, names, transports—and I needed to ensure these girls got rescued before they got used and the others rescued and given a new life of some kind. American immigration can be harsh, but I didn't think they'd want this story broken to the press.

I jolted awake as the truck braked. Our driver, Abdul Kareem, opened the rear doors and ordered us out. He looked me up and down, clearly wondering if he could get away with it. I hissed at him, "You know they pay for virgins, don't you?" He looked startled and pushed me forward so roughly I almost fell. He followed us down as he shouted directions to a splintered dock where a rickety launch lay tethered. A hooded figure stood facing us, arms akimbo. He waved at the driver before making his way to the prow and starting the engine without turning back around. I looked at the sky, noted the exact position of the sun, and made my calculations.

"Enjoy the sky while you still can, bitch," the driver said quietly in such an even tone that I knew what he intended. As planned, I was last in line, so well placed to deal with him. After the last girl had clambered aboard, I whipped around and grasped the brute's shoulders, dislocating them both before hurling him into the marshy growth at the path's edge. He screamed and writhed while I leaped into the boat.

The other man turned briefly. "Where is Abdul Kareem? What was that noise?" he asked.

"He fell and hurt his arm," I said. "He told me to tell you to go ahead."

He looked at me hard, allowing me to imprint his desert-abraded face in my mind's gallery. He went about his business of steering us to the freighter that lay anchored just over the horizon. He wasn't too good at riding the chop, but it could have been worse. Didi looked green already.

The ladder up to the freighter's deck, rusty and precipitous, gave rise to some wailing and gasping on the part of the girls. I had no problem scaling it, of course. The captain, clearly European, spoke basic Arabic and English with a Germanic accent. I pretended not to understand English when he shouted orders to the crew. We stood quietly until he turned to face us, sweeping his cold blue eyes over our bodies.

"You will stay below deck. Keep quiet and give no trouble, or you will be very sorry. Come."

We climbed behind him down into the bowels of the ship. He opened the door to a cabin with six bunk beds, three stacked on each of two opposite walls. There was barely room to move.

"I need a bathroom," Didi told him, her hand only leaving her mouth long enough to speak.

He laughed and pointed to a large, covered bucket under a barred porthole. "Someone will collect twice a day." He then pointed to another bucket, this one full of water, with a ladle attached by a chain. "In case you get thirsty."

He laughed again at our horrified expressions. "Nothing fancy on my ship." He left and slammed the door.

Didi rushed over to the bucket, tore off the lid, and vomited. "I'm sorry," she said, wiping her mouth with the back of her hand, tears streaking her grubby cheeks. Houdah and Sussann started to whine, and the others quickly followed suit. But I shut them up, telling them that they must make the best of it. This was the price we had to pay for a better life.

I thought I should try to get to know the two new girls better, as they'd just been a blur until then. My former tent mates got on my nerves. Later. Now, my mind needed a rest, so I claimed one of the top bunks and lay down. Muffled noises above our heads told me the ship was beginning to move out. The other girls listlessly chose their bunks, and our cabin stayed restfully quiet until an hour or so later when one of the sailors eventually delivered some chicken curry with rice. The smell didn't do much for Didi. She turned to the wall in her bottom bunk and held her shawl over her nose and mouth. I ate enthusiastically, the others sparingly.

By the time night closed in, after we'd been chugging along most of the day, they were all vomiting. The smell and sounds of vomit had set off a chain reaction, starting with Didi, who resumed her earlier performance. Then Houdah succumbed, soon followed by Mariam. We were in for a nasty ride.

I'd heard the door lock engage but wondered if I could get it open. I blocked my machinations with my body, so they couldn't see my little awl work its magic. I could have broken it, but that would have brought the captain's wrath down on our heads, and I'd never get out again without giving myself away. Now for some air. When the girls started a clamor, I shut them up by promising to look for fresh water.

I crept around and found a couple of sailors having a few drinks on the main deck, so I hid behind a lifeboat and listened. Fortunately, their common language was English, although obviously not their mother tongue.

"I cannot wait to visit Madam Violet's," one said with a dirty laugh.

"Gott, don't you think about nothing but women?" said the other, his voice a rough grumble.

"I hate Cyprus, so there has got to be some nice times, don't there?"

"I think it is quite good. Better than that sand hell we just left. I wish they would let us over to the Greek side, though. Everyone says it is nicer."

So that's where we were headed. North Cyprus, Turkish territory.

"What will happen to the girls after that?"

"They get taken off the boat to some house, I suppose. After that, who knows? It is none of our business. Best not to ask questions."

The captain was clearly a dangerous fellow, so it wouldn't do to upset him. But maybe I should try to cozy up. If I saw or heard too much, he'd try to kill me, so I'd have to kill him. I could seduce him. But how would that help? I needed to know where we were going, and if he died, the supply chain would be broken. He was only useful if nothing changed. Knowledge and saving the girls was my goal. *Keep focused, Lin. Keep focused*; I kept reminding myself.

I looked for water and only found one can. The girls were in a bad way, and the stench was appalling. I've never done well with bad smells. Of course, I lived in the Middle East and Far East for several lifetimes, not to mention suffered the horrific swathe of the Black Death, and one gets used to it to a point. America is so sanitized you become spoiled. Americans are always showering, deodorizing themselves and even their pets, fussing about garbage, and offering food for sale in tightly wrapped packets. You get used to people and places smelling good, or at least neutral. Even death is tidied up as soon as practicable.

The girls' seasickness improved gradually over the next few days, but their spirits remained low. Having frequent bowel movements, thanks to daily curries, in a small room containing five other people proved demoralizing above all else. I managed once or twice by stealing out during the night. Hanging over the side of the ship, making sure I wasn't over any portholes, was quite awkward but better than the alternative. It assaulted my dignity, even though no one saw me. Ah, the price of gluttony! I also needed time alone to reinforce my persona. That itchiness manifested itself more often when the sea got rough. Something to do with equilibrium?

One night, we were about to get ready for bed when I heard the unmistakable sounds of the ship coming into port. The engine slowed, commands rang out, and the clamor increased as the ship eased into the dock. No climbing the ladder to a launch this time, thankfully. The girls weren't up to it.

"Girls, I think we are docking very soon. I don't know if we will disembark here or not, but we'd better be ready. Gather your things." They looked apprehensive, and each stuffed a cloth bag with her paltry bits and pieces. They followed my lead without question or comment these days.

Sure enough, the captain banged on the door and flung it open. "You have reached the end of your voyage, ladies. Out you come."

"Good evening, Captain. They don't need you on deck?"

"My crew is very well trained. And you have a smart mouth, which is not safe for a young woman in your position. Move."

He led the way. I brought up the rear as usual. We climbed the stairs up to the next deck and down the gangway to the well-lit dock, where a crowd of brawny characters rushed around, achieving very little that I could see.

A small man in a uniform festooned with gold braid shook hands with the captain and palmed a wad of notes.

"Goodbye, ladies," said the captain with a mock salute. Follow Mr. Osman. He will take you to your resting place for tonight."

The magnificent Osman hustled us into the back of a waiting van and slammed the door. The girls remained silent, frightened. The windows had been painted over. I thought of scratching a peephole, but that would take time, and I should concentrate on memorizing the route. We hadn't driven longer than twenty minutes before the van stopped, and Mr. Osman opened our door. We seemed to be behind a large house, almost a mansion.

"Keep very quiet. Go over to that door." He pointed to an old wooden door with iron studs and handle. It creaked open, and an old lady in a floor-length beaded black gown and raven hair piled on her head, Japanese geisha style, beckoned us in. I turned to Mr. Osman, but he was already back in the van and pulling out.

"Come in and do not say one word," the old harridan ordered. "I am Madame Thierry. You may simply address me as Madame." Trying to appear French, but just an old Turkish whore. At least she spoke Arabic, but not with any accent I recognized.

We walked through a dark passage lit by Madame's oil lamp. Something smelled good, and we instinctively slowed down. "Faster!" We passed a door with a glass window that showed a tiled, steamy kitchen in full frenzy. We climbed four flights of back stairs into an attic filled with dusty, broken furniture and padlocked trunks. Madame opened a door to a large room with bunk beds. She pointed at a closet in the far right corner.

"That is your lavatory. Use it as little as possible. It gets stopped up. The shower has only cold water. Better than nothing, is it not? I will send food soon. There is a caftan, a nightdress, and underclothes on each bed." She locked the door behind her.

It was time to pep up this sad crowd. "Well, girls, choose your bed and get some rest. We've had a difficult journey, but at least we are on dry land." Didi started to wail. "Hush, Didi, we were told to be quiet."

The key in the door turned, and Didi cried harder as it slammed open. "I said quiet!" Madame slapped Didi's face so hard she cracked her head on the bedpost. She left again, closing the door quietly this time. The woman must have been eavesdropping, waiting to make an example of the first to breach the rules. I held Didi in my arms while she whimpered quietly into my clothing, which was neither comfortable nor appetizing. Oh, well, none of us were especially fragrant by that time. Even my clothes smelled of food spills and other unmentionable things. The other girls remained silent, eyes wide and mouths compressed. I went to inspect the shower. A hard nub of soap rested on a ledge. Two rough, graying towels had been folded on the lavatory seat.

"One at a time, take a very quick shower."

I was the last out of the shower and had just toweled off, which was not easy considering all those who went before, when the key turned in the lock again. This time, a barefoot young woman in a striped cotton caftan appeared. She picked up a large tray from the floor outside and put it on the ramshackle table in the center of the room, which wobbled alarmingly. Either the floor was uneven, or the table had a broken leg.

"What kind of place is this?" I asked in Arabic. She shrugged and shook her head.

The food tasted heavenly: chicken chunks in a delicately flavored sauce, a pilaf with herbs and pine nuts, and roasted eggplant slices smothered in yogurt. It must have been left over from the evening meal downstairs. They wouldn't have prepared it especially for us. I ate with relish, but the others were too miserable to do anything but peck at it.

"You must keep up your strength," I urged. "We don't know what lies ahead."

They ate a little more and drank the tea. At least it was boiled water. Dysentery was to be avoided at all costs under the circumstances. We each used the lavatory, mercifully without complications, and settled down for the night. When they all seemed to be asleep, I lay on the rough wooden floor and pressed my ear against it. Laughter, music, men's loud exclamations, and women's purring entreaties filtered through. Intermittently, the unwelcome sound of whipping and entreaty rang loudly, then low rumbles of ecstasy, arguing, cursing, and earthy cries of pleasure. As I suspected, a whorehouse. I hoped the journey would not end here. Suddenly, widespread shouting and cursing … the key clanged in the lock, so I leaped back into bed, pretending to be asleep.

"Quickly, before they have a chance to cry out. They usually don't come up here, but if there is noise…"

I opened my eyes enough to see Madame, the maid, and two men come at us with cloths. I turned my head to avoid a full dose and fought to ward off the effects of the chloroform, but it left me feeling foggy for a few minutes as they'd held the cloths on our faces for at least five minutes, and I couldn't give myself away by fighting them off. The others were out. I heard furniture being moved across the floor and banged against our door. They? A raid?

After about fifteen minutes, I got up and pushed against the door. It didn't budge. The chloroform must have sapped my strength. I closed my eyes and concentrated. I pushed again. Slowly, whatever barred the door screeched back, and I stuck my head out, crept to the attic doorway and turned the handle. Locked, as expected, I ran to look out of one of two small, barred windows. There seemed to be vans with flashing lights gathered in the courtyard, although I couldn't see as clearly as usual. I'd never taken drugs of any kind or needed anesthesia, so this was an interesting experience, albeit an inconvenient one. I found a few old tools on the ledge of the other window and went to work. These old locks were made strong and solid. Footsteps coming up the stairs had me running to hide behind an old, oaken armoire that leaned like a drunk.

It was the little maid who gasped when she saw the table in the middle of the floor and the door open. I removed my shawl, threw it over her head, shoved her into the room, and pushed the table against the door. Her shrieks were barely audible, so the builders had done a great job of soundproofing. I crept downstairs. The place seemed strangely quiet. I moved up and down corridors, peeking into garish rooms where mirrors and purple velvet abounded, all beds except one hurriedly abandoned, the smell of sex everywhere. I decided to try the lower level. I'd just turned toward the kitchen when a hand clutched my shoulder. I turned. The captain.

"Well, well, who is this pretty miss?" I wondered why he spoke in English.

I decided to answer in English. "You don't recognize me? After all that time?"

He looked puzzled. "We don't see beautiful blondes so very often. I'd remember you, for sure." He picked up a lock of my hair and rubbed it between his fingers. Blonde. The chloroform had dissolved Noor, caused my strength to ebb, rendered my eyesight human, and explained why I hadn't heard him behind me.

"How did you escape the raid?" he asked.

"I hid in the attic," I said. "You?"

"I arrived just as they were pulling away. I needed a little recreation after a long voyage. I suspect Madame did not pay the right people all she was supposed to. But perhaps I am not going to be disappointed after all."

I had no choice. I needed this man alive to keep the network in place. If he disappeared, the rest would take fright and disappear. It had to be done. Anyway, he wasn't bad looking and had clearly bathed recently.

"I saw one clean room," I said, leading the way. "And I must bathe."

He left at dawn after a surprisingly pleasant interlude. Brutes sometimes surprise you with hidden depths of sensitivity.

I went back to the attic carrying an armful of clean caftans and shawls. Sitting outside the lockup, concentrating on my form, I felt the welcome stretching and tingling as I shifted and was finally able to stand up as Noor. I pushed the table away from the door and opened it. Everyone was crying, including the maid.

"Why did you do this?" So she spoke Arabic. Not Syrian, not Egyptian.

"The police were here," I told her. "I put you in here to save you. You'd better go home. They've all been arrested." She sobbed louder.

"My mother will whip me if I lose my job."

"She'll whip you worse if you end up in prison. And your family. Where are you from?"

"Algeria. Things got hard for my family."

"Do you know what they are planning to do with us?"

"Madame said you are all going to be moved on today. The men arrive at noon."

"Where are they taking us?"

"I don't know. I heard something about a plane."

I gave her the money the captain gave me. "Go now." She scuttled out.

I turned to the five sniveling girls in front of me. "Pull yourselves together. They didn't chloroform us to hurt us but to keep us quiet. There was a police raid."

"Why the police?" asked Sussann, a quiet, anxious girl who rarely spoke.

"I don't know, but it had nothing to do with us."

"How did you get out?"

"I am good at these things. Remember how I would get out of our cabin in the boat to get water? I'm just good at it, that's all."

"How come you didn't sleep like we did?"

"I held my breath and managed to push the cloth away before I got too much of it. I was still awake when they came, you see."

"You are very clever," Sussanne said. It came out like an accusation. Maybe I wouldn't bother getting to know her.

Two men in mechanics' jumpsuits arrived a few hours later, clumping up the stairs and throwing open the door. The girl hadn't bothered to lock it. They looked like brothers.

"Where is everyone?" one of them asked in Arabic.

"Police raid," I said. "Nothing to do with us. I suppose Madame didn't pay the right people."

"Time to move on. And keep quiet."

"We haven't eaten," I said.

He shrugged. "Too bad. We have our orders."

"It is better if you let us all use the lavatory first."

He shrugged again. "Very well."

Our sad little procession wended its way down the staircase and into another van, this one windowless, that was parked in the courtyard recently vacated by the police. One of them handed each of us a bottle of lukewarm water. This trip lasted at least two hours, maybe longer. When the van rolled to a stop, I heard a plane's engine start up, a turboprop.

The men shouted at us to get out and climb up the stairs to the plane doorway. They saw us on our way before driving around the back of the building. A young woman pointed us each to a threadbare seat and fastened our safety belts for us. She closed and locked the cabin door.

"Ready, Gunther," she called into the cockpit.

"Where are we going?" I asked.

"Never you mind," she said harshly, actually wagging her finger at me. Cheeky cow.

The plane taxied out to the runway. None of the girls except Houdah had flown before, so little squeals and frantic prayers accompanied our ascent.

"Don't worry, I've flown lots of times. Just relax. Take a nap. I will. I'm tired, so don't disturb me." I couldn't take much more of them, which wasn't fair of me, but I was mentally exhausted. I needed to concentrate on my form, too, as that damned itching had started up. The chloroform must have really done a number on my system.

I listened to the captain's garbled exchange with air traffic control. Finally, he mentioned a destination. It sounded like Avignon. I closed my eyes and visualized Penelope Gay, feeling my skin relax and my hair tug a little at its roots. My fingertips felt sensitive, though, as did my ankles.

I wondered if Hunter was a brute. As cold-blooded as Lin? He was absolutely huge and sometimes klutzy. But that sweet smile. He almost certainly has hidden depths. I hope so. Funny she used the term "hidden depths," like my mother. Uncanny.

"Avignon. I have never spoken of this since I returned home without my little boy. It is going to be very difficult. Those two children were so precious. Their faces have become blurred in my memory, but I remember how they loved the wooden Dutch toys their father bought them in Venice. A doll for Marie and a boat for Jean. They would go down to a nearby pond in Avignon and float the boat, making up stories of long, exciting voyages. I can still hear their shrill voices, conjuring up countries and barbaric natives, whom Jean would conquer bravely, saving his sister from certain death. Little did they know they would soon embark on a long journey, deadly in its own way."

She heaved a great sigh, ending with a little moan.

"We started off in Venice, and what happened there is why Hunter is so paranoid about anyone knowing anything about us, especially our wealth." Her mouth twisted a little before she composed herself.

I had never been a mother, but I could not imagine outliving my children over and over again. If this was going to be a sad tale, I hoped I could hold it together. I cried easily.

Tape 15

I sometimes dream of Avignon, but only on lazy summer afternoons when I am quite alone and can reminisce undisturbed. I've only ever let myself remember the good times—until now.

Hunter chose Venice for the adult period after a rebirth, I think about 1340. Venice was the center of naval power in Europe, so he had notions of making his fortune by sending magnificent ships laden with unspecified goods to trade all over the known world. He'd become a man of substance, rubbing shoulders with the Doge and other powerful elders. We already had a fortune, but he was always keen on not revealing that in case people started asking questions. He still is. To spend big, he had to be seen making it big. It's not as if we could tell anyone the truth—that we absconded with the dwarfs' treasure when their mountain rose from the sea once more and, luckily, they failed to come back up with it. After leaving Hel, we made a short detour to collect it.

Aetna was yet another deep dark place, but we were happy to reach her rumbling caves and shed that load. The walk had sorely tested Hunter, so he lolled about most of the time. I could pop out and walk under the sun through soft emerald grass every day, which delighted me after such a long sojourn in the cold, gloomy underworld. Hel was even colder than northern Midgard's usual climate. I don't know how humans endured all that ice and snow, only to be followed by a short and grudging spring merging into a fleeting summer. Hunter sometimes joined me on my walks as he grew stronger and more cheerful. Rough-looking humans threatened us with violent gestures several times, but after a couple of families saw the monstrous faces we could pull, followed by other super-human antics on my part, the wiser ones learned to keep away. Three or four headstrong young men periodically felt they should hunt us down and take an impressive trophy home to the clan. A few fatal tumbles down Aetna's rocky black slopes finally deterred them. After the last episode, I caught Hunter looking at me funny.

"What?"

"You have changed," he said.

"Of course I have."

Many lifetimes later, Hunter set his heart on Venice. He had no idea what was to befall us. Naturally, we spoke old Norse at home, and one of our maids tattled to another maid, and so on up the line until we became objects of suspicion. Spies, probably, speaking a language no one had heard before. That's when he became even more paranoid about us not drawing attention to ourselves. Protestations of innocence did no one any good in those days, and our children could be left destitute or worse, especially when we proved nearly impervious to the usual torments. Time to leave.

We fled to Florence, then to Avignon. Avignon had been something of a backwater until a French pope was elected and decided to stay in France, making it his permanent residence, as did the five popes who followed. The pontiffs developed the town and built monuments to their glory. With its pretty houses, magnificent palaces, and the picturesque River Rhone, it was the sort of charming place you see on postcards nowadays. We were happy once more. There were many discussions at all levels of society about whether the city should be ruled by Pope Boniface or King Philip. The dispute got quite nasty at times. We didn't care one way or the other and kept out of it. We just wanted a quiet life with our two children, Marie and Jean—in Venice, Maria and Gianni. Life was good in this bustling metropolis.

Hunter found employment at a candlemaker's shop and learned the trade from its old founder. He seemed to enjoy the work. When the old man became too crippled by arthritis to continue, he was only too glad to sell us the business.

I should have known it couldn't hold.

The Black Death scourged the world. It probably came up to Avignon from Marseille, paired with terrible tales of horrors suffered in other great cities. People knew nothing of germs then. They ran away from the sickness, only to carry it with them to other poor souls. Once it hit Avignon, astounding numbers of people died within the first few weeks. I had to get my children away, but Hunter refused to leave his precious shop. It took me a century or more to forgive him for not putting them first. I didn't allow myself to conceive children in my next life. Why I allow myself to continue bearing mortal children, I can't tell you. It's some kind of urge I can't explain in any logical terms.

I took Marie and Jean on a tough journey by carts, small boats, and, finally, a ship. In normal circumstances, Marseille would have been the logical place to sail from, but it had become a death trap. I couldn't show my face in Venice. I headed for Nantes, a town on the Loire River, from where we could take a ship north.

The first ship north was going to Bergen in Norway, which I hoped was still free from the plague. The poor children suffered a miserable crossing. The North Sea is a malevolent beast, and that spring was in a particularly spiteful mood. They looked wan and thin by the time we stumbled off the gangplank. The kindly captain directed me to a decent hostelry not far from port. Fru Soderstrom, the proprietress, welcomed us warmly, clucking sympathetically over the tired little ones. We spent a fitful night. The children kept waking up crying and sick, thinking they were still at sea. After the second such episode, I stayed awake to watch over them and saw how they rolled from side to side in their sleep. I tried to still them, and finally, they managed to drop off sometime toward dawn. They ate a reasonable breakfast of dark bread and cheese in Fru Soderstrom's warm, blue-tiled kitchen, getting fierce looks from me when they wrinkled their noses at the smell of pickled herring. I needed the landlady to like us, as she'd be a useful source of advice. I love pickled herring—a taste of my heavenly home. Not that I ate it or anything else in my handmaiden days, but later I would buy it in England, where Swedish sailors brought in barrels of it to keep them going in that rough country. They were always willing to share with a close friend.

I conversed with Fru Soderstrom in broken English. She said she'd heard about this plague, although it had not reached Bergen. She shook her head in disbelief when I told her that could change soon, as ships seemed to carry it all over the world. She suggested we go into the mountains, cold and rough but far from port. Getting to a mountain community would take at least three days, and it wouldn't be easy. She knew of a family leaving for a village called Tusededal in two days. She would make inquiries. The children needed a break, so that sounded ideal.

The stolid family of seven gladly accepted my offer of payment, and we set off in one of their two wagons. They were not unfriendly, merely uncommunicative. Even the children seemed subdued. They may have been frightened by the horror stories going around town about the Black Death. My children had also become withdrawn, staying close to me. They were not used to such cold weather either and glad to snuggle up to each other under the rugs.

On the second day, as we got farther up into the mountains, trees became scarcer, and the track got slushy, then by the third day, icy. The thaw had not yet arrived at these heights. Two sons in their late teens plied the reins expertly and got us through in one piece, although the leading wagon once almost overturned going around a rocky ice-slicked bend. The horses were not like any I'd seen before—on the small side, but improbably strong. A drafty hard-floored wagon, even with marvelously thick blankets in that climate, soured me on camping forever. Relieving ourselves in sub-zero temperatures turned out to be an exercise in endurance, too. I've never intentionally spent a night outdoors since—except for that Turkish refugee camp. Preserved rations sated our appetites more by the effort of chewing salty mystery slabs than filling our bellies. The parents and I slept in one wagon, sensibly leaving all the children in the other. There wasn't a night when they didn't indulge their marital bliss, annoying in such close quarters—tactless, too, since they weren't the sharing kind.

Finally, we reached our destination. Our companions offered us lodging at their new home, a substantial house in town they had recently bought from the family of its deceased owner. A stout maid welcomed us. She had kept fires going in all the rooms and prepared a simple meal. A big bed in one of the spare rooms was made up for us. I regarded the family with new interest. They had seemed like simple people, but this place was luxurious by most standards in those days. I came to learn that these northerners tended not to strut their wealth as people did in other cultures. When I was fulfilling my mission with Lady

Frigg, almost no one in Midgard had wealth except the great chieftains. She didn't bother herself with them as they achieved their status by brute force and, in her view, had earned any misfortune that came their way.

The meal that evening was much more to the children's liking. They wolfed down the rich venison stew. Jean fell asleep sitting up at the table, swaying from side to side to everyone's amusement until the beefy maid carried him up to bed.

After a few restful days, we found our own lodgings, and the children went to school, although the language made it hard for them to learn much. It came easily to me, as while Norse is more complicated, there are many similarities, so I helped with their homework. I have a picture in my mind of those dear blond heads bent over their tablets at the candlelit kitchen table. I haven't thought about Marie and Jean for many years. I loved them deeply, as I have all of them. Some of their faces are misty at best, though, and I get them confused because, unsurprisingly, all our children resemble one another. I must have borne and lost a few hundred by now. That is my tragedy.

I can hardly bear to think more about that time in Tusededal.

Lin clenched her teeth and lay immobile. After a few minutes, I noticed tears on her cheeks.

"Are you all right, Lin?" I asked, nervous she might resent the intrusion.

"No, I can never be all right with so many dead babies. Never."

I switched off the recorder, went over to her, sat on the chaise, and stroked her head. She grasped me as if she were afraid I might leave her. I held her as she rocked, crying.

She sat up abruptly after a few minutes. "Well, enough of that. Let's get on with it."

I went back to the table and switched on the recorder again, my face wet with tears for this desolate mother. She drew a deep, shaky breath.

In hindsight, the Black Death must have hitched a ride with us. Little Jean went first; his fight for each breath, his cries of pain, his attempts to be a brave boy, intolerably heartrending. Marie seemed fine for a while, although sad. Not only sad for her brother, but so many school friends, so many fine young people, and all the good people who had brought us here. Marie finally came down with it and suffered worse than her poor little brother. She survived.

The fact that I did not get sick made me an object of suspicion. The few survivors blamed me, considering my arrival in the village a curse. I caught their looks and mutterings. When I pointed out to a couple gossiping and throwing me evil looks that they should deem all those still alive as possible culprits, it only deepened their enmity. When they started whispering about witches, I understood we should leave immediately. It wouldn't be long before they came for me. Only me, though, as they didn't seem to blame Marie. As if I hadn't suffered myself, losing my darling little Jean.

I took a dead neighbor's wagon and horses, which I'd presciently kept fed and watered, and returned to Bergen. Fru Soderstrom had succumbed, as had many hundreds of others. From there, we made the hard trek back to Avignon. At least Marie was safe with me.

Stories of that time tell that only one girl survived in Tusededal. These reports possibly refer to Marie, but four other families and I made it through. I'm guessing they probably left the mountains soon after I did and were presumed dead. It's not as though any of the victims had individual graves or headstones when things got really bad.

Hunter finished serving a wealthy customer before he acknowledged my arrival. He glared at me when I told him about Jean. His mouth became a thin white line, and he went off to get drunk, leaving Marie and me weeping from grief and exhaustion in the big marriage bed. Hunter lay down on the kitchen floor once he got home and passed out.

We stayed thirty more years in Avignon, seeing Marie wed and happy and, eventually, the mother of a wonderful little boy she named Jean because she thought he looked just like his uncle. He didn't. He inherited his father's dark hair.

Inevitably, friends began to avoid us. People were very superstitious in the Middle Ages, and our youthful appearance gave rise to gossip. Once more, it was time to leave. We decided on England next. Marie knew only that her friends remarked on how strange it was that her parents hardly looked their age. Humans, especially women, aged quickly then.

So, after much sorrowful discussion, we decided to disappear on a journey to Marseille. We told her we needed to buy provisions for what was now a successful factory, which Hunter had already willed to his daughter. She was lucky he'd moved the business out of our home ten years before, so we no longer had to endure the sickening smell of sheep tallow that stuck to our clothes and hair.

I wonder what became of them all. Do churches still keep ancient records of births, marriages, and deaths? Too bad I wouldn't have time to check. One day, perhaps. Should I make a list and try to track down all of them and their descendants? Curiosity gnaws at my mind some days. But what a thorny path to madness, one I should never go down.

Whew, that was a tough one. Poor little boy. And poor Lin, who rushed away immediately after the session. She didn't come to dinner, either. Hunter came to the table, wolfed down his food, and disappeared without a word. Had she told him she was remembering that time? He probably mourned, too, just buried it deeper.

I could have comforted him.

17

"The journey was tedious but at least reasonably comfortable. I like comfort. Insist on it.

That was all she said that morning. Was the project getting too much for her? I needed the job.

"I'm sure things get more interesting as your story goes on," I said.

"Yes, in fact, it does. I accomplished a lot."

A faint smile hovered, and she seemed to cheer up.

I felt cheerful, too. Lin had come down to breakfast after Hunter. He kissed me on my forehead and said I seemed to be glowing. As soon as I saw him in the mornings, I did feel myself glowing.

Tape 16

The plane began its descent. I'd hardly touched my lunch. I loathe pasta salad—chilled macaroni, slimy with cheap oil, never feels right on my tongue. I checked on the girls, whom I'd ignored. They were all asleep. Good, because I wasn't in the mood for any whining or sobbing, even my own.

There was a great flurry on the tarmac, unloading and loading crates of god-knows-what. I focused on a rapid conversation between the pilot and a sallow character slouching at the bottom of the steps. Italian. My rusty Italian barely sufficed, but I gathered we were to be driven to a house near another airfield and held there for a night before our next flight. But where? Then I caught it. Aviano, not Avignon! Oh, well, they say you can never go back.

Aviano rang a bell. Something about a ski-lift accident, an American plane cutting the wires, or something like that. Then I remembered; Aviano housed an American Air Force base in Italy. Were they really that nervy, using an air force base? But clearly, we had not landed at any air force base.

Two fellows appeared at the head of the aisle. They looked like B-movie renditions of mafia hoods with their white ties and socks, topped off by wide-brimmed felt hats. They hustled us down the steps, led us at a brisk pace around the shack that seemed to serve as a terminal, and down a baked dirt road lined with woods, where weeds straggled through numerous cracks and holes. No one seemed to find it necessary to hide us.

After about half an hour of complaints and lagging (at one point driving the fellow bringing up the rear to swat poor Didi hard on the backside), we arrived at a concrete box that proved to be a hostel where we were to spend the night. We were shown to our two rooms up a flight of stairs to drop our bags and use the nearby toilet.

When we got downstairs to the large table in the kitchen, four other girls were there; three plump women in black supervised us with sullen vigilance during dinner, barking, "*Silenzio*," accompanied by much finger-wagging if any of us tried to make conversation. The other girls were Asian and had the delicate features of Vietnam or Laos, but I couldn't be sure. Where were they going? They looked cheerful, which was more than our lot did after such an exhausting journey.

We were allowed to clean up in the bathroom after dinner, a dormitory affair with two shower cubicles and two toilets with door openings top and bottom. One toilet contained dark, malodorous water and wads of paper, clearly clogged. I wondered what would happen if we needed the facilities at night as we were sure to be locked in, but whom could I ask? I understood a lot of Italian, thanks to a good command of both French and Spanish, but my spoken ability was Venetian, and old Venetian at that—unintelligible to most Italians. Hunter and I have had to learn many languages and learn them fast. Adopting a new language seems to be an inbred talent for us. I decided to try Venetian on these women, anyway. One of the women could be from Venice, after all, as it wasn't that far away. My overtures were met with incomprehension and derision. If we needed anything, we'd just have to bang on the door.

I was bunked with Houdah and Mariam and relieved to be shot of Didi's waterworks for the night. We went to bed at once, turned out the lights, and the other two immediately started chatting about the other girls, the excellent pasta dinner, and the weather.

"Noor," said Mariam, "They served us a nice dinner, don't you think?"

"Italians are incapable of producing bad food; it's against their principles," I said.

The next morning, the three harpies served a breakfast of brioches and coffee before a corpulent man came in and led us to yet another closed van. I've never since passed a passenger van lacking side windows without wondering who might be shut in there and why. We drove for about an hour and arrived at what was clearly an airport as a jet screamed low overhead. We slowed down and finally came to a stop. The driver opened a sliding window at the back of his compartment.

"You are going in with the luggage, so be quiet and do as I say." American but fluent in Italian, from what I'd heard in the hostel when he flirted with the harpies.

The baggage hold didn't appeal, although they transport animals in baggage holds, so they must have warmth and air down there. I told the others, "We have to go in the underneath part of the plane for now. Keep calm." Houdah looked at me, horrified, but the others didn't know any different.

The van had drawn up right outside one of the holds, which had a baggage trolley next to it. "Three at a time, stand on the pallet," said the American. It raised us up to the hold, and we stepped in. It was cavernous and half empty.

"Are we going to be down here all the way?" whispered Houdah. Mariam looked ready to unleash a flood.

"I don't know. All we can do is wait," I whispered quickly as Didi and the other two were coming in.

"No chairs?" Didi cried. "Are we to sit on the floor? Is this how they treat us respectable young ladies on our way to a new life?"

"Shut up, Didi," I said as quietly as I could but firmly. "Don't make them angry. He told us to be quiet. They are clearly hiding us."

The American appeared at the entrance. "Get away from the doors so no one can see you when the van leaves. While the plane taxis to the runway, you'll be taken upstairs to the cabin. Now, like I said, be quiet!" He glared at Didi, who had no idea what he'd said.

Once he'd left, I relayed his instructions, so they quieted down and kept out of sight. Mariam looked at me with her eyebrows raised. "I wondered if you knew English," she whispered. The others were too wrapped up in their misery to notice. I listened carefully to the goings-on outside. The van's door slammed, and it took off. Indistinguishable sounds of action and people moving in and out of the aircraft went on for about a half hour before the engines started and the hold doors closed. The plane began to move. A clatter on the other side of the hold drew our attention to a trapdoor that had opened over a ladder-like contraption. A young man climbed down.

"Come on up, quickly," he said in Arabic, beckoning. I went first (making a nice change from bringing up the rear), clutching my and Didi's cloth bags, and watched the others toil up more painfully. Didi needed a firm shove to get her moving when she froze near the top. Tears rolled down their well-worn grooves in her cheeks. I ignored her after shoving her bag into her arms. We were hustled into seats and belts and given bottles of cold water. The young man disappeared. There were no other passengers. If we were going straight to the U.S.A., I estimated we'd be in the air for at least eight hours.

The young man came back with an armful of magazines and bottles of water. "My name is George. Get some rest. I'll bring food in a couple of hours. Here, I brought you some magazines to look through." Lebanese. The girls were excited to have the magazines, as some of them showed the latest fashions. I would have loved a newspaper but didn't want the young man to know I spoke English.

The flight was a welcome respite after all we'd been through. A toilet that worked. A halfway decent lunch, afternoon coffee and cake, and most of the girls fast asleep for the last few hours. No turbulence. The itching necessitated another meditation.

The pressure in my ears meant we were losing height. George came back and told us to go to the bathroom, then fasten our belts. Once the plane slapped the runway, George led us back down to the hold.

"You will be here for a while, so keep out of sight and keep quiet. Good luck." The way he looked at us with pity in his eyes, I understood he knew exactly what was in store for his passengers.

"Doesn't it bother you?" I asked quietly. He looked shocked and shot back up the stairway like a frightened rabbit. I immediately regretted my stupid impulse and hoped it hadn't ruined things.

It seemed like hours before the hold doors opened, and we wearily stepped onto another pallet and climbed into yet another van. The driver didn't speak. After about twenty minutes, we bumped along what felt like a dirt track. We got out to find ourselves at the door of a big old shed in the middle of a field. At least I could see a line of trees edging the field. After so much time, either in dusty dry areas or locked up indoors, I hungered for green. The man swept his arm to indicate we should enter. The place had a strange smell, and many of the side wall planks were propped open. He went out and came back with paper bags, which he put down on the floor. He motioned towards his mouth, by which I guess he meant it was food. Then he went out again. I didn't hear the van start up.

"Girls, I think we have to wait here for a while. At least we have food. My guess is that they are waiting until dark to take us where we need to go."

"I have to use the toilet," Didi wailed.

"Then I suggest you find a good corner," I said impatiently. She did, as did the others, shielded by some farm machinery in case the man came back.

I sat on the floor and leaned against the wall. Would we end up at Olive's? I hoped so, as it would be easy to get out and use the phone. Rustling dry leaves caused me to open my eyes slowly. A snake with beautiful markings and a triangular head wound its way toward where Sussann and Mariam still flipped through their magazines. I knew all hell would let loose if they spotted it before I caught it. I stood up in one fluid motion and leaped on top of it, holding its neck in a vice-like grip. The girls saw me brandish the creature over my head as I made for the door. Their screams rivaled the output of a dreadful soprano the Salton Symphony hired one year. Our minder flung open the door and recoiled when I shoved the snake in his face.

"What the f—"

I marched past him since he clearly wasn't going to handle the matter and carried the wretched thing to the edge of the woods. He followed at a safe distance. I threw the creature into the brush and strolled back, smiling at his stricken face. How was he to know I didn't want to escape? By the time I'd joined the girls, they had calmed down to a shaky, panting state, sitting close by me and jumping at any sound, real or imagined, for the rest of our stay. The driver shut himself in his truck.

Near dusk, we set out again. I found this van business really tedious and couldn't wait to get out and get on with things. After about an hour and a half, we stopped. Yes, Olive's house.

Reality struck home. If there was room for us here, that meant the others had been moved on. No longer useful as virgins, they'd be prisoners in some awful brothel.

Jerry opened the door. "Come in, come in," he said jovially, no doubt looking forward to fresh treats. We trooped downstairs to their little bordello, and he locked us in. It wasn't long before Olive showed up with a young woman to translate. She had a suitcase with her, which she set on the floor.

"You will each choose your room. There is a kitchen at the end of the corridor and a bathroom too. I expect you to keep yourselves and your rooms clean and tidy and do as you are told. Underwear and clothing are in this case. Pass them out tomorrow. There are simple clothes for daytime, nightdresses, and nice caftans to wear for guests." I guess the caftans I'd stolen in Cyprus were too flashy.

"When will we go to our new jobs?" asked Sussann.

"Soon enough," Olive said with a smile. "It's Thursday today. We have guests coming tomorrow. You will help us entertain them."

I wanted to hurt her, and I would soon enough. Mariam gasped. She probably had realized the situation but said nothing. I had only one day to get the police involved. After that, I must find Reema and the others and fulfill my mission to rescue them.

Late that night, when all was quiet, I put on the light in the narrow hallway to open the door. Of course, the padlock was on the outside. Now what? Footsteps. The padlock clicked open, and the doorknob turned. Jerry was in pajamas and robe. He just couldn't wait, although despoiling a virgin was quite a financial sacrifice.

"Why are you standing out here?" he asked.

"Eh?"

"No English. Well, you'll do."

I went into my room and flicked on the light switch, turning to face him. I pushed him onto the bed, climbed on top, and looked him in the eyes. He was excited to be made so welcome—uncomfortably so, from my point of view.

Fury intensified my mesmerizing abilities, and he was soon out. I had to call Joe; no time to lose. After a quick search, I spotted a phone in a small bedroom. There was only one problem: the bed was occupied by Kate, the housekeeper. I picked up the phone, fortunately wireless, and crept out, shutting the door gingerly like a sinner sneaking out of church early. Would there be a signal in the utility room? It seemed the best place to hide, assuming one could circumnavigate mousetraps.

The signal was weak, but it worked. I needed to cool down and remember Joe's phone number, which I'd memorized weeks ago. *Close your eyes and think. Pluck it from within. It's there.* I managed to retrieve it and dialed. *Come on!* It went to voicemail. I left a long message explaining the situation and asking him for help. I mentioned the guests arriving the next night, that I had observed them before and spoken to the previous group of young women they had used, one of them recently killed and dropped into the Potomac from Ludley Park. Maybe I should have had a quiet word with him before I left. He might think me crazy and ignore my plea for rescue. I couldn't do more. I didn't want to risk going back into Kate's bedroom, so I left the phone in the small bathroom next to it.

Jerry was beginning to stir. He sat up suddenly. I smiled broadly. "Mmmm," I said.

"I'll be back," he drawled before scuttling off, forgetting to secure the padlock. Would he wonder later why he still wore his robe? And I was puzzled the virgin thing hadn't seemed to matter.

The next morning, we heard quite a hue and cry outside our dungeon while we were enjoying breakfast, which starving Didi had whipped up with eggs, canned diced tomatoes, and a tin of baked beans.

"You stupid bitch, you could have ruined everything. How could you be so careless?"

"But I know I locked it, Jerry. I know I did. What about Kate? You don't think she knows, do you?"

"She must have guessed there's something going on down here, but she'd have no idea what. It's too well soundproofed." I'd forgotten about that. The door must be ajar. "What about that son of yours? Been helping himself, has he?"

"He's your son too, asshole. Let's go look."

The door swung open, and the girls, shocked at these angry shouts, all stood, trying to edge their way behind me.

"Well, they're all here, Jerry. No harm done." Olive peeked into each room. "No Chad, either."

"Well, be more careful in the future."

They left, Olive slamming the door in passive protest as she went, the lock engaging with a vicious clang.

"Why were they shouting?" asked Nadia, her voice shaking in fright.

"The lady forgot to lock the door properly. Her husband was angry." Mariam frowned at me and beckoned me to her room. She perched on her bed, and I leaned against the door.

"Do you think we are really here for a proper job, Noor? Have we been deceived?"

I was torn because I didn't want to start a panic. But she was too smart to be fobbed off by white lies. "No, Mariam, there is no job. We are here to please men." She cried out before clapping her hand over her mouth. "You must keep quiet for a little longer because it will be a problem if the others find out."

"How do you know? Don't they deserve to know?"

"I am not who I seem. I know about these people. Last night I got out of the room. I telephoned a policeman I know and left a message asking him to come for us tonight. It's too bad I couldn't speak to him in person, but I told him everything. Let's hope he believed me and isn't out of town."

"If he doesn't help, we are doomed, ruined," she cried.

"Shush, keep quiet. I have strength and skills you can't imagine. I can prevent the worst from happening. But you might have to fight, too. I'm going to tell the others you have a headache. Pull yourself together and put on a good face."

I could probably fight off all the players. I would give it a damned good try, but in such a melee, the girls could get hurt. If only I had confided in Joe before I left. Of course, he would have stopped me, and I would have lost my big chance. I wanted to roll up this gang like an old carpet.

The day dragged on like an old donkey at the water wheel. I couldn't stop pacing. Mariam stayed in her room most of the time, even when Didi produced a halfway decent bean and rice lunch. The kitchen hadn't been stocked with fresh vegetables or even sweets. I like sweets when I'm tense. I hadn't tasted anything sweet since I started this junket, except a cookie at that little wrecked coffee house in Syria. They hadn't even given us dessert in the whorehouse, the kind of place I'd have thought would have been choc-a-bloc with it.

Oh damn, that reminded me of chocolate. There was no such thing as chocolate when I lived in Asgard in my Lady Frigg's service. Imagine that. No chocolate. If we ever regain our heavenly kingdom, I will introduce the joys of chocolate. There's no going back in some respects. Sex too. There wasn't any of that for handmaidens, either. We didn't think about it, even though the gods were deeply engaged in carnal activities. It's hard to believe we three handmaidens were so pure—and content to be so.

We had no way of telling the time, but it must have been close to evening when the door opened again. Olive entered alone and went into my room, pulling the good caftan off the hook. She carried it out to show the others. I wondered about her interpreter. Complicit? "You all wear these now. Shower first. She made motions as if soaping her body and hair and pointed to the bathroom. You'd have to be really dumb not to understand this, but we'll see. And you'll meet my lovely son, Chad, tomorrow. We'll give him his pick. He's going to college down south, and the poor boy needs a treat."

I vowed to kill this woman, but I fought to keep my face deadpan because it would make life more difficult if they felt the need to conceal their moves.

She looked at me hard for a second or two. Perhaps my eyes radiated hatred. "You need taming. I think I know just the man to do it." She tittered like a schoolgirl, turned on her heel, and left.

Any man who tried to tame me in the way she meant would be inviting the attention of an orthopedic surgeon. Dear Olive. What treats should I plan for her?

"Okay, I'm going to New York tomorrow for a long weekend, so I'll see you on Tuesday."

I said, "Oh. Is Hunter going, too?"

"Yes, sorry." She laughed.

"Whatever do you mean?"

"Well, you might feel lonely in this big house. Of course, you've got your Auntie Peggy, so have a nice relaxing weekend with her. Lucky Sam, having all those cuddles."

I felt she was toying with me. I knew she was.

And, damn it, I wanted to know what happened next.

18

She was in fine fettle that morning.

"Did you have a nice time?" I asked.

"Oh, yes. Hunter met up with some investment bankers, and I went to the theater with friends a couple of times."

"Did you see anything good?"

"Can't remember."

Ah ha, so what were you up to?

"Well, time to get down to work. This is where the Goodalls get their comeuppance."

"Oh, splendid," I murmured.

She looked downright combative the way she crossed her arms after flinging herself down.

Tape 17

We had all showered and changed, although our hair was wet as Olive had not seen fit to provide hair dryers. She came back down, dolled up like many a Salton doyenne in silk and pearls.

"Wet hair! Stupid girls." I looked theatrically puzzled, spread my hands, and shrugged. She disappeared again and came back with two hairdryers, which she proceeded to demonstrate as if we had come from another planet, one innocent of small appliances. Finally, we met with her approval and were led upstairs. We entered the hallway, and she lined us up like a reception committee. She stood nearest the door. Jerry stood with his hand on the doorknob. A ponderous grandfather clock struck nine excruciatingly slowly—just like ponderous old Big Ben.

At the first knock, Jerry peered through the peephole before admitting the young Japanese man I remembered from before. He moved down the line before picking Didi. He took her by the hand and headed downstairs.

"What does he want?" she called back, frightened. No one answered. Even me. I was getting worried.

Joe Paglietti, where are you?

The cadaverous creature came next and picked me, to my delight. He was probably the one who killed Yasmine.

He led me downstairs, ushered me through the door, and I led him into my room. He suddenly cracked me across my face with a closed fist, grinning as he did. He never knew what hit him as I returned the favor in spades and much faster. I rolled him under the bed and went to Kate's room. Didi's piteous cries rang in my ears as I closed the door, but I couldn't risk waiting any longer. I picked up the phone and dialed 911.

"I want to report a rape," and reeled off the address.

I heard that click we all read about, but most of us never experience, as a cold metal object poked the back of my neck. I should have locked myself in.

"Hang up. Who are you?"

"Someone you'll wish you'd never met, Jerry." I didn't hang up but jabbed Jerry in his doughy gut with my elbow, whirled around, and grabbed the gun. I fired it just past his ear so the 911 dispatcher would hear it. Jerry wouldn't hear much of anything for a while. People don't have time to react physically or mentally when you move so fast. Then I hung up. I kept the gun on him while I searched for something to tie him up with. Olive rushed in at that point.

"What was that?"

She took in the scene and glared at me. "They all left when they heard the shot. I doubt they'll return."

I said, "Don't worry, Olive. We know their car registrations. We'll find them. It's over." I loved that. I should have been on TV. "Now, come with me into our little dungeon." I waved the gun and chivvied them into our erstwhile rooms.

I flung open Didi's door and waved them in. The client had his pants off and was still trying to finish undressing Didi, who had two rapidly blackening eyes. I waved the gun at him.

"Get lost." He drew a knife from his pocket, so I shot him in the gut. Olive's eyes rolled back, and she dropped like an elephant turd. Jerry ran into the kitchenette.

"Get upstairs, Didi, and open the front door when the police get here."

She fled, hopping and skipping as she tried to adjust her dress on the way. I backed out and locked the door on my hateful hosts.

Lin had to come back now. I hid in the utility room and focused. The tingling and adjusting happened in less than five minutes. It's easier to go back than forward.

The sirens tapered off as I ran upstairs. The girls opened the door, and the first one in was Joe.

"Lin! What's going on?"

I explained the situation. I told him that I'd been working on the case, my first as a private detective.

"Private detective? Since when?"

"Later. There are two injured men in the basement. A Japanese fellow, one of the Goodalls' clients, was raping one of the girls. He pulled a knife when I tried to stop him, so I had to shoot. The other hit me, so I returned the favor. I think he's still out. And Jerry, he's not hurt except for a jab in the gut, but I left him down there. He put a gun to my head when I phoned 911. I managed to get it away from him, and that was the gun I used to shoot the Japanese guy. They are both locked in the girls' quarters.

"The Goodalls are part of a sex trafficking ring, as I told you. The other clients fled, but I have their car registrations from a previous visit. These girls have been smuggled in from a Syrian refugee camp. There was another batch here before, but they've been moved on. They must be found." I paused to draw breath.

It was a lot for him to take in. He looked a tad flustered, even after it occurred to him to close his mouth. "Show me."

I led him to the basement with a contingent of cops with their weapons drawn. I gave him the key, and he unlocked the door.

"You!" Olive spat at me. "What are you doing here?"

"Exposing what you're doing here!" I retorted.

The cops marched Olive and Jerry upstairs and out. I followed. A new siren announced the arrival of the EMTs. It wasn't long before the two unlucky clients were borne off, one moaning softly, the other hooked up to an IV and still breathing, blissfully unaware of the mire he'd stumbled into.

"We need to find their son, Joe. Chad is not one of the organizers, but he uses the girls."

Without waiting for a response, I ran up the stairs, Joe scrambling behind, calling me to stay back. *Not a chance!*

Where was that little sod? I moved along the corridor, opening bedroom doors until I found one that was obviously his, judging by the dirty clothes on the floor and old rock group posters tacked on the wall. I looked under the bed before sliding open his closet. There he was, huddling in a corner.

"Mrs. Thoren? What's going on? I heard a shot and sirens."

"Your parents are under arrest, Jerry, and so will you be."

"But I haven't done anything! I don't know anything about those girls!" God, that kid was dumb.

"Know anything about what girls, Chad? Those kidnapped young girls you raped in the basement?"

"Let me handle this, Lin," said Joe behind me.

I ignored him, hauled Chad out by the scruff of his neck, and dragged him downstairs. The cop waiting in the hallway moved his hand to his holster.

"Don't worry, officer, this is the owners' son," I said as I shoved Chad into his embrace.

"Take him away," Joe said. As the handcuffs snapped around Chad's wrists, he sobbed like the spoiled brat he was.

"Lin," said Joe, "I need to know everything."

"I will tell you everything. I know the routes they took and how they did it. I have to tell you, though, that certain people working for the U.S. Air Force are involved, so it's sticky. Tell you what, isn't it better to do this at home? I've been gone for a while, and I need to check on my family."

"No, we have to do this by the book. Video, the lot. Could I ask you to come in early tomorrow morning?"

"Sure. Nine all right? And don't let them call their lawyers. We don't want anyone tipped off."

"Eight. I'm glad we got these leeches. Who would have thought the Goodalls would be involved in anything so tawdry?"

"Who, indeed."

"But what about evidence? Do you have any besides what we might find here?"

"Oh, I've got all the details. A few police raids here and there should provide all the evidence you need."

Dear Joe. When he first got involved with the orchestra, I tried to seduce him, but he was too professional to get involved with anyone before the Rose Hale case was solved. And now he's devoted to his girlfriend, Helen. She only got out of law school the year before, and her firm has her working all hours, so I hoped at first he might be just a little lonely. He's cute. And useful. But no dice. Well, I like Helen, so it's all good.

"Hey, Joe, where are the girls?"

"They're downstairs. We're waiting on Immigration."

"You might tell Immigration to keep open minds. They should be allowed to stay. Americans are deeply involved in this, including Air Force personnel, as I mentioned. I don't think anyone wants that being made public."

"That sounds like a threat," he said, grinning.

"You should know it's not in my nature to make threats," I said with a straight face.

Now I could say hello to Hunter and the kids, sleep in a good bed, eat decent food and leave those girls in someone else's hands.

Hunter was watching a riveting police chase on TV when I walked in. At least he had the grace to get up for the couple of minutes it took to give me a rib-crushing hug.

"How did it go?"

"Better than I could have hoped."

"I'm glad to hear it."

"Where are the kids?"

"In bed. They are fine. Sven got detention for fighting in the playground."

"Oh, not again."

"Yes, again. I'm proud of him for standing up to that bully."

"He's being bullied?"

"No, another kid, a little girl with her leg in a brace. She limps. Sven has taken her under his wing. This group of boys has been teasing her, and one pushed her over at recess this morning. Sven punched him on the nose."

"Well, good for him. I hope he told the teacher what's been going on. They need to keep a better eye on vulnerable kids."

"That's what I told them once I'd heard his side of the story. They called me in, you know. The other boys also got detention. They said Sven has to find a better way to handle things."

"Sometimes, there isn't a better way." *The apple doesn't fall far from the tree, huh?* "I need to get showered and into bed. I'm dog tired. I'll tell you all about it tomorrow."

"I had a quiet word with Bob, by the way. He won't bother you again."

"What did you do to him?"

"Oh, nothing permanent. At least, I don't think so. I followed him home from the neighborhood watch one night and got into his car after he pulled up in his driveway. I grabbed him by the nuts and told him to keep his hands off my beautiful wife. He fainted. You know how it is. I sometimes forget how strong I am, especially when I'm mad."

"Oh, Hunter, you look after me so well. Thank you." I doubted Bob would be bothering anyone at all for a long time.

Hunter didn't come up to bed before I fell asleep, by which I gathered his needs had been fully taken care of by Dora. The next morning, dressed once more in my own clothes, I went to the police station to give my statement. I took my notes from the time I first saw the clients go to the Goodalls' house and what the girls there had told me. I entreated Joe to do what he could to trace the girls who had been moved on. I gave him coordinates, descriptions, Mary Wilder's tactics, the name of the ship, the whole lot. It took several hours. Poor Joe would be weighed down with paperwork for days.

"This is FBI territory. I can't keep it local. We don't have the resources. I'm sure you'll be hearing from them."

"I'm sure I will. Let me know what Olive or Jerry say about the other girls. They must be in some awful brothel somewhere."

"I will. By the way, I don't understand how someone who looks like you could get away with posing as a Syrian refugee. And what about the language?"

"Oh, I'm very good at disguises, Joe. I was in the theater in another lifetime. And I spent a large part of my childhood in Egypt. Bye-ee!"

Believe it or not, in all my lifetimes, I've never worked in the theater. I must think about that for the next time. Anyone can see I'm star quality.

I got home too late to see the children off to school, although I'd woken them up with kisses and hugs. Well, I'd hug them again soon enough. I found a lovely little note on the kitchen table with pictures—a flower by Margareta and a helicopter by Sven—welcoming me home. I sat and mooned over it while sipping the best cup of coffee I'd had in days and nibbling on English chocolate biscuits.

I suddenly remembered my belongings in Istanbul. I'd hardly taken anything and, fortunately, had kept important things like my passport strapped to my body. The jewelry was fake. I called and asked to speak to the manager.

"I was unavoidably delayed dealing with a refugee camp issue." I could almost hear his ears prick up. "Please feel free to give away the belongings I left in my room. And, by the way, I'm sure you have had some burglaries recently. The Englishwoman who works in the health spa gave a passkey to a young man. I saw her let him in the back door just before I left."

"Oh, my god! I implore you to keep this to yourself, Madame. Our reputation!"

"Of course, you have my word." None of my business, anyway."

Now, where should I start looking for Reema and company? I should have gone to Turkey first and saved school for later, although they would have moved them once they had a new batch of girls coming in. The house would be off-limits now. Maybe I should let the FBI take a crack at it first. I certainly hoped they'd find Mary Wilder's bank account. I'd sworn to empty it, but I didn't have the computer skills to do things like that. It's something I've always meant to learn but never got around to. Most likely, the transactions would provide vital evidence.

The fate of the new girls bothered me. If they were deported, where would they go? I'd go to the media with the Air Force story if they tried that. Were the Goodalls just cogs in a bigger wheel? I'd better be careful. I had to think of my children.

"Did the man you shot die?"

"No idea. The FBI kept us at arm's length once they took over. He deserved to die, anyway."

God, she could be cold-blooded. And speaking of God, I hadn't been able to explain to Auntie Peggy why I didn't go to church with her anymore. It seemed so hypocritical. I mean, I was working with gods. Other gods. Was there room for so many in one firmament?

Not for the first time, I wondered if Hunter was quite so cold-blooded. Probably, if he felt the situation called for it.

"I was a good sleuth, you know," Lin told me. "I miss it sometimes."

"But you still work from time to time, don't you?"

"Yes, which is cool because it's usually just the tricky cases when Lettie needs help. The theater's success made up for it, but I still get a thrill seeing the plaque outside the office door and my nameplate on my desk. It's truly a success I made for myself, and helping people still makes me feel good."

Would I make a success for myself? I had always known without a doubt what success would look like: lots of readers, good reviews, awards, good money, and name recognition. My novel was feeling staler by the day. I could use what I had already as a framework for a mystery. Forget the snobbery of my professors and fellow students about genre novels. Or maybe I should try fantasy. That might be fun. But I could see myself settling into a rut here. That wasn't always a bad thing, though. Was it?

Dora still treated me like an intruder, Hunter still whispered his promises, and Lin enchanted me one minute and appalled me the next. It was beginning to feel like home, although I had yet to meet the children.

Tape 18

I spent the next few weeks setting up my detective agency. There were so many details to attend to, like renting the office for a start. I'd wanted to be close to the county court-house in Fairfax but couldn't find a decent place. Was that location really such an advantage? Close to home might make more sense; much easier with the family. I found a nice little condo townhouse in an office complex near the post office and decided to buy it, as that might prove easier than dealing with credit checks for a rental. All I needed was a bank account and a Social Security number, which I'd bought years ago. Since it was a cash transaction, it went to closing in a couple of weeks. Then there was signage to arrange, furnishings, and stationery. An office manager had to be next.

I couldn't concentrate on all those details when Reema and her friends were in such dire straits. Joe told me he hadn't gotten anything out of the Goodalls about the girls. He believed they didn't know much and were clearly very frightened of whoever was behind the scheme. If I'd had some time alone with them, they would have soon spilled their guts, but now the FBI had taken over, and that wasn't going to happen. If only I'd had more time at the house before the cavalry arrived.

On impulse, I pulled out our class list and called Lettie.

"Hi, Lin. How nice to hear from you. What's up?"

"Long story. I've got lots to tell you. First, though, do you have a job yet?"

"Yeah." Such a sigh.

"I guess that's a 'yes, but I hate it?'"

"Uh-huh. I'm a security guard at a factory in Loudoun County. The manager's an asshole, a beer-sodden loser who was always hitting on me. When he doesn't get his way, he puts me on night shift. And know what? P.I. school doesn't qualify you to be a security guard; that's a whole other course, so they just pay me minimum wage. I can hardly afford my rent."

"Well, guess what?" I said. "I've got a better job for you. I need an office manager for my new agency. Lots of setup to start with, then you'd have to run the office, although there shouldn't be too much clerical stuff. But you could help with some of the P.I. stuff if you like. Interested?"

"Yes!" was her high-decibel answer.

"I've got this new office I'm setting up in Salton. It's a little townhouse. It might not be quite legal, but you could live upstairs until you can afford something else. There's a bathroom and a couple of rooms, including one that might once have been a kitchenette. We can get everything fixed up. I can't give you much to start because I haven't got any clients yet. Twenty-five thousand?"

"Oh, Lin, you're an angel. When can I start?"

"Right away."

"Ha! I've got tomorrow off. I'll go to HR first thing and give them my notice and a piece of my mind. After that, I'll come straight over."

We arranged a time, and I gave her directions. I knew Lettie was a woman I could get along with. She'd pay attention to detail and be someone I could brainstorm with. And become a friend? It was many years since I'd had a real friend, not since Penelope.

"You haven't met Lettie yet, have you?"

"No, I've not had that pleasure."

"I'll arrange something. Maybe movie and dinner."

"Cool."

I'd been on several outings with Lin. She never let me pay, and she was always lively and fun. I can get a little depressed sometimes, so it did me good.

Auntie Peggy had noticed the difference. "You've perked up, dear," she said. "Are you in love?"

"Oh, good heavens, no!" I said, annoyed to feel a blush rising.

"I see," she said.

20

"It's a wonderful feeling to put money in the bank that you earned yourself." Lin looked pleased with herself. She'd only come down once that whole week, telling me that Hunter was restless because the market had fallen.

Hunter hung around all week, restless and grouchy, suddenly darting into his office every couple of hours. On Friday, he announced at lunch that he had an appointment with his broker at three and might be out with him for dinner, too. I found it strange, but Lin didn't seem concerned.

"Yes, I know what you mean." I'd deposited my check this morning and bought a new top straight after. Nothing too flashy because I needed to save for my future, but I was happy with it.

"Blue suits you, Mary. You should wear it more often."

Did she miss anything?

Tape 19

Lettie finished setting up the office quickly and well. A discreet brass sign at the door announced our presence, as did ads in the local papers. I decided to give the Washington Post a miss for the time being, as it was so expensive, and there was a lot of competition. There'd been nothing in the papers about the Goodall business, although the family's sudden disappearance had tongues wagging. The FBI had not requested an interview, either. I'd hoped for the publicity, but maybe later when the affair came to trial. Joe would have given them a very full set of notes, but it was nevertheless surprising they hadn't wanted to talk to me. A massive cover-up was no doubt underway, and they'd only call on me to tell me to shut up. Maybe there wouldn't even be a trial.

At least the rumor mill in Salton hummed like a swarm of bees. The first time I found myself amidst a knot of gossiping symphony board members, I inserted a few *bon mots*. I mentioned my new career, which garnered mixed reactions—running the gamut from surprise to distaste—and managed to imply I'd been in on some action concerning the Goodalls but couldn't possibly comment further. Everyone looked at me differently from then on. I was even invited to return to the neighborhood watch, which I accepted graciously as they were short a couple of people.

Bob's wife had called to say he was unwell and could not continue.

Lettie called one Monday morning a couple of weeks after we opened the office.

"We've got an appointment! A missing teen."

I got into the office about twenty minutes before the client was due to appear. Lettie made coffee and set out her notepad and pens at a small table in the corner of my office. I found myself unaccountably excited, and I could tell from Lettie's flush that she felt the same way.

A sad gray couple walked in at eleven sharp. I sat them at my desk, and Lettie served coffee, which they accepted gratefully.

"Mr. and Mrs. Grandison, how can I help you?"

It was surely a commonplace story, although to them, painfully extraordinary. Their daughter was a freshman studying theater at New York University. She was in the habit of calling them every Sunday morning at around ten. She didn't call the day before, so they became concerned and finally called her roommate, whose number they had in case of emergencies. Apparently, the roommate hadn't seen her for almost a week. She'd told her friend she had a date and might stay out overnight. The roommate hadn't seen fit to let anyone know.

"You were recommended to us by a friend, Doris Freeman," Mrs. Grandison said in a toneless voice. Doris was one of the symphony clique who had heard me mention the agency. "We want you to go to New York and see what you can find out. We can't afford much, but we have this check, and we will pay your expenses, naturally. We just want our little girl home safe. We wouldn't know where to start."

"I will do my level best to find her for you," I said. Not that I knew where to start, either.

I collected phone numbers, the dorm location, and the girl's description. To hear her parents tell it, Susan Grandison was a petite brunette with features of great beauty and delicacy. They had brought a photo from her high school graduation. She was, indeed, a lovely girl, although her features looked generous rather than delicate, with a touch of Mediterranean. I wondered how these drab parents had produced her.

"She's adopted," said her father, as if he'd read my mind. I couldn't help blushing. That seemed to be happening more. I used to be inscrutable.

"Do you know anything about her birth parents?" I asked.

"No, the records are sealed. But she's been very curious lately. She really wants to know where she came from."

"I don't understand why. She's had such a happy home with us," her mother added.

I told them I'd leave for New York first thing in the morning. We shook hands and said goodbye. As soon as they were out of sight, I endorsed the check, which Lettie took straight to the bank. While it's true Hunter and I are not short of money, having money you've earned is quite another thing.

"Was it a tough case?"

She sat up suddenly. "Yes, it was a tough case. But I solved it. There were repercussions, though. My children..." She heaved a great sigh and studied her hands. "Let's go out for lunch. Do you like Thai? I need a change."

"I haven't eaten Thai food before. I love Chinese."

"You'll like Thai, then. It can be hot, but you can choose how hot with most dishes."

It was so tasty, tastier by far than Chinese, or at least the college town Chinese food I'd sampled so far. I tried a shrimp from Lin's green curry and felt as though all my tubes were on fire, shooting from stomach to ears. She laughed while I finished her water after downing mine. She'd chosen wisely for me. I guess you can get used to spicy food, but I don't think I could ever aspire to that devilish level.

"Just to let you know," she said, "you'll notice it tomorrow."

Indeed, I did, although I hadn't realized what she meant at the time.

21

"I had no idea what I was doing. But I mostly did the right thing in the end. After all, helping people is my destiny."

I guessed that was the best any of us could hope for. But one doesn't always recognize the right thing at the time.

She'd come downstairs right behind me, singing a lilting song in another language. It was a happy song, and she wore a happy face. It promised a good session.

"I'll be spending tonight with an old friend of mine. Dora will serve dinner as usual. She usually goes to her room after she's finished clearing up. We'll start a little later in the morning. Eleven or so."

"Have a nice time," I said. *Hunter, will you come?*

But her statement was oddly specific. Letting me know the coast would be clear?

Tape 20

I took a taxi to Union Station. Hunter offered to drive me, but I knew he'd get lost and make me miss my train. In all fairness, it's a tricky place to get to if you're not accustomed to finding your way around D.C. The train wouldn't take much longer than flying once you take into consideration the required early check-in and so on, not to mention arriving way uptown when my destination was downtown. Besides, I could use the ride to plan my strategy.

I settled into my grubby, scratchy seat in the quiet car and got out my notepad. I started with a list:

> *When seen last, and doing what with whom?*
>
> *Friends? Anyone especially close?*
>
> *Boyfriend? Sexual orientation?*
>
> *Good student? Been cutting class?*
>
> *Interests?*
>
> *Search closet: New clothes or jewelry?*
>
> *Laptop*
>
> *How to draw out roommate if unwilling to "spill the beans":*
>
> *A good meal, promise confidentiality, be understanding, and agree that parents don't get it.*

I told myself there was no point in worrying too much. Susan had probably gone off with a boyfriend. Needless to say, what really worried me was whether I'd measure up. This was a more complicated world than the one where I'd fulfilled my ancient missions. Only in one dire situation did I beg Thor for a thunderbolt. He delivered it after he heard my story, nailing the depraved little rat who loved children much too much. Yes, even in those days.

I stopped for an espresso in Penn Station, watching people hurrying to and fro while the indecipherable announcements flowed like background music in this crossroads of tumbling humanity. I should have proceeded directly downtown, but the city's frantic pulse captivated me. After a half-hour, I tore myself away and went out to line up for a cab.

After a stop-start exhaust-filled drive, we pulled up outside at my hotel in the East Village. The cabbie popped the trunk and sat like a lump while I retrieved my suitcase. He'd earned only a meager tip, which earned a dirty look. Another downside to city life. I checked in and went up to my room to freshen up.

The concierge directed me to the main campus entrance. I was nowhere near the dorm, a shaggy, breathy young girl told me. I plodded over in accordance with her directions and finally found Susan's room. I could have run but wanted to take it all in. Being on a university campus feels different from any other environment, and it had been a long time. I showed the young "gatekeeper" in the dorm lobby the letter of authorization I'd had Mr. and Mrs. Grandison sign.

"I don't know about this. I mean, she has her rights, you know?"

"And she's been missing for more than a week," I replied. The guy looked like a linebacker, the kind who enjoyed a good deal of female adulation, so I flashed my best smile. "You wouldn't want to cause a delay if she's come to harm, I'm sure. You look like a good guy. The type of man who would want to help a girl in danger."

He blushed a lot, smirked a little, and let me go through to the elevator.

"Glad to help, ma'am," he called as I waited. I sent him one of those wiggly finger waves Marilyn Monroe performed so endearingly.

I finally found Susan's room after taking a few wrong turns in the dank labyrinth so often found in such buildings. I knocked a couple of times, but there was no answer. The door was locked. No problem. The only signs of life were blasts of music emanating from a couple of rooms farther down the hall. I picked the lock. I treasure that little awl, which I'd managed to hold on to through thick and … thick, and sidled in, making sure the door was closed behind me. It didn't take much detective work to figure out her side of the room, largely owing to the hand-sewn labels on all the clothes in her closet and the printed labels pasted in all the textbooks arranged in neat piles on her desk. And, hallelujah, a laptop, which disappeared into my tote.

I rummaged through her desk drawers, looking for any clues about friendships, love affairs, and meetings. Everything was abnormally neat, very different from her roommate's chaotic side of the room. I searched her closet more thoroughly. At the back of the top shelf, I found the sort of cardboard box used for men's shirts, which I pulled down and opened. It contained only pale pink tissue paper, printed all over with "Little Secrets" in silver. My mind roved around the range of little secrets that might be wrapped in pretty pink paper and held in a plain white box.

A key turning a couple of times in the lock made me realize I was going to give someone quite a fright. True enough, she let out a zesty comic book "eek" when she saw me. I hugged the box as she dropped the tome she'd been hugging. She stood goggle-eyed, her strangely sculpted black hair, striped with emerald green, standing up around her face like a rotting topiary.

"How did you get in?" She seemed unduly frightened.

"Forgive me, but time is short. I'm a private investigator hired by Susan's parents to find her. They are very worried. My name is Lin. What's yours?" I knew, of course, but I had to do it by the book. I was a professional, after all.

"Oh!" She collapsed onto her bed amidst its rumpled blankets and discarded clothing. "I'm Virginia. Ginny."

"Nice to meet you, Ginny. Did she tell you anything about her other friends?"

"She really didn't have many friends. We weren't close. She was always so fussy about everything. She got on my nerves. And I got on hers because I don't care about stuff being so neat and orderly all the time." She stared moodily at the huge book lying splayed out on the floor. "She was very critical. She was friends with a couple of girls who were into chess, though. Chess was her thing."

"No boyfriend?"

"Nope. She's very attractive, so boys often ask her out on dates. But never twice."

"That bad, huh?" She nodded. "I'd like to meet her chess mates. Can you direct me to their rooms?" She burst out laughing, to my surprise.

"What's so funny?"

"Chess mates? Good one! They're in a different dorm. I can take you."

"Thanks. I'm taking her laptop."

"Okay. Don't forget the charger."

After another slog across campus with Ginny, I found the other girls' room in a dorm closer to the main entrance. Their door was locked, so I left a note with my hotel number, said goodbye to Ginny, and went to find a bite to eat. I thought it prudent to look for a place off campus, as I'd heard discouraging stories about modern college cafeteria food.

I found a hole-in-the-wall Chinese restaurant nearby where the food was surprisingly good, unlike most mid-priced American Chinese restaurants. I was lucky to find a seat, as it was clearly very popular. Next to a college campus with good prices and good food, it could hardly fail. I had to share a table with a couple of young men but didn't mind, and they ignored me anyway.

I began to tune in when they started arguing about chess moves. The day before, they had watched a game in Washington Square between a middle-aged woman and Pat, the girlfriend of one of the guys. The older woman seemed highly skilled and won easily. Pat was flattered when the woman waylaid her on campus later and offered to coach her at her home nearby because she displayed great potential. They were to meet back in the square tomorrow morning at ten. Pat had confided to her boyfriend that the woman instructed her to tell no one, not even her boyfriend, because she was a very private person. They went on to speculate about who this woman might be and if she was legit. The boyfriend didn't want Pat to go, but she insisted.

I would go. This woman's behavior sounded very fishy. Could this be the stroke of luck I'd been hoping for?

Reception passed me a message when I got back to the hotel. The girls were in their room.

Delores and Greta could have been sisters. Their long, brown, straggly hair with bangs, dark-rimmed glasses, calf-length skirts, and shapeless tops looked like some kind of "don't touch me ever" uniform. Their room was drab and tidy. Not a single poster. Yes, they knew Susan—a bit uptight but nice and a good player. I asked about the middle-aged woman who'd been seen hanging around the chess players in Washington Square. Delores had played a game with her once and lost. The woman was really good. No, she had not offered her any tutoring. She seemed surprised by the question. Greta said Susan had mentioned a challenging game she'd played down there recently with some woman but didn't know any details. They didn't think Susan had a boyfriend. She didn't seem that interested.

I had one last question that occurred to me over lunch. "Susan was studying theater, I understand. The obsessiveness I observed in her room doesn't seem to fit in with that world. How was that working out for her?"

"Oh, she hated the department," said Delores. "In high school, they mostly put on selections from Shakespeare and other classical plays. Here, it's much more far-ranging, usually more gritty than she is comfortable handling. She just didn't fit in. Her roommate bothered her, too. A real slob and always putting goo in her hair, a new color each week. She said it disgusted her."

"So, was she planning on dropping out?"

"No, she's switching her major to accounting. She said you know where you are with accounting. Anyway, she did well in high school math."

I couldn't help laughing. They looked at me reproachfully.

"I hope she's all right," said Greta.

"I was only laughing because I just saw her half of the room and her roommate's half of their room. So I can see her comfortable in accounting. I will do my very best to find her," I said, the smile tactfully wiped off my face.

I went back to my hotel. Washington Square was the obvious starting point the next day. I freshened up and went downstairs for afternoon tea. They did quite a good job, offering commendable scones and clotted cream. After a fruitless search through Susan's laptop, I took a nap before going in search of dinner.

"I guess private detective work can be quite boring sometimes."

"Yes, like anything. But just you wait. It's going to get pretty hair-raising soon."

"So, you solved it."

"And how!"

I didn't like it when she smirked. It made me feel bitchy. My impatience for Hunter's promised visit wasn't helping.

"You seem a little tense, Mary."

"Oh, I'm fine. Just a little tired. I didn't sleep well. I had a cup of coffee too late, and that never works out well for me."

"Well, perhaps go to bed early tonight, then."

"Yes, definitely."

22

"I was thinking last night about my introduction to America, not yet the United States. Not a happy story. I have to say it's improved, though."

"Glad to hear it," I said. She shot me a reproving look. Last night? Didn't she have better things to do on her visit?

Hunter had paid me a visit the night before. Finally! He knocked on my door quietly.

"Come in," I said calmly, praying it would be him. Lin never came down unless we were having a session. Hunter must have felt awkward. After a minute of nothing, I opened the door myself.

"Come in," I said again, my stomach flip-flopping as my pulse raced.

"Thank you. May I?" he said, taking a seat on my bed.

"Of course." I sat next to him, thinking that would signal my willing state of mind.

He put his arm around my shoulders and pulled me to him. I won't say more except that it was soul-lifting, nothing like the puerile fumbles I'd experienced at college. I hoped it would happen again. I also hoped Lin wouldn't find out. Was he a god or a devil?

"You still look tired, Mary."

"Oh, I'm fine. Feeling quite good, actually." *Very fine and good!*

She cleared her throat a tad theatrically. "Anyway, about the old America."

Tape 21

America has come a long way, although more than a whiff of puritanism remains on the surface of public discourse. Racism wasn't an issue when I came over the first time because the slave trade hadn't begun, at least in that part of the continent. Many people fled England to escape religious intolerance, only to find they'd landed in a situation just as bad.

Women were subordinate and scantily educated, as in most places. America didn't yet have colleges for anyone, let alone women, the first time I arrived, so that is a huge advance, although my college experiences all over the world in different eras vary tremendously. American universities are more informal in their approach than in other countries, and the professors are more approachable.

My sojourn in the Massachusetts Bay Colony didn't last long. We traveled over in a sturdy ship, which wasn't badly appointed given the times, with a group of Quakers looking for freedom of religion. We pretended to be Quakers because Hunter had worn out his welcome in England, thanks to his drunken imitation of a roundhead making love to his wife in the tavern one night, which he reenacted for me when he got home. I knew there'd be trouble. Early the next morning, the soldiers' clumping march got louder as it neared our dwelling. I hit Hunter until he woke up—fortunately, he hadn't bothered to undress—and we hightailed it out of there. I always had a bag of essentials ready to go. We ran to the docks a few miles away and found the Quakers waiting to board. I handed a few gold pieces I kept in my bodice to the captain, and we were all set. I know I overpaid, but time was of the essence. He was a good-looking chap and clearly appreciated my generosity. I would have liked to have basked in his approval, but the ship was too crowded to allow me to evade prying eyes, not to mention Hunter's proximity.

After a rough journey via Barbados, we finally arrived in the colony. Our group sadly discovered only too soon that there was no freedom of religion in the New World, either, at least in Massachusetts. The Puritans harassed all of us from the time we landed. Only a few months before, they had trumped-up charges against several women for witchcraft. They hanged them, poor things. Nooses slung over a tree branch don't make for a merciful death.

We'd spent a few months working the land, backbreaking for humans, when one of the women was arrested for blasphemy. The poor woman hardly spoke at all, even at meetings, so I couldn't imagine her uttering anything she shouldn't. I called a secret meeting at my house. The Quakers would never refuse anyone entrance to their weekly meetings, so there was usually at least one spy in attendance, hence the secrecy. I laid it out. This was just the start. They would arrest everyone and confiscate their possessions, one by one. Our ship had docked again in the harbor, as the captain had decided to trade between Barbados and the new colony for a while. We should get on it and go back to Barbados. I offered to make the arrangements. We would board late at night.

I told the captain what was going on. We had dinner together, drank some spiced wine, and spent a thoroughly pleasant evening getting to know each other a whole lot better. A few more gold coins ensured our journey. The ship would set sail in two days.

Unfortunately, there was a full moon on the night of our departure. Some of our party could not quiet their children, while others insisted on carrying too many belongings. A militia of ten men headed us off just outside the settlement. Hunter and I fought like the gods we used to be and killed them all. The Quakers prayed in a tight circle.

"Come on," I said, "we have to move quickly."

"Who are you two? We cannot condone your violence," said one of the older men.

"They will hang you all," I said. "Is that what you want for your children?"

In the end, two older couples stayed behind, and the rest boarded the ship, leaving without further incident. The captain told me later that those four were hanged for murder. They got short ropes. I never told the others, although they must have guessed their friends would not survive. But it was their choice, their sense of right and wrong. The whole episode certainly put me off America for a century or two, especially after slavery took hold.

"Their god didn't take care of them, did he?" I mused.

"Gods can't do it all, you know," Lin said.

"Well then, what's the point?"

"We just are, that's all. Our time is past. No one worships us anymore. But we used to do our duty as best we could. I certainly saved a few. And I would have saved all those Quakers if they'd let me."

"We are told that God sees all, everything is his will, and we just have to believe in him and try to do good to get into heaven."

"There's no heaven that I know of. Olympia is probably still limping along, but it's no paradise. Our Norse heaven has gone. I haven't come across any other. Of course, I may have missed something."

"What about hell?"

"Oh, I'm sure that's still there. Dreadful place. But only a real god can send you down there, and you have to upset him or her very badly to warrant that kind of punishment. It's not really accessible to the likes of us. Hunter and I only went there to escape the void."

"Did you ever meet Jesus?"

"No, although I remember hearing about some nomad who was creating a ruckus in the eastern provinces when we were visiting Rome a couple of thousand years ago. Apparently, he was put to death. He's the one who started Christianity, right? Martyrdom always does the trick."

"Yup, that's the one." Martyrdom always does the trick? How cynical. Catholics make martyrs saints, it's true. But what a price to pay.

I was troubled, though. I'd never thought about religion much, just went to church on Sundays, Easter, and Christmas and left it at that. But still, it was my bedrock in a way. If I were honest, I'd say most of us only do the minimum to hedge our bets. Now I had all kinds of questions. Or did I? I never cared before, so why should I now?

It was just that I felt as though the rug had been pulled out from under me.

23

"**S**hocking discoveries!"

My stomach clenched. This was it. Lin paced briskly as if she had to do something drastic rather than lie on the couch and reminisce. Did she know? Finally, she lay down, quite still, her eyes closed as usual, but said nothing for at least five minutes. I sweated.

"Are you all right?" I finally ventured to ask.

"Yes, let's get on, back to the case. I mean, I can still hardly believe it. After all this time. Time you can't conceive of in your human terms. And of all people, it had to be him. He's not even..."

This valley girl rant didn't sound like a reprimand. I relaxed a little. It wasn't a good idea to annoy Lin, but her indignation didn't seem aimed at me.

"Well, turn that thing on."

So snappish.

Tape 22

At 9:30 the next morning, I sat on one of the benches in Washington Square that offered me a view of the tables where people ate lunch or played chess. My container of espresso was so tall I couldn't do anything but clutch it. It wobbled precariously if I set it down next to me. This meant I couldn't fold my newspaper in a way conducive to reading one-handed. I walked over to a table, set down my cup on one of the smoother patches of concrete, and folded my paper into quarters with a snap. Sitting at this table, I could keep an eye on all the rest. Much more convenient. I didn't have to wait long. A tall, pale woman with a tight blond bun, wearing a cream pantsuit, sauntered to the tables and looked around. She looked vaguely familiar, but I couldn't place her. One meets so many people over the centuries. She looked me over, so I wished her a good morning. She did not return the compliment, instead walked down the path and sat as far away as she possibly could with her back to me. Good, at least she wouldn't notice me watching her.

At about five minutes before ten, a young woman arrived and sat across from her. She looked rather similar to Susan. Dark hair, olive skin, beautiful. She could be Indian. Did this woman recruit a type of girl? *Please, not sex trafficking again* was the first thing that crossed my mind.

After a few minutes, they got up and left. It was too early for most college students, so I was alone except for a few families in the distance. I delved into my tote for a raincoat and dark wig, donned them along with a pair of large glasses, and got up to follow.

Within twenty minutes, they entered a large brownstone. I made a note of the address so I could look up the public records later and find the name of the owner. I memorized the registration plate of the van parked outside, too. It might not belong to this woman, but one should cover all bases. It was an easy area to blend into, with boutiques and a coffee shop across the way. I looked in a few windows before going into the café. My order of mineral water earned a sullen, "Will that be *all*?" from the waitress. That tall coffee had proved too, too much. I could manage a Danish, probably, but I'd better spread it out in case I had to stay awhile.

Five minutes later, a man emerged from the house and drove away in the van. He'd gone so fast, I had a hard time seeing his face. My impression was of a thin, lithe character who moved at a fast-paced slink, like a prowling panther.

I waited another half-hour before deciding to try talking my way in. I let the knocker drop only once before the door swung open. The lunk who occupied most of the doorway must have seen me coming. He stared. I stared. It couldn't go on.

"I've heard the lady of the house offers chess tutoring?" I asked with a valley-girl upward inflection.

"Yes."

"Could I come in and speak with her?"

He edged aside so I could squeeze past him. He smelled of sandalwood, a surprising vanity for a bouncer. I looked for a cauliflower ear, but he lacked that badge of honor, and his nose lay straight, too. The hallway was paved in black-and-white marble, and the walls were painted a deep red, not the kind of rich red that glows, but an opaque hue that sucked light.

"This way." He pointed to a doorway on the right. This room was equally gloomy. It looked like a doctor's waiting room, lined with cast-off dining room chairs interspersed with plain wooden tables. No magazines. But the dark girl also waited.

"Sit, please. The doctor will be with you shortly."

Well, well. And who was she doctoring today? When Lunk left, I got up and paced, looking for some idea of the purpose of this establishment. I leaned close to the young lady and whispered, "Are you Pat?"

"How do you know?" She looked scared.

"This is a dangerous situation. Leave while you can. Just get out."

"But she's going to tutor me..."

"Chess, I know. It's a setup. Get out." She looked confused and ready to cry, clutching her backpack to her chest as if shielding herself from some sort of onslaught.

"I'm a private detective. They've already kidnapped my client's daughter," I hissed.

To my relief, she rushed from the room, and the front door slammed seconds later.

Lunk opened the door and peered in.

"Where has that girl gone?"

"She said she had to go. Something about an exam."

He ran out. I hoped he didn't plan to give chase.

A closed door stood opposite the one I entered by. I reached out, gently turned the handle, and poked my head in. The room contained a leather-covered medical couch, empty, many bookcases, full, and a desk occupied by the woman I'd followed. Only she looked glamorous now, glossy hair touching her shoulders and cosmetic touch-ups.

She looked up, surprised. "I wondered when I was going to see you again. It's been too long. Come and sit down, Lin. Tea?" Had one of the girls talked?

"What's going on? How do you know my name?"

"Oh, I've caught sight of you very occasionally, Hoenir too, lucky fellow. You didn't notice me because I'm so changed. But you look almost the same. Harder, maybe, not the innocent little savior you once were, but still beautiful. That wig doesn't suit you. You were born to be blonde."

She had switched to Norse, and the measured cadences of her speech, not to mention the fact that she was a doctor, stimulated my memory.

"Eir! Is it really you?"

"It is, sister Lin, it is. I am not as strong as I once was, but still a force to be reckoned with. And still a physician, although I have to keep getting new degrees and diplomas. So tiresome."

"How did you get away?"

"I made a deal with Loki. I told him it was prophesied that he would be fatally wounded and only I could save him. So he hid me in a cave deep under a volcano in the ice land. Even there, I heard the battle and the cries of the dying. When the long silence told me it was over, I crept out to find him. I carried him back to my cave and nursed him for an eon. We have traveled down the ages, sometimes together, sometimes on different paths, but here we are.

"I saw you carrying Hoenir, by the way. You weren't easy to keep track of, but I sometimes caught up."

I couldn't contain myself. "Loki? The trickster god? You really met him again?"

Lin opened her eyes and glared at me. "You know how I feel about interruptions. Yes, the vile Loki. Thriving in New York when he should have sunk into the void forever. And he's not a god. His father was Jotun—that's a giant—and no one really knows who his mother was. Some say she was Jotun too, but Loki is too small for that to be true. Odin made him a blood brother after some small favor and granted him immortality. And that creature abused his adoption almost from the beginning. The betrayal!" Her voice rose to a wail as she clenched her fists and banged them on her thighs.

"Shush, Hunter will hear."

She almost spat out her answer. "He's out. He needs to replenish the wine cellar. Didn't he mention it?"

"No, why would he?"

"Oh, I just thought he might have. In passing."

"Nuh, uh."

"Anyway, just shut up and listen."

Might have mentioned it in passing? She knows.

I could hardly believe such terrible betrayal. I banged my palms on her desk and leaned forward.

"Loki was wicked. Why didn't you save the good ones? My dear lady Frigg?"

"A deal is a deal."

My anger amused her and she couldn't quite hide a smirk. Saving Loki was unforgivable. Eir's godly ethos must have changed beyond imagination.

"What is going on in this house? I am a private detective now, and I'm looking for a missing girl. A chess aficionado. Is she here? Her parents are frantic."

"What does she look like?"

"Somewhat exotic, name of Susan. I was tracking some Syrian refugees who were tricked into prostitution in Northern Virginia, too. They were moved before I got back from uncovering the kidnapping ring."

"So that was you, was it? Loki will insist you be severely punished. He'll be back soon. In the meantime, I will show you to your room."

"I'm going back to my hotel."

"No, my dear, you are not." She picked up an elegant cut glass spray bottle even faster than I could react and sprayed a sweet-smelling mist into my face. My senses began to cloud, and I felt my strength ebbing. She hauled me to my feet and half carried, half dragged me out of her room and into an elevator.

"It's no good struggling. Anesthesia drains our strength. We are all the same."

I vaguely remember being shoved onto a cot in a dark room.

24

"That creature is a scourge. Not Eir, you understand. Her partner, the one the Goodalls were so afraid of."

"Exciting," I said.

"Yes, indeed."

I let out a sigh. Hunter had visited me again. I was foolish in love, no doubt like many before me.

"I don't mind about Hunter, by the way. He needs a change from time to time. We've been together for eons, you know. I enjoy a change sometimes, too."

I was too shocked to answer but sat with my hand still on its way to the recorder, gawping like a halfwit. She didn't open her eyes.

When she started talking, my hand flapped to the record button, almost knocking over the recorder, making quite a racket.

She smirked.

Tape 23

My head felt so muzzy; I didn't want to open my eyes. The bed was warm and cozy, the pillow cloud-soft, and a warm, purring body lay across my chest. I've always loved cats.

My mind meandered to Greece and an island we lived on for a few years, where cats were revered and fed by all the villagers. Those people were primitive and superstitious. A jealous young woman turned them against us when a cat and her litter were found drowned one morning. She pointed out that the foreigners were the most likely culprits. We had to get the children out of there.

The fog began to lift from my mind, but I still didn't feel like moving. The bed at home wasn't this cushy. Where was I? Recent memories began to filter through—the girl, the doctor Eir, the mist.

The cat stretched, and its back leg reached down my body. What a long cat. When it started scratching around my genital area, my eyes snapped open. A yellow feline eye winked into mine as the scratching intensified. I shot up, heaving the large creature off the bed. It yowled a mixture of meows and human epithets. "Meow-grr-shit!"

"Loki, you son of a *Jotun!*" My mind was clearing rapidly. "How dare you touch me? Murderer!" I clutched the duvet close to hide my nakedness.

The size of a puma now, he sprang to the other side of the room.

"Stop showing off and come out of that."

I'd only shifted within the human spectrum but soon realized that moving between species probably took longer. I glared at him for the quarter hour or so it took to go from sleek and gorgeous to wiry with thin, pointed features—a feral little man. When I knew him, he was the skinny bad-boy type, eyes set a little too close, charm shining brighter than a summer solstice sun when it suited him.

He laughed like a hyena. "Well, aren't you the prude."

"I have standards, and half-Jotun doesn't cut it. And let's face it—for a half-giant, you are somewhat deficient in height and bulk. To the tune of a couple of yards and a hundred kilos or so. Don't you think?"

He reddened and pouted. "You won't be so cheeky when we've finished with you. You messed up a nice little thing we had going with those Syrian girls. Now you want to meddle with our home-grown ones, too?"

He flopped down into an armchair and pouted some more.

I stayed quite still, what with me being unclothed and him quite without principles when it came to ravishing young women. At least he stayed on the other side of the room.

"I can see why you got into this, but why Eir? She healed the sick and wounded and always gave wise counsel. How could she save a traitor like you and go along with your wicked schemes?"

"In our old world, you gods were trapped in your allotted roles, enmeshed by the prophecies. Since I was only Odin's blood brother, not a god, I felt free to play around all my days. But in the end, even I was subject to fate. I've always been able to make my way." He smirked and crossed his legs. "Eir was a goddess and revered by all. She wanted for nothing. Then, when the world came alive once more, she found Midgard the only world reborn, Asgard extinguished. Where did that leave her? I saw it all coming, so we struck a deal. I'd get undead, and she would get all the help she needed to regain position and comfort. We all have our price."

"Of course you saw it coming," I said, "You started it!"

"Well, someone had to do it. It was preordained, remember?"

"You always were a troublemaker. I suppose you have other sidelines besides human trafficking?"

"Well, I'm quite popular with the ladies." He straightened out and grinned.

"You? You don't look like my idea of a lady-killer."

He curled his lips, reminding me of my precarious position. I drew the duvet tighter.

"Oh, I can be really charming. I might even break down your defenses one of these days. But even if I don't ..." He snarled.

"Oh, stop it. You're not a cat anymore, remember?"

He gave no sign of hearing me. "I aim to have many children to carry on my line. I've been visiting Manhattan since the forties. This town makes me feel on top of the world. Many young New York matrons are married to successful men who neglect them shamefully. Poor things; they get pathetically sappy about carrying my child.

"My first conquest was when I visited the city for the first time. Some kind of Britisher, funny accent, low-born, from what she told me. Rather plain but quite sweet. Her husband was a real estate developer who got filthy rich. A hustler if ever I saw one. I'd done a couple of deals with him, and he invited me to dinner. That's how I met her. They're both dead now, but I keep track of my son, who's not too bright, but turned out street smart and a real shit. He makes me proud. There are twelve or fifteen more, all sharp characters, and now they're spawning my grandchildren."

"You are truly shameless."

I'd heard footsteps tiptoeing up to the door. Loki didn't seem to register them, so maybe his hearing wasn't as good as mine. He probably never had godly hearing. One sometimes forgot Loki's low origins because of his incredible shape-shifting and certain other magical abilities. Odin conferred immortality on him, but Ragnarök taught us that immortality isn't guaranteed, even for those born into it.

"And what about Eir? Doesn't she object? I'm sure she's a fine woman and a wonderful doctor, in spite of what she's done to those girls. Your idea, certainly. I always loved her. I'd still welcome her as a friend." I was banking on it being her outside the door.

"Eir has her limitations, and she bores me, frankly. She doesn't care to bear children either. I only stay for the convenience. She makes a good business partner. It's not as though we came out of Asgard with anything. Fenrir destroyed everything. I hadn't counted on that."

Strange, he must have known about the gnomes' treasure. I suppose he thought it had disappeared into the void.

The nearly silent footsteps retreated. After a minute, they came back louder, and Loki turned toward them.

"That must be Eir."

She opened the door, brandishing a hypodermic. I shrank back.

"Don't worry, Lin, it's not for you. Loki needs his tonic. It keeps him from aging. Come along, my dear," she said in a tone a good deal sharper than her normal lilt.

"Thank you, dearest," he said, not seeming to register her mood. He looked at me with a nasty, lopsided grin. "We all have to take our medicine, you know. Soon you will swallow yours. Hoenir, too. And the children won't want to live without their parents, will they?"

Loki bounced through the door ahead of Eir. She lingered for a few seconds and looked back at me.

"Don't worry, we'll talk," she said.

But I did worry. Even goddesses cry sometimes. Dear old Hoenir, I wouldn't want any harm to come to him. And my darling children. Loki would stop at nothing to destroy us. I shouldn't have mocked him.

Lin tore up the stairs as if she had a bus to catch. Talking about Loki had clearly rattled her. Me too. Two more Norse gods—wow! And where were they now? Lin would have had to do something drastic about Loki. But Eir?

I went upstairs for lunch. Dora had set out a cold selection of wonderful cheeses and homemade bread. Lin opened a bottle of white wine, and we finished the lot.

"This wine is so delicious," I said.

"Yes, this one is hard to find. From Germany, you know. My favorite. I think I'll take a nap."

"Me too. I shouldn't really drink wine at lunch because it makes me sleepy."

"It doesn't make me sleepy; it makes me want to dream of the old days."

"Lin is too nostalgic," Hunter said, clearly uneasy. "I am going to my study."

Lin and I enjoyed the smiles of conspirators after he left, although I felt a nagging sense of disloyalty. I hoped I'd dream about him.

I did, and it was lovely.

25

"I had to forgive her. She's one of us. I love her. He was never one of us."

I heard the loneliness. No kindred spirit but Hunter. Wonderful in love, but not the sharpest knife in the drawer.

As if she read my mind, she said, "Hunter has his drawbacks, but he's clever in some ways, especially with money. He makes a killing on the stock market. He'll probably make our fortune last forever. If anything lasts forever. But it doesn't, does it?"

A veiled warning?

Tape 24

Eir returned later that day, trundling a trolley bearing dinner for two. It smelled wonderfully fishy and savory.

"Eat," she said. "We'll talk afterward."

I nibbled and gobbled, overcome with pleasure at these tastes of home, which I'd never actually tasted in Asgard, but smelled and watched others devour. Eir ate in a more restrained manner, obviously pleased by my enjoyment. My goblet contained something I didn't remember. Something ice cold, tart, and sweet-scented with herbs.

"What is this?" I asked.

"My own concoction. It has healing properties. It will make you strong again."

"Why would you risk me being strong again?"

"I've had a change of heart. Loki no longer serves my purposes. I am dealing with him. The last syringe didn't contain his usual medication. I hope by the time he realizes what I'm doing, he will be too feeble to do anything about it."

So she had overheard. "Good. You heard him threaten my children."

"Yes. Don't worry; they will be safe."

But I did worry. What if he concocted something before he had significantly deteriorated? I felt helpless and terrified. But I had to act strong.

"And what about the girls?"

"The one you seek is still here. You can take her. But we have to wait until Loki is weaker. A few days at most. You are interested in other girls?"

"In particular, there are five who were imprisoned in the Goodall's house in Salton, Virginia. They'd been moved on by the time I got back from Syria. There was a sixth, but one of the clients killed her. I saw Jerry Goodall dump her body into the Potomac. It still hasn't been found, as far as I know."

"They told me the missing girl had a heart condition and collapsed during the night. Why these girls?"

"I found them and promised to save them. That's my quest."

"Ah, still the faithful handmaiden at heart. Well, they were all sent to the same house. We could get them out, but it won't be easy. Then what do we do with them?"

"I don't know. There's a detective in Salton who might help. He knows their story, after all. The immigration authorities have the five I came back with, and I hope they'll be lenient. As you may know, Air Force personnel were involved, which I'm sure they will want to keep quiet, not to mention the American woman in the camp, Mary Wilder. Joe can hand the others over to them, too." I hoped that would be the case. They didn't deserve to go back to the camp.

Eir got up and started pacing. She seemed agitated.

"What's the matter?" I asked.

"I've established myself here. I've got a lot to lose. Much more than you. I'm not sure I want to start again right now."

Now I felt agitated myself. She couldn't chicken out now. Granted, this turnaround had seemed too good to be true. But ... a woman scorned and all that.

"Why don't you sell your practice, sell this house, and get out before the authorities can discover your involvement? That way, you'll have a good bit put by. And I'm sure you and Loki have built plenty of assets over the years. Then come and live near us. Practice medicine in Salton. It's a nice place."

"It isn't New York."

"No, it isn't. But it's near Washington, and lots of important people live in our town because it has upscale housing and an easy commute. And you'll be near your own kind. That's important, isn't it?"

"True. I'll think about it. I don't know how long it will take for Loki to become incapacitated. Odin conferred the gift of immortality on him. But the immortals themselves died in the final battle, so they are vulnerable. Incapacity may be the best I can do. That means I'm stuck with him." She slumped before taking a deep breath and drawing herself straight once more. "I'll let you know what I decide."

Eir dumped the empty dishes back onto the trolley any old how and wheeled it out. I thought I'd persuaded her but couldn't be sure. I hoped Loki declined quickly before he realized what she was up to. Could she fool a trickster like him?

My children, my love. I didn't sleep that night, remembering the good times, and banishing the bad to the end of the queue.

26

"I hate Loki. He deserves to linger and suffer." Lin's hands clenched into fists. She did a lot of that when she talked about Loki.

I sat back in silence, waiting for the next installment. I still couldn't quite believe she didn't mind about Hunter and me.

Tape 25

Loki played many hateful pranks on the gods. When he cut off Sif's beautiful golden hair while she slept, her husband, Thor, threatened to kill him unless he restored it. The gnomes got him out of that one by manufacturing new hair out of pure gold. Its magical properties allowed it to meld to her scalp as if it had grown there. It shone even brighter than her real hair. To further mollify the gods, he'd had the gnomes make valuable gifts that rendered them even more powerful—for Odin, a spear that could never miss its mark, and for the other gods of Aesir, a ship that could carry them all, yet be folded small enough to fit into a pouch. But after his role in murdering our beloved Baldur, he'd gone too far and knew his time in Asgard had come to an end.

He discovered a sheltered hollow next to a waterfall and built a house out of the stones he found, with doors on each side so he could watch for anyone coming to avenge Baldur. Odin discovered Loki with his all-seeing eye and sent Thor and other gods—including Hunter/Hoenir, which is how I know all about it—to capture him.

Thor's group crept down to the hollow one day, just as Loki had finished crafting a fishing net he'd invented. When he spotted them, he threw his precious discovery on the fire, ran into the river, and turned himself into a salmon. When the gods arrived at his house, they realized he had escaped and pulled the half-burned net out of the fire. It didn't take long to mend, although Loki claims it took the gods all day and night to learn how to make a new one from the ashes they found.

Needless to say, they'd heard all about this miraculous "secret" invention on the grapevine because Loki was such a braggart, so it didn't take much brainpower to figure out what they'd found. Loki was a clever rogue, no doubt about it, and I've never seen anyone so good at shape-shifting. Later, he loved to talk about how he invented the net while hidden away in his hollow. He actually invented it much earlier after watching a spider weave her web on Midgard during one of his forays down there looking for human maidens to despoil.

To be fair to Loki, his invention turned out to be an incredible boon to succeeding generations of humans who depended on fishing nets for their livelihood. Later, Odin instructed my lady Frigg to make sure the idea was carried to Midgard, and I was one of the first to demonstrate its benefits to a poor fisherman who'd lost his boat and lines in a fire.

Thor realized Loki must be in the river because there was nowhere else he could have gone without being seen. There was still enough netting to catch a fish, so down to the shore they ran. They soon spotted Loki, as he was the biggest, shiniest salmon they'd ever seen. Typical. He had to be a standout, even in those dire circumstances. Loki thought he was too well disguised to be caught and swam around the pool at the bottom of the waterfall, laughing at the peering eyes above. His fishy chuckles produced all kinds of bizarre bubbles, further confirming their suspicions.

Hunter crept down to the pool and blocked the pool's outlet with huge boulders. Loki darted here and there frantically when he realized what was happening, infuriated by the gods who mocked his desperation. Thor cast the net over Loki, who darted deep and came up the other side. This happened several times until Loki took a mighty leap over the boulders, but Hunter caught him by the tail, so he couldn't wriggle away this time.

Thor changed Fenrir, one of Loki's two sons, into a wolf, who immediately mauled to death his own brother. Odin had Loki bound to a boulder in a dark bat cave on Midgard using the entrails of his dead boy. They chained the wolf-son Fenrir to another boulder. They fastened a snake to a stalactite over Loki's head that dripped venom onto his face every few seconds—drip, drip, drip. Loki's faithful wife, Sigyn, held a bowl out to catch the venom but had to go to a nearby underground stream to empty it before it overflowed, leaving Loki to suffer the burning venom until she returned. When he shuddered in pain, the earth around the cave shook and heaved. And that's where Loki and Fenrir remained until Ragnarök.

Eir heard of these earthquakes and the injuries they caused and descended to Midgard to explore their source. The gods had not spoken of Loki since his capture, so she had no idea of his torment. She discovered the disturbance was centered in that cave and entered. Dark and cold, the stones dripped moisture onto the slippery moss below. She heard Loki's cries and felt the world around her tremble as Sigyn emptied her bowl into the boiling stream.

Eir could not bear to let Loki suffer for eternity, despite his crimes. She placed a cloth over Loki's face that neutralized the poison until Sigyn could return with her bowl.

"Set me free," he implored.

"I cannot thwart Odin's will," she replied. "When he discovers I have relieved your torment, he will be angry enough. But humans are suffering, too. It is my duty to help them."

"Next time, then. There will be a next time."

Eir didn't know what he meant, although she discovered later after Loki escaped and began exacting his revenge. I was attending to my lady Frigg during the time Eir related her tale. None of us knew exactly what was coming, despite the prophecies.

Odin grew quiet as she kneeled before him and confessed what she had done.

"I can forgive your wish to help the humans," was all he said.

The father seethed, and the son grew, straining his bonds until they ripped apart. The earth trembled once more as Loki cackled with anticipation, and Fenrir roared his hungry threats.

27

Lin and I didn't meet for two weeks because Hunter wanted to look at investment properties in the Northwest. Lin seemed eager to go, too. I was nervous she might opt out of our project, but I relieved my anxiety by cleaning up the garden with Aunt Peggy and walking Sam. The fall had gone by so quickly. It was November already and chilly. I had another stab at my novel too but finally had to realize it was a lost cause. Maybe I should read some mysteries with a more analytical approach. I liked to get lost in the stories and sort of inhaled them. I needed to find out what made them work. There must be books on the subject, too.

Lin had a gardener who took care of their property. Dora didn't do much except loll around and eat chocolates, then start marathon cleaning a couple of days before they got back. She bought so much food she had to have it delivered. I stayed out of her way because she'd turned absolutely vitriolic lately. Did she still have the hots for Hunter?

I missed his attention horribly. He was so goofy-sweet, enormous, and tender; he could make me see shooting stars, too.

I needn't have worried. As soon as they got back, Lin started up again.

"I've been neglecting my reading, Mary," she announced at breakfast. "I'll start up again this morning. I hope it won't disturb you to have me down there." Her sweet smile was so fake.

"Of course not, Lin, any time. It's your house, after all." I also smiled sweetly.

"I do not know what you want to do all that reading for," Hunter grumped. "I will be in my study until lunch."

Lin ran downstairs, flopped onto the couch, and wiggled herself comfortable.

"I've been through old age many times, but at ninety-eight, I have the body of a well-kept woman of thirty. I never suffered like humans do, like Loki does now. I pity the humans but not him."

Ninety-eight? "Don't you get tired of it all," I asked.

"Oh, no. There's always something, someplace, someone new. Not that anything is truly new and different, rather a fresh aspect of what came before."

"The Internet is different. Medical discoveries. They were unimaginable centuries ago."

"It's true. But people communicated differently and in a smaller range. What good has all this global connectivity done? People used to have pretty effective folk remedies, too."

"It's inevitable that people will branch out and find new places and things. It's human nature. It's your nature too, come to think of it."

She laughed. "True."

"And folk remedies couldn't deal with most things. Many died before they had time to get other serious diseases because they died of bacterial infections."

"I suppose you're right. But in this country and other undeveloped nations, medical treatment is only available to those who can afford it."

Other undeveloped nations? I decided to keep my mouth shut.

"Anyway, Hunter is always there. And now I have Eir. It's a comfort to have fellow travelers. They know.

Ninety-eight? Sweet Jesus! I could see the toll arthritis was taking on Auntie Peggy at seventy-five. I took groceries over there whenever I could to save her a trip. And dear old Sam would soon start slowing down, too.

Tape 26

Loki brought me breakfast. "A taste of New York," he warbled.

Bagels, lox, and cream cheese. "None for you?" I asked.

"That is supposed to be for two. You'll notice the two coffee cups." He made a sweeping gesture to present his offering.

"Oh well, I suppose I can share if I must."

He ate as hungrily as I, wiping his mouth with the back of his hand. He slurped down his coffee.

"You know, you have disgusting table manners. Is that how you eat when you're having dinner with your rich friends?"

"Of course not. I know how to behave. But why should I bother around my nearest and dearest?"

A resounding "Huh" laced with contempt was the best I could come up with.

All of a sudden, Loki froze, his face sliding from surprise to horror.

"What is it?"

"I feel strange. My stomach..."

He rushed out, failing to lock the door behind him. I waited a decent interval before venturing downstairs, figuring the stairs would be a safer choice than the elevator. The first flight brought me to a balcony that overlooked a large living room, where Loki complained to Eir like a whiny child. I watched their interaction while crouched behind the low wall that supported the railings.

"It all came out of my mouth. All my breakfast. I've never done that before. It was terrible. What's going on? Help me, my darling."

"I don't know why that happened to you. It's so strange. Let me get you something to make you feel better."

"It must be that Lin. She did this to me! We should kill her."

I got chills. Maybe Eir's plan wasn't going to work out so well for me.

"Don't be silly, dear boy. Where on earth would she get her hands on poison? I'll be right back. Perhaps I should just give you your medication early. I wonder if it's becoming less effective."

Loki's face scrunched and twisted into an ugly caricature. "You'd better see to it that it works. You need me. What kind of doctor are you that I suffer so?"

Eir looked shocked. "How can you talk to me like that? Of course, I will keep you going. Of course, I need you. Have I ever given you cause to think otherwise?"

"Well, there was that time in Olympus—more than two hundred years you were gone."

That was a shocker. So they'd visited Olympus too? After or before us?

"That wasn't entirely my fault, Loki. We sought haven with Zeus. You played your usual pranks, and we were no longer welcome. In fact, you may recall he threatened us with an unpleasant and permanent death."

"Didn't he know we are immortal, silly fool?"

"You must realize immortality can end. Where are Odin and Thor, after all? Zeus was never a god to trifle with. The

Titans learned that the hard way. Even you should have realized that."

Eir was losing her temper. A big mistake. Loki needed to be kept calm, not put on the defensive. Or angered. That might prove deadly from my point of view.

Loki collapsed into an armchair. "I'm ill. You shouldn't shout at me."

Eir went over to him and took his hands. "I'm sorry, darling. I'm going to get your medication now. Just rest. I'll be back in no time."

Loki closed his eyes, his head lolling back away from her. Eir looked up at me and made the thumbs-up sign. So much for stealthy, at least where another god was concerned.

I leaned against the wall, waiting for her return, popping my head up again when I heard her voice.

"Loki, sweetness, I'm going to give you your shot now."

He sat up groggily. "I still don't feel good."

"I know. I've put a little sedative with it so you can take a nap."

I watched with some pleasure as she jabbed his arm with the needle. To my disappointment, he didn't react. I've never had a shot, but I'm told the needles they use nowadays are so sharp you hardly feel them. Not that you'd know, the way my children used to carry on when they got their vaccinations.

"Let's get you to bed, dearest." By the time she got him to the doorway, she had to take most of his weight. That must have been some powerful sedative. I stood up, tempted to make a run for it. But the girls. I had an obligation to save the five I'd left behind.

I decided to brazen it out. I went down to the next level and made myself comfortable on one of the cream silk-covered loveseats. A selection of magazines lay fanned out on the coffee table in front of me. I selected *Vogue* and leafed through the ads, which informed me that my wardrobe was no longer *au courant*. Here I was in New York, a great place for shopping, but I had to get that girl back home. Of course, I could always tell her parents to fetch her. I'd completed my first official case successfully, after all. Fifth Avenue awaited!

Eir returned after about twenty minutes. She didn't seem surprised to see me. She sat in the matching loveseat opposite. We both sat like statues, not willing to unbend until we'd assessed each other's intentions.

"I would have let you go."

"I have to save the girls."

"Still the do-gooder."

"Like you used to be."

"Now, now, Lin. This isn't getting us anywhere." She sat a cushion on her lap and fiddled with the tassels. She no longer looked me in the face.

"Look, Eir, I have a job to do. Will you help me? You know, you could wrap up everything here and leave. It doesn't look as if Loki will last much longer."

"Oh, he'll last for years. He just won't enjoy it. He'll get old and decrepit very soon because I have destroyed his life potion. I'll be my own mistress, although he'll be a millstone around my neck. I don't dare leave him to his own devices, even in that condition."

"Why don't you look for a permanent solution? As you pointed out, even immortality can end."

Eir got up and contemplated a Scottish landscape on the wall next to us. It seemed to calm her. "It will take a lot of research, but maybe I'll find a way. It would be like putting an old dog out of his misery. I'll try to figure out what poison the great serpent used at the end times."

"How do you suggest we proceed with the current situation?"

"Well, you can have your girl. She won't remember anything; I've made sure of that."

"I was thinking of telling her parents to come get her, anyway. I need some new clothes."

"Well, they can't come here."

"I can take her to my hotel. But I must tell them where I found her. A house where she was being kept prisoner before being moved on? But then I'd have to report it to the police. That won't work."

Eir got up and paced back and forth behind the loveseat before turning on a lamp in a room already bright with sunshine, straightened the magazines I'd left in disarray, and finally inserted a CD into the player. Bach, I think. I'm not wild about that kind of piddling string music, always in such a hurry but never actually getting anywhere.

"I know of a condo that's only used for assignations by one of Loki's hateful sons." She saw my surprise. "Surely the twerp bragged about planting his seed for posterity."

"Yes, of course, but I wasn't sure you knew."

"Oh, yes. I know what he is. I only realized how little he cares for me when I overheard your conversation. I was touched by your declaration of friendship, by the way."

"Eir, we need our own kind—people who understand us. We are all we've got, real family. I have children, but it's not the same. And sadly, they are not immortal."

"Oh, Lin, that's horrible; I'm so sorry. Yes, you're right. That son is in Thailand right now. I'll get you in there, and you can plant the evidence, which I'll have ready by that time. Fake records, and so on. Have a good look around so you can describe where you found her. Leave the front door wide open. And leave fingerprints. The doorman will be out for about ten minutes, so you'll have to be quick."

"I don't have fingerprints."

"Damn, I'd forgotten that. Well, leave some sort of trace. I'll incapacitate the doorman. Then come back here and take her to your hotel before calling the police. You have the afternoon to think up a good story for them."

"When shall we do it?"

"Tonight. Stay in your room until dinner at seven. I'll have lunch brought up. I think Bjorn is loyal to me, but I'm not sure. I'll get him talking this afternoon. I have my ways."

"Who's Bjorn?"

"My butler, the big fellow. The dining room is through that door and to the right." She pointed at the door where she'd come in. "Is your watch still working?"

"Ten-twenty?"

"Yes, good enough."

"I'd better call my hotel. They haven't seen me for a couple of days. They may have given my room to someone else."

"I'll take care of that. I'll tell them I'm your secretary, and you were called away on urgent business."

I gave her the name of the hotel and asked if I could borrow some magazines before heading back upstairs the way I came. I felt her watch me until I was out of sight.

Lunch came and went. The magazines didn't last all afternoon. I napped and dreamed I was a model mincing down a runway, wearing an outlandish ball gown constructed of feathers that made me sneeze so often and so hard that I fell off the end of the catwalk and woke up.

I looked at my watch. Six-thirty. I finished an article in one of the magazines—hardly *Vogue*, I'll have you know—about how to please your man. Utter twaddle. I doubt the author could have pleased a dildo.

28

"Old friends are the best," she declared as she trooped in once more, pulling back her hair so she could fan it across the cushions like a Hollywood goddess. "Eir made a huge mistake tying herself to Loki. She told me why she went along with it, but I still wonder if she told me the whole truth."

"I guess she had to choose someone she felt would be practical in a new world. The other gods might have been too idealistic to manage their new circumstances," I said.

"That's a good point, Mary. He certainly knows how to flourish. But we all knew he was trouble. And she went along. She should have gotten rid of him years ago. She has a lucrative profession, after all."

"But, like you said, one of the old ones. You're right about old friends. I met someone I knew in high school last year. She was one of the popular girls then and not someone I ever hung around with, but it was great to reminisce. She'd matured and had an entry-level job with a TV station, which she loved. Most of the other friends left town and didn't come back. Those who stayed had nothing to talk about with someone who'd broadened their horizons. They were well and truly mired in high school football, babies, and church picnics."

I suddenly felt morose. My old friends had scattered far and wide. Still, Hunter made up for it. Often.

Tape 27

Eir and I enjoyed a companionable dinner, reminiscing about our homeland and our favorite godyarns. I told her some stories of humans I'd helped in Midgard. Bjorn served, so I assumed he'd passed Eir's version of the polygraph.

"Well," she said, pushing back from the table. "It's time to get going."

Bjorn dropped us off a couple of blocks away from the Park Avenue condo. Eir had dolled herself up in a mink coat, diamond drop earrings, and my brunette wig, so she looked the part. I wasn't sure how she'd get in, but I knew she would somehow.

The doorman, an older man dressed up like a Balkan dictator, raised an eyebrow when we stopped outside the door. People who mattered didn't approach this palace on foot.

"Good evening," she said with a sweet smile.

"Good evening, madam," he replied, his voice crackling with suspicion.

A quick spray, and he started to get wobbly.

"Oh, you poor thing," she exclaimed. A passing couple turned to look but pressed on. She helped him into the foyer, where a young man stood landlocked behind a desk.

"He's terribly heavy. Help me," she cried. The concierge sprang a bolt and hurried around to help his colleague to a chair. He hurried back to his station.

"I'd better call my boss," he said.

"Well, we'll be on our way upstairs," Eir said, her voice certain and chirpy. "My friend here has a job interview with Mr. Wheeling in 800. We mustn't keep him waiting."

"But he's in..."

With another spray and a quick push, he slid under the desk. Eir took his keys and selected the one for the elevator and another labeled with the apartment number.

"Go on, quick."

The elevator soared, speedy and smooth. When I turned the key, it opened opposite the front door of number 800. I guess they didn't feel they needed a personal security system with the ironclad system they had downstairs—two comatose watchdogs—so no trouble there. The foyer led into a living room with a panoramic view of the city. But the bedrooms were my main focus. I looked in all four and memorized the contents of the one that looked most suitable, mostly because of the four-poster bed.

I opened my large bag and placed a glass with Susan's fingerprints on the dresser and threw a couple of used towels and a toothbrush in the adjoining bathroom. Too bad we couldn't have brought Susan here to leave other fingerprints where one might expect to find them, but we had deemed that too risky. And it wasn't as if we had the time to transfer them using my unique methods. Huh, such an adventure that was!

The master bedroom was a monument to some tacky but expensive decorator. Mirrored ceiling, party tub in the bathroom, and lurid furnishings throughout. Totally at odds with the traditional look of the rest of the apartment.

I guessed Mommy didn't get invited in here. I placed transaction records in the bedside table drawer and handcuffs and a whip in the closet. Then I left, checking my watch in the elevator. Five minutes.

When I got downstairs, I found Eir sitting in the chair next to the doorman, who was swaying from side to side, mumbling to himself. The concierge had not reemerged.

"Not a moment too soon," she said. "I can't believe no one has come in or out."

I tossed the keys over the desk. They landed with a soft thud, which suggested a warm body. We hurried down the block to find the car.

"Where in hell is he?" I wanted to get far away fast.

"Don't worry. You can't just sit in a car around here. He'll be circling."

Bjorn showed up in a couple of minutes, and we were soon safely indoors.

"Now you must meet Susan," Eir said as she pulled off her wig, coat, and earrings. She tossed them onto a chair next to the hall table.

She led me to the elevator, and we went down this time. The passageway it opened onto looked uncannily like that at the Goodalls', but I thought it best not to bring that up.

Eir unlocked the nearest door. A young woman crouched on a cot, shrinking against the wall. She approached her slowly. I stayed in the doorway.

"No need to be afraid, my dear. We won't hurt you. In fact, this lady, Lin, has come to take you home."

"Where's Luke? He said I was going to be a treat for someone who will pay a lot for a virgin. He said he'd be second in line."

Luke—Loki's Americanized name.

"Luke won't bother you anymore, my dear. He's quite out of the picture. Lin will take you to a hotel, and she'll call your parents to come and get you."

Susan's face registered horror as a pair of bony hands gripped my throat. The element of surprise cost me a few seconds before I reacted.

"Not such a strong little goddess nowadays, are you, my pretty?" His voice croaked like an old man's.

I jabbed my elbow into Loki's gut and flung my arms up under his to break his grip. He faltered. I wondered why Eir wasn't helping. I spun around and brought my knee up where it would hurt even a nonhuman like him. He vomited and passed out just as Eir appeared, brandishing a syringe.

"That little weasel is tougher than I thought," she said as she delivered a vengeful jab to his thigh. "This is double the dose I gave him this morning. He'll be twenty years older by the time he wakes up."

He could still get at my children, though, was my immediate thought. I rubbed my sore neck, only gradually registering the sobbing in the room behind me.

"Are you sure he's out?" I asked. "We need to get Susan out of here."

"He had a room down here fitted out with special restraints. He might like to see how efficiently his design turned out," said Eir. She laughed, something I'd never heard her do before, even in the good old days when she floated around in an aura of wisdom and serenity. Quite the goody-two-shoes, like me. Knowing what she'd been up to since this had been a façade. Even the good gods disappoint. I'm not without my faults, I'll be the first to admit.

"Don't forget how he broke loose once before when he was lusting for revenge."

"He doesn't have the strength now. This is the third day without his life nectar. He'll go down fast."

A timid voice behind us said, "Who are you people?"

"Two people who are going to set you free," said Eir, going over to the bed and taking the girl's hands.

"But aren't you the chess lady who brought me here?"

"No, she's my sister, Luke's wife. She's gone away. It's okay."

Eir needed her to cooperate until we were safely in my hotel room. She took the girl's hand and led her to the elevator. We went out of the front door and stepped into the car. Mercifully, my purse lay on the back seat.

"There's a small spray in your purse," Eir whispered. "Use it when you get settled in. She'll remember nothing. Mention date rape drugs."

"Why are you whispering?" asked Susan. "Is anything wrong?"

"No, no," Eir said in a soothing tone she probably used on patients. "I was just telling Lin to call me if you need anything."

Susan nodded, clearly too traumatized to question further.

When we got to the hotel, I guided Susan to a deep armchair facing away from the front desk. She slumped, which gave the impression I wanted.

"My key, please," I said to the receptionist. "I believe my secretary called to explain my absence."

"Welcome back, madam," she said. "There are two of you?"

"Yes, there are two beds in my room."

"I'm afraid we have to charge for an extra guest, madam."

"Of course, no problem. You have my credit card details."

We got upstairs.

"Take a nap, Susan. You're safe now."

"Will you call my parents?" she said as she stretched out on the bed. She didn't even take off her shoes.

"Of course. You'll be home in no time."

"I don't want to go back there." She glared at me as if I were the enemy.

"Why ever not? Have you any idea how frantic they've been? They paid me a lot of money, probably more than they can really afford, to save you."

"They are really boring. Salton is really boring."

"Well, maybe go back for a few days just to make them happy. It's the least you can do."

"I've got tests."

Okay, this I could do without. She closed her eyes, and I got out the spray bottle. I crept over to the bed and squeezed out the contents. Her eyelids merely fluttered before she stilled. Time to make a few phone calls. It's a good thing hotel rooms still have regular phones.

The mother cried, the father cried, and could I possibly bring her home? Funds were a bit short, you see. I told them their retainer would cover their train fares, and my office would book their tickets. I had a few more loose ends to tie up here; I added.

I called Lettie to fill her in and have her take care of the reservations. Next, I called the police, and that became very tedious, not helped by the fact that Susan didn't wake up for three hours and remembered nothing—thank the gods. They carted her off to the hospital and me down to the precinct.

The parents' arrival the next morning and their grateful utterances helped, as did the cops' visit to the condo. They hadn't been keen to follow up on such a prominent citizen, but a cleaning lady had reported a break-in when she found the front door open. The police, heartened by the discovery that the condo's owner was safely out of the country, sent a couple of detectives over, who found signs of recent occupation in the small bedroom. They also found the little black book in his bedside drawer. Things went from sticky for me to sticky for the hapless absentee. They let me go, warning me I'd have to testify in court. Good publicity for the price of a train ticket.

The parents came to my hotel to thank me and say goodbye before they headed home. Susan thanked me, but looked sulky, knowing her parents would object to her returning to New York. I forecast stormy weather in that household.

I called Eir. "It's over. How's it going with Loki?"

"He's sick, or at least he thinks he is. Actually, he's just old. Arthritis, tremors, you name it. Unfortunately, he's going to be very old for a very long time. Still, as we discovered, even immortality has its limits, so maybe he won't last forever, especially if my new research project proves successful. I've hired him an ugly nurse. He can still cause trouble, so I'll wire his rooms.

"I'll start the process of selling my practice soon. Because I have to devote myself to my elderly spouse." She laughed. The merry not-quite-a-widow. "Then the house. Who knows, perhaps whoever buys the practice will want the house, too."

"That's great news. I can't wait to see you in Salton."

"Yes, if I think it's safe to leave Loki, I'll come for a quick visit."

"Now we have to get the other girls out. Can you rent a van with covered windows? Once we get them out, we could just drive to Salton, and I can leave them in my detective friend's hands."

"As I said, it won't be easy. I'm almost out of spray. It takes a couple of days to make."

That wasn't good news.

"We'll have to resort to brute force, then. Can you arrange a visit to whoever manages the house?"

"Sure. But we'll have to work quickly. I've got enough spray for her, but not for anyone else. She's sure to have a couple of bouncers around. The johns might be a problem, too."

"We can say we're the vice squad. They'll evaporate as long as the goons are incapacitated."

"All right. Tomorrow night. Check out of the hotel and come over here in the morning. I'll rent the van and have them deliver it. We'll start out around nine in the evening."

"Loki has a van, doesn't he? I noticed him use it that first day."

"It's registered in my name. I'll sell it later."

"Sounds good, Eir. I'll drop you home after the operation, then drive the girls straight to Salton. I'll put my baggage in the hotel office because I'm going clothes shopping up and down Fifth Avenue tomorrow. I might need a new suitcase."

"Good for you!" she said with a small laugh that sounded more like a bark. I guess she was tense, which was hardly surprising.

"You must come see us soon. Bring Loki and the nurse. Safer that way. We don't have a big house, but we can free up a couple of rooms. Actually, I'm thinking of buying a larger place. One you might know. The Goodalls' house is in the market." I wasn't sure how she'd react. Heck, I wasn't sure how Hunter would react since I hadn't told him yet.

I needn't have worried. Eir laughed long and hard, properly this time, before hanging up. Music to my ears, as they say.

I finally got to bed. Fifth Avenue would find me well-rested and ready for a massive outlay of hard-earned cash. Well, plastic. We certainly suffered in the getting and keeping of that money. We earned it.

"My first shopping spree. I have never forgotten it."

"But you and Hunter are rich. You could buy whatever you want."

"Hunter gets so mad if I splurge. He had a fit when he saw the credit card bill after my New York trip. He wants me to get just one thing at a time. No flashing the cash!"

"He really is paranoid."

"Well, one thing that worries him is the IRS. He says that if they become too interested in the source of our money, it'll be worse than the inquisition. And believe me, that was very bad."

"Quite. No one understands gnomes ... unless they live in Zurich."

Lin laughed long and hard. "That's a good one. How do you know about Swiss gnomes?"

"My grandfather. He used to have a few investments, and about all he ever talked about was the predators in New York, the nobs in the City of London, and the gnomes of Zurich. I asked him about the gnomes, and he told me a horrid story about these gnomes, who live in Alpine caves and sell little girls for huge amounts of money. He laughed when I declared I'd never ever go to Switzerland. It gave me nightmares."

"Did you tell your mother?"

"Yes, she told me what the term meant, but I wasn't sure until I heard her on the phone with Grandpa the next morning, yelling at him for telling me silly made-up stories."

"Naughty grandpa. After I tell you this story, I'm going to get the shopping itch again. What about it?"

"Oh, Lin, you're too generous. It's embarrassing."

"Nonsense. Every girl needs special things."

"Sounds like fun."

"Today or tomorrow. Or both."

What I really wanted was pretty underwear. In the circumstances, that would define embarrassing.

Tape 28

I walked into the first store and quickly became over-whelmed by the selection, not to mention the prices. I could afford to splurge, but this level of expense seemed absurd. I spotted the sales lady out of the corner of my eye, a bony, impeccably turned-out woman with bluish hair and a one-track mind—sell, sell, sell. She was quite a frightening woman actually, the sort one doesn't like to disappoint. Fully articulated consonants, almost British vowels, and subtle cadences of voice and expression indicated certain-ties and doubts one could hardly miss. She reminded me of the English headmistress in my boarding school in India, so I automatically toed the line, as one does.

I tried on so many outfits I could hardly keep track, nor could I make up my mind, so I turned over the final word to Mrs. McMasters. Although no one talks about little black dresses anymore, having one can certainly take Madam to a lot of places, she informed me. And you can't go wrong with a pair of slim black linen pants paired with a classic ivory silk blouse—with good cleavage potential, I noted. I timidly mentioned that I am fond of blue. Yes, blue is an excellent choice, given Madam's coloring. This went on for a couple of hours. As I looked at the bags, I wondered aloud how I could possibly carry them all. Of course, they could be delivered to Madam's hotel. I should bloody well think so after spending that kind of bundle. Mrs. McMaster even cracked a smile when she wished me a *very* good morning.

Next stop, shoes and a helpful young assistant who was enthusiastic rather than intimidating. I love shoes and can never have enough, although I came pretty close that morning. They sold bags too, which saved me another stop. The girl told me where to find a place to buy luggage nearby.

I found a case that would accommodate my purchases, shoved my shoes and bags in it, and marched off in search of lunch.

I ate in a chi-chi bistro near the hotel. There was some awkwardness in seating due to the place not being set up for suitcases, but they managed to put mine against a wall where I could keep an eye on it. I ate a delightful lemon and thyme risotto and drank prosecco. I discovered all those lovely shopping bags waiting for me in my room, the handles of each secured with a blue organdie bow. I'd pack everything in the new luggage and leave those bags for the staff. None of them could afford to shop at that emporium, but they'd love swanking around with the bags.

A short nap, pack up, and leave.

"I've never been on a real spree like that. It sounds marvelously fun."

"Well, I told you I'd get the shopping itch. You could do with some nice things. We'll go to the mall this afternoon."

"But I never go anywhere. I've got all I need."

"Nonsense. We go to nice places quite often. And on holidays. You will come with us sometimes."

"That sounds wonderful."

It did sound incredibly exciting. I hadn't ever been anywhere special. My tummy fluttered with excitement. Holiday? Abroad, maybe? The Kennedy Center? I'd looked at tickets for the ballet, but they were exorbitant, out of reach for the likes of me.

"Do you like ballet? I love it, but Hunter can't stand it, so I'd love someone to go with me."

Was she a mind reader?

30

"I was so happy to see them. Especially Reema. She's not much like my own little Egyptian girl, but they have something in common. Brains, for example. You have brains, and you are quiet, think before you speak. That's why I like you."

Her words warmed me. I ate my meals with the family and gradually got to know their foibles. I hoped I'd get to know their children when they came home for the holidays.

"I told Hunter why you didn't want to model the little things we bought yesterday, by the way."

"Really? What did he say?"

"Just that you were too modest. Well, they'll just be a nice surprise." She arranged herself and shut her eyes.

Lin, you're so embarrassing.

Tape 29

When the taxi dropped me off at Eir's house, it double-parked by a large passenger van, which looked as if it could seat eight or ten. I'd never driven anything that large, but I'd manage. I always manage. Five girls and their bags, Eir for a short time, and my luggage. About right.

Bjorn opened the door and looked at my luggage. "Is it just you, Madam?" he said.

"Yes, Bjorn, I'm afraid I've been shopping."

"Indeed, Madam."

"I will be leaving this evening, so you may as well leave my cases by the front door."

"Certainly, Madam. The doctor is in her study. You know where it is, I believe."

Indeed, I did.

Eir appeared behind him. "Let's have a cocktail," she said. "It's early enough; it won't affect our little performance. Or doesn't it go to your head?"

"Drinking has never affected me. It gives me pleasure in some obscure way but doesn't go to my head. It's more taste and sensation than anything else. Sort of like sex."

She laughed and asked Bjorn, whose face had momentarily registered a marvelous confusion of shock and titillation, to bring champagne cocktails before leading me through to the living room.

We spent a few hours going over the plan. Eir said she had enough spray for the brothel's owner. We'd have to deal with any bouncers she employed using other means. There would definitely be one man at the entrance, so the element of surprise would allow her to deliver a knock-out shot. She'd have a second one ready, but we'd have to play it by ear.

"I'll have my pockets full between the spray and the hypodermics. Have you ever used a gun? The one I have is not large or heavy, but it does the job," she said.

"I haven't used one for years, and it was a pretty old one even then."

She went to a desk drawer and brought out a small revolver. "It's loaded." She showed me around the little weapon. It was pretty simple and not heavy. "This is only a last resort. We don't want too much attention drawn to the facility."

We enjoyed a pleasant few hours before setting out. I drove to get the feel of the van, and Eir navigated. I did quite well, only side-swiping a parked Hummer that protruded unnecessarily into my lane. An hour or so later found us in Queens, trundling along a road lined with white clapboard houses penned in by chain-link fences. I didn't want to draw unwelcome attention, so I kept to the posted 25 mph. These tired little houses seemed to stretch out to the horizon.

"Nearly there," she said.

"Here? Funny place for a brothel. Don't the neighbors complain?"

"She only allows three visitors each evening. Besides, it's down a secluded lane, just up here on the right. It used to be a horseback riding school. Violet, the manager, lives in the house, and the business operates in the stables."

I laughed. Couldn't help it. She got the joke and laughed, too.

"Don't crack that joke in front of Violet," Eir said. "She takes her profession very seriously."

"Profession? You must be kidding."

"No, I'm not, and she has no sense of humor, even though she's a Brit. Turn off by that sign."

The sign read, "Violet's Herbs and Lavender." The rutted dirt road made for an uncomfortable drive. Maybe that was part of the pretense that this was a rural undertaking.

"Doesn't anyone drive in here looking for herbs?" I asked.

"Oh, yes, during the day, she gets quite a few people. She has a good little side business with her plants. One of the bouncers is her gardener."

The road forked to the right, up to the house, and to the left, out to the stables. The moonlight was sufficient for me to note greenhouses near the path and gardens melting back into the night. A parking lot lay off to one side of the entrance, where a bulky man sat, watching us. I parked, and we got out and strode toward him.

"Good evening, Stuart," Eir called out in an uncharacteristically chirpy tone. "My friend and I wanted a quick word with Violet."

"She didn't tell me," he groused, getting to his feet.

"I know. I'm sorry, I forgot to call."

"I'll ask," he growled, unwisely turning his back. Eir jabbed him in the backside, which afforded me a moment of childish glee, and dragged him around the side of the building.

We went inside. Eir knocked on the first door to the right.

"Come!"

The woman looked surprised to see us. "Well, if it ain't the good doctor!" she exclaimed. She sat behind a polished oak desk like a gaudy toad, her bulk decked out in green velvet, bangles, and vivid, cakey makeup. "Why didn't you give me a bell? I would have baked a cake." She laughed, a process that set bangles jingling and flesh rolls jiggling. "And who's yer friend?"

"I'm sorry to barge in like this, but I have some urgent business. This is my new partner, Lin."

"Urgent? There's trouble?"

"Yes, I'm afraid so. The Syrian connection has been shut down, at least for the time being. Long story. We're going to have to do some recruiting elsewhere."

"'Ell's bells, I've got a very particular clientele, you know. Very particular tastes, they 'ave. Lin, was that yer name? Any ideas?"

"Well, I have some connections in Malaysia. Some of those girls should fit the bill. I've got four or five ready to go." I was quite proud of myself for that spur-of-the-moment whopper.

"Ah, yes, that might work. Oh, 'allo George!"

We hadn't heard the door open and turned around to see a fairly short fellow, easy to take out—except for the gun he pointed at us. It was no lady's gun like the one I carried, but a serious-looking, heavy number. I turned back to Violet to find her also pointing a gun at us.

"You don't think I run a place like this without security, do you?" she said, roaring with laughter and setting off all the jingling and jiggling again. She pointed to her computer. "I saw you take out poor Stuart. And a handy little button under this 'ere desk summons help. I'd've thought you smarter than that, doctor. And just who is this Lin?"

Eir looked at me and raised her eyebrows. She had the spray, so I guessed George was all mine. I whipped around and bent double, going for George's knees. He got off a shot but aimed at where I was when he pulled the trigger. I got the gun away from him and threw it into a corner. I grasped his head and twisted until I heard the telltale snap.

Eir sat still, calmly watching the proceedings as if it were a tennis match. Violet's head lay on her desk, the blotter well placed to absorb her drool.

"Well, that's messy," she said. "And I've been shot."

"What? Let me see."

"Never mind. When we get home, I'll attend to it."

Liquid, the color of young ivory, oozed under her cuff. "No, you are really hurt. We have to go."

"Not before getting the girls. Such a waste, otherwise. I'll leave you to find them. Remember to tell the johns you're from the vice squad. They'll scatter like cockroaches. I need to meditate."

She sat there as if nothing had happened, but it must have hurt. I hated to leave her like that, but I had to get those girls, and fast. I took the extra hypodermic out of her pocket and slipped it into mine.

I went down to the end of the aisle. Each former stall was fully enclosed, with a solid wood door and a small, stained-glass window. I listened at each door until I heard voices behind one. I turned the handle slowly and peeked in. Reema. She saw me over the man's shoulder. He appeared to be asleep. I put my finger to my lips and closed the door behind me.

"Rise and shine!" I said, punching him on the shoulder.

Groggy at first, he looked around, but shot up when he saw me. "Who the fuck are you?"

"Fucking vice squad," I said. "We can do this the easy way or the hard way." I love a manly cliché. "You can leave quickly and quietly while I take care of business here, or I'll have to take you both in and call your wife to explain the situation."

He dressed and left in sixty seconds flat.

"No questions, Reema. Where are the others?"

I sent Reema to get Iman, Laila, and Muna first, as they had the evening off. Zara's client fled, clutching most of his wardrobe rather than wearing it. Nazli's fellow turned belligerent. I remembered the revolver in my pocket and drew it. He raised his hands, making him quite vulnerable since he was naked. I lowered my gun to crotch level.

"Okay, okay, I'm going," he cried, dancing around as he twisted this way and that to angle his private parts away from my aim.

"I'll raise my gun a little if you get dressed now," I said.

I listened to make sure he got all the way out. I didn't hear a car start, though. I might have to deal with him again.

"Is there anything special you girls need to take with you?" I asked. "We have very little time. We can buy toiletries on the way."

They shook their heads, only wanting to get out.

"Reema, that caftan is too conspicuous." She changed into pants and a shirt she had on a shelf by the bed.

The two not entertaining were wearing civvies, and Nazli and Zara had pulled on jeans and tees. "You'd better get warm jackets if you have any." The three darted off and got back in minutes. We hurried down the corridor to Violet's office. Eir wasn't there. Violet still drooled over her damp blotter, her double chin folded under a slack mouth—absolutely revolting.

"Wait here and keep quiet," I whispered to the girls.

I crept toward the door. I heard a little scuffling sound. I poked my head out to find Eir, held in a headlock by Nazli's john. He smirked at me.

"Well, what're you going to do now, lady? You're no cop. What's going on? I'll break her neck if I have to."

Under normal circumstances, there was no way he could have overcome Eir. That's when I realized how badly hurt she must have been.

"All right. What do you want?"

"I want to know who you are. And don't tell me vice. Some of my best friends are in vice. I'd have noticed you."

"You're a cop, huh?"

"Never mind that. Tell me who you are, or your friend gets it."

He shouldn't have watched so many gangster movies. I edged a little closer. I wanted to make him loosen his grasp on Eir's neck. I'd done it before, and it always worked like a charm, given my super strong grip. He'd forget everything once I grabbed his nuts, which I did with one lightning leap. He screamed and collapsed. I put him out of his misery with the second hypodermic. Eir looked shaky but straightened her back.

"You found them?"

"Yes. We'll have to spend the night. I can't leave you in this condition. Does Violet know where you live?"

"No, certainly not."

"Come on out, girls," I called. Nazli had tears running down her face. Not much more than a child; she'd been through too much. Reema put her arm around her and helped her into the van.

I remembered how to find my way back to Eir's place. I asked Bjorn to get rooms sorted out for the girls, telling him they'd help make the beds. He assured me the bathrooms contained plenty of toiletries.

Eir and I went through to her office. She took a vial from a small refrigerator concealed under her desk and went over to a cabinet to retrieve a hypodermic.

"This will numb my arm sufficiently to get the bullet out. You might have to help me bandage afterward."

"Of course."

She gave herself the shot and opened a sealed packet containing a scalpel and another with what looked like large tweezers and placed them into a metal dish. Next came disinfectant pads. "I've never had an infection of any kind, but we are not so strong anymore—look how we even feel pain now. It doesn't hurt to take precautions." Her voice sounded weak. "Would you mind taking this over to the table? Oh, and this bandage."

She sat at the table and took off her shirt. The wound in her upper arm looked jagged and angry. She calmly opened about an inch through the bullet hole with the scalpel, took up the tweezers, and started probing. Even my strong stomach turned rebellious.

"Ah, there it is," she said, drawing out the bullet and dropping it into the dish with a loud ping. "Oh, damn, I forgot the butterfly strips and big bandages. Over there, top drawer to the right of the fridge."

I found what she needed, unwrapped them, and handed them over as she progressed. After wiping off the incision with the disinfectant pads, she closed it off and covered the whole thing with a large adhesive bandage. She leaned back in her chair, clearly exhausted.

"You must go to bed and get some rest," I said.

"Yes, but first, a shot for Loki. The last thing we need is for him to regain his strength." She got up and prepared the hypodermic. "Why don't you come downstairs with me?"

We walked slowly to the elevator. I didn't want to see Loki, but if he wasn't as weak as she hoped, he could easily take advantage of Eir after her ordeal. The door she led me to had a small, covered window like a jail cell, which I guess it was.

"He's in there, dozing in a wheelchair," I told her.

We went in, and he looked up at her, confused.

"I think we've met. What was your name again?" Loki's voice sounded childlike.

"I'm your nurse, Daphne," she said. "I've got your shot. It makes you feel better."

He began to cry. "I don't like needles," he said.

"There, there. I know how to do it so it doesn't hurt."

He quietened down. Luckily, he was wearing a short-sleeved shirt, so there was no hassle with rolling up sleeves and so on. He soon nodded off to sleep.

We locked him up again and went upstairs. Despite Loki's evil ways, the change in him saddened me.

"Will he always be like that?" I asked.

"No, it's the combination of drugs I'm giving him until he is too aged to be dangerous. He'll lose a lot of that mental fog, so I'll have to watch he doesn't get other people to do his dirty work. But he'll never be able to do much physically."

"How long will he last?"

"Hard to say. Too long, I suspect. He's not fully immortal, but probably not far off. Well, I'm off to my room. I need to meditate to hasten healing. You'll attend to the girls? Maybe I'll see you at breakfast."

I heard Reema and Nazli chatting nearby and looked in on them. They had a big bed to share and an adjoining bathroom. A tray with the remains of supper sat on a table by the window. Nazli seemed more relaxed, but Reema looked pale and tired.

"Get some rest, girls. Dr. Eyre is fine. We leave for Virginia in the morning. I'll tell you everything on the way." Not everything, but enough.

The other girls were in two other rooms nearby and were already half asleep. I was starving and went in search of the kitchen, where I found Bjorn clearing up. He heated me some soup and French bread, which I ate daintily since he sat watching me before heading off to bed.

31

"It's always nice to come home after a trip," Lin declared.

"I guess so, although I've never been anywhere much."

"Where would you like to go?"

"Italy. I've always wanted to go to Italy."

"Very well. When we've finished enough tales for a whole book, we will all go to Italy once you get it in shape. You need a break."

"Wow—thanks so much!" was all I could manage.

It took a supreme effort to pay attention to what she was telling me. Fortunately, the recorder was going strong, despite its age.

Italy!

Tape 30

I collected the girls from their rooms the next morning and ushered them down to the dining room. They seemed in better spirits, except for Reema, who still looked sad. The girls enjoyed the food—eggs, good bread with Danish butter, and Swiss black cherry jam. Everyone but Reema ate ravenously and exclaimed over enjoying good coffee again. We'd been sitting there for about a half-hour when Eir joined us. She looked rested and healthy.

"How are you?" I asked.

"Oh, much better, thank you, almost healed."

"How is that possible?" asked Reema.

"Dr. Eyre has some remarkable medication that aids healing," I said hurriedly. We couldn't reveal our heritage to these girls. I wasn't sure how much Bjorn knew, although Eir must have explained a lot. If he had the Scandinavian background his name and slight accent suggested, he'd know the old tales.

"I brought you a map to study. What time are you leaving?" asked Eir.

"I thought around ten to avoid rush hour," I said. "The trip will take about five hours. We'll stop at a strip mall on the way, buy some necessities, and have lunch. Maybe the girls can get some new clothes, too."

They all looked pleased. Their clothes looked as if they'd been bought at Goodwill. I should have remembered to buy a little something for my own kids. Perhaps I'd find something nice for them, too.

"Excuse me, ladies, I need to study the map. Carry on eating. We've got quite a long way to go before stopping." I memorized our route in about ten minutes.

Breakfast over; it was time to say goodbye.

Eir kissed each girl on both cheeks and wished them well. I was still shocked by how well everything had worked out. Eir had behaved abominably with the sex trafficking business. Had the fear of being poor and inconsequential overcome her scruples? Or had she never been empathetic in the first place, merely playing a role? It's one thing to obey the ethos of your own civilization but quite another to transport it to another world that must have seemed crass and corrupt in comparison.

Look how much I've changed.

She drew me aside, speaking quietly.

"I know you must have been wondering why my life evolved the way it did, how I went to the dark side, how suddenly I came out. It's all about fellowship and fear of loneliness, my dear, all about finding someone who knows who I was and who I can be, someone I don't have to hide myself from."

"You'll join us, then?"

"Yes, I will. It will take some time to settle everything, but I will be there. Phone me when you get home safely." She hugged me tight.

I turned to Bjorn. "Thank you for your assistance, Bjorn." I reached up to give him a smacking kiss on the cheek. He stood even stiffer and blushed like a virgin bride.

"Thank you, Madam," he said, his voice unsteady.

I noticed Eir trying not to laugh. I kept a straight face.

We got settled in the van, with Bjorn's help, and set off. Once I got clear of the city, I began to tell the girls what I'd been up to, why I couldn't rescue them in time, and how I came to find them. I didn't want to tell them Eir's part in their plight, though, only that she was an old friend who came to my aid. I did some elaborate embroidery of the facts. Reema gave me a few strange looks—she was more intelligent and less gullible than the others, but she voiced no doubts.

Lunch was fun, involving hamburgers, fries, and coke—a real American meal. They enjoyed Target, too. I told them to each take a cart and buy underwear, toiletries, and a couple of outfits, and I'd meet them by the cash registers. I found a video game for Sven and a fun top with glitter for Margareta. They ended up with enough bags to fill the aisles of the van. Reema just got one simple long-sleeved top, a pair of jeans, and a few other necessary items. I suspected she had been used to much better than this.

She was last in line. I whispered, "I'll take you to a better place for some clothes when we get home."

"Oh no, please, it's quite all right. I have all I need," she said, polite as ever.

I just let them chatter for the rest of the way. I'd done enough talking.

Finally, we pulled up outside my house. I looked at my watch. Four o'clock, the kids must be home. Hunter opened the door as we were all getting ourselves and our packages out. The children ran out to hug me. Sven nearly knocked me off my feet. Then he got shy with such a large audience, hanging his head and shuffling his feet while the girls tried to make his acquaintance.

Hunter just stood there, arms crossed. "What is this?"

"Mission accomplished. These are the young ladies I found at the Goodalls'."

I introduced them all, and Hunter crushed their hands with great solemnity. "Welcome," he said to each. He has a good heart, you know.

We all went inside. Dora came to see what all the fuss was about.

"These young ladies will be staying with us for a few days," I told her. "Would you please make coffee for everyone? And start thinking about dinner."

She frowned and disappeared.

I quickly took my cases upstairs to our room. The bed looked mussed. The girls would have to sleep in the basement on air mattresses, which, fortunately, we had in abundance for children's sleepovers. We had plenty of sleeping bags, too. That was when the children were young enough that their friends wouldn't recognize our strangeness.

When I got back down, the welcome smell of brewing coffee made me feel I was truly home again. The girls all sat in the living room while Hunter held court. He can be very charming, as you know.

My kids had disappeared, probably to their lairs. I found the bag with their gifts and took them the half-flight down to their bedrooms. They were pleased, and I received more heavenly kisses and hugs. I'd missed them in what little time I'd had to think about it.

Time to call Joe. He was there in fifteen minutes. He interviewed the girls, and I translated. I persuaded him to postpone calling Immigration until morning.

"They need a good night's sleep," I told him. "Stay for dinner. It's probably only going to be pizza, but we'd love to have you."

He looked doubtful. "I should call the authorities," he said. "I could get fired for this."

He paused and looked at the girls, fixing on Nazli's face. "She's just a kid," he said, his voice sad and low. "Very well, I'll hold off."

We had a merry time, if exhausting for me, given all the translating I had to do and the fact that my Arabic was so out of date, I had to double-check quite a few words and phrases, not to mention contend with their Syrian dialect. Even Reema cheered up. The girls had been wary of Joe because he was a policeman, but he seemed to have won them over with his relaxed manner.

The girls started yawning by ten. Joe, ever tactful, took his leave.

"You are something else," he said. "You know, you'll have to tell us exactly how all this went down."

"I know. I'm just worried about what they'll do with the girls."

"I don't have much influence, but I'll do what I can. Good night, everyone!"

It was time for bed. Dora helped me find pillows and blankets, and everyone settled down. I went up to bed, and Hunter soon joined me. My news about Eir and Loki could wait.

The next morning, we cooked a couple of cartons of eggs. The kids ate their usual cereal before scooting off to catch the school bus. The girls took turns showering, and all put on new clothes.

"Let's go for a walk," I said. They didn't seem keen.

"Come, I will walk with you. We can go to the park," said Hunter, a proposition received more warmly than mine.

"I'd better stay here. I'm sure we'll get some visitors," I told him. "Don't be too long."

The doorbell rang at around ten. Joe and two stern, dark-suited fellows stood there. I invited them in. They introduced themselves.

"Where are the girls?" asked the older one.

"My husband took them for a walk. They haven't been out much. They've been prisoners, essentially."

He questioned me for some time. I was glad the girls were absent for this, especially as Reema seemed to have a working knowledge of English.

After a while, Joe said, "These officers have read my reports, and I guess it all adds up. Is there anything you want to add?"

"Only that they were abducted by the same group that abducted the girls I came back with a few weeks ago. As you know, there was some involvement on the part of U.S. Air Force personnel—civilian, I believe, but nevertheless an embarrassment. And that an American was responsible for picking out the girls and sending them on this journey to hell."

"Your point?" asked the only officer who seemed to talk.

"Only that I trust you will grant them refugee status, given the potential international attention this may garner. It's not as if they can go home. They are no longer virgins, you see. Not marriageable. Ruined in their cultural milieu."

"Miller?"

"Environment, customs."

"I see. No promises, but we will certainly give the matter all due consideration. Where are they, anyway?"

"I think I hear them coming." That was a mistake, as while I could hear them, no human could. I saw the guy cock his head and frown. When they arrived five minutes later, I caught how the two suits exchanged looks, clearly suspicious.

Fifteen minutes later, the girls, subdued now, had gathered their new possessions, said goodbye, and been herded into the kind of long, sinister black SUV those people drive.

Mission accomplished indeed, hopefully with a happy ending.

"You are such a soldier, Lin. Superwoman!"

"Thank you. Yes, I did quite nicely."

She'd killed someone, though. Snapped that guard's neck. And he was one of her luckier victims. She'd shown empathy for these girls and others in need but none for the bad guys. She had her own ideas about justice.

I wondered again if Hunter was also that ruthless—my sweet Hunter. It was hard to envision, but they saw things differently, so who knew?

32

"Dirty cops deserve what they get. And this one threat-ened our Sven."

"Oh, my God—really?"

"Yes, for sure. The silly man thought he could win."

Yes, I could see how that would set her off. Hunter, too. What new ghastly revelations were coming my way?

Tape 31

I enjoyed an uneventful few weeks playing mother and housewife but was beginning to get restless. If only Eir could get herself sorted out and move down to Salton. Or at least to Washington. She obviously preferred city life. The agency hadn't received any other cases. The plight of the Syrian girls had not yet hit the media, so I couldn't drop hints about my involvement and maybe would never be allowed to. I hadn't heard anything about the girls, either. I was particularly eager to hear Reema's news and hoped she would be able to continue her education.

All this made me edgy. Hunter said I reminded him of Aetna.

One day, while the children were at school, we had a particularly acrimonious lunch. I had made some egg salad as Dora had the day off. Hunter pouted and said he wanted ham salad. I didn't have any ham. He said to get some. I said he should go get some if he wanted it that badly. He sulked some more before devouring five egg salad sandwiches, then stomping upstairs to take a nap.

About fifteen minutes later, the bell rang.

"Well, hello there. I do believe it's one of our good Samaritans." The cop from the brothel in Queens, wearing a wide grin that rivaled that of a shark. He held Sven by the scruff of his neck.

"What are you doing with my son? What do you want?" My stomach contracted with fear. Sven's mouth was clamped tight, his eyes wide as they looked into mine. Brave boy.

"Keep quiet if you want your son to live. Let me in." He pulled a gun and held it close to his body so it couldn't be seen from the street.

That filled me with the kind of hot anger he couldn't imagine. I moved aside and motioned him in. I hoped my yelling had alerted Hunter.

"I've been asking around—lots of rumors about the girls. Your name came up."

"So?"

"You did some damage. I'd like to return the favor. Let's discuss it upstairs. Cooperate, or I'll just wait for the little girl to come home. Where is your husband?"

"Out shopping for a new car. Let my son go!" I spoke as loudly as I could without seeming too obvious.

"Excellent. Let's go upstairs now."

"Why?"

"Three guesses."

I plodded upstairs with the gun to my back.

"Take me to your son's bedroom."

He threw Sven on the bed. "If you move an inch, I'll kill your Mom." He pushed me out and slammed the door behind him. "Now, your bedroom."

"How about the guest room? It's very comfortable."

"You really are some kind of stupid."

I threw open the door to our room with great panache, expecting some kind of grand finale. No Hunter.

"On the bed. I want to enjoy myself first. Show you how much you didn't manage to ruin my manhood."

I laid down on the bed.

"I don't even know your name."

He laughed. "You can call me Dick. I am going to put the gun over on the dresser. If you try any funny business, the children will suffer. Really suffer."

I smelled Hunter, so he was around, probably in the bathroom. Dick threw himself on top of me, tearing at my clothes. I stayed quite still, watching Hunter creep up behind him for the smackdown. Hunter grabbed Dick's arms and threw him against the wall.

Only slightly stunned, the cop made an ill-advised lunge for the gun. I got there first and hit him over the head with it, failing to do much damage because Hunter had begun to shake him, giving full vent to his rage.

"So, you sniveling little coward, you want to rape my wife, and you want to hurt my children, do you?"

The cop, clutching his head, sobbed out, "She interfered with an investigation. She hurt me badly. I'm a cop. I'll have you both arrested."

"You are a dirty cop." Hunter grinned as he said it, no doubt identifying with his TV heroes.

"I'm going to call for backup." The cop reached for his cell phone. Hunter snatched it, flung it to the floor, and stomped on it. The guy went berserk, rushing Hunter, who picked him up and shook him again until he lost consciousness.

"He has to go," Hunter said. "He will talk."

"I know. Is he still alive?"

"Just."

"You'd better repair the drywall before Margareta gets home."

"We had better get rid of him before she gets home." For once, he had a good point.

"We've got a few hours. Let's lock him in the basement until we've made a plan. Maybe Eir can make him forget."

"Is Sven all right?" Hunter asked.

"Yes, the bastard shut him in his room and told him he'd kill me if he came out."

Hunter swelled with fury, picked up Dick, and threw him down again.

I went to Sven's room, where I found the little chap hugging his knees. I sat down beside him and held him tight.

"You are a very brave boy, Sven."

"Where's the bad man?"

"He will never hurt anyone again. Mama and Papa have some things to take care of. You are going to have to stay in your room for a few hours. I'll bring you some milk and cookies. You must never tell anyone, even Margareta, what happened today. Understand?"

"Yes, Mama. I'm sure glad he didn't kill you."

"I'm very hard to kill." I hugged him again and went back to our bedroom.

Getting a potion from Eir would take some time, but I hesitated to simply snuff the man, even though he knew all along about the circumstances of those Syrian girls and used them anyway. And he threatened my son.

As far as Hunter was concerned, Dick had stepped way, way over the mark when he threatened our children, and he deserved what he got. Maybe he was right. A dirty cop, a rapist, a sex trafficker, perhaps a killer. I found him sitting on the bed, staring at the man.

Dick looked inert. Even his chest wasn't moving up and down.

I edged closer, half expecting a trick. His eyes were open and glazed. Brain damage? I placed my hand on his chest. No movement. No pulse, either.

"Hunter, he's dead."

"Oh, well. That is that, then."

"No, it isn't that simple. We've got to get rid of him. Bring your SUV into the garage."

Hunter went downstairs and got back quickly. I was still changing out of my torn clothes.

"You closed the garage door, didn't you?"

"Uh, no. I forgot."

Hunter sometimes makes me wish alcohol could make me tipsy. "Do you want the neighbors to see us loading him?"

He went back down, then appeared again, slung the cop over his shoulder, and started downstairs. The doorbell rang. He wheeled around to answer it.

"Get him into the garage right now," I said in a whisper somewhere between a hiss and a squeal.

After Hunter and his burden disappeared, I answered the door.

"Would you like to buy Girl Scout cookies?" asked a little girl, all dressed up for the occasion, her beaming mom waiting at the end of the path.

My situation had made me a little irritable. "Goodness me, why aren't you in school today?"

"Oh, I go to St. Helen's. It's private, so we get different days off from the public school kids."

"Well, you can put my name down, but I'm very busy right now. Since my children are public school kids, this is my time to get things done."

"We're supposed to get the money."

"It'll have to wait. Or maybe I can just do without the cookies."

"But I want to win for best sales."

I was about to shut the door in her face when it occurred to me it wouldn't be a good idea to thwart the child, an event especially memorable to one so keen. Her mom would remember and hold a grudge.

"How much for two boxes?"

"Seven dollars."

I went and got my purse and gave her ten, telling her to choose what kind of cookie and keep the change. She beamed and thanked me. I waved with a happy smile to the mother and shut the door.

When I got to the car, I found the cop—I couldn't bring myself to call him Dick—lying in the rear, uncovered. I didn't express my feelings, as this was no time to start a fight.

"I'll be back."

I found an old blanket in the hall closet, Hunter's bowling bag, and a few other children's sports items to strew around the back.

"We don't want people to see him asleep in the back there, do we, my love?"

"No, no, quite right."

"Just wait while I take Sven his snack. He's had a shock."

"Okay, but hurry."

I was soon back. "I'll drive. I know just the spot." I thought of the bluff where I saw Jerry throw poor Yasmine into the river. Her body still hadn't been found, or at least it hadn't been reported.

It would take a while, but we should make it home before Margareta. Hunter still had to work on the drywall repair, too. He'd slammed the cop into the wall hard enough to dent it, certainly hard enough to kill him outright.

I usually pushed the speed limit but didn't want to get a ticket, so it took even longer than I remembered. After well over an hour, we finally pulled into the parking area, where an elderly couple sat on a blanket having a picnic. They didn't look as if they'd be able to get up off the blanket under their own steam, but I supposed they must have thought of that.

"Shall I get rid of them?" Hunter looked eager to make an impression—most unwise, given the delicacy of the situation and his general cluelessness.

"I've got a better idea. See that little grassy area just behind them? Let's settle down there."

We sat down, and I drew Hunter to me. We canoodled and petted, really getting into it hot and heavy. I made lots of good noises. He forgot about the old couple, but I kept an eye on them over whichever of Hunter's shoulders the moment dictated. Their muttered disapproval and backward glances were hilarious. After about fifteen minutes, they heaved themselves off the blanket and packed up.

"Old enough to know better. Disgusting behavior!" The old woman shouted at us as they staggered back to their car, laden with the blanket, bags, and a hamper. As soon as they'd driven off, I pushed Hunter away and sat up.

"What is the matter? What did I do?" he said, looking as if he were about to weep.

"Nothing, we just needed to make them leave. Get the body out."

Still sulking, Hunter opened the back of the SUV and pulled out the cop.

"Now what?"

"Over here." I guided him over to where the other body had gone over. "Throw him over."

I waited for the splash. Nothing. I crawled on my stomach to the edge. Chicken wire festooned the cliffside, probably in an attempt to halt erosion. The body rested on a piece that had come loose as if on a hammock, one arm draped over his head like a swooning damsel.

"Quick, find a long stick. He's all caught up."

Hunter tore a branch off a sapling. I pushed and shoved and almost got him once or twice, but he kept swinging back.

"Get another stick." The denuded sapling bowed in defeat with the force of Hunter's yanking. "Now, lie down like me and help me push him over." A couple more heaves, and he toppled into the river with an impressive splash, fast disappearing from view. I'd replaced his gun in the holster, so between that and his steel-capped boots, I hoped he'd stay weighed down, at least for the immediate future. If he were found with rocks in his pockets, that would have been a dead giveaway. As it were.

"Come on, we have to get home. This has taken too long."

We arrived home about ten minutes before Margareta.

"Where were you? You were gone a long time," asked Sven after I called him downstairs. He still looked shaky.

"We had to take the bad man to the police. Now, remember, not a word to anyone."

"I remember. What's all that banging?"

"Oh, Papa knocked a chair against our bedroom wall. He's repairing it."

"Was he in a temper?" Sven looked concerned, as his father's tempers could be frightening, although he's never laid hands on any of us.

"No, sweetheart, everything's okay."

"Can I have some cookies?" The back door opened and slammed. "Here's my sister. Can she have cookies, too?"

I settled them in the kitchen, where they told me about their day to the accompaniment of much hammering and cursing overhead.

"Why did Sven leave early? I looked everywhere, then Miss Worger said his uncle picked him up. I thought you said we don't have any uncles."

"It wasn't an uncle. I'll be speaking to Miss Worger. You must never, ever, go with someone you don't know, no matter what he or she tells you," I said.

"Oh, Sven, was he a bad man?"

Sven looked into his milk. "Yes," he said in a small voice. But Mama and Papa saved me. The bad man has gone away."

Margareta looked dumbstruck for a change.

"We are not going to talk about this anymore. You are not to tell your friends or anyone else. Understood?"

"Yes," they chorused, looking confused and anxious.

"Not even the police?" asked Sven.

"Not even. Not a word!" They nodded solemnly.

"Sven got detention again," Margareta announced.

I sighed. "What did you do this time, Sven?"

"Well, Tommy Baker said I was a clumsy oaf and dumber than a rock, too. I shoved him into the bushes. Then he said you had a bunch of plastic surgery because his mother said no one has a face that perfect without help. I couldn't let him get away with that, could I?"

"Oh, Sven, it's nice of you to stick up for me, but you can't go around shoving people who say things you don't like. Just ignore them. He's just a silly boy who likes bullying people. Anyway, I've never had plastic surgery. I don't need to." I couldn't help smiling. Tommy meant it as an insult, but I saw it in a different light. "What did you do to him next?"

"I opened my PBJ and smacked each piece of bread into the side of his face and rubbed it in his hair. He looked like an idiot, and all the other kids laughed at him. Then he cried and went running to Mrs. Roberts. What a sissy."

"Did you tell her what happened?"

"Yes, but she said the same sort of thing you always say. And gave me detention for tomorrow."

I drew him close and kissed his forehead. "Well, control yourself next time. It's best for you that way. Detention's no fun, is it?"

He shook his head.

Margareta smirked. She is far more subtle than her brother. She went on to tell me the story of her worst enemy in the class, Maurine, who claimed loudly and often to be prettier than her, resulting in a fairly even political divide. The girl took violin lessons immediately after school was out. When one of Margareta's friends asked to see her violin, she opened the case and let out a shriek to shame the banshees when a traumatized baby garter snake slithered out and made its break for freedom. Of course, all the other girls shrieked too, and probably some of the boys. Not Margareta, though. Maureen accused her of doing it, and my darling daughter replied she wouldn't ever touch a snake, let alone do such a wicked thing. I can imagine her gazing up at her teachers, beautiful blue eyes wide and innocent. When I asked her if she did it, she just laughed. "Such fun!" was all she said. I simply warned her that even garter snakes can bite and cause bad infections. I mean, what can you do? Girls will be girls.

I sometimes wish our normality could be less turbulent, but how can even the mortal children of gods be anything but off the wall in human terms?

So Hunter could be violent, too. I knew it must be a possibility. But the cop threatened his children and saw him trying to rape his wife. Fair enough. He was quite the hero. I'd enjoy a little fantasy that night about Hunter rescuing me. Just the thought of it gave me shivers.

33

I t seemed to me that the main story was over. Girls all rescued, trafficking ring exposed, dirty cop dead. But Lin had more to say.

"Not long after we got rid of the cop, another case came along. This one proved easy and put us on the map, which is why I want to get it down. The business came along steadily after the papers got hold of it. And I was good, you know. I earned my success."

She was a little puffed up that morning. She said how good she was several times in one way or another, and I really didn't need to hear it again.

My novel still wasn't going anywhere. The beginning was okay, although hardly riveting. I had no idea how to proceed, though. A local murder my protagonist gets blamed for? That's been done. Several times. A hot love affair? That always goes down well. I was getting some experience to base my story on, after all. A big, overpowering lover with all kinds of interesting ideas and abilities. My fellow MFA students would turn their noses up, but I really didn't care anymore. A pen name might be wise for when I eventually publish Lin's stories, too. I've Auntie to consider, after all.

Food for thought.

On the other hand, after I'd typed up the notes from our sessions, I was quite happy with the way I managed to arrange the stories into a fluent narrative. Did that mean I was good? Perhaps ghostwriting was my strength.

Lin and Hunter seemed distracted. They were friendly but obviously had something on their minds. Lin's sessions had become intermittent, and Hunter hadn't visited for nearly a week. Was he tired of me? I hoped he didn't suspect we were deceiving him. We didn't actually lie *per se*, only by omission.

Lin came down on a Friday, the first time since Tuesday. She just laid down and said, "Ready."

Tape 32

Lettie called. "We've got a case. Missing girl. They're coming in at ten."

"Hallelujah!"

Don't think me callous, but my nerves can only take domesticity for short periods. I'd become so lackadaisical that I was still in my pajamas at nine.

I raced upstairs to get ready before tearing out the door and into my car. I got into the office with ten minutes to spare and sat behind my desk, catching my breath while assuming the mask of a cool professional. I, of all people, out of breath? It must have been psychological. Lettie got out her notebook and pen and looked similarly poised.

To my surprise, an elderly lady opened the door and stuck her head around.

"Is this the detective agency?"

"Yes, ma'am," said Lettie. "Do come in."

She was followed by a roly-poly old man with more hair over his upper lip than around his head. She, thin as an eel, was clad in one of those shiny brown rayon travel out-fits. Wash and wear; I guess there's something to be said for convenience.

I wished them welcome and invited them to sit.

"I am Lin Thoren, and this is my assistant, Lettie Fitzgerald. How can we be of assistance?" Crisp and impressively professional. I was really getting the hang of it.

"My name is Ellen Crater, and this is my husband, Peter. It's our granddaughter Diane, you see. She's missing. Her parents work late a lot, and they're not sure if she was home Tuesday night or not. They didn't check."

Peter snorted.

"Now, now, dear, they have very responsible jobs, you know."

"One of their responsible jobs is being parents," he said, his voice a low growl. "Did you ever not check on our son at night?"

"How long, roughly, has she been missing?" I asked in a firm voice designed to keep us on track.

"Either three or four days."

"Didn't her parents call the police?"

"We had to nag her mother to do it. She ran away once two years ago, so the police are not taking it seriously. And she's twenty," Pete said.

"Does she get along with her parents?" I asked.

They looked at each other, clearly uncomfortable. Pete patted his wife's hand and took the reins again.

"It's a little awkward. They've never had much time for her, you see. They live only one street over, so she's always come to us after school. She confides in us. It seems she doesn't tell her parents anything. Says they don't listen. She had this boyfriend they didn't know about. Gary. Says they won't like him because he's not from a well-to-do family." Peter looked uncomfortable again. "Not that my son is a snob, you understand. It's just that they have high hopes for her."

"Have you met him?" I asked.

"Yes."

"Well?"

"I'm afraid we didn't care for him. He seemed very controlling."

"In what way?"

Ellen chimed in. "Well, one time, they were going out to a nice restaurant for dinner. Diane had put on a pretty green dress that came to about an inch above her knees. Gary told her to change into something more respectable, with a longer skirt. And she did!"

"And Ellen, remember that time she wanted to go out to the movies with her friend one evening," said Peter. He turned to me. "Her best friend had been away all summer, and they wanted to catch up. He insisted on dropping her off at the theater and picking her up again after. I don't think she saw much of her friends while she was going out with him."

This was like a ping-pong match, with each of them patting the other on the hand for reassurance every time they spoke.

"When did they break up?" I asked.

"A couple of weeks ago," said Peter. "She came home one night quite upset. Said she couldn't take it anymore. She wanted to have fun with her friends again. He smothered her. She told us he was so angry she'd been a bit scared of him."

"Did you tell the police about him?" I asked.

They said they had, but the young man had all kinds of alibis and had impressed the investigating officer as upstanding.

"I will start with him, I think," I said. "Would you please write down his name and address? And yours. Lettie here will explain our terms. I will begin straight away if the terms suit. Excuse me, I must attend to a few pressing matters."

I like to disappear while Lettie talks money. I knew, even in those early days, she could be pretty astute in reading our clients' reactions to what they considered reasonable fees. Whether they could afford the full whack or not, I planned to find this girl. The boyfriend sounded like a classic control freak, but I knew I must keep an open mind.

A clean-cut young man, coifed, and dressed like a Mormon missionary, opened the apartment door early that evening.

"What do you want?" His voice was sharp, his eyes equally so.

I gave him my card and explained I had been hired by Diane's grandparents to look into the girl's disappearance. He assumed a woebegone demeanor and invited me in. The narrow corridor led to a small sitting room that was spotless, cream all over, and its furniture arranged in barracks room order. No pictures, ornaments, or photos. A *Washington Post* lay folded on the coffee table.

He sat on the sofa, and I took the armchair to one side.

"I'm so worried about Diane," Gary said, leaning forward and looking earnestly into my eyes. His eyes were the flat gray of the North Atlantic in one of its quieter moments. I stared back until he gave up.

I decided to cut to the chase. "Why did you break up?"

He looked startled. "Well, she is very young for her age. I cared deeply for her—still do—but she felt she was not ready for a commitment. I guess she wanted to explore the field." Definitely a sour note.

"I'm sorry," I said, forcing myself to sound sympathetic. "This must be very upsetting for you. Do you know anywhere she might have gone just to be alone? Any particular friend she might have run to?"

"No, I don't. I'm afraid she's rather spoiled. Her parents give her money and no attention, and her grandparents treat her like a princess. She could be in Paris for all I know."

"Her credit card has not been used, nor has she drawn any money out of the bank."

"Oh dear, oh dear, that is worrying." He heaved a great sigh and let his shoulders slump. "You will let me know if you find her, won't you?" He stood, indicating the interview was over. I continued to sit.

"Where do you work?"

"At Holley's, that new department store on Madison. I run the men's department."

"You got off early today?"

"I have Mondays off because I work all weekend."

"Very nice. Were you two intimate?"

He colored. "That's none of your business."

"Oh, but it is. She's missing. Maybe she's pregnant."

"Certainly not. She didn't want to. Wanted to wait. Wasn't ready. Now, I have to get ready. I have somewhere I have to be in half an hour."

I let him guide me to the door.

"Thank you for your time. I can assure you, you'll be the first to hear if I find her."

He nodded, scowling. I went down the two flights of stairs and out to my car. I got in and looked up at the second floor. Gary stood on his balcony, arms folded, watching me. I waved. He didn't move a muscle.

Guilty. But of what, precisely? Now that he'd seen my face, I'd have to put Lettie on his tail.

Lettie found out the store closed at nine. So the next day, we camped in the store's parking lot a few minutes after eight-thirty. I'd decided to join her since I could identify him. I huddled down in the back seat when he finally emerged. He seemed to be in a hurry.

He first visited Safeway. Lettie went in to make sure we didn't lose him. She came out before him and got in the car, hugging a six-pack of Guinness.

"You really like that stuff?"

"Oh, yes, food of the gods, my old gran used to say."

"Well, what did he buy?"

"Two mac-and-cheeses from the frozen food section and a ready-made salad. Two bottles of water."

"Ah, dinner for two. But nothing fancy."

"Okay, there he goes."

We drove through the narrow winding streets of a town west of Salton that aimed for country posh—mansions on five acres—and out to a new retail strip with several vacant storefronts just before a major highway. He pulled around the back of the strip. One restaurant was open, so we parked in front of that and slid down in our seats so the car would look empty.

I got Lettie to call Joe. "Hi, it's Lettie. You know that missing girl Lin told you about yesterday? We think we might have found her." She told him where we were.

"Lettie, tell Lin not to do anything until I get there."

"Okay. I'll tell her. We're parked in front of the restaurant. There's only one."

"I'll be there as soon as I can."

I asked her to turn her phone to silent and keep watch. I got out.

"Tell Joe I've gone to assess the situation. I'll try to let you know what's going on."

I crept around the corner of the end store, which was unoc-cupied, and down the side wall to the first back entrance. I concentrated my hearing. He had to be in one of these empty stores. On to the next. Nothing. But I registered a faint scuffle from the entrance next to that, a green metal door with a frosted square window. A light flickered before what must have been a neon strip came on fully.

I sidled closer and listened.

His angry voice, her crying, "No, don't, let me go! I don't want to."

A slap and a scream.

I rushed around to Lettie. "Third store round the corner. He's hurting her. I'm going in."

I ran back. The door was locked. What next? I could try to pick the lock, but he'd hear me. I could break it down. She was crying again.

I knocked. Silence. I knocked again.

When he opened the door a crack, I slammed it into his face. He screamed and came for me, punching and stab-bing with the knife he'd been holding behind his back. One broken arm and a glorious kick in the nuts—I seemed to be doing that much too much lately—had him weeping on his knees, hardly knowing what to clutch with his one good hand.

I kicked the knife out of the way and went over to the girl, who sat on the floor, one wrist cuffed to a radiator. She stank of urine and worse.

"Diane?"

"Yes," she whispered, her tear-stained face looking at me in bewilderment. "Who are you?"

"Your grandparents hired me to find you."

"Thank God ... oh no!" Her face twisted in horror as I whipped around to see Gary, his face contorted by murderous rage, aiming a gun at her. I remembered he was righthanded, and he was using his left, but I couldn't assume he'd miss. I flung myself at the gun to deflect the shot. The red-hot bullet went through my thigh and into the wall.

It hurt like hell. I never knew hurt before Yggdrasil withered and am still not used to it. I don't think I feel it nearly as much as humans, but still, the invective I hurled his way was well-earned and made me feel a tad better.

The cops came thundering through the door, probably after hearing the shot. Joe followed on their heels. He ordered the cops to arrest Gary, which resulted in more screams as they yanked his broken arm to the back and cuffed him. I didn't enlighten them.

"Lin, I told you to wait for me." His voice sounded like the resigned reproach of someone who knows he's wasting his breath but is obliged to say it, anyway. He ended with a fake sorrowful sigh, too.

"He was slapping her around."

"He said he was going to rape me," Diane broke in. "He said I was becoming a liability." She was sobbing again now. "So I'd better enjoy my last experience, he said."

"For God's sake, get that handcuff off her," shouted Joe.

One of the cops produced a key and unlocked it.

"Interesting," I said, "a police cuff."

"Not necessarily," Joe said. "Many handcuffs on the open market these days have universal keys. Where in hell is the ambulance?"

"I just want to go home," Diane whined, rubbing her wrist.

"I'm sorry, miss, but we have to get you checked out first."

"Thanks, Joe. I'll call her grandparents to let her know she's safe."

The EMT guys came in and loaded her onto a stretcher.

"Fairfax?" I asked.

"Yup," one said.

"I think I'll go home now, Joe. Thanks again."

"I'll need your statement in the morning."

"Sure thing. Ten?"

"Nine."

"Hey, what's that liquid running down your ankle? Oh, I guess ... sorry!"

"I'm all right. Don't worry. Bye!"

I couldn't disclose that my blood wasn't like his but as clear as my lady Frigg's gazing pool. We goddesses are pure through and through. Not pure in the way that human religions like to glorify, you understand, but in our physical attributes. But damn, he thought I was peeing!

When I limped back to the car, I found Lettie leaning against the hood, arms crossed and frowning.

"Are you all right, Lin? That Joe said he'd arrest me if I didn't stay here."

"Oh, he means well. Just trying to protect you. Yes, I'm fine."

I needed to call Eir. Physician to the gods once and recently shot herself, she'd know what to do.

By the time I got home, Hunter was snoring in bed. I went into the bathroom and took off my clothes. The hole looked ugly. I washed it and wrapped a bandage around it as best I could. Sleep. But first, call Eir.

"I'm so sorry to call so late, but I've been shot."

"Oh, Lin, what happened?"

"I'll tell you another time. The bullet went through my thigh, but it didn't hit the bone. It feels very stiff and tight. Can you tell me what to do? I washed it."

"I'll be there before lunch tomorrow."

"Oh, that's too much trouble."

"No, I'll be there. I have special potions, you know."

"Yes, I remember."

The next morning, I told Hunter what had happened. He insisted I stay in bed and told Dora to bring me tea and toast with honey. Eir arrived at about eleven with her horrid gnome, Luke, in tow. Calling someone a gnome is our worst insult, by the way, even worse than Jotun.

I'd come downstairs to greet her, but she made me go back to bed, where she numbed my wound and cleaned it before binding it with a few yards of white gauze. "Good as new." We sipped the strengthening tea she brought and chatted while Hunter babysat Luke.

"Well, I'd better go downstairs and see what kind of yarns Luke has been spinning."

"Yes, Hunter is easily confused."

"I know. You should feel well enough to come down."

"Yes, as a matter of fact, I do. Let's listen in."

We tip-toed downstairs to hear the old man's quavering voice saying, "Hoenir, all I need is for someone strong to force her to make me young again. I'm so unhappy; it's so cruel."

"Oh, poor Loki, I am so very sorry." To my horror, Hunter sounded sympathetic. "On the other hand, Loki," he said, his voice hardening, "I remember what you did to us, how my entire family died, how I almost died. You deserve to die, but this way is better. You will suffer forever."

We entered the living room. Hunter stood over a cowering Loki, fists clenched and alarmingly tall.

"Catching up, boys?" I said airily as we took our seats.

We struggled through a tense afternoon of conversational starts and stops before they left for the airport. I felt much better, though.

That case was the easiest and quickest one we ever took, but it paid great dividends. We were well compensated by Diane's grateful parents and grandparents, and my role in her rescue made the papers, especially when former girlfriends came forward to relate his stalking and occasional violence. Then a *Post* reporter got a whiff of the Syrian affair—Joe?—and my part in it. He got most of it wrong, but it was good publicity. We were launched. We landed several smaller cases over the next few months, but then, a big one hit. But that's another story.

34

"I love this house," Lin said, spreading her arms and twirling around. "It was meant to be, I know that."

"It doesn't have bad vibes for you?"

"Oh, no, that's all gone. Only nice things happen here now. You're happy, aren't you?"

"Yes, of course. I love it here."

"It'll be Thanksgiving soon. We should be done with this book before Christmas. By the way, I'll be away all of next week."

"Anywhere nice?"

"Oh, nothing special. On my own." Her tone and abrupt turning away to lie down warned me not to inquire further. Besides, a week of Hunter's undivided attention was an attractive proposition.

Dora had become a problem, thumping my plate down in front of me at meals, burning my toast, and spitting at me whenever she thought she could get away with it. Lin said nothing—in my presence, at least. Hunter was oblivious, of course.

"Mary, you and your aunt will join us for Thanksgiving, won't you?"

"Thank you. How kind. Naturally, I'll check with Auntie, but I'm sure she'll be delighted." She absolutely would.

Tape 33

I had a welcome respite for a couple of weeks. Lettie, ever the eager beaver, reorganized the office space and painted her upstairs rooms. She was careful with her comings and goings, as our cluster was zoned commercial-only. She wanted to save for the security deposit on an apartment. She needed a new car too, as she would only be able to afford an apartment some distance away.

I actually had my eye on a one-bedroom apartment in a medium high-rise in town within walking distance of the office. I told Hunter it was a good investment. I'd not charge her much rent, and Hunter wouldn't pay attention to such a small investment.

Buying the Goodall property was another story. I had to rope him in on that one.

"But people will wonder where the money has come from."

"No, they won't. We can sell this house and hint at how my business is booming. It's priced to sell. God knows I earned it."

He finally came around. My Irish realtor was practically jigging around town. Two cash sales in a couple of months, soon to be followed by a listing. I didn't want any of their furniture, so an estate sale took care of that.

The first task was to renovate and clean. That basement had to be different. Quite different. Chad's bedroom should probably be fumigated, too. I'd take my time, as I wanted to move in before I put our house on the market. I couldn't have buyers poking around in our stuff and seeing anything they shouldn't.

The contractor was a little perplexed by the basement layout in the Goodall house.

"You didn't read about those Syrian girls who were brought over here?

"Er … well, heard about something like that."

"These little rooms are where they were held prisoner."

"Oh, wow." He scratched his head as he let out a stream of breath fetid from nicotine and beer. He'd have something to tell everyone he knew and a few more.

"These walls between the rooms have to be torn down. I want the space to be a kitchenette and eating area. The little bathroom in back can have the shower removed and be made into a powder room. There's already a separate bedroom and bath down here. And remove the door leading to it and make an archway over the opening into the space. I know it's partly underground, but can you do a half-window?"

Well, he couldn't do the window because it was too far underground, but the other half of the space was once a walkout, closed in by the Goodalls. They'd boarded up the windows and door. I wanted to let in the light.

He was as good as his word, and it only took a month. We packed up some of our most personal possessions—like the golden chess set—and moved them separately. Would you believe I almost forgot Yggdrasil? The new people wouldn't have noticed because it was nothing to look at. Not yet. They might have pulled it up, though. Horrors! I found the perfect spot in a small bed on one side of our new home. I put a little protective cage around it, just in case someone thought it was one of those weed trees. My carelessness had unnerved me. Lots of what-ifs.

The kids fussed and fumed because they would be living farther away from their friends. Hunter complained unendingly about the disruption to his routine, whatever that might be. Dora griped because she would have to clean the old house after we were out, then have a larger house to take care of. I hoped that would sap some of her excess energy. Maybe that was Hunter's main objection.

A couple of weeks later, I was able to tell Lettie I'd closed on the apartment, and it was hers for a modest rent. She went pale, then reddened as reality took hold.

"I'll be living in Salton! In my own space! With a separate bedroom!" She hugged me tight. I've never liked hugging much, except with the children, but her almost delirious joy made me happy. Was I going native? You have to admit, though, that I've done a fair amount to help people in need. I'm not really that callous, as gods go."

This sounded tentative for her, for whom certainty was almost a trademark.

"Whoever said you were callous, Lin?"

She sat up halfway. "A fair number over the years. I just don't look at things the same way as people do. One woman in Texas said I probably have Asperger's! Gods don't have syndromes. They just have their roles to play. Mine was to save those in peril and punish their tormentors." She looked sad.

"Lin, you've been so kind to me. And look at all those girls you saved. So, a few heads got broken along the way. Can't be helped. What else could you have done?"

Well, listen to me; I'd embraced the narrative. She rewarded me with a dazzling smile and my favorite dessert for dinner—peanut butter pie. And a lovely German white wine.

She lay back down, cheerful now, and resumed.

Finally, we moved. I had made sure the TV was set up, our phone number stayed the same, the kids had equal-sized rooms, and Dora's room was between them rather than in the basement. Hunter said he would have preferred Dora to sleep in the basement, conveniently separate, complaining about privacy. I knew whose privacy he meant. The children still huffed and puffed, and Dora continued to pout, but an order of several large pizzas quieted everyone down for the moment. I sat back and enjoyed the irony. I think Joe did, too. I invited him and his girlfriend Helen for dinner a few weeks after we moved.

"You have a lovely home here, Lin," Joe said, looking around.

"Would you like to see what we've done with the basement?" I asked. I knew he would.

They liked the open plan, the ping-pong table, the light colors, and the patio outside the French doors.

"I love it," Joe said, grinning at me. "Such a change."

"Indeed."

Helen asked, "You've seen it before?"

Joe hesitated, so I chimed in. "Yes, those Syrian girls were held prisoner down here, beyond that archway. Joe arrested the Goodalls right in this house."

"Oh, I didn't realize this was the same house. Wow! Hateful people."

I guess Joe didn't like to bring his work home.

We had a pleasant evening, as always. Dora had cooked one of her lamb specialties, and they both tucked in with gusto. Helen was an associate at a local law firm and, still low on the totem pole, was every partner's slave. Joe is always busy too, so I assume good meals are few and far between.

"Anything new at work?" I asked Joe.

"Well, we did get a circular about a body that washed up near the old boathouse downtown. Turned out to be a New York cop who went missing a couple of months ago. He told his wife he was coming up this way to see a friend.

"One of our sergeants said that, yes, he'd had a drink with the fellow, who hinted he had some business to take care of. Said he asked about the Syrian girls, who was involved, and so on. Apparently, your name came up."

I heard a crunch from Hunter's direction and a gasp from Helen as red wine dripped down Hunter's sleeve and onto the tablecloth from his crushed wine glass.

"Oh, Hunter, you don't know your own strength," I said. I called Dora, and she took him into the kitchen to get cleaned up.

"Yes, Joe, you were saying?"

"Is he all right? He hurt himself."

"Oh, yes, he does that all the time. Such big rough hands, such delicate glasses."

He looked at me as if I'd said something bad.

"What?"

"Oh, nothing. Just thought you might be worried about him."

"He's as tough as old leather. No need to worry." Dora would be patting and consoling him all he wanted.

"Well, as I was saying, your name came up."

"My name? How extraordinary. I don't know any cops apart from you. What possible business could he have with me?" I perform innocent puzzlement quite well.

"I have no idea. I investigated him quietly. I heard he was suspected of being a dirty cop. I'll be taking a look at our sergeant and his friends, too. It's very hush-hush, though. Very unofficial. Anyway, it seems whoever he was involved with was upset enough to put a big dent in his head."

"Oh my goodness," I said. "Any ideas?"

He looked into my eyes. "None."

Joe is, I suspect, one of those intuitive cops who goes with their gut feeling. I've been tempted on and off to tell him what I am, especially since I know how tight-lipped he is. But I can't, especially after seeing that glimmer of understanding. He'd treat me differently. Maybe he'd feel honor-bound to report me to his superiors. People treat humans and animals badly enough. Whatever would they do to gods who threatened their sense of superiority, not to mention their religious certainties?

The next morning, I was just out of the shower when the phone rang.

"Mrs. Thoren? It's Reema."

"Reema! I've been wondering how you're all doing. How are you? Where are you?" Still naked, I paced the bedroom carpet while Hunter's sleepy eyes followed me hungrily over the edge of the duvet.

"I am well, thank you. We are all in Michigan, even the other girls you brought over. There are a lot of Arab families here. We are each staying in a different home. The others, except Nazli, are learning English at a local evening school. I am too, but at a higher level so I can get a certificate. I am trying to get into college. They say I have to do a bachelor's degree to get into medical school. And that is four whole years! And it's hard to find one that will accept me because I have no high school transcripts. I must find a scholarship too, and that's nearly impossible without transcripts."

"So why isn't Nazli in evening classes?" I felt concerned for this poor waif.

"Oh, she's only sixteen, so they put her in high school. She's had a lot of therapy and seems happy. She loves her host family, and it's unbelievable how well she speaks English. Almost better than me. I call her our little American."

"I'm so glad. I was worried about her. Look, do you have to have permission to move?"

"Yes, why?"

"Give them my name and phone number. You must come and live with us."

Hunter bolted upright, eyes wide, and made wild gestures indicating NO in a variety of ways. "We will send you to college. Only one thing." I took a deep breath. "That house you were kept in. We live there now."

"Oh." She said no more, but the weight of her trauma came through.

"It's completely different now. That basement, where you were, it's renovated, those little rooms are gone, there's a door to the outside and windows. No locks inside. And you can sleep upstairs if you want. We can move the maid down there." I faced Hunter and smiled my best. His face showed a variety of emotions as the wheels started turning. Dora would be in a more conveniently accessible space. He slid back down under the covers.

"You are very kind." She sounded better now. "I will give them your number. Thank you. I owe you everything."

"You are like my daughter, Reema."

Dora would grumble again. An attractive young woman and another person to clean up after.

35

Lin returned from her trip after I had gone to bed. I hadn't yet fallen asleep and couldn't help hearing the raised voices. They hardly said a word the next morning at breakfast.

I wanted to bring up the subject of Dora's jealousy because it was getting on my nerves. But how could I without bringing Hunter into the conversation? I had to put a stop to the pranks she'd started playing, though. Given Lin's mood, it obviously wasn't a good time, but it couldn't go on.

"Lin, I found worms on my pillow last night. Who could have done it but Dora?"

Lin looked irritated. "Dora gets above herself sometimes. I'll put a stop to this nonsense. She's jealous, you understand. She's rather fond of Hunter, and with you being young and pretty—well, you know. Dora has had a hard life. She wasn't created lowly."

"What's her story? How did she come to work for you?

"We first saw her in a place you have probably been led to believe is just mythological. Not so, although, looking back on it, fantastical would describe it. We met up years later, purely by coincidence."

"I'd love to hear about it."

"All right, I guess this will be my story for today."

She lay back on the couch in her usual sleeping beauty pose. When I turned on the recorder, she took a deep breath and began.

Tape 34

We were wandering around the area people call Greece now, trying to decide where to settle next, when we met a charming man called Hermes. One day, we'd watched as he offered up honey in one of the shrines honoring Zeus. When he'd finished, he introduced himself. While not as huge and Nordic as Hoenir, I nevertheless found him attractive—fair-haired, tall, slim, and lithe. He wore the usual Greek loose robes and unusual sandals that looked like part of his feet. I couldn't see where leather ended and flesh began. A smile that seemed to always hover around his lips caught my interest at once. Altogether, a lovely lad.

We were curious about these gods who had taken over the business of religious adoration and smiting the unfaithful while conveniently overlooking the taking-care-of-the-world side of things. We later saw for ourselves what a narcissistic and hedonistic bunch they were. After enjoying a few picnics together—and I enjoyed a lovely afternoon with him once while Hoenir (he still kept to the old name in those days) claimed to be getting a house sorted out for us—Hermes came clean. We asked him several times about the gods, but he always managed to divert the conversation.

The three of us were chatting about where we'd been and so on when he blurted out,

"You are not human, are you?" We gaped at him.

"How do you know?" asked my genius husband.

"This and that. But don't worry, only another god would recognize the signs."

"Well, who are you, then?" I demanded, not willing to give myself away just yet.

"I didn't try to hide it. I told you. I am Hermes."

"Oh, Hermes..."

"Do you mean to say you have not heard of me?" His mouth turned down, as did his eyebrows.

It was time for us to come out. "We are the old ones," I said. He looked puzzled. "You must have heard about Asgard. And Valhalla. And Odin."

"I seem to remember hearing stories. But why are you here?"

"Our heaven has long been vanquished. The final battle nearly finished earth, too. We escaped and have wandered the world ever since."

"You poor dear things! You must visit us in Olympus. Zeus will be delighted to meet you." He fairly bubbled with excitement.

"Well, Hermes, pleased to really know you," I said. "What are you doing here?"

"Oh, I often come down to enjoy earthly delights," he said, shooting me a meaningful look that thankfully went over Hoenir's head. "I am frequently asked to take messages here and there—that's part of my job, you know—and so I often wander the earth looking for nice things to do."

"How will we get there?" I asked.

"We will journey to the foothills of our mountain in my carriage tomorrow night. From there, we will fly."

I'd been spirited from Asgard down to Midgard often enough, but that had been in our old world, our own old magic. I couldn't help feeling apprehensive. Hoenir was thrilled by the idea. You have to realize he'd lost a very privileged position as the son of Odin after Ragnarök killed everything and just about everyone. He craved the chance to bask in a godly world.

At dusk the following evening, we waited for Hermes by the shrine. I noticed a cart drawn by a mule standing nearby and hoped having a stranger around wouldn't interfere with anything.

"Good evening, friends." Hermes had materialized behind us. Only another god could do that. "We are ready to leave."

"Where is your carriage?" asked Hoenir.

"Right over there," Hermes replied, pointing at the cart.

I was annoyed and wondered if he'd been spinning a scam of some kind. Hoenir just laughed like a carefree youth.

We jumped in, and Hermes tucked a blanket around my lap. "It gets cool later on," he said. I just sulked, which seemed to amuse him.

The mule started off, lazing along for a while. I felt even more grumpy when I realized what a long, bumpy trek I would have to endure. Hoenir wasn't enduring anything. He and Hermes chatted and laughed about everything and nothing the whole way. When we passed the outer edge of an olive grove and entered a barren stretch, the pace picked up. The mule's ears perked up, and the road became smoother. After another few minutes, the little I could see by the light of the moon flashed by, just like what you see from a train window these days. Back then, it was shocking. It took us only about half an hour to reach the foothills and the end of the trail.

Hermes helped me down, even though he knew full well I could simply have leaped over the side, as Hoenir did. Hoenir was happy as a gnome fondling gold after his fun ride, anticipating glories to come. It crossed my mind that maybe he'd decide to stay up there. I'd have to see whether I could be satisfied with that life. I'd reveled in most of our adventures so far and looked forward to more.

"Follow me," said Hermes.

We hiked up a narrow trail to a small, flat outcrop flanked on each side by ancient olive trees, its edge showing a steep drop into the valley below—surprising since we hadn't walked far uphill. Hermes wrapped us into his embrace and jumped off the ridge. We might be immortal, but we feel pain now. Our powers have weakened, so I didn't fancy a messy landing. I held myself rigid, hardly daring to breathe.

"Be still, little one," he murmured into my ear. "You will come to no harm."

I realized we were soaring rather than dropping, and in minutes, we stood in bright sunlight on solid ground once more. Sort of solid ground. It was white, fluffy, and hard to walk on with any semblance of dignity. Hermes took my hand to help me find my footing.

Always up to a challenge, Hoenir simply blundered through. Soon we came to a pathway, really solid this time, that led to a palace that glowed and sparkled, sunlight bouncing off what looked like glass tiles. Glass was still rare on earth at that time, so it was a wondrous sight—and still would be.

We went through a massive arched gateway and continued up to the door.

"Where is everyone?" I asked.

"Feasting in the great hall, I imagine," said Hermes.

"Are there no guards?" asked Hoenir.

"Why would the most powerful god need guards?" *Good point. We'd had other worries, though. Rogue gods.*

We walked for some minutes through what seemed like a maze of corridors that led us into and out of chambers, some simple, some sumptuous, until the sounds of music and laughter spilled out of the next doorway.

"We have arrived at the great hall," said Hermes. "Be sure to show great respect and reverence. He may not know of your old world."

When we entered the hall, we stood behind Hermes at the end of two long columns of marble tables, one on each side, with one stretched across the top. An ancient, who looked as if he were wrought from an oak tree, sat at the head of the table. A stunningly beautiful black woman sat on his right, and an array of servants stood at attention behind them. Dancing girls writhed in the wide aisle between the tables, accompanied by musicians in a gallery above. The gigantic size of the hall, the tables, the dishes, the crowd, and the noise were overwhelming, even for me.

Zeus noticed Hermes waiting and bellowed, "Hermes, what news do you bring?" Then he noticed us. "And you dare to bring mortals to our realm? Come forward."

Hermes walked us up to the table to stand opposite Zeus. "My father god, I have delivered your message to the centaurs. Allow me to introduce my new friends, Lin and Hoenir. They are the old ones, from the far north, from Asgard, now no more. They wander the earth and are honored to meet you."

Zeus looked at me. "I have heard these stories. Are you Odin's kin?"

"My lord, I served his wife Frigg as handmaiden in Asgard all my life. I am a goddess, but not as high ranked as my husband." I gestured to Hoenir. "He is the brother of Odin."

He smiled—leered—at me, stretching leathery lips to alarming proportions before turning to Hoenir. "And you, you seek another kingdom? I rule here."

"My lord," Hoenir said, calm and poised. "I seek no kingdom but am destined to wander the world until the end of time. Hermes has brought us here in friendship. We ask for nothing but the honor of your exalted company for a short time." He bowed. My heart swelled with pride at the way my husband conducted himself. He is not the brightest of souls, but his breeding showed through bright and clear.

"You are welcome to my dominion. Please be seated next to me, Lin. Hoenir, please sit next to my wife, Hera. Hermes, you and I will speak later."

Hermes bowed. We had to walk all the way to and around the end of the tables to get back up to the top again. Hermes found himself a seat between a couple of beauties, one of whom sported a pair of small, gossamer wings. We sat as commanded. Hera and Hoenir soon became fully engaged in conversation, as did Zeus and I. The old god was mesmerizing in his ancient omniscience and magnetic presence. I told him about Asgard, the final battle, and Hoenir's injuries. It didn't occur to me until later that we spoke the same language. Which language? I have no idea. One of the mysteries of the gods.

We were assigned a suite of rooms, one of which contained a pool fed by a spring that we used for bathing. A full chest provided fine clothing that fit us as if made to measure.

Our days were peaceful and comfortable. Being surrounded by beauty and amusement is a wonderful life—for a time. Both of us did our share of cavorting, but we felt restless. I don't know how long we were there in earth time. I don't think much more than fifty years or so, although I saw later that our aging process had halted for the duration.

Zeus took a liking to Hoenir, as well as to me—and my word, that was interesting. A mountain of a god.

I loved the gatherings in his magnificent great hall. The last time I'd been in a god's great hall, it was Hel's. We had fled down there after the final battle, knowing she would never harm another god. Hel had designed her hall to look just like Odin's except for the ghastly trophies that adorned the walls—her version of macramé, comprising strands of shredded souls knotted into intricate designs. I used to take a break to attend her when I got tired of nursing Hoenir. She liked attention and would turn that ghastly face to me and smile with the good half of it. That was such a long millennium.

Zeus's hall shimmered with light that tumbled off nacred walls as torchlight caught the pastel curves this way and that. He liked to surround himself with beauty, perhaps to remind himself of what he had once been. Even immortals age eventually. His beard had turned grizzled, and his hands ropy with green veins. It was whispered by some foolhardy gods that he could no longer please a woman. Not so. Hermes, always so competitive, often hinted at it, but what could I say? He would have nagged me incessantly to compare notes. Hermes was a lovely creature, but no one could compare with Zeus—even Hoenir—and I wasn't interested in fomenting a male ego trip. Hera didn't always attend the feasts. While I kept a watchful eye on her, she didn't seem at all jealous. Probably because she was enjoying getting to know my husband. I wondered how Zeus allowed it. He had many dalliances, of course, but that was different. Gods got a pass; goddesses, not so much.

Anyway, we were watching an entertainment one afternoon when a girl burst in. The music tapered off as the gods' heads pivoted to stare at this apparition—someone dressed like a nymph and trying to glide along above the surface of the floor like one, although her feet kept bumpety-bumping along the marble. Shockingly, she was fat, disheveled, and tear stained. The circlet of oak leaves she wore on her head showed she was a dryad who belonged in woods and glens, not here in this grand palace of intrigue and debauchery. The immortal dryads are all slender and beautiful. No one had ever seen anything like it.

Zeus recovered himself after taking in this spectacle. "What do you want here, girl? And why do you look like that? You are a disgrace to your kind!" His face got redder as he clenched and unclenched his massive fists while thundering at her. He didn't appreciate nuisances. Besides, everyone knew he liked to go down to the woods on earth now and then to play with the dryads, frolic around in the streams, and dance naked in the woods before taking his pick. This girl's appearance offended his sensibilities.

The girl was sobbing a flood by this time, no doubt hoping to arouse pity in her lord. She was barking up the wrong tree.

"Pan did this to me. Look at me! How can I appear to travelers like this?"

"Well, since the only reason you girls show yourselves to travelers is to frighten them, I don't see the problem," was his callous reply. With that, she wailed like a Fury, not realizing that female scenes enraged Zeus. "So, girl, why did he do it?"

She gathered herself somewhat, perhaps noticing that Zeus's scowl had only deepened.

"He wanted to despoil me, and that is not my destiny. Besides, he's ugly and stinky. When I ran from him, he said he'd make sure no one else would want me and cast this spell."

Zeus burst out laughing, and the whole court joined in. I kicked Hoenir when I noticed him guffawing. It wasn't funny. The girl had been humiliated and ruined.

When Zeus stopped laughing, everyone else stopped too, as if he'd blown out a candle. We all stayed still and silent, waiting to see what the big bully would do.

"What is your name, girl?"

"Dora."

"Well, Dora, you cannot fulfill your destiny looking like that. You will walk among humans. You are to serve them for the rest of your days. That is your new destiny."

"But Lord Zeus, can you not remove the curse? Please? You know I am immortal. You would banish me forever?" Her voice rose to an ugly shriek, her eyes swollen and piggy in the rolls of fat.

"You are a stupid girl. Would it have hurt to give a god a few moments of pleasure? Who are you to refuse any one of us? I will not insult Pan for such a lowly one. You will become a serving wench to humans."

The poor girl drooped, pale and shaking, shocked into silence.

"Go!" he shouted, thrusting forward his right arm to point at her and then down to earth. She disappeared.

Zeus was a bastard. I tried to warn Hoenir when he started to play around with some of the court favorites, but he wouldn't listen. Hera wouldn't have appreciated it either, and she would probably prove a deadly woman scorned. That's when I left, since we didn't have children to consider in that life. Hermes spent an entire evening trying to talk me out of leaving while Hoenir was otherwise occupied. Finally, he agreed to take me as far as the Bosphorus, where he claimed to have a mission.

I thanked Zeus, apologizing for any trouble we'd caused him. He had the good grace to take me to his private chambers for a last goodbye and presented me with a fabulous gold armband that I still have. I sometimes get it out to caress its finely wrought olive leaves and snakes. Armbands aren't fashionable at the moment, unfortunately. I used to wear it when dressed up in my flapper outfits for a night of dancing, though. I wondered why no one ever complimented me on it until I understood that no one could see it but me.

Hermes spirited me to a simple house on a clifftop over-looking the Bosphorus. The weather was warm, the garden scented with lemons, the house with jasmine flowers that floated in crystal bowls of many hues. Ducks and goldfish swam in a large pond among pink and white waterlilies the size of dinner plates. Most evenings, he'd take me in his arms and swoop down into the deepest part of the straight, one night diving deep enough to dine with the mermaids who guarded the waters against monsters always trying to invade from the Black Sea at one end or the Sea of Marmara at the other. Their palace, a dreamland of many hues of blue and green, undulated unceasingly, and our hostesses served us gracefully, a mere flick of their tails transporting them to our sandy recliners from the kitchens beyond. The fish wasn't cooked, of course—no fires down there. But it was cured somehow and delicious, as were the greens offered with it.

One night, we rose to the surface to find a few drunken locals prancing on the beach, wielding any primitive weapon they could find. We'd been seen entering the water several times, it seems, naked and often ending the eve-ning with a romp on the beach—very much against the customs of that time and place. We walked out of the water onto the shore, where they waited to punish us for our wanton behavior. Hermes picked me up, and we soared over their heads back to the house. This gave rise to ter-rified prayers to their god for protection. They saw which garden we landed in, so we knew it was only a matter of time before a mob arrived to vanquish the evil spirits.

"Are the servants safe?" I asked Hermes.

"They are immortal," he replied. "But we should cut our time here short. We shouldn't attract more attention than we already have. I know of a ship we can travel on tomorrow. It is bound for points west, but I will depart at the first port of call.

We sailed for three days before I wished Hermes a very fond farewell. He wept a little, which I found gratifying. I watched until he disappeared into a motley crowd of passengers, hawkers, and sailors on a filthy dock somewhere in Africa, I think, although that wasn't west. I never went back to the Bosphorus. I wonder if the house still stands.

Hermes tracked me down in Malta about thirty years later. He was always full of mischief and trickery, but romantic for the time we were together. I know he forgot me the moment he left. Although he had searched me out. I had to move shortly after because I looked too young for the amount of time I'd lived there. People were talking. It was lucky our aging had been set back fifty years. I didn't feel like being reborn alone. It's a painful, exhausting business.

I'd left a note for Hoenir when I left Olympus and hadn't seen him for nearly a century by the time he showed up at my villa in what is now Sardinia, properly contrite. He'd been lucky to survive Zeus's wrath. I let him back into my life because he was family. I'd been lonely, too. I'd had friends and lovers in the meantime, but there were so many things I could never share with them. They wouldn't have understood, and fear might have led them to destroy me—or try to. Then I would have had to destroy them.

It was time to move on, so Hunter and I traveled to a savage land in the far west of Britannia, where we laid low for a few years so as not to attract unwelcome attention from Zeus. It was so damn wet and cold—and hasn't improved by all accounts, although the people seem to have evolved nicely. Celts weren't so bad when you got used to them—a superstitious lot with their own gods, though, so we had to watch ourselves. They still believed in witches and demons and all that claptrap. They couldn't know that Fenrir swallowed all those creatures as he rampaged through the worlds during the final battle.

Once or twice we thought of going farther west to an island not far over the sea, but learned from travelers that it wasn't much better. Of course, we'd have to pull up roots soon, as it was nearly time for rebirth. I wanted to move south to sun and warmth and where I could find good nannies.

Anyway, several lifetimes and relocations later, we were free because Zeus had closed his doors to the world. After Ares went on a murderous rampage on earth—they say rivers turned red from human blood—the gods declared war on him. Ares won, to his own surprise. Zeus was allowed to keep his throne but vowed never to have anything to do with earth again, mostly because many humans stopped believing in him, which sapped his power. So depressing for the poor dear, but he'd had a good run.

We occasionally came across an old Olympian acquaintance who'd been marooned on earth, but the poor things had somehow lost their immortality. I have no idea what that was all about, although Zeus, no doubt eaten with bitterness, had always been spiteful. I never saw Hermes again. I guess his messenger service had folded.

After the Roman empire overtook the Greek as another foundation of western civilization, they came up with their own mythology, but it wasn't anything real, merely a repackaging of the Greek pantheon. Different names, same portfolios. I wondered about Dora from time to time but never expected to find her. I wouldn't have known where to look.

Before we moved here to Virginia, we lived in Texas. We made some friends, although they had a funny way of looking at things. Their Christianity was full of strange stories from the Old Testament rather than the New, telling of a vengeful god, like all the Greek gods rolled into one. I haven't noticed this disturbing phenomenon much since because farther north, they don't go on about it so much. I must say most of our Norse gods were much nicer.

One of our friends down there was always trying to get us to church to be "saved." I didn't quite know what she meant, but considering I used to do a great deal of saving in my role as protector of Frigg's favored mortals, I thought myself justified in giving the whole thing a miss.

The way they treated blacks appalled both of us. One day, Hunter came home shaking with rage. He'd been "taking a walk in the woods"—which I doubt he ever did unaccompanied by some fair maiden—when he heard the wails of a child and the laughter and taunts of men about half a mile away. He ran over there and found four white men trussing up a black boy of about ten. A noose hung from a hefty tree branch. The men didn't live to see sunset, but the boy did. Hunter told him never to breathe a word about what happened.

It was the final straw for us. We'd heard plenty about such atrocities, but this was the first time it had touched us.

However, I digress. We made quite a few friends over our twenty years in San Antonio—acquaintances would be more accurate—and attended a dinner one night at the house of a couple we'd just met at another party. They were wealthy people with an enormous house full of wannabe *Louis Quinze* furniture. The place seemed to be curiously devoid of the usual cadre of black servants. It was our host who took our coats upon arrival and led us into the drawing room. I guess he was cheap, and, as with many of the wealthy, excessive thrift helped him to his goal. At some point during the cocktail hour, our hostess needed more ice.

"Dora!" she bellowed through the door.

Hunter and I turned as one. Yes, it was her. Merely plump now, an overworked and probably underpaid maid. As I found out later, the only maid.

I excused myself to go to the powder room and caught up with her in the hall. "Dora, stop. I was there when Zeus banished you." Her mouth dropped open, and she looked ready to weep. "I've thought about you a lot." I like to make people feel good. "We're going to leave town soon. Would you like to come with us?"

She paled, and the tears started to roll. "Who are you?"

"We are Norse gods who were guests of Zeus for a while. We saw your banishment and felt very sorry for you. You know Zeus closed the doors of his heaven to earth, don't you?"

She broke down then. "There's no hope for me, then."

"Pull yourself together, or people will talk. At least we know who you are, and you know about us. No one else does. And we will never have such a big house as this to clean. There are woods you can play in, too."

"Yes, yes, please take me away from here. Please."

I passed her my card. "You can read English?" We'd been speaking ancient Greek.

"Yes, I can. I've been in the South since 1925. I came over from Italy with a rich family, but they lost all their money in 1929 and had to let me go. I said I'd stay for nothing, but I suppose they couldn't afford to feed me. I eat like a human now, you know. We used to enjoy only fruits and berries, but now I've discovered much more. Humans have some good stuff."

"You're not fat anymore."

"No. Now the gods are no longer with us, I suppose Pan's curse weakened. But I'm still a servant and can't seem to think of doing anything else."

"Well, come and work for us when we go next Wednesday."

She looked brighter and wiped her eyes on the corner of her apron. "Yes, I will. Wednesday is my day off."

Our hostess was calling for her again. "Off you go, Dora. My card has my address. Until Wednesday."

Dora arrived in the middle of the moving chaos and helped empty, pack, and carry. We hadn't told anyone we were going, so no one else came, although curtains twitched along the street. We'd planned to fly up to Washington, and I'd bought a ticket for Dora, hoping she wouldn't get held up. She was terrified the whole time we were in the air, letting out little squeaks and squeals at every bump and announcement. I thought it odd until I realized she'd been transported to earth rather than suffered an arduous journey, then, no doubt, only traveled by road. She settled down once she, I, and the children were in a taxi on our way home to a house we'd bought sight unseen. Hunter followed in another taxi with the luggage.

So that's how Dora came to us and, I suppose, will always be bound to us. At least she knows the score and can help with the rebirths. I truly feel born again coming back to a clean house. And dinner. And someone to help bring up Hunter.

Dora played an important part when I gave birth to Sven and Margareta, too. Nowadays, there have to be records with signatures, and so on. You can't just show up one day with a baby. So, I had to take a trip each time and claim the babies came early—a stretch since they're always on the large side—and pay someone to forge the papers, often a nurse who can get her hands on the necessary paperwork. It's all so complicated. I register the birth myself because Hunter might give himself away.

Dora has proved a godsend. We're always hungry too, and she's a good cook.

Poor Dora. And Hunter dropped her for me? No wonder she was jealous. What a guy. I'm like a lovesick teen.

And Zeus on Mount Olympus? Really?

A few days later, we were watching the news after dinner, and a segment came on about some scandalous behavior in our local park, which is mostly wooded. Parents of teenagers had become aware that their children were having little parties in the woods. I think one of them overheard their son discussing plans on the phone. One phone call to his friend's parents led to another, and soon enough, they cracked. Apparently, a young woman was in the habit of dancing around in a copse not far from the road, naked but for a crown of leaves and flowers and playing something like a little harp. A couple of parents were interviewed, expressing horror at such scandalous goings-on their children had been exposed to. I'm quite sure their children thoroughly enjoyed themselves.

Lin and Hoenir exchanged horrified looks, and he rose from his chair incandescent with rage, looking even bigger than usual. I suddenly realized who the culprit was. And given the fact that Hoenir was paranoid about drawing undue attention to his family, I knew poor Dora was in big trouble. He stormed out, and explosions of recriminations and sorrowful sobbing soon filled the house. Lin looked at me, sighed, and shrugged. After he'd worn himself out, Hoenir returned and slumped into his chair.

"She is grounded for a year," was all he said.

36

"Nothing stays hidden forever," Lin said, looking out of the sliding glass door to the patio. "Think of the things archeologists have dug up after thousands of years."

I wondered what had brought on this philosophical mood. "Yes, I think you're right."

"Sometimes they pop up when you're not really looking, though."

"What are you thinking about?"

She sat on the sofa without taking up her usual position but gazed out at the patio with its potted plants, most well past their former glory on this chilly November day.

Thanksgiving had been special. Lin and Hunter were so kind to Auntie Peggy, and Lin even said to bring Sam, who slept under the table during dinner. Hunter didn't comment. Sven and Margareta, home from boarding school, loved playing with him and took him on a long walk. Sven complained that Margareta made him pick up his poo in the special bags affixed to the leash. I finally met Lettie, too. She was a feisty young woman whom I liked instantly.

Sven and Margareta turned out to be fun, and both were exceptionally good-looking, hardly surprising given their parentage. Sven was good-natured like his father and easygoing, although I sensed he could stick in his heels if pushed too far. Margareta was bubbly and affectionate, with an edge that inferred steely determination. These were fleeting impressions gained over a four-day break, but I looked forward to getting to know them better when they stayed home for longer.

Joe and Helen were also there, of course, although her daughter had to go to her father's, Helen's ex. Auntie made a comment about how those two were just made for each other, which raised a fierce blush in both of them. I wondered if Joe was close to popping the question—it was about time.

I went home with Auntie and Sam later and stayed the night with them. Lin told me to take the next day off so I could have a long weekend. It poured rain most of the time, but I had a good book, slept in, and ate pot roast, pies, and all kinds of other Auntie-spoiling goodies.

Tape 35

We love this home, once a prison, now a haven. When we moved in, the house was surrounded by transplanted old trees and shrubs that looked manicured but commonplace. I like flowers and had grown quite a few in our old house. I wanted perennials in the main garden and annuals in big pots all around the deck and patio. I enjoy buying plants and looking at them, but messing in the dirt, not so much. And everything should be finished well before the hottest months arrived. I hired a landscape company run by Reynaldo Ramez.

I chose the pots and plants at a nursery in Fairfax and arranged for the landscaper to pick them up. As well as the big deck off the living room upstairs, there was a haphazard arrangement of pavers outside these sliding glass doors with little white daisies growing between them. I found it strange since the door down there had been walled over by Olive and Jerry, the original owners. I figured a few shade-loving plants might cheer the spot up, so I asked Reynaldo for suggestions.

"Well, Miss Lin, they don't look so good."

"They're not very pretty, but I think a few pots of plants will help."

"Look how unevens." He put his full weight on one, and it sank a couple of inches. "See, not evens. Someones can trip over. And the pots will be wobbling. And they may falls."

I could see his point.

"What do you suggest, Reynaldo?"

"Digs. Throws away. Sands. New stones. I show you samples in my trucks."

"How much?"

"Cheaps at two thousand dollar."

"One thousand."

"Okay." *Damn, too easy*

We went out to his truck. Only one truck. The guy had a strange habit of tacking an "s" onto everything. I picked out a nice paver and told him to do it after all the other work was finished.

The pots for upstairs and all the plants were duly picked up and installed. It was going to be great, and it lifted my heart to think about how the garden would look in a couple of months. Yggdrasil still lived on in its secluded spot that caught the morning sun but was shaded from Apollo's afternoon assault. I'd added some liquid fertilizer, although I didn't know if it would appreciate that. Reynaldo had strict instructions to leave it alone.

"But Miss Lin, there are better trees."

"I like this one."

He shrugged and disappeared around back.

Reynaldo and his assistant went to work on the patio downstairs. They raised the old pavers and put them in the truck, no doubt to resell. The new ones would definitely look better. Now they had to dig a foundation.

Hunter didn't see the point of all this disturbance and expense, so had shut himself in the study for most of the week. I had no idea what he got up to in there. He mostly did nothing but watch TV and eat. Now might be a good time to find out.

I climbed the steps up to the deck, which conveniently wrapped around most of the side of the house and under his study window. I tiptoed around and listened at the open window. He always opened the windows, even when it snowed, which annoyed everyone. Silence. I risked peeking in.

He sat as still as a tree, staring into a glass ball I'd never seen before. He whispered something in the old language so softly that even with my hearing, I had a hard time catching it all until, "Come to me, children, come to Papa." My heart broke for him. So he did remember them. He did grieve. And someone had taken advantage of his sorrow with that stupid crystal ball. Did he remember more of them than me? Did he have favorites? I felt like going to my bed and crying an ocean.

"Miss Lin, Miss Lin!" It sounded like a herd of elephants rampaging up the outside stairs.

Reynaldo appeared on the deck, his face as white as snow, his terrified assistant Julio sweating not far behind.

"There is a foots in the patio. It shouldn't be foots in patios." My heart sank. If he panted much harder, he'd hyperventilate. That I could do without.

"Calm down. What do you mean, a foot?"

"Is a foots. And there's a legs on it, too. "

I went down to check for myself. They followed at a discreet distance.

There was indeed a blackish, big foot with a hairy ankle attached. I'd been expecting a female appendage, so I heaved a sigh of relief.

"Thank goodness," I said too loudly.

"No goodnesses, Miss Lin, what do you mean?" Reynaldo, reaching the end of his tether, looked and sounded hysterical.

"Leave everything, Reynaldo. I will go and call the police."

"Police! They will punish me!"

"Of course, they won't. I was here. I know you didn't do anything. Calm down, for God's sake! Come upstairs and sit on the deck while I call."

Julio, who had never uttered a word in my presence before, said, "No visa." His voice shook.

I looked at Reynaldo. "Can he drive your truck?"

"Yes."

"Go," I told him. Reynaldo handed him the keys, and he scuttled off.

"Julio left two hours ago. He was sick. But only if they ask."

"Yes, Miss Lin."

As I entered the living room, Hunter emerged from the study. His eyes were red, and I yearned to hold him tight.

"What was all that noise? It disturbed me."

"There's a body buried under the patio downstairs."

"I knew it was a mistake buying this cursed house! I am going to take a nap." He plodded upstairs.

I called Joe, who told me he'd be with me shortly as he was just finishing an interview at a house a few streets over. He looked harried when he arrived, lips and shoulders tight.

"Thanks for coming. How are you?"

"String of burglaries. Irate householders. Blaming us." was his terse description of the situation.

"Well, this should make a change." I led him downstairs to the patio.

"I'm just happy it's not a girl," I said.

"I doubt this fellow would share the sentiment."

The crime scene people arrived shortly thereafter. I left them to it since Joe was so snappish.

He came up to the living room a half-hour or so later and plopped down in an armchair.

"Coffee?" I asked.

He nodded. I went to the kitchen, and he followed. We sat at the table, waiting for it to brew.

"Guess what?" he said.

"What?" What else can one say?

"It's our missing husband and father. His health club card had slipped through a hole into the lining of his jacket pocket. You remember, I told you about the missing body."

"You mean from the funeral home?"

"Yup!"

"That's odd. Why on earth would they bury him here instead of just cremating him? Oh! That means the Goodalls were involved with all of that, too."

"Quite so. It's all become very complicated."

"Well, good luck unraveling the mystery!"

"It's out of my hands. I was instructed to call the FBI, so they'll take it from here."

"How do you feel about that?"

"Relieved and annoyed."

"Things okay with Helen?"

"Yes. Why do you ask?"

"You are not yourself."

"It's these burglaries. The guy's clever. And careful. My professionalism has been called into question."

He finished his coffee and left.

I wasn't expecting that. Those Goodalls were into all kinds of nastiness. I was touched by Hunter's grief, too. Immortality carries a heavy burden. I was glad to know how loving he is—loving in a deep and meaningful way.

After Lin left, I looked out the window, wondering what other unpleasant surprises might turn up.

But then Hunter appeared. "Lin has gone to spend an afternoon with a friend," he said. "So, I would like to spend an afternoon with mine."

37

"I know Reema is not my daughter, but there is something special about her."

Reema, by the time I met her, was on the verge of finishing medical school in Washington and had a punishing schedule. I liked her. She was a thoughtful young woman and obviously very fond of Lin, who insisted on dragging her protesting protégé to the mall to buy her clothes. Hunter seemed fairly cool around her, and the bonhomie he showed when she arrived carried a false note. Maybe she'd turned him down?

Sven was a sophomore and Margareta a junior at boarding school, so it wouldn't be long before they'd be off to college. I sensed Lin mourned her empty nest.

"My children are special too, of course. But will they stay close when they start their careers? Will they come home?"

"Children have to follow their own star, Lin," I said. "Even if they settle far away, there's nothing to stop you from traveling to see them. And there's always Skype."

"You are right, of course," she said, with a note of resentment. Not quite what she wanted to hear. I wondered if she would become difficult if they moved far away. Almost certainly.

What would happen if Yggdrasil thrived once more and Asgard reappeared? She'd go back in a heartbeat, for sure. On the other hand, how could Asgard function with only three gods? They'd have to get rid of Loki, too. Quite a conundrum.

Tape 36

Reema had quite a spring in her step that Saturday she walked off the plane. We embraced and went to look for her luggage. It was more than she left us with, but still only one suitcase. That would soon change. As we chatted on the drive home, I was pleased with how fluent Reema's English had become. On arrival, she received varying levels of welcome.

The children, home for Thanksgiving, were reserved, but she had won them over by the end of the evening. Hunter was a little stiff but polite—he wasn't happy about sharing his home with a stranger who didn't know who we were. Dora saw more work.

We had a good weekend, though. I invited Joe and Helen over for a barbecue on Sunday, and that seemed to break the ice. Joe brought a set of horseshoes with him, giving rise to much hilarity—for most of us. Sven and Hunter missed by yards, with Hunter managing to decapitate a crow as it swooped down for a bit of hamburger someone had dropped, which made Sven cry. Helen looked a little green, too. Reema did well, and Joe beat everyone. He'd done it before, of course. If I'd had more practice, I would have done better. He said the game was a gift, so I could always practice. I only like games I can win.

We had an appointment at a local Catholic college on Tuesday, so I took Reema shopping on Monday. I knew she'd be unwilling to let me spend money on her, but I told her flat out that I wasn't going to have her looking like a refugee. If she felt she looked good, she'd act with more confidence. I was also afraid of her getting picked on, although she no longer wore a hijab. After the Twin Towers debacle, many Americans had become very bigoted and considered all Arabs potential terrorists. Most of them haven't experienced other cultures in any meaningful way and can't relate to any customs but their own. They've always been isolated by oceans too, so they haven't before been subjected to attack on their own territory like most other nations. Fear has a way of undermining democracy.

Reema seemed a little nervous about her interview, although I know she felt good in her navy suit and white silk blouse. I was allowed to go in with her in case further clarification was needed. My heart sank when I set eyes on the president, Sister Mary Margaret O'Connor. A tall woman, she had a scrubbed, no-nonsense look about her. I saw a couple of nuns like her in action in Naples once, and it wasn't pretty. The unfortunate schoolboy could only hobble home crying for his mother by the time they'd finished with him.

"Well, Mrs. Thoren, how do you do?" Her smile transformed her face into a kindly, softer arrangement. "And you, my dear. Reema, isn't it? You are most welcome."

Everything went smoothly. We had missed the enrollment deadline by months, but Sister Mary Margaret felt that exceptions could be made in Reema's case, so she would enter in January. Reema handled herself well. I kept forgetting she was about 22 by then and had experienced one semester of medical school, not to mention a war.

It was soon settled. Forms were filled in. I handed over a semester's fees, and Reema managed to meet with her new advisor. It was a small college, so I guess that made things easier than if it had been one with thousands of students.

Reema had about a month free before starting her studies, so I looked forward to taking her around. She fitted into the household smoothly and seemed happy. The museums awed her, although she was surprised that most of the contents weren't older. She and I think of "older" as thousands of years rather than hundreds. I occasionally saw a shadow cross her face. Not every sorrow can be forgotten. I should have taken her to the natural history museum. Dinosaurs qualify as old, even to me. They lived before my time. Gods came with people, and that hadn't happened yet.

Reema befriended Dora too, and often helped her with the laundry and cooking. We enjoyed some Syrian specialties from time to time. I was about to enter the kitchen one day when I overheard Dora ask Reema about her home while they made the dark bread Hunter loves.

"So, you're from Syria?"

"Yes, I am."

"Why did you leave?"

"Because of the war."

"What war?"

"You don't know about it? It's on the news a lot."

"I don't watch the news. It's boring."

"Oh. Well, there's been a terrible civil war in my country, so I managed to escape to a camp across the border in Turkey. I was lucky enough to be brought to America from there."

I was glad she didn't elaborate.

"What about your family?"

I edged into the kitchen silently. Neither girl noticed. Dora thumped dough as if she were making a statement. It didn't bode well for the bread or the family. Reema's hands, which lay flat on the table now, looked floury, so she'd clearly been helping. Now she sat staring into her lap, her shoulders hunched.

"My brother was killed when he went to the market to buy our dinner. A bomb. Dear Tarek was only fifteen."

She paused and took a few deep breaths. Her voice had started strong but grew strained as she continued. The silence stretched unbearably. Dora looked up as if she'd only just taken in Reema's words. She wiped her hands on a towel and patted Reema's shoulder.

"My mother had a fatal heart attack not long after. I tried to save her with what little training I'd had in medical school, but I was not successful. My father disappeared while I was at my university classes. I came home one evening to find the apartment empty. I waited for weeks, aching to hear his heavy steps coming up the stairs. I don't know what happened to him. The university closed. Our apartment building was bombed while I was visiting a friend for lunch. I suppose I was fortunate. There was no reason to remain. I joined a group on the long walk to the camp. And here I am."

"Zeus almighty!" was the best Dora could come up with.

"I think I'll go and take a little nap," Reema said and got up. She gasped when she saw me. I put my arm around her shoulders and took her upstairs. Her face was blank, and she said nothing. Once I'd tucked her in, I went down to get her some tea. Arabs drink as much tea as the British.

Reema's numbness bothered me. She didn't cry. By the time I got back upstairs, she was asleep. I sat in her room and drank the tea myself, watching her as she slept.

Christmas was coming. Hunter and I love Christmas, and so do the children, of course. With many people, it's got nothing to do with religion. With some, it's all about excess, but with others, it's about enjoying a festival with family. I get a tree for which we've collected ornaments over the years; we have a special meal and exchange presents. Just one for each. Besides, I wouldn't want the children to feel left out when all their friends talk about their celebrations.

38

"I go all out with Christmas," she said. "You'll see. It won't be long now."

"I'd love to spend Christmas with you, but I can't leave Auntie Peggy on her own."

"Of course not. She will be very welcome."

Auntie would love that. She'd been curious about this household since I started working for Lin. She'd had a glimpse of it at Thanksgiving but was longing to come back. A few things might have seemed odd to her—Dora, for example—but not enough to cause concern. It was just a different kind of existence from any she had seen.

"I'm a little surprised you celebrate Christmas. Since you're not a Christian. Since you belong to another god group." God group? Well, how else could I put it?

"Oh, yes. We love it, more for the traditions than the religious aspect, of course. But isn't that true for most people?"

"Yes, I suppose it has become a cultural celebration, although many would deny it."

"Let me tell you about my first Christmas." Lin sounded excited.

Tape 37

When we lived in San Francisco after leaving Tunis, our lives became downright dull. I found the frequent tremors troubling, particularly as Hunter had a tantrum every time one hit. His nanny was astonished at how early he was learning to talk. He was only just over a year old. She claimed he was a genius. If she only knew.

"Go away! Must go!" he screamed each time and ran to the front door.

Once, when we took him for a walk near the Bay, we felt quite a strong one. "Out there, coming here!" he screamed, pointing out to sea. He locked his eyes on mine, eyes full of terror. He sensed a threat he could not articulate. *Should we go?* It was beginning to worry me.

I wasn't that enamored of San Francisco, anyway, although I'm told it is quite lovely now, so I sold the house and wandered for a while. In 1905, trains were the way to go, so I tried out Boston, Chicago, and New York over the next year but couldn't find my niche in any of those places. New aristocracies or new hustlers. Too much new. The nanny came too but quit in New York when she found a settled place with a wealthy family. I didn't blame her. Hunter was a handful and huge for his age. She complained of back-aches, among other things. It was July now, and I wanted to get settled before Christmas, usually a lonely time. We had never celebrated Christmas as it seemed to be an event for Christian families, and we didn't catch the spirit.

I cast my mind over Europe. I knew the Scandinavian countries were still somewhat undeveloped. Spain and Italy might prove pleasant. Decent weather for the most part and not too staid.

Then I met Stella.

I'd taken Hunter for a walk in his baby carriage, well-harnessed to keep him contained. I sat on a park bench to gather my thoughts. I'd never had to look after the boy on my own before, and it was driving me crazy. I couldn't let him out of my sight for a minute, as he was godly fast and devilishly inventive. Just that morning, he'd run into the kitchen while I was getting dressed, pulled out all the drawers partway to form a ladder, and emptied the cookie jar into his ravenous maw. It didn't make him sick—nothing did—but I could swear he grew an inch. And I love cookies, so he'd caused a double nuisance.

Anyway, Stella came along and asked very politely if I'd mind if she joined me. She sank down with a heavy sigh. We began to chat; she spilled out all her disappointments, and I told of my frustration about no longer having a nanny and being sick of New York with only a lonely Christmas and a harsh winter to look forward to. I told her about the fearful San Francisco earthquake that April, which probably destroyed our former home. I have to give Hunter credit for sensing the danger and letting me know.

Stella had come over to New York as a nanny with an American family who had been stationed in London for a few years. Stationed to do what, she never discovered. She'd had enough and wanted to go home. As it turned out, she'd thought she might find a rich man to marry in New York because most American men were rich, weren't they? Poor Stella was not outstandingly pretty, and if a rich American man were to take an English wife, he would most likely look for one with a title. That wouldn't endow him with a title, but such a match added social advantage, particularly if his money were very new.

We came to an understanding right then and there. Stella was under contract until the end of the month. She'd come to me, get to know Hunter, and help me pack up. To make a long story short, I got myself a new nanny, and in October, the three of us were on our way to Liverpool in the new ocean liner, RMS *Lusitania*. Stella was so happy on that journey. She'd see her mum soon and meanwhile reveled in luxury.

We stayed a couple of dreary nights in Liverpool before traveling by train to London. I'd arranged for rooms at the Russell Hotel, where Stella's parents came to see her. They had a teary reunion in my suite while I ordered tea for five.

"Is someone else coming?" asked her mother.

"No, Mum," Stella said, laughing. "You just wait and see how Hunter eats."

They were indeed astonished. Being the center of approving attention, the boy bucked up no end and actually behaved himself. He had liked Stella from the start too, so he probably didn't want to disappoint. As far as nannying was concerned, she was the no-nonsense type. We discussed my plans, which involved house hunting, beginning the next day, and Christmas. They hoped Stella could come home for Christmas. Of course, I agreed, but they must have noticed I was a little downcast. By now, loneliness had become an unwelcome state of mind.

"What do you usually do for Christmas?" asked Stella's father, a comfortable shipping clerk clad in a tweed suit with one side pocket bulging with a pipe whose mouthpiece peeped over the top. When I took his overcoat, it had been pleasantly redolent of good tobacco.

"I've never really celebrated it," I said. They looked surprised, and I realized there had better be a good reason. "I was an orphan, and my late husband didn't believe in it. Thought it was all a waste of money. It sounds lovely, though."

"You must come to us, my dear," Stella's mother exclaimed. "We'd be delighted, wouldn't we," she said, looking at husband and daughter, who didn't look so sure.

"Mum, I think Mrs. Thoren is used to … well, grander places," said Stella. "Not that it wouldn't be wonderful to have you," she added hastily.

"I'd be delighted," I said. "But I tell you what. Why don't you come to me? Stella can teach me how to do Christmas properly. How does that sound?"

It sounded good, and no one had to feel awkward. I had a project and only about two months to carry it out, including finding a home. Ideally, I would rent one furnished, although Hunter had a propensity for disaster when it came to delicate artifacts.

After a tedious day looking at houses, I chose the first one my solicitor's clerk took me to. Conveniently situated in Knightsbridge and reasonably furnished with solid oak pieces that would probably withstand Hunter's attentions, we moved in a few days later. Hunter seemed drawn to the attic, but the door was locked and bolted. The solicitor said the owner, who was traveling in Mesopotamia, needed to leave a few possessions behind. I, too, sensed something strange up there, but it was none of my business. Mummies, perhaps.

We unpacked and settled in. I shopped for new sheets and towels, as the ones left for us had clearly been used for a lifetime. Stella's task was to make up a Christmas shopping list. It took up a couple of pages. Some things could wait. She said the Christmas tree would drop its needles if we got it too soon. But we could start gathering the fruit for the Christmas cake, which should be made soon and kept in an airtight tin. It could be iced—with royal icing, if you please—closer to the big day. We would buy a pudding since they should be made a year ahead. These English have some funny customs.

Gifts could be bought well ahead to avoid the worst of the crowds. That was fun. I got Hunter a train set with all kinds of accessories that would maybe last a couple of weeks. I thought of a tricycle but decided that would invite catastrophe on London streets.

It turns out I thought right. The next summer he grabbed another child's trike and went on a joyride down the middle of Pall Mall. King Edward's car happened along, and I was treated to the embarrassment of watching the royal entourage driving at snail's pace behind a thuggish little boy pedaling toward St. James's Palace as if being chased by an army, which I feared he might soon be. I ran at a human-fast pace, passed an astonished His Majesty, mouthing, "Sorry," grabbed my boy and the bike, rounded the next corner, and sped back to the howling child Hunter had dispossessed.

I couldn't help giggling.

Lin opened her eyes and asked me what was so funny.

"Well, the image of Hunter pedaling furiously down the road with a King following behind is very funny. He must have been such a cute little boy."

"Hmm, well, yes, he could be cute sometimes. But that was a major embarrassment, and I was not amused."

"Now you sound like his mother."

"Whose mother?"

"King Edward's mother. Queen Victoria."

"Oh, for heaven's sake. Let's get on. Where was I?"

Ah, yes, presents. Stella would get an afternoon frock, her mother perfume, and her father a warm cardigan. I had everything wrapped by the shops, as I didn't expect that to be an amusing pursuit. Hiding the parcels presented a challenge as Hunter was not to be trusted. I got back to the house when I knew Stella would have taken him to the park.

Now what? There was a little maid's room off the kitchen, I remembered. I had put our maid on the floor above our bedrooms in a larger and more comfortable room. A large trunk from the box room filled the bill and was plenty large enough for all the presents. It had a solid lock, too.

Our cook lived out and came in five days a week. On the other two days, Stella and the maid either heated leftovers or prepared simple meals. I took Stella and Hunter out for an early dinner once, and only once. I don't think the restaurant would have allowed us back.

Anyway, by Christmas Eve, we'd iced the cake and unwrapped the pudding to soak with brandy, and the cook prepared a goose to be roasted the next morning. Stella and the maid saw to the vegetables. I had decorated the tree, issuing strict instructions to Hunter to leave it alone. He kept eyeing the glass balls and ribbon curls with too much speculation for comfort, so I decided against candles. I waited for Stella's parents to arrive before putting the gifts under the tree because they would have to be opened immediately to avoid desecration.

The parents arrived, we opened presents, and everyone was delighted and excited. Stella's mum played the piano for carols, which I still don't know the words to. Christmas lunch—which they called dinner—was served around one o'clock. The parents left a couple of hours after tea.

That Christmas cake was a wonder. I'd never tasted royal icing before. I'd liked the pudding at lunch too, with its glorious brandy sauce. What a festive sight when Stella poured a jigger of brandy over it, applied a match, and blue flames licked the sprig of holly on top. We all clapped and cheered. Mince pies were a revelation, too. It was all absolutely splendid, and I found myself happier being part of this family celebration than I had been for decades.

We've celebrated ever since, although for me, nothing has been quite as special as that first time. Well, that's not strictly true. The first time each of the children became old enough to understand what was going on was very special.

Stella stayed with me for nearly twenty years. She was full of questions about how I kept my skin looking so young, as was her mother. "You haven't changed since the day I met you!" Soon it was time to move on, especially since Hunter was now mature in every sense of the word. I would miss my friends terribly but couldn't stay in touch for obvious reasons.

London used to be such a fun place, but the Great War put a damper on that. I didn't know a single family that didn't lose someone dear. And believe me, whatever the whitewashed announcement said, those deaths would not have been pretty. The city's nightspots still maintained a certain desperate gaiety, but a grim streak of misery ran through daily life.

I'd met a Texan family at a friend's grand dinner. The place sounded very different, fascinating. Stella was sad, although she was married with a son of her own by that time, so she was living out. I explained that some distant relatives had made contact and asked us to come over and live with them while we decided if we'd like to make our home there. I also made a very generous pension arrangement for her. She'd done so much for us. I still think of her, although we eventually stopped writing. I'd never bought the house, and the owner had never come back wanting to live in it, so no complications there.

That attic. After we'd finished packing up, I was checking the study desk drawers when I pressed a latch I hadn't noticed before. A small drawer slid out of the underside, and in it lay an old key. I knew it had to be for the attic door. I couldn't resist.

The cobwebs were thick, draping over chests and a mummy case that stood at least eight feet tall. The worst odor came from there, as did a miasma of angry chill. I walked around, opening some chests and peering in without touching anything. This man was a collector. Or a plunderer, looking at it another way. I kept away from the mummy. I didn't want to know. I locked the door and returned the key to its hiding place.

Now my Reema must experience Christmas. I'd invited Nazli, but her host family was taking her to Florida for Christmas and New Year's.

As a Muslim, Reema felt doubtful at first. I reassured her that for many people, Christmas has become a secular celebration rather than a religious one. I knew her soul needed a joyous family party. I had most of the meal catered; Hunter would pick it up on Christmas morning.

There were things that Americans didn't do, though, that had become part of our tradition. I could buy a pudding and even mince pies. But bread sauce was an English staple to go with the turkey rather than cranberry sauce. I'd provide both. Bread sauce is quite easy—breadcrumbs, milk, pearl onions, and cloves are the main ingredients. Reema and Dora helped me with the cake. Loads of fruit, generous additions of brandy and ale, a good stir, and a silent wish for everyone in the family. Then, six hours in a low oven, which I reassured Reema would burn off all the alcohol.

I planned the decorating and icing. There would be a little Santa on his sleigh and a miniature deer, which I'd brought from England all those years before, alongside a stream lined with fir trees. The white base would have wavy drifts, like snow. It looked magical. When Reema saw it, she began to perk up. The children were beside themselves with excitement and impossibly hyper, especially after they saw me stack a few boxes of Christmas crackers on the dining room sideboard.

Reema and I set the table the night before. The guests—the usual crowd—would arrive at eleven. I let the children open their presents "from Santa" first thing to vent a little steam from their valves. I still maintain the Santa fiction, and no one questions it. When it was almost eleven, I started the Christmas music to add to the ambiance.

Joe, Helen, and Helen's daughter arrived first with a bag of gifts they added to the pile under the tree. Our next-door neighbors came next, closely followed by Lettie and Freddy. The adults had champagne, the young ones and Reema had fizzy grape juice, also in champagne flutes, and happy chatter filled the room.

I took it all in, my heart full as I saw Reema sitting with my children, relaxed and happy. I noticed Hunter looking at me with his special little smile, and my heart filled even more.

"I can't wait. I'll help, of course. All those traditional foods! Did you make a pudding?"

"No, it's enough trouble making the cake. I've got it, though. I always order one from Harrods."

"Howards?"

"Harrods. It's a famous old store in London. You wouldn't believe that place. So many departments of everything you can think of and the most incredible fancy food offerings imaginable. We'll go one day."

London! Oh, yes please.

39

"I hate that slimy creature!" Lin was wound up. Surely the upcoming holiday couldn't have rattled her. She had all the help she needed.

"What slimy creature?"

"Loki, of course! I manage to forget about him for months, then something reminds me. I must tell you about him today. Of course, you will hear more when we start in after the holidays, and that won't be pleasant. I'm still not sure it's completely over."

"You know, I think we have enough for the first book now. You may want to take a break and think of the way you want to start the next."

"Really? I could do with a break. A vacation, in fact."

As could I.

"Somewhere warm. After Christmas. Let's save Italy for the spring."

She lay down and wriggled around as if unable to find a comfortable position, finally heaving a great sigh before launching into her narrative.

I had missed my period. Three weeks. What would I do? What would she do? What would he do?

"You know, Mary, you look a little tired. Is everything all right?"

"I think so."

"Good. It will be lovely to have a little one in the house again."

"What? How...?" I found myself shaking like jelly.

"I sense things, Mary. Don't worry. You'll always have a home with us."

My God. Beyond weird. What on earth would I tell Auntie Peggy? I certainly couldn't admit it was Hunter's child.

"Calm down, Mary. Agitation is bad for the baby. Are you ready to begin?"

I could only nod, my eyes pricking with tears.

Tape 38

We were getting a lot of cases now, often small nuisances with a small payoff, but some more meaty. Hunter drove Reema to her classes, and we agreed she would take driving lessons next summer, although she'd also be taking extra classes to graduate early.

Between work and home, I was very busy and relying more and more on Lettie to help with some of our sleuthing, finally hiring a new office manager so Lettie could have her chance. I was happy the girl was dating Freddy, a colleague of Joe's. He was a nice guy who clearly appreciated her, and they seemed happy. He might prove useful at times, too. They met at our house. We hosted quite a few dinner parties then. Whenever Hunter grumbled about having to socialize, I always said, "Networking."

I got up early on Easter Sunday. I was sipping coffee in the kitchen when Dora came down, still in her robe and holding out an envelope.

"Someone slipped this under the back door," she said. "Very peculiar."

"When? You only just got up."

"Last night. I went to bed before you got home."

"You could have just left it on the table."

"I thought I'd better keep it safe. Because it was peculiar."

The envelope was the normal kind you buy anywhere and was addressed "TO LIN." I ripped it open. The contents made my blood run even colder than usual.

Dear Lin,

My dear master Loki wishes me to tell you that he will visit you and your beautiful family very, very soon. But first, he must deal with a little problem in his own household.

No signature.

"Bad news?" asked Dora.

I couldn't answer. Hunter needed to know. I ran upstairs with the letter and woke him. He showed little reaction besides crumpling the letter in his fist.

"Call Eir."

I picked up the bedside phone and dialed. I hoped Eir would answer. Her practice and home were under contract but would not settle until summer.

"Lin? I was about to call you. There's a problem."

"I know," I said. "I got a letter under my door from someone who seems to be working for Loki. Where is he?"

"That's the thing. They've left."

"They?"

"Loki and his nurse. He must have promised her the earth to spirit him away and hide him. Hiring an ugly nurse may have backfired. Too vulnerable to flattery."

"He said he would visit my family very soon. But first, he was going to take care of a problem at home. You, I suppose."

"I don't know what he can accomplish in his condition. But that woman could make trouble."

"How can she go against gods? My children!"

"Lin, keep them close. I'll do my best to track him down."

"Can he ever recover his powers without your treatment?"

"I don't think so. But that scheming mind of his can come up with all kinds of evil with a faithful servant to do his dirty work."

"Keep in touch."

I told Hunter we must keep the children close. Thank heavens it was a holiday. I went back downstairs to prepare for the day.

"Oh, god, Loki was free and after you? Did he do anything bad?"

"This is enough for now. You'll have to wait until the next book. As you can see, we are all well."

"That's so annoying!"

"You have enough to occupy your mind. Christmas is only two weeks away, so we have things to do."

"Yes, I still have shopping. How's the cake coming along?"

"Oh, it's safe in the tin, wallowing in good brandy and ale."

"You told Reema the baking burned off the alcohol."

"I wanted her to feel comfortable with the whole thing. It burns off most of it and just leaves a good taste. Besides, it preserves the cake. Don't worry; there's not enough left to be harmful or intoxicating."

I'd helped make the cake the day after Thanksgiving. Reema had been able to take off the long weekend, and the children were free for a few days. None of them wanted to miss the stir-and-wish tradition and the fragrance of the long bake. Hunter loved it, too. We all had a merry time. Families and traditions are wonderful and memorable. I'd had some growing up, to be sure. But everything always seemed overshadowed by anxiety—about plant closures, strikes, rising prices, aches and pains, and so on. Mom and Dad could never seem to reach a carefree state of mind. I think they felt it would be tempting fate.

So sad not allowing yourself to be happy.

"What are you moping about?"

"Oh, just thinking about my parents. They were always so insecure, worrying about layoffs and all the things that could happen to make them lose everything. It's a shame to always have that shadow hanging over you."

"I can't imagine. You'll never have to worry, though. Have you told Hunter yet?"

"No, but I'll do it this week."

"We've got tickets for Aruba. We leave on January 15th. Unfortunately, the kids will be back in school, so they can't come with us. But the three of us will have a jolly time together."

"Good heavens, that's marvelous."

My life was going off like a Roman candle, sparking out in all directions. I was going to the Caribbean. Italy in springtime. Baby in the summer. Would Hunter be pleased? Or angry?

"Now, Mary, let's get down to it. We're almost done with this volume. Switch that thing on again."

I knew Christians like to eat a family meal with roast lamb at Easter, so we had twelve around the table. Joe, Helen, and Helen's daughter were there, of course, as neither adult could spare the time to travel to their families. Reema seemed as delighted with this celebration as she had been with Christmas. Everyone had a little basket of chocolate eggs on their placemat, and I'd decorated the table with ceramic rabbits and spring flowers.

Joe happened to be sitting next to me.

"Hey, Lin," he said quietly. "They finally identified that headless corpse."

"What? You should have called me."

"Well, it's not really that important, is it?"

"Well, if you recall, I was the one who found it. Not to mention it was a stand-in for the body under my patio."

"You found that corpse? What's that supposed to mean?"

"I mean, I found the corpse under my patio." Oops. "Why wasn't there anything in the papers?" It was hard to believe that was only eighteen months ago.

"The powers-that-be wanted to keep it quiet because of ongoing investigations. Between you and me, he was a Mafia hitman. New York family. I guess someone put a contract out on him. Now I come to think of it, I don't think they ever discovered who phoned in the tip about the funeral home." He gave me one of those looks I give Sven when he denies raiding the cookie jar.

"What about the bereaved family?"

"They were distraught. First, the funeral home mess, and then your partial corpse. The funeral home owner was obviously complicit, and now we know the Goodalls had some hand in it."

"Or his so-called bereaved family."

"They're keeping open minds. I am no longer involved, as you know, although a friend close to the case feeds me tidbits now and then."

"So, was it DNA that nailed it?"

"Yes, because they had a sample on file. His fingerprints too, of course. Too bad someone removed them, but DNA was enough in this case. I'm looking forward to the new fingerprint database coming online in a couple of years."

"Database?" If I'd been wearing pearls, I'd have clutched them.

"Yes, results of fingerprint searches at the tips of our fingers, so to speak. In seconds. He laughed at his little joke.

"Watch out! Your wine glass! Lin!"

Given my new aquamarine silk dress, thank the blue heavens I was drinking chardonnay.

40

I told Hunter about the baby on Christmas Eve. Lin had gone to visit one of her mysterious friends, and he arrived in my room shortly after dinner.

"I have something to tell you, Hunter," I said, sitting on the edge of my bed. He sat down beside me.

"That sounds serious." He looked apprehensive.

"Yes, it is. I'm expecting a baby."

His face glowed with happiness. "That is wonderful! When?"

"Summer. About the beginning of August." He enveloped me in a bear hug.

"Does Lin know?" he asked.

"Yes and seems happy about it."

"The house needs another little one. We must be careful now. I will be very gentle with you."

"I asked the doctor about that. He said lovemaking would be fine as long as we aren't rough." He hugged me again. We laid down on the bed in each other's arms and discussed names instead of making love. I was the happiest I'd ever been.

Despite a rough month with morning sickness (sometimes 24-hour sickness) after being officially declared pregnant, I managed to whip the manuscript into shape by New Year's.

"Are you and Hunter doing anything special for New Year's?"

"No, we usually just watch a movie," Lin said.

"We do not believe in looking back or too far forward," Hunter added. "We just wake up in the morning and start another year."

"I see what you mean." I did, although anyone else would have found Hunter's remark odd. Why would they be interested in celebrating? The idea of starting a new year would have lost its attraction centuries ago. And Lin certainly liked to look back.

Auntie Peggy said she'd be going to bed early. I shouldn't drink, anyway. Sven and Margareta invited me to go out with their friends, but I had to face the depressing reality that I was too old for their set. I'd turned 25 in September but hadn't said anything to Lin. It fell on a Sunday, so I'd stayed the weekend with Auntie Peggy. She made me a scrumptious chocolate cake and gave me a soft coral cashmere sweater, which must have cost her a pretty penny. I wore it at Thanksgiving and again on Christmas Day. Lin eyed it but didn't say anything, which surprised me. Perhaps she thought I was becoming extravagant.

Christmas was just like she said it would be. The food was terrific, even the bread sauce.

"No turkey, Mary?" Lin asked, surprised to see only sides on my plate.

"Oh, I'm not much into meat these days." I didn't think Auntie knew or had noticed. The thought of meat nauseated me.

Lin said she'd decided to do the Secret Santa thing with so many people coming, which was a relief. Her guests being scattered, she said she'd have to match the donors and donees herself, which no doubt suited her just fine because I'm pretty sure she provided most of the gifts. I was assigned Hunter and found him an alpaca scarf. Auntie got Margareta, so I helped pick out a snazzy top. I received a scarlet designer jacket—definitely Lin's doing, as it fit perfectly—for the time being.

Everyone laughed and chatted all afternoon. I thought I couldn't eat another thing but had to try that cake.

"Don't cut the part with the Santa!" Margareta said.

"Idiot," Sven said.

"Dork." So predictable.

"I will remove the Santa now and put him on the side of the plate," Lin said in her crispest manner.

I wasn't sorry I ate that slice of fruity, boozy heaven, even though it gave me a stomachache. To be accurate, overeating gave me a stomachache.

"A glass of champagne to finish off the day?" Hunter asked around nine o'clock.

"No, thank you, I've had more than enough," I said.

Auntie Peggy gave me a funny look. I'd refused wine with dinner, too. Did she suspect?

Lin and Hunter made fine hosts. I didn't feel jealous as I watched them with their children and friends, passing out gifts, offering food, and making everyone welcome, including Auntie and Sam. I'd shifted my boundaries when this strange family became my life.

Joe drove Auntie home, and I collapsed into bed soon after they left. I'd visit Auntie tomorrow. Poor Dora looked wiped out, but she'd get no help from me. Her dagger looks in my direction became sharper by the day.

On January 15, we boarded a plane for Aruba, just the three of us. I wondered how it would all work out. Fortunately, my queasiness was a thing of the past.

"You know, I have an old friend in Aruba," Lin announced halfway through the flight. "Her family has invited me to stay for a couple of days."

Aha! Just her?

"They're local people who only have a small house, so it'll just be me. You two don't mind, do you?"

"Not at all," I said. "It would be a shame to travel all that way and not see your friend."

Hunter grunted at both of us before turning back to his iPad, no doubt reading some financial report, making no show of interest in this friend. Lin looked miffed.

The island was a dream of palm trees and warm water, and the sand looked almost white, especially under moonlight. Lin took off in a taxi several times to meet her friend, to whom she never saw fit to introduce us. Hunter and I enjoyed the leisurely swims and languid lovemaking her absence allowed. He was fond of stroking my bump—more of a curve at that point—and singing to it. He was so excited about this baby.

"That sounds like a sad song. What language?"

"No, not sad at all. It is a lullaby. I am singing in Old Norse. We are from a certain village that still speaks the old language, the only ones left."

"I never hear you and Lin speaking it."

"Only in private. It almost got us into a lot of trouble once, a long time ago. We have been very careful ever since. People have suspicious natures about things they don't understand."

I had opened my mouth to say, "Yes, Lin told me," but remembered not to spill the beans.

Our two-week sojourn was over all too soon. We arrived home to the beginning of a snowstorm, which turned to freezing rain during the evening. Our taxi barely made it up the driveway. I called Auntie, worried about her having enough supplies, but she said she was fine, had heeded the weather reports, and stocked up. I felt guilty. How that warmth would have eased her joints.

"You sound brighter, dear. I think your holiday has done you good. You looked downright peaky last time I saw you."

"It was wonderful, Auntie. I was thinking how you would have loved it. So warm."

"I don't get on well with the heat, Mary. I like winter better, even this mess."

I'd forgotten that. To me, feeling warm air on my arms was blissful, cold air downright hostile.

How in hell was I going to tell her about the baby?

Book Club Questions

1. How does Mary's outlook change as Lin tells her tales of mythology?

2. How does Mary and Lin's relationship fulfill a need for them both?

3. Is Lin affected by her connection with humans in Salton?

4. Is Lin likable?

5. Is Hunter really as dumb as Lin says he is?

6. How do the losses suffered by Mary, Lin, and Hunter affect them?

7. What makes Lin happy?

8. What makes Mary happy?

9. How does Dora affect the family?

10. What makes Eir abandon her criminal enterprise so willingly?

11. Does Loki change?

12. Auntie Peggy is a good soul. Is she wise or oblivious?

13. How do the various accounts of gods complement each other?

14. How does Lin and Hunter's status as gods affect their approach to life?

AUTHOR BIO

D. A. Spruzen grew up near London, U.K., graduated from the London College of Dance and Drama Education, and earned an MFA in Creative Writing from Queens University of Charlotte; she teaches creative writing in Northern Virginia when not seeking her own muse. Her publications include a historical novel, *The Blitz Business*, and a poetry collection, *Long in the Tooth*. Her poems and short stories have appeared in many online and print publications. She resides in Northern Virginia and Southern Maryland.

ROBERT J. LEWIS
Shadow Guardian and the
Three Bears

VALERIE WILLIS
Cedric: The Demonic Knight
Romasanta: Father of Werewolves
The Oracle: Keeper of the
Gaea's Gate
Artemis: Eye of Gaea
King Incubus: A New Reign

FANTASY

D. LAMBERT
To Walk into the Sands
Rydan
Celebrant
Northlander
Esparan
King
Traitor
His Last Name

LOU KEMP
The Violins Played Before Junstan
Music Shall Untune the Sky

R.J. YOUNG
Challenges of Tawa

SYDNEY WILDER
Daughter of Serpents

DANIELLE ORSINO
Locked Out of Heaven
Thine Eyes of Mercy
From the Ashes
Kingdom Come
Fire, Ice, Acid, & Heart
A Fae is Done

VALERIE WILLIS
Cedric: The Demonic Knight
Romasanta: Father of Werewolves
The Oracle: Keeper of the
Gaea's Gate
Artemis: Eye of Gaea
King Incubus: A New Reign

J.M. PAQUETTE
Klauden's Ring
Solyn's Body
The Inbetween
Hannah's Heart

KYLE SORRELL
Munderworld

DISCOVER MORE AT
4HORSEMENPUBLICATIONS.COM